THE

Guests

OF Crooked Neck

Also by Danielle Williams

Bad Tidings from Queen Sophie
The Bureaucrat
The Capramancer Next Door
Chrystine's Sleep Solution
Day of Silence, Day of Sound
Debuts and Dragons
A Gingersnap Cat Christmas
The Girlfriend Who Wasn't from Delaware
Growing Shadows in the Desert
The Guests of Crooked Neck
Hello, Wizard
Love Potion Commotion!
Midwinter Magic
Out Where the Sun Always Shines
The Purrfect Christmas
Steel City, Veiled Kingdom
Side Effects May Vary
What the Cat Brought Back
The Witching License

Available at PixelvaniaPublishing.com

The Guests of Crooked Neck

by Danielle Williams

Published 2024

Published by Pixelvania Publishing.

Cover illustration and design by Danielle Williams.

Published by Pixelvania Publishing.

ISBN 978-1-7326308-1-9

TROUBLE'S IN PARADISE

THE
Guests
OF Crooked
Neck

AUTHOR OF *STEEL CITY, VEILED KINGDOM*
DANIELLE WILLIAMS

PIXELVANIA PUBLISHING

In loving memory of David R. Booker.

1

KEONAONA

THE AIR SMELLED HEAVY tonight. Of course, the iron-darkened sky (which had eclipsed the sunrise that very morning and later had completely hidden the sun's setting, fusing the waking hours into a single scrum of heather grey clouds) foretold the impending rain.

But not a drop had yet fallen through the humid air, so the scents around—of the minted ferns and waxy-leafed rubber plants; the neighbors' familiar, timeworn footsteps permeating the ground; the plastic tang of the forsaken playset in his front yard; of the coatimundi paths and sweet ripening jubal fruit and the musty-twiggy aroma of the woven nests of the oropendolas—all were pressed together into a sordid mishmash, dense with information, images.

And memory.

He clacked at himself once. No good. It would do no good to dwell. It would all wash away with the rain. When it came.

He had only one task tonight. The gold-crested squargling scanned the dark yard before him, breathing with his beak parted so he wouldn't fog up the window glass. The brighter ceiling of clouds above made the nodding of the forest palms easier to track than if the night had been clear; then, all of the dark shapes would have blended together.

Still, his eyes were not meant for darkness. His tail curled, uncurled. Some of the greenery had bowed, but had it been the wind? He curled his blunt claw on the wooden shutters so they opened more, but the adjustment didn't help him determine the cause of the movement. And his long ears were too filled with the river-water sound of the wind as it pushed its way past the branches and moss of the dense forest. From time to time it would find voice in a crack of an eave of the house, giving rise to brief howls that would have greyed him if he hadn't grown up with them.

There! The trees had moved again, not shouldered to one side by a unidirectional wind, but split apart from each other, as though someone were clearing a path through.

A path to his house.

Keonaona crouched down even farther behind his window. His bright eyes swept the darkened landscape before him. But only when silent lightning flashed and lit up the two figures trudging up the neighbor-flattened dirt street was he sure it was them.

His eyes readjusted. Now, even in the dark, he could make out their shapes, bent under heavy-looking packs. The tall human opened Keonaona's front gate. The smaller human shape passed through in front of the tall and kept going. The tall followed, after a careful moment to shut the gate behind himself.

Keonaona slid to the floor, gliding the shutter slats closed with his claw.

He waited.

He couldn't smell them coming up the walk. The air was too heavy; their scents weren't passing through the air, but melding into it, adding a strange, hungry perfume to it. But some minutes later, he heard their weary steps on the gravel walk, then the creaks of the lanai steps. They came inevitably, but slowly. Footsteps stopped at the front door, hardly three feet away from the window where he kept watch.

Keonaona steeled himself. He wouldn't open to them. They couldn't scent things the way his kind could—they wouldn't have seen the shutters close in the dark. They'd think the place empty. That he'd forgotten the arrangement made with their handler. Then they'd have to go away—

Knock. Knock-knock.

Keonaona raised his eyes to the efficient, polite rhythm. The tall one was *really* high off the ground, wasn't he?

No. Keonaona's claws clenched. *I won't open to them. No matter what they threaten.* They couldn't hurt him—their handler had said that two or three times in the course of making the arrangements. And Keonaona had been agreeable, then! So, big as that fist sounded, he had no reason to fear. Besides—he might be tall, but he was scrawny as a palm tree. From the pictures anyway.

"HELLO?" The tall man again. Raising his voice, but not yelling. Not yet.

Another efficient drum on the door, but longer, louder. "ALOHA? LANE HOʻOKANO?"

Keonaona held his breath in the pause that followed. Footsteps moved off the lanai, down the stair, crunched on the gravel—from the sound of it...maybe he was checking to see if a light was on?

He thought he heard a "halloooo" out in the yard, but if the tall man shouted it, it was assimilated by the wind.

Gravel crunch. *Squeak, squeak.*

POUNDPOUNDPOUNDPOUND!

"LANE HOʻOKANO, WE, HRIANA'S GORGON, HAVE ARRIVED." He shouted the announcement in full voice now, yet not even a drop of ire colored the words. How could someone so polite—as polite as any on his home-world—be a war criminal? "WE ARE READY TO MAKE USE OF YOUR HOME FOR OUR STAY IN YOUR VILLAGE, PER THE AGREEMENT YOU MADE AT THE BEGINNING OF THIS MONTH WITH KŌKOʻOLUA EZ. IF YOU'RE THERE, PLEASE OPEN UP."

Silence. Inside and out. Then: muttering.

Keonaona scooched closer to the wall, trying to listen. He couldn't tell if the tall man was muttering to himself or if the female was speaking—

WHAM!

Something struck the wall outside, exactly where his ear was pressed up against the baseboards. Keonaona barely held in his shriek of alarm.

"I SEE YOU IN THERE!" That woman—or whatever—could roar like a jaguar.

Keonaona trembled.

I will...not...open!

More muttering.

They can't break in. The Kōko'olua told me. They were adopted, they're family now, they can't harm us anymore!

But the silence that followed the muttering outside slowly strangled Keonaona's resolve. That silence felt more dangerous than even her fearsome blow at his head (a lucky guess...right?) had.

A tiny muscle in his arm was just beginning the motion that would allow him to push himself to his feet and answer the door when their footsteps clomped across his lanai. Then, with the creaking that had become so familiar to him over the years, they took the steps, leaving.

Keonaona listened as the crunch of his gravel walk receded.

When he thought they were at the gate, he nosed the shutters opened once more. He peered out in time to see the tall man opening the gate for her. She took a step towards it, then stopped.

Keonaona froze like a squab beneath a hawk's shadow.

Stop it. They can't see you from here, he thought, at the same instant the woman turned and faced his window.

He went grey. If it weren't for the dark, he would have sworn she had somehow felt his gaze on her and had decided to look him in the eye.

The sky flashed, revealing the tall man. He, too, now faced Keonaona. But the darkness returned too quickly for Keonaona to decipher either of their expressions.

The woman went through the gate. The tall man followed and closed it (again, carefully) behind him.

Thunder crashed. The man looked up. The clouds unburdened themselves with a deluge that would turn the yard into soup within minutes.

The man hunched and hurried after the woman, returning to the forest from whence they came. Keonaona prayed that would be the last he saw of them.

The rain continued pouring out from the heavens. As it did, the compressed scents in the air loosened, began sluicing apart, to be forever washed away by the fresh rain.

Like the memories would be.

Keonaona bolted to his feet, flew to the door—almost threw it open, almost called to them *Come back!*

But no.

His hand dropped from the door handle. The rain battered the roof. The way it echoed through the empty house made his walls sound brittle.

Keonaona turned away and stalked into the depths of the house, where a bed for him lay.

What those two offered wasn't meant to be shared with him.

2
GORGON

THE TALL MAN THOUGHT seeing the single light on in the window of the motel would fill him with relief. Instead, it made the pack on his shoulders suddenly feel like it was filled with concrete blocks.

And that's a trick, he thought, *seeing as half the weight's been enchanted out.*

He glanced beside him at his wife, his Queen, the one who had done the enchanting. Her head was bowed, her mane of shoulder-length black hair plastered to her head by the constant barrage of wet. She, like him, was soaked to the bone. Unlike him, she was a creature who hated and feared water, a creature who was advancing forth only because he could take his own human instincts (not happy with the water, but not in mortal dread of it) and shove them into place over hers. But her instinct fought with his in a way that reminded him, ironically, of wrestling a submerged beach ball in the pool, thinking you had it securely under you, only to have it slip aside an inch and jet to the surface to pop you in the face. After a full day of hiking through the rainforest and a week of sleeping in the tent, he was exhausted.

That little troll. He made an agreement. Not a written contract, granted, but still—an agreement! Ez will hear of this.

But right now the charge on his mobi was low, and the water too thick to see a screen through to dial anyway; only a quick step under an umbrella palm leaf earlier had let him consult the mobi's GPS and find this motel, but then the water had flooded the leaf and doused them but good. Who knew? Maybe it had gotten into his mobi.

Oh, boy, his head was swimming.

/Are we going?/ His Queen sent the words to his mind—though these days, they were so blended together, it was easy to think the words were also his own. /Or are we staking the tent here?/ Red annoyance flared underneath the sentiment.

/Hell, no. Not when we're in sight of a hotel. We're sleeping in a bed tonight—human OR squargling, I don't care./

She took the heat of his anger and recirculated it, like a current, into his legs. He strode forward in the mud, and her body did the same. To an outside observer, they appeared to be moving towards the motel in perfect synchronization, as though they were one body moving to an inaudible rhythm.

But the late hour and the rain meant there were no outside observers, despite the light on in the motel. They dragged themselves up the stairs—the place was on stilts painted blue, made of the same wood as the siding—, shambled to the front door next to the light, ignored the clearly-marked *No Vacancy* under the *Crooked Neck Canopy Motel* sign, and, after a wordless sigh between them, the tall man raised his fist.

Knock. Knock-knock.

In less time than they'd feared, the door opened to them, warm light spilling out from around the edges of the squargling hen.

She was a typical squargling specimen; stocky with muscle but not squat, with a large head that was topped with (in her case; he'd seen longer) a short rubbery comb. The long rabbity ears, fluff coming off her round cheeks, and large bright eyes always gave the impression of a mascot costume come to life, but Jerimin knew better than to dismiss her as harmless: the tip of her parrotlike beak was sharp enough to slash through flesh when needed, and the claws on the end of her three-fingered hands could also do damage.

Luckily, as a whole, the race was friendly—*though that counts for little when you were their mortal enemy just months ago.*

She squeezed her smoky purple body forward into the gap she'd opened, large wings spread—*like she's hiding something.*

He pressed the suspicion-flavored thought over to his Queen, so he could draw upon the last dregs of his manners.

7

"Good evening, Lase. We are the Gorgon of Hriana, and we seek shelter for the night. Our assigned host...did not seem to be in to receive us."

He waited. From the way her large eyes had popped, the hen had recognized them as soon as the door had opened. He thought he could hear shuffling behind her somewhere, but couldn't be certain. They were (blessedly) standing beneath a covered porch, what they called a lanai on this world; the monotonous drumming of the rain on the wood was just as effective as the hiss of it on the leaves for blocking out spare noise.

She glanced back over her shoulder, then said, "Lane—Gorgon—I wanna help you, but we been full up the brim three days already. Folks from E-city come in droves when they heard you were on the way. Never seen anything like it. Who's supposed to be keepin' you?"

When she got a blank, tired stare in return, she clarified, "—I mean, your host, who is she?"

"Lane Ho'okano."

Her violet face broke into a smile. "Oh! Keonaona! He just moved back from Pillars Beach. I'll have my husband call. Maybe he didn't hear you over the storm."

While she turned to call her husband, the tall man and his Queen shared a knowing look.

"He's on the mobi now. If Keonaona's keeping you, you're in for a treat, he—"

"Would it be possible for us to wait inside while he calls?" asked the man. He felt his marrow standing up in his bones and leaning, hungrily, towards that warm, dry light.

"I would, but—see, we're so full up, my sister-in-law's squabs are sleeping in the office here, on the floor. Had to high step around 'em just to answer your knock."

At this, his Queen drew a little more energy off him and opened her third eye. The veil sight (as they called it) showed a dozen sleeping young squarglings packed tail-to-beak on the floor behind the motel-keeper; the shorter form of her husband behind a front desk, calling on the phone; and the awkward lift of the motel-keeper's tail, raised high so she wouldn't bean the squab sleeping directly behind her in the face.

His Queen opened her perception wider, and now they could see the entirety of the motel itself, three separate long buildings coming off the point where they stood, like three prongs of a bird's foot. More clearly than that (for her veil sight was especially keen at detecting living things around her), they could see that not only did every room house at least two squarglings, but that there were so great a number of occupants that they spilled out onto the covered porches outside, with little more than their wings and a few light blankets to warm them.

Everybody wanted to meet the Gorgon.

She extinguished her veil sight with a slam of mental force that made him flinch.

The hen opened her mouth—maybe to ask him what was the matter—when her husband, muffled, spoke from the back. She turned away. "Whaddat?"

Her husband repeated himself.

The hen turned back, warbling softly, troubled. "No answer. That's really not like him...Anyway, I'm sorry, but I can't take in another soul."

"That's all right." The man's hand slipped into his pocket. He pulled out his mobi. "Could we trouble you to call our Kōkoʻolua? His number is..." He bit down on a curse. The device wouldn't start. Not even a low-battery image.

He smiled at the hen, but the edges of it were wearing thin. "Sorry. Looks like the rain got to it. By chance did he happen to call you? Perhaps to make arrangements for tomorrow?"

The hen shook her head. "No, sir. No Kōkoʻolua's ever called here, not in all the time I been running the Canopy."

Of course not. This was some little podunk town out in the wilds of Osider. Which meant the tall man already knew the answer to his next question before he asked it. "I don't suppose there's another motel in town?"

Back straight, the hen slowly shook her head. And the way she had her claw on the door—she must have thought they'd get upset and force their way in. Do something stupid.

"Sorry," she said. "And all our neighbors are full up with family, too."

He wanted to scream.

Instead, he gave a little bow and said, "Well, we'll figure some-thing out. Thank you for your time, Lase."

She began to shut the door. But just before it shut completely, his Queen's hand shot out, grabbing the door and holding it open with inhuman strength. A shrill of terror escaped the hen. The sound set off a cacophonous chain reaction as the squabs around her awoke and repeated the alarm cry.

The tall man slammed his hands over his ears. He expected his Queen, with her hypersensitive hearing, to do the same. But to his surprise, she leaned in towards the bedlam. Looking into the hen's face, she asked something, but he couldn't hear it.

Loud, birdlike scolding from behind the hen quieted the squabs.

When the silence was complete, his Queen, eyes still locked onto the hen's face, asked her question again.

"Are there any fae living in this place?"

"I don't..." started the hen, but she stopped and turned at something said by her husband. She turned back to the strange guests on her doorstep. "Actually...yes."

An awful grin began spreading across his Queen's face; Jer-imin felt his own teeth bare in the same way at the same time.

From the slow stare of horror growing in the hen's eyes, the tall man knew he ought to be fighting his Queen's influence, but he couldn't help it; the corners of his mouth drew up in the same maliciously gleeful shapes as her own.

And it felt *good*.

Thunder crashed behind them.

"Tell us where we can find them."

3
SIZZLE

SHAYNA "SIZZLE" VISWANATHAN'S FIRST instinct, when the hammering at the cabin door woke her out of a dead sleep, was to flinch instantly into a tight ball. There she froze, heart pounding while her thoughts scudded to and fro in her rattled brain.

What was that? Where am I? This isn't my bed. No, I'm on vacation on Osider. With my friend Jewel, and her sister Treasure and her human friend Lisa and her roommate, Seppy. We rented a cabin from a squargling, and that's where I'm at. With the girls.

She heard the bedroom door open. Frosty purple light glowed through her blanket; must be Jewel. Sizzle poked her head out of her cocoon. It was actually both pixie sisters on the wing, hovering just above the cool wooden slats of the floor. Their winglight cast strange shadows on the walls. Sizzle wished they'd drop to their feet—what if whoever was outside could see them?

The hammering started up again.

They looked at each other. Sizzle thought the winglight didn't help the alarm in their faces any—they looked a little like corpses in light that pale.

"The owner's not 'sposed to be back till tomorrow, right?" said Treasure. The worry on her plump-lipped baby face made Sizzle want to gather her up in a hug.

"Not till tomorrow *late*," said Jewel, pulling on her silky hair.

Sizzle checked the glowing clock on the nightstand. 1:20 AM. So who could it be?

Lisa the human entered the room, belting her grey fluffy robe around her waist. The frown on her plain, round face seemed more bothered than worried.

"Treasure," said Jewel, "did you invite a boy?"

"No! I don't know anyone around here!"

"Well, I didn't invite any, and Sizzle doesn't have a beau right now." The remark stung a little—Sizzle was too busy in culinary school to work on a man presently. "Lisa," Jewel went on, "would Seppy have invited a guy up?"

"What? No...and even if she did, who'd want to come out in this weather? We're an hour's walk from town on a nice day."

And only a ten minute flight away, but no faerie would want to go flying in this weather. It'd ruin her blowout.

The fae glanced out the second-story window. The palm trees leaned dangerously in the moaning wind. And now that she was up, Sizzle could hear the creaking as the old house tottered. It wouldn't break apart in this wind, would it?

"Where's Seppy, anyway?" said Jewel.

"She said she was going downstairs to see," said Lisa.

"What?"

"She kept her flight silent, if that helps."

We're alone in a house that isn't ours in a storm that sounds like it wants to take the roof off, it's butt-o-clock in the morning, and help is an hour away, if we're lucky.

Sizzle thrust the covers off.

"I'm getting my knives."

She hit the floor running—almost trampling Lisa in the door-frame, *sorry, Lisa!*—saw the loft banister overlooking the bottom floor—decided she'd risk being seen to get downstairs quicker. Sizzle spread her wing casings and jumped into the air. The pastel yellow glow of her wings lit her way as she went over the banister and down safely to the first floor parlor. But she extinguished her light as soon as she touched down, so when she arrived in the kitchen, only the pale light of the storm through the window lit the cold granite countertops.

Sizzle heard the other girls hurrying downstairs on foot, and the front door being assailed again, but she pushed all that aside as she rushed to her black fabric knife roll, lying on the counter next to the sink. Sure, she and the other pixies could burn any weirdos, but only if they made contact with bare skin. And if the intruder's skin was wet, that'd just turn their attack into steam. All that rain! Seppy would only be able to fly away, and Lisa would be helpless. But there were enough knives in here for each girl to have one, and maybe a hot knife or three would scare a bad guy off.

Thunder fell onto the house, deafening. Sizzle pulled out her favorite knife, then took the roll.

She left the kitchen and returned back to the main hall where the girls were crouching around Seppy. Normally tall and slender like most sirens, Seppy was bent over double in front of the door, surrounded by the other girls, whispering something. Fear was in all their faces.

Sizzle raced to join them, feet slapping across the floor. She reached the circle in time to see the front doorknob wriggle. The girls shrieked and recoiled, all except for Lisa.

"Oh, sparks! Oh—" Treasure began hyperventilating.

Sizzle knelt and unfurled the roll in the middle of the group. The others stood for a moment, staring at the gleaming shapes hanging from it.

"I brought my knives." She held up her free hand, strangling her trusty chef's knife in a death grip.

Seppy began shrieking uncontrollably.

"Put those AWAY!" said Jewel. "It's the Gorgon outside!"

Sizzle's thousand-jen, professionally-forged chef's knife clanged to the floor. Her gaze darted towards it—then away, as if by looking at it too long, her guilt would become visible on her. "Oh, gods—don't tell them—"

"Who? The Gorgon?" said Lisa, puzzled. "That's a royal title, right? And aren't there two of them?"

"Oh, whetstone, I don't want to die. Not here! Not now!" said Jewel.

"Should we answer?" said Lisa.

"We have to!" Jewel and Seppy hissed at her.

"You do?" said Lisa.

"Hurry, Sizz, wrap 'em up, wrap 'em up," Jewel whispered, hands flailing over the fallen knives.

Sizzle reached for the roll, only to have it disappear. She squeaked, hand freezing in midair.

"Seppy, no!" said Jewel. "Don't make them invisible, she has to see them to put them away!"

The knife roll reappeared. Sizzle snatched it up.

"*Oh girls!*" came two voices from the other side of the door. "*We're* WAITING."

Sizzle dropped the roll again. Treasure grabbed her head and whimpered. Jewel and Seppy looked at each other, but could do no more.

The Gorgon of Hriana knew they were there. Never in Sizzle's worst nightmares did she imagine this could happen. They weren't even supposed to be in till tomorrow! That's why Jewel'd arranged to be gone in the morning! Leave the keys disguised on the lanai for the owner...

Lisa stepped past all of them, flipped on the porch light, and unlocked the door.

"No—no!" cried Treasure.

Lisa opened the door.

4
LISA

LIGHTNING FLASHED. FOR THAT moment, the Gorgon was only a black shape, devoid of any relatable qualities, taller than the door, wider than it, looming there while the wind hissed and the rain spat angrily behind.

Then, Lisa's eyes adjusted, and the Gorgon was a boyish-faced Netron man whose incredible height was augmented by a seriously heavy-duty Osidern army jungle hiking pack. His completely sodden hair was plastered to his skin, and rivulets ran down the sides of his narrow face, but otherwise Lisa easily recognized him from the cover of *Novus* magazine last year. Jerimin Icarii. Traitor to Netron, co-perpetrator to the first war in generations (which had ended with their capture, thank Hera), and a murderer. But he could just as easily have been a junior professor (or perhaps a TA) at her uni.

Next to him, the other half of the Gorgon duo: the former queen of Hriana, the one who'd started the war in the first place. She was surprisingly small and strikingly pale, except for that unkempt shock of black hair. She looked at each of the fae behind Lisa in turn with a stare as hot and piercing as a laser.

I've seen these people on feeds and on TV...how is it they're standing in front of me in the middle of this rainstorm? They don't seem so scary.

"Ah, a reasonable person," said Icarii-sir, with perhaps the slightest bow—or maybe he was just staggering under the weight of his pack. His tone was as polite as any of the young uni men she'd met, but there was a glassiness in his mismatched eyes that prickled the hairs on the back of Lisa's neck. *Odd!*

He blinked hard; the glassiness seemed to disappear. Lisa got a strange thought: *he knew I saw that in his eyes, so he hid it away.*

But no, that couldn't be. That was irrational.

"We are the Gorgon of Hriana, and we're taking your house now, as our royal position permits," he said, and took a step forward.

Lisa nearly shut the door on him, but his hand (a huge hand! Just how tall was he, anyway?) shot out and thrust it back with enough force that Lisa felt something in her shoulder tweak.

His foot was in the door; now he ushered the former queen in ahead of him. The small woman squelched inside. Those burning eyes raked across the room. How could she even see out from beneath her waterlogged black hair?

"You can't come in here," said Lisa, faintly, stupidly.

Two sets of small hands clutched Lisa's arms painfully from behind. Her shoulder twanged again.

"Milady Gorgon!" Jewel and Seppy chorused, but the music in their voices strained, then went mute.

Lisa heard movement behind her. She turned her head. Sizzle had gotten to her feet.

"Milady Gorgon." Her voice was shaking. "Please forgive, uh, our ignorant friend. Here. We...uh, would be...privileged! To host you tonight." She dropped suddenly in a curtsey that the rest of the faerie girls fell over themselves to mimic.

"Thank you."

Lightning lit the room through the still-open door. Icarii-sir, standing in it, shifted his weight to step inside, but there was no room for him to enter, not with the former queen, Lisa, and the fae all clotted up in front of the door.

The former queen, still dripping from the rain, snapped her head to Seppy.

"Windborne Deception Morris, move your bony ass aside so that the Gorgon may enter!"

Seppy shrieked and rocketed to the ceiling. But before the former queen could move forward and let Icarii all the way in, Lisa stepped into Seppy's old place, blocking the former queen.

If looks could kill!

"You can't!" said Lisa.

The former queen replied with blazing eyes and a growl, but Icarii coolly answered, "Why not?"

"Because—because a Gorgon's authority is over other Hriannens, and only Hriannens. I saw the news. I'm a citizen of Netron. You can't make me do anything I don't want. I don't want you in this house—neither of you. And you can't make me. You are not authorized."

The man slumped to one side, making his head tilt. He read Lisa—in a distant way, she thought. She set her jaw.

"It's poor manners to refuse assistance to travelers in n—who ask for it. I'm certain your parents taught you better than that," he said.

"They taught me my rights as a citizen—and to be true to my world."

If the jab at the treasonous man bothered him, it didn't show. "Fair enough. Let's return to your newscast, shall we? It's true the Gorgon technically can only command other subjects of the Hriannen crown. But..." He waited for the latest drum of thunder to fade before he continued. "But did you miss the part of the reports that said a Gorgon also enjoys over fifteen kinds of diplomatic immunity? And it's all backed with several millennia of Hriannan judicial precedence."

Beside her, Treasure groaned.

"Of course," said Lisa. She was a hundred-mark student. She was thorough. "What does that have to do with..."

While she spoke, Icarii-sir's hand, the one holding the door, slid forward. It came towards Lisa gradually, languidly. She watched it, curious but unafraid. And then, it was around her neck, squeezing just as languidly.

His eyes had gone dead as a shark's.

"What it has to do with this situation, Plattman-miss, is that right now I could keep squeezing, until you are dead, in fact, and not a government on the four worlds could do anything about it."

Lisa gulped and gulped as his thumb began to dig into the soft flesh under her chin.

"I wouldn't even have to feed your body to her"—he lifted his chin at the former queen—the *not-human* queen—, who wasn't even watching this, but who was pinning Jewel, Treasure, and Sizzle down with her stare—"though it would make things cleaner, don't you agree?"

Lisa couldn't see past that dead stare. Next to her, Treasure's breathing began coming in rasps, as though screaming for her.

She'd never before been so aware of the sheer strength in a man. The boys at uni were all—just like her, in essence—harmless. She was harmless and this man was so huge, he held her entire neck in his one hand! She could fight, but what would it do? Nothing.

She stood there, mouth agape, his hand around her neck, unable to move, like some newly-encountered species of bird that had never before known a predator.

Then, like he had flipped a light switch, the amiable, uni student-esque light came back in his mismatched eyes.

His hand seemed to have disappeared. Lisa touched her throat. She swallowed. Nothing was the matter.

For now.

He spoke gently now, with a patient smile.

No, look at the edges. There's something wrong with that smile.

"So...do I have to keep standing here like a drowned rat, Plattman-miss, or may I come aboard?"

There's no way he could have known my name. There's no way...No way...

Lisa took a staggering step back. Luckily, Sizzle was there to catch her before she fell. Sizzle hauled her back from the door.

The former queen stepped forward and Icarii stepped in. He shut and locked the door behind him, dropped his pack with a groan, then helped the former queen out of her pack.

Seppy sank back to the ground floor. The girls watched on, the storm rumbling outside.

"You can only stay the night," Lisa blurted out.

They stepped out of their muddy hiking boots.

Lisa listened to herself babble on in horror. "We were only renting for our vacation. The owner comes back tomorrow, he's a squargling. We leave in the morning. You'll have to leave."

"I know someone sleeping on the porch tonight!" Icarii sang.

The four girls began gabbing for mercy upon their poor, stupid friend.

"Stupid friend"? Wait—they're talking about me! How dare they!

The former queen, having hurled her wet socks to the floor, watched them bounce to where Sizzle's knives lay. She picked up the roll, the lone knife Sizzle had dropped.

"Idothink they all should pack their things. Right now."

"Oooh, those are nice! Belong to you?" Icarii asked Jewel.

"They'm—they're mine, milady," Sizzle answered quickly.

Was she really calling him "milady" to his face? thought Lisa. But to her surprise, Icarii didn't wrap his hand around *her* throat.

Why? Why single me out?

The former queen handed Icarii the knife, the roll. Lisa couldn't understand why the sight of the knife in his hand made her shake. But all he did was slide the knife back into its spot. "Knew it had to be one of you pixies," he said, rolling them up. "Very nice. Think we'll keep them for now."

"You will make us a breakfast tomorrow. A savory one," said the woman Gorgon.

"Yes, milady Gorgon."

"Tell you what," said Icarii, "you ladies promise us in your vow names that you won't kill us in our sleep, attack us, poison us at breakfast, or make any other kind of trouble for us, past, present, or future, while we're here—"

"—and make us a breakfast."

"—and make us a breakfast tomorrow before you leave, and we won't make Plattman-miss sleep facedown in the yard tonight."

Lisa opened her mouth to protest—only to have Jewel clap her hand over her mouth, as though Lisa were a child!

The fae nodded eagerly. "Yes, milady Gorgon!"

"Of course, she'll still need to be tied up."

Lisa trembled again.

5

GORGON

JERIMIN ATTEMPTED TO PEEL open his eyes. His body, eyelids included, felt like lead—no, felt like each extremity had been dipped in wet concrete, then put through a forced march while it set.

He stopped fighting. Ah, sweet darkness.

The knocking at the master bedroom door—ah, right, that's what had bothered him awake in the first place—repeated, and a trembling voice said, "M-milady Gorgon?"

He willed himself to concentrate on her voice, though he still couldn't summon the motivation to open his eyes.

"It would help me...very much!...to make your ladyship's breakfast quickly...if I could have my knives back?"

He could hear her wincing at her own request through the door. He listened to rain tapping at the window, occasional plaps. He may have dozed off again.

"...Please? Milady?"

Next to him in the sunken squargling bed, his Queen's warm body attempted to burrow beneath his. Even if he could have skipped breakfast, she needed as much fuel as she could get. He didn't think this sublevel town—if it were so inclined—would have the means to properly honor them with a feast the way the last one had. Ez was really putting them through hell (though Jerimin would be the first to admit he was well within his rights to), sending them to the distant, rural jungles of Osider first.

It was both a curse (see: no decent infrastructure, decent amenities, or kinet-trains between locales) and a blessing (how many hours would she have to spend in session in a city as big as Ranel? The squarglings had thrown a lot of sons and daughters at them in the hopes of defeating her).

In more comfortable circumstances—or at least with a tonnage more rest—he could have seen to her needs himself. But hunting on the trails had been poor, and by the end of their daily jungle march, he was too exhausted to help her the other way. Though heaven knew the spirit was willing.

The spirit is willing, but the body feels like smashed watermelon.

So. Breakfast.

With eyes still glued shut, he pushed himself upright.

"Coming," he called.

He went to the bedroom doors, where both packs were placed on the floor. Between the vows, the locks, the heavy packs blocking the doors, and the fear instilled the previous night, he'd hoped none of the girls would be able to get the drop on them while they were sleeping. He certainly hadn't been in any shape to stay up for a watch.

He was excavating his way to the core of his hiking pack, where he thought the clothes would be the driest, when a song began playing in the room somewhere. One of Prin—no, *Queen*—Jantessa's songs, some poppy thing with a tune that stuck in your ear like molasses with a grappling hook.

He whipped around, scanning the room. He'd confiscated the girls' mobis and put them...oh right, lined them up on the shelf in the headboard. He scrambled over, but his wife was already growling, no doubt recognizing her sister's dulcet tones before the first measure ended.

He snatched up the offending mobi. The Netron girl's, if he remembered right. The alarm had the note, "Get girls up for TP home." He silenced the phone with a tap.

Odd. Going to a teleportal bank—or, no, they'd use waystones—well, wherever it was fae kept their waystones—it wasn't like a shuttle launch, where they could miss their flight. All they had to do was stand in line, and they'd be transported offworld, first come, first served.

His Queen (or rather, Queen-shaped lump of covers) wormed around a little in the circular bed, then stilled.

Good. He turned, mind already back in his pack.

Then the second mobi went off—with yet another one of the new queen's songs, blasted out at twice the volume anyone needed.

And then there was another knock at the door.

"Milady Gorgon, I hate to rush you, please forgive me, but Lisa—our human—really has to pee, could you please come untie her?"

His Queen threw off the covers. Irritation, gritty red, seeped into the edges of his mind. "Idosee the flavor this day will take."

He silenced the other mobi—this annotation read, "DON'T MISS YOUR RIDE"—so that's why they were in a hurry to feed them. Made sense—he couldn't imagine the buses or whatever stopping in a town this far out too frequently...But why not fly?

/Too noisy to chat and squeal and giggle on the wing./

He turned, caught the clothes from his pack that his Queen flung at him without looking, then put them on while running through the sequence of events the girls might have originally planned.

If the transport is in town, they'd fly out—so...hm, let's say fifteen minutes on the wing...before that, packing...could be fifteen to thirty minutes, depending on if they're clotheshorses, and if they got a head start the night before...

He came up with a final estimate, reached in his shirt pocket for his own mobi, scoffed in disgust when he remembered he'd laid it out on a nearby nightstand to dry last night.

Maybe they could raid the pantry for rice (though the squarglings he'd known never ate it, to his knowledge), or maybe couscous (??ditto??) to help dry it out...maybe...Even if he did find any, it'd be a week in this humidity before he dared turn it on.

After checking the time on one of them, he tucked the girls' mobis into whatever pockets were on his person. Then he turned again to the double doors. His Queen was already dressed—pity—in her traveling clothes and boots, and waiting. He took the chef's roll of knives from the bed (she'd decided it would make a nice enough pillow...exhaustion had made it so for her, he hoped) and squared his shoulders.

They shared a look and a thought before hauling their packs to either side and opening the doors.

The faerie girls waiting for them on the other side of the doors took off like startled flies, hovering high up against the far wall.

Jerimin held the knife roll out.

The Chef (as he thought of the short-haired, dark-eyed pixie) swooped before him and dropped to her feet before taking them.

"ThankyoumladyGorgon," she said, before flying out of the hall and zooming over the second-story railing. His Queen turned away.

/I'll watch her. Go tend to little-Miss-My-Rights. Or don't./ His Queen followed the railing, descended downstairs, leaving him with the youngest-looking pixie, the hysterical one, whose cream-colored wing casings spotted with rainbow dots reminded him of confetti cake. With his reach he could easily grab her ankle, but he was trying not to be a bully if he didn't have to be.

She was still plastered against the wall, her cherub lips pulled tight and pale.

He gestured in the direction of the girls' room, opposite their corner of the upstairs. "Shall we?"

He watched her throat bob as she gulped, was relieved when she took off in the right direction.

The door to the room they'd stuck the four of them in last night was open, but he knocked anyway.

"Everyone decent?" he asked.

The tall siren appeared at the door, already dressed for travel in white shorts and an orange halter top whose bottom was clipped to the belt loops of the shorts. All the better to keep the garment in place in flight, he supposed.

She glanced at Confetti Wings before answering. "Yes, milady Gorgon, please come in."

They'd put Plattman on her side on one of the two beds lining the room, still in her pajamas and robe from last night. The fae had kept the tape over her mouth, he was pleased to see.

She watched him approach with eyes widened in apprehension—but remained soundless and still.

Fast learner.

He undid the complicated knots (a new skill he'd been doggedly working on during what little downtime they'd had these past three months; his woeful bushcraft needed all the help it could get) and the siren grabbed her hand immediately to lead her to the attached bathroom.

"Come down as soon as she's dressed," he said.

"Yes, milady," she replied.

He left them and followed the smell of warming butter downstairs to the kitchen. (Confetti Wings tried flying behind him on the way, but he gestured, "Ladies first," and that was one less faerie at his back to worry about.)

His Queen sat atop a barstool, watching the two pixies scurrying to and fro in the kitchen.

It was a cramped affair—fridge standing opposite a deep and oversized sink; stove and bar all together as one, wood-paneled cabinets lining the walls opposite. This whole place had a tired air to it (though the overcast day blearing through the windows and washing everything out wasn't exactly improving what little rustic charm the place did have), and aside from the mango-colored fridge, and admittedly expensive-looking countertops, everything was wood, with chipped corners being the order of the day. It was clean enough, though, he thought, catching sight of the dust-free top of the fridge when the taller pixie pulled a box of Double Crunch Honey Puffs off it.

What was left of the girls' vacation food appeared to have been rounded up on little counter next to the giant sink: three cans of passion orange guava juice, a plastic jug of milk with only an inch or two left in it, one orange, two bananas, one sad bread heel, a single black takeout container, and a lopsided block of hard cheese.

The Chef was at the stove, pouring liquid (fake) eggs from the carton into a fry pan. The liquid tore the air with a sound like angry static when it hit the pan. On the cutting board next to the stove sat a pile of chopped greens, julienned red pepper, and the knife roll, all wrapped up. The stools looked too short for him to sit on comfortably, so he leaned over to whiff the greens.

"Cilantro, green onion, and red pepper, milady," said the Chef, stirring the custardy eggs.

"Smells good," he said as his stomach roared. Once their room had been secured, they'd dropped into sleep without a bite to eat; dinner had been easily over twelve hours ago.

A beautiful wooden bowl containing the cereal and milk was placed before him, followed by a biodegradable takeout spoon. The taller pixie, in purple backless tank top and matching purple scrunchie holding her plum-colored hair, bobbed in a curtsey. He'd call her Mauve. "Your—milady Gorgon said you would like this."

Out of long-ingrained habit, he started to bow to Mauve in return. Catching himself, he stopped short, but he still wasn't quick enough; his Queen slammed a nasty mental sting of pain into his back as punishment. Old habits died HARD, and now that he was Gorgon, bowing was one he was trying to kill.

Mauve was giving him a funny look. He quickly wiped the wince off his face and went on. "As usual, she's right," he said, picking up the spoon. "But could you also please start the kettle? I like tea in the mornings."

Mauve's eyes bulged and her mouth worked, but the Chef barked, "Treasure, kettle. Jewel, cheese, now, like we planned."

This kicked Mauve/Jewel into gear and she spun in the air to grab the sad block. Confetti Wings/Treasure stopped hovering at his arm and blew into the cramped kitchen, flinging open the topmost back cabinets, going, "Where is it? Where is it?"

"Where's what?" asked the siren in the orange blouse, entering the living room. (*Tangerine. That's a good one.*) She still had a firm grip on Plattman's hand, like she was a small child prone to wander.

"The teakettle!" said Confetti Wings.

Plattman broke free and darted into the kitchen. "It's down where *I* can reach." She crouched beside the fridge and removed a canary yellow teakettle from the cabinet there. "Do you want me to make the tea?" she asked the kitchen. "I have a teabag left..."

"No," he said.

"Lisa, *give Treasure the pot* and come here."

Feeling a shimmer of power in the siren's voice, he gave Tangerine a dark look. But a soothing cool cloudiness, like milk pouring over his consciousness, distracted him, and then his Queen pulled his attention away. He tried to squirm out of it.

/You must have felt that! She's using her power to order her around./

The Netron girl had handed over the kettle the very next instant and left the kitchen to be held by Tangerine again.

/*Ja*, I felt it, but there's no real.../—he felt the familiar rummaging in his head while she looked for the word she wanted—/*juice* behind it. Members of the court are trained in the strong use of their power. Their...volume is turned up. It is expected. But these ones...learn what they learn, and only practice what is useful to them./

The Chef leaned aside to let Confetti Wings put the kettle on the flat electric stove

/So you're not worried about them stabbing us in the back?/

/No. One kills us, she becomes Gorgon—and a target is painted on her back. A puppy doesn't kill a wolf, then run the pack. Though I purr at your caution. Now eat your cereal before it is cold worms./

/Ugh, thanks./ But he began shoveling it in anyway, only pausing to watch the Chef toast the remaining sliver of bread to golden perfection with a glowing hand. Pixies, being aligned in the direction of fire and heat, were supposed to make good cooks, but growing up, his conservative Netron family had never eaten anything by a pixie chef, and if he'd eaten a meal produced by one in the past couple of years, he hadn't known it.

She buttered it and placed it on a worn green plate next to the freshly-cheesed eggs before serving it to his Queen.

She took a bite, then held out a forkful for him to take. He ate off the flatware without missing a beat, enjoying the warm blossom of her delight as he did it.

Ritual completed, he drank the too-sweet milk out of the bowl. *Eugh. But today we need all the fuel we can get.*

"Hand me that banana, will you?" he said to the Chef. "And the orange and cheese too, please."

The girls stood in silence, watching them eat like they were at a graveside. He felt a twinge of guilt, hearing their stomachs rumble—but his Queen sent a flash that burned between them, with images of the grueling day to come. They—the girls—could eat on the bus. Which reminded him...

/Who's got money on them?/

Her stare went distant, perception searching the house. He got an image of purses in the bathroom above, in blue-edged silhouette, set out on the counter. /All but the youngest, Idothink./ She made the faerie girl, standing beside them, extra colorful to indicate her. /It is a little difficult to see. —Confetti, really?/

/Like confetti cake. Listen, I was hungry. Am hungry. Can you tell how much they have?/

"Mmngh," she grumbled aloud, causing the girls to straighten at attention, but he ignored them to focus on the purses she was seeing.

It wasn't quite like an eye-doctor's exam, for the way her attention sharpened the parts of what was being seen was far smoother and more natural than the clicks of "one...or two?" that changed the quality of vision in the optometrist's office, but it was the closest thing he could relate to the sensation of first seeing the outside of one purse, then moving past its outer walls to see its insides, then finding the wallet tucked away (in...was that a zippered pouch? It was hard to see through everything, and this spiritual x-ray vision saw all), then looking through the wallet's own exterior to the paper money within.

All of that in less time it took him to glance upon a familiar word and read it.

He could see the problem, the thing that had made her grumble. He should have known; it was the same problem she had with seeing books through the veil sight: she could tell by the shape and spiritual makeup/character/texture that it was paper, but couldn't read any of the print on it.

She turned the veil sight on each purse in turn. One had a fat wad of bills coiled in it, but the way their time in this town was going, it was likely to be a fistful of ones.

Still, something was better than nothing—which is what his wallet was close to holding right now.

/Show me the purses again? Just the outsides. Hm, no, can't tell if one's the Netron girl's or not./

/Idothink they all live there. All Netron things./

/I thought fae all liked to, you know, show some Hriannen pride. Buy realm-made products./

/Court fae are different from city fae are different from country fae, different different. Or so I was taught. But also, you disremember you are not seeing the physical form of these things. This shape is typical, but its color is…ferocious./ She sharpened one of the purses in the lineup, held it in focus between them for a moment. /Few things shout the difference between Hriana and Netron than an accessory in a color that screams./

He chuckled.

Wordlessly, he thanked her and told her to relax. The image faded from before him and he was left staring at the irregular shapes of the orange peel in the empty wooden cereal bowl. (Really, it was big enough to be a serving bowl. And unlike everything else in the house, it had a beautiful patina to it. He got the feeling it was used for special occasions only—maybe it was the last clean one?)

He finished the banana he had been eating during the search of the purses and laid the peel neatly into the bowl.

The kettle whistled. The Chef jumped out of the line and picked it up, but paused before she poured the hot water into a mug.

"We have no tea left, milady," she said to Jerimin. "Unless you want Lisa's."

"No, thank you. I brought my own." He fished around the phones to pull a glass vial out of his crowded pocket.

He let himself grin at the horrified face she made when he poured the slow-oozing, oil-black substance into the hot water. He stirred it with his cereal spoon until the black blood of his Queen was blended into his morning pick-me-up. *Not all of us were born immortal, miss.*

He took a deep, steaming drink, the raspberry-dark-chocolate-but-not flavor comforting to him. "Thank you," he said to the Chef. "Your care is much appreciated."

But before the Chef returned to the line, his Queen snapped her fingers and pointed at the takeout box in the corner. The pixie grabbed it from the corner and delivered it to her.

"Fries, milady. Shall I warm them for you?"

"*Nein, danke.*"

A curtsey, and then the Chef returned to her place with the girls. His Queen began picking the fries out of the box.

/Why were you looking for Miss My-Rights' purse?/

/Because the Gorgon can't confiscate her money,/ he sent, disgust coloring the thought a putrid brown-green, veined with lava orange.

"Hmmm..." she said, chewing thoughtfully.

He looked at her and grinned. He knew that tone. She was cooking up something.

When the black blood was drunk and the fries obliterated, they looked around the kitchen.

/Do we need them for anything else?/ she finally sent.

The remains of the vacation food were all gone.

/They ought to do the dishes for us./

/Yes, that, but after?/

He could think of nothing more.

The Queen turned on her barstool. "You, girl," she said calmly to Plattman. "Take care of the dishes. You others, go upstairs and gather your things to leave."

"Yes, milady," chorused the fae before lifting off. He caught Tangerine sending a meaningful look to Plattman before zipping away.

Plattman reached for their plates like they were in a container full of venomous snakes. And she practically lurched to the sink like her joints had frozen.

His Queen observed the movements of the girls upstairs while Plattman tossed the food waste into the compost and scrubbed the plates clean.

"Plattman-miss, I assume you're attending uni right now?" said Jerimin.

"Yes, sir."

"Where at? If I may ask."

"University of New Athens."

"Oh! I considered that school, once." Wow. That felt like a lifetime ago. "What are you majoring in?"

She levered open the dishwasher. It was full to bursting. She attempted wedging the elegant wooden bowl in anyway. "With all due respect sir, I don't see how it's any of your business."

He smiled like he'd bit into a lemon. *I play nice, and this is what I get in return?*

"You remind me of the people I worked with at White Hall. No, I take that back. You might be more insufferable."

She stopped forcing the bowl in and looked at him, aghast. "You can't say things like that!"

His Queen laughed in the back of her throat.

"What, does it infringe on your rights?" he asked. "At least when they were treating me like gutter trash, they were my superiors. Do you need a lesson again about where you stand, Plattman?"

"I—you—"

"Put that bowl down," said his Queen.

Startled, Plattman froze and stared at his Queen.

"The machine cannot eat it at this time. Clearly."

After another moment of standing there like an empty-headed cow, Plattman set the bowl on the counter with a too-loud clunk. "Then...may I go up now? I'd like to get my things."

"You may," said his Queen,ignoring his glower.

Plattman dried her hands on a rust-red towel, then left for the stairs.

Quickly, his Queen left the bar and took the wooden bowl Plattman had left on the counter. She set it next to her in plain sight—but he knew it could be hidden from the girls with just a light clouding of their minds.

He gave her a questioning look.

/You'll see./

That brightened his mood a little.

A hum of wings announced the faerie girls' return. Soft-sided suitcases were in hand, and specially-designed flight purses were buckled around their thighs. Sure enough, Confetti Wings' purse was an upsetting shade of nuclear green. Her bedhead had been tamed by pulling the mass into two pigtails.

Tangerine had pulled her hair back into a messy bun. She had Plattman's hand clenched in her own again.

"Everyone ready to go? Did you double-check to make sure you didn't leave anything behind?" he asked.

"Yes, milady."

"You all have your tickets?"

A little hesitation. *Must be on their mobis.*

"All right, all right. Who has the house keys?"

Mauve stepped forward and set them on the counter in front of him.

"Thank you." He slid it into his fingers, traced the metal shape. "How old-fashioned," he said. He handed it over his shoulder to his Queen, who secreted it somewhere into the depths of her traveling cape before stepping off the barstool.

The fae stopped breathing. Jerimin fought a smile. From the mirthful hum in his head, something fun was about to happen.

"There is a last thing before you go," said his Queen. /Take their machines out./

One by one, he removed the girls' mobis and set them on the bar next to the knife roll. He watched closely to see whose eyes locked on which device, just to confirm the owner.

Confetti Wings began chewing on her thumbnail, eyes positively glued to the one wreathed in a furry yellow duckling case.

/Can you show them they are on?/ Not a request, but a Luddite's question; her power didn't allow her to handle electronics.

He held the first up and activated it so the time screen displayed clearly, did this for all five.

"Youdosee we have kept these safe for you this past night. I imagine you want them back, yes?"

Silent nodding.

/Pick up a one that's NOT Miss My-Rights'./

He held up the ducky.

"The cost for keeping this one safe overnight is six hundred jen."

Utter silence.

He worked to keep his face as blank as his Queen's.

"That's extortion!" said Plattman.

Her fly-winged keeper jerked her hand—hard enough that the girl gasped in pain. "Stay out of it, dummy!" she hissed.

He thought he could see a friendship dissolving in the look on Plattman's face.

"She doesn't have that much money, miss. —Milady," said Mauve.

"I did not ask you for it. I asked"—she nodded at Confetti Wings—"that one."

Confetti Wings squeaked wordlessly a couple of times before she gave up.

"Milady," said Mauve, "What I meant to inform Your Excellency is that we—we all don't even have that much money together."

The mental connection between them tugged at him, feeling like a wire snare embedded in the back of his head. *Pay attention*, it urged.

"How much *do* you have?" asked his Queen.

"I—I'm not certain. —We all brought our own spending money."

A little orange annoyance. "How much do *you* have?"

Though she'd only asked Mauve, some fast calculations must have occurred, for she showed him yellow numbers suddenly floating above the girls' heads.

/Make sure they don't lie./

"About one fifty," said Mauve. "One hundred fifty."

His Queen turned to Confetti Wings.

"And you?"

"T-twelve dollars, milady. I bought a lot of spicy candy to take back."

"You?" to Tangerine.

"Two hundred."

Three hundred was the number over the siren's head.

/Guess she's well-named./

/Mm. Sirens are named Deception the same way Netron women are named Persephone. It means nothing./

"You sure?" he asked the siren.

She nodded—*and by Hera, if she doesn't look absolutely sincere...*

"Count it," said his Queen.

"Milady?"

"Take your money out. And count it."

The siren's long lashes kissed her cheeks as she looked down at her feet.

"I—I remember now. I have three hundred left."

"That's what I thought," they said together.

Now his Queen addressed the Chef. "And you?"

"I'm not exactly sure, milady. Maybe fifty?"

This tracked with the number hanging over her head, which was one number one moment, then a few less the next, then spinning to a new amount.

"Let's see it," said Jerimin.

They watched her count out her money, red paper bills rasping as she passed the counted notes into her awaiting palm.

/Forty-seven fifty-three,/ he sent. /Not off by too much. Now what?/

A flurry of thoughts were exchanged between them as the question turned into a debate, turned into a settlement. She addressed Confetti Wings once more.

"Treasure Verette. For showing the realm's defender appropriate respect this entire visit, the charge on your mobi has been discounted to seven jen."

The girl did little more than tremble until Mauve (/her sister/, his Queen informed) fluttered a wing casing by her ear. The little pixie dipped in a wobbly curtsey. "Yes, milady!"

He held out his hand for the money. She zipped forward in the air, pressed the bills in his palm. He took it back at the same time his other palm extended out with her mobi. She clutched the furry thing with both hands and said a hoarse, "Thank you," before retreating back into the lineup.

"Jewel Verette," said his Queen to Mauve, "we appreciate your prompt obedience and your good example to your sister. For this, your payment has been reduced to one hundred forty-five jen."

She curtseyed. "Thank you, milady."

The exchange was made. The same deal was made with Tangerine—"for protecting the well-being of an ignorant foreigner" (he could practically see the steam shooting out of Plattman's ears)—and a final time for the Chef. Each faerie was left five jen—enough for a small lunch each, he thought, or more if they pooled it together. Osiderns were good about family meal deals. Besides, once they reached real civilization, they could use their mobis to access their bank accounts.

Fae taken care of, Jerimin handed Plattman's mobi back wordlessly.

That left the expensive chef's knives right next to him.

/Let's see if she's brave enough,/ she sent. /Else we can pawn them./

"Very good," said his Queen. "If that is all, you are free to leave for your waystones home."

The Chef gave pleading looks to each of the girls on either side of her. Though he knew they could not speak to one another in their minds like he and his Queen could, he nevertheless observed a discussion taking place in those few silent seconds.

Mauve spoke. "Milady? How much for the return of my friend's knives?"

"One hundred seven dollars and fifty-three cents."

The number over Plattman's head turned atomic red before going up in flames. She turned on Jerimin.

"YOU SKINNY RATBAG!"

The fae swarmed her, but she threw off their mouth-covering hands and shouted over noisy wings, "How did he know? *How did he know?* He must have looked through my purse, hacked my mobi—"

"I did no such thing," said Jerimin.

"Liar!"

"So you will not pay?" said his Queen.

Mauve turned on Tangerine, the siren liar. "She's *your* roommate, you have to make her—"

"She won't listen!"

"Sizzle fed us this whole time! We can't—"

"She made my favorite cake! Seppy, do something!"

"*Take it upstairs,*" said his Queen.

The gaggle of girls levitated as a single mass—hauling Plattman horizontally—and seethed upstairs. A door shut, muffling the heated bickering.

His Queen glanced upwards before taking the homeowner's bowl from the counter, going over to the corpse-grey backpack and unzipping it.

"Are we certain that's hers?" he asked.

She sharpened focus on the luggage tag hanging off the side (*if lost, please return to L. Plattman*, followed by an address) while uprooting clothes by the fistful. A few of them got wrapped around the bowl—as camouflage or padding, he wasn't sure—before she wrenched it into the backpack. The displaced clothes got stuffed back in on top.

The few articles that would no longer fit (mostly underwear, he noted before quickly averting his gaze) were simply fwapped onto his Queen's barstool before she sat on top of them like a hen on an egg.

Her cape seemed to cover the evidence, but even if one of the girls noticed, he knew they wouldn't dare ask. None of them had a death wish, not even Plattman. She just didn't know what to make of them, and when his people—well, maybe, his former people—happened upon something that upset their idea of how the world was supposed to function, they tended to cling on to protocol for dear life.

Still infuriating, though.

His Queen glanced up again.

"They come," she said, a moment before the door upstairs opened and the wingbeats elevated in volume.

The flying raft of fae landed as a single unit right where they had started, in the archway between the kitchen and the front parlor. He wouldn't have been surprised to see prissy Plattman trussed up again, but they set her down on her own two feet, unrestrained.

With the barest inclination forward (*you call that a bow?*) she pulled her wallet out of her purse and emptied it out on the counter, face set and bland.

She didn't step back when he grabbed up the red bills to count them (they were creaseless, like she'd gotten them straight from the bank), but she also didn't flap her lips any.

For once.

He double-counted the amount, then handed it back to his Queen.

"Sizzle Viswanathan, you may collect your tools."

The little pixie chef floated forward and took the knife roll. He looked over them all.

/That's it, right?/

Earthy-colored agreement soaked into his brain.

"All right," he said. "Get out of here."

The fae grabbed their things (and Tangerine, Plattman) and threw themselves at the front door like children released from detention early. A handful of strides took Jerimin to the doorway, where he watched them zoom away into the pewter sky, reducing to dark flecks within the blink of an eye.

A breeze wafted the invigorating smell of warm rain into his face, but his bones reminded him that it was no match for their weariness. The boost was quickly fading.

He heard his Queen enter the parlor behind him.

The fae were completely out of sight now. Without their fear, the air felt empty. Finally, they could relax.

He slumped back on the parlor couch. After double-checking they were gone, his Queen cuddled her warm body to his side, leaning her head against his chest. He slid his arm around her.

"Were we too hard on them?" he asked.

"Kind, sweet Gorgons do not live long."

"You're right, but...I don't enjoy intimidating people—"

"Liar," she said, and he felt the smile in it, knowing and approving in his head.

He had to smile back. Couldn't hide anything from her. "Okay, well, let's say—I don't enjoy it when it's unnecessary. Those girls were terrified of us! For no reason."

"They were *respectful* of us. We upheld the reputation of our office and did them no true harm."

"We took their money."

"We needed it. Subjects of the crown must give aid to the Gorgon when she requests it. They know this law. They followed it, and were left unharmed. The only one we nipped at was the girl who gave you lip."

Jerimin suddenly noticed his clenching jaw. He released it. "That's true. Hearing her talk down to me like that..." He shook his head in disgust. He'd once risked life and limb to keep his people safe. But no matter what he'd done, he always wound up covered in their contempt.

Now he was Gorgon—*Gorgon!*The Horror of Hriana, a real-life Fury, the hippity-highest ranking official on Hriana, top of the (metaphorical) (and possibly literal) food chain, untouchable! Responsible only to Queen Jantessa herself!

...Yet, to people from his homeworld, nothing had changed.

"You'd think being knighted one of the most powerful people in the galaxy would make them rethink how they treat me. But no!" His jaw was clenching again. He swallowed, couldn't quite relax it. "I can't win with these people."

"*Ja*, you are sick of it. You don't must to—"

"—have to."

"—have to smile and swallow snideness anymore."

"I know, but...am I always going to be the bad guy? It's not like I grew up saying, 'Hey, when I grow up, I totally want to betray my people!' Don't they get that?"

She looked up at him. "Youdowant to go back to the way things were?"

Hell, no! The words were barely formed in his mind (and they certainly hadn't reached his mouth) when she grabbed the sentiment and held it up, hefting it, shaking it approvingly, triumphantly, *rah-rah-rah!* Then the golden glow in his head faded.

"Then this is the prey you must eat."

She was right.

"Still. I'm not a monster," he said.

This earned him a look.

"Not unless I have to be," he amended. "I just wish they—people like Plattman, I mean—could see that."

"Your people are uninterested in seeing any more to you. You are Gorgon now. Your image is set."

"Permanently?"

"Permanently," she said with finality.

But he just wasn't sure. It didn't sit right, anyway. But it was a moot point; they were on Osider now, and unlikely to meet any more Netrons in this neck of the woods. Better to focus on the day ahead rather than theoretical encounters with imaginary adversaries.

He gave his Queen a squeeze and stood up. "I think I'd like to get cleaned up a little more. Who knows where we'll be sleeping tonight."

6

MERCURIO

MERCURIO MAXIMINO MACOYA TURNED his floating cameras on the fiery orange bus as it came coughing up to the Crooked Neck transport "station" and hit *record* on the remote. His beak quivered at the strangely enticing tang of the exhaust and the hint of greasy synthetic oil pluming invisibly into storm-heavy air.

Gotta wonder if even an Incensario could bottle all these scents up. Could make a nice add-on to the premiere release, though. He pulled his screen out of the bandolier that held his one-square filming gear and quickly texted himself a note—COMM INCENSRO—RECREATE SCENZ? (AIR ROLL). His claws depressed the sunken buttons at the bottom of the device with hollow chucks, but he kept his eyes trained above the screen ninety percent of the time. He didn't want to miss them when they disembarked.

The bus puttered in place long enough that Mercurio had time to hook his screen back on, do two checks of his other equipment, and rewrap the very tops of his puttees for the umpteenth time since he got here.

His tail thumped the bench leg three times when he saw the shadowy figure of the driver moving out of her chair through the bus's tinted side windows.

C'mon, c'mon! You've got a schedule to keep, and so do I!

But the bus kept rumbling, doors sealed shut.

"What's she doing in there, givin' an orientation?" he said aloud, making the little group of fae (oh, and one human...he'd smelled her earlier) turn their heads. But they said nothing, didn't even start whispering among themselves—kind of weird, he'd thought when they'd arrived a half-hour ago, but one came over and asked him where he'd gotten his mangoes earlier, and he'd caught the notes of anxiety in her sweat-scent, so maybe they were in a hurry to go home? Maybe to a funeral?

He'd filmed them, for B-roll, but didn't think he'd use it. No good energy there. Bad vibe. But it didn't matter. He was here at this pathetic bus stop to make a very specific connection—one that'd lead to lots of vids—multiple, huge, must-see series on his feed, MercurioMaxFilms—until he became king of the feeds.

But first, they had to get off the stonking bus!

He glared at the sliding doors from his seat under the green-peaked shelter, willing the bus to open.

Nothing.

He pulled his digital recorder off his belt and did some voiceover to the scene:

"The grey sky overhead is pregnant with rain, but I'm gonna have kits any second now if the bus doesn't open up soon. The Gorgons of Hriana are on it. I can feel it."

The *stop* button made a satisfying *click*! Maybe he'd use it (follower engagement went up whenever he appeared exasperated—but only if the duration was short, under thirty seconds), maybe he wouldn't (pregnant with rain??), but that was the beauty of the medium: most sins could be erased in post.

He was tapping the wafer-skinny machine against the tip of his beak tip, trying to decide if he had anything else to say when the doors finally slid apart.

With one quick, unconscious motion he reholstered the voice recorder and slipped the camera control stick into his claw, zooming in with one of the floating camera spheres, repositioning the other two to get a better shot.

Squarglings came pouring out. More than a few must have been seated on the floor—he took deep drinks of the air—beneath the vegetal odor of tiredness layered atop travel, he thought he smelled city smells—of rubber walkroad surfacing and coffee nut habits—

He slid the recorder out again.

"These travelers have left their comfortable homes in the city and traveled hours on a cramped bus to the humble town of Crooked Neck, A'ina Muliwai, all for the chance to reunite with their loved ones lost in the war one last time." He trained his eye on a squab, hardly out of the egg—one of the few, most leaving the bus were grown—widows, widowers, close friends, parents, grandparents—and winked, his control-contact lens setting the focus on her head, which turned every which way to scent the air of this new place. He hit *zoom* on the remote. "Some for the first time." That would be poignant. He held on her face for as long as he could, then winked focus back on the bus' doors. "But for any reunions to happen, they are forced to rely on the powers of their most reviled enemies, the very assailants who killed their loved ones in the first place."

He turned the recorder off, *click!* Then, thinking of posterity, Mercurio switched it on again. "For the aggressors of the Cáscaramida War, the monstrous former queen of Hriana and her human paramour, Jerimin Icarii, were adopted as 'ohana to the Osidern people, thanks to the extraordinary deal made by Warfather Rodor Alwitz. Now, despite their lofty Hriannen title, the Gorgons of Hriana humbly serve Osider. Crooked Neck is just one stop of hundreds..." Was that accurate? Better cover himself, "...one stop of thousands...in their globe-spanning tour to make restitution for the evils they've committed."

Click! Too much? Not enough? Eh.

He'd need some great music for that part.

The bus was empty now. The offloaded squarglings were making their way past the covered waiting benches beneath the shelter, probably towards (from the smell of it) the awaiting fruit vendors for a quick breakfast. The merchants would make a killing.

Mercurio kept his eyes locked on the bus doors. They had to come out sometime.

But he waited. And waited. And the only person to come out of the doors when they opened again was the popsicle hen, wheeling her cooler expertly off the lip of the bus to the awaiting ground.

His wings sank in dread. Was the tip bad? But the screenshot had looked real!

Mercurio waited until Popsicle Hen finished her conversation with the driver, then sprinted to catch the driver before the doors closed.

"Excuse me, Lase?"

But she was already on the external speaker system.

"Aloha, travelers. This bus leaves for 'Ehanua City in about twenty minutes, but riders able to show a valid ticket are welcome to board at any time. *Mahalo* for riding with the A'ina Muliwai extended transit system."

"Lase? La—hey!" Mercurio jumped aside to avoid being stampeded by the depressed fae. He only narrowly avoided being walloped by their luggage.

The driver grabbed a steady bar and swung herself out of her chair to meet the fae at the bus threshold. Mercurio looked her up and down with a smile.

I bet she's a great dancer.

"Looks like you wahinis need a vacation from your vacation!" said the driver.

The fae pressed their ticket screens on her without a word. The smallest one—with rainbow-speckled wings, how cool—glanced behind her with a hunted look. She gasped, looking ready to start a heart attack when she saw Mercurio there. He peeped reassuringly at her, but her attention was already back on the bus driver returning her mobi.

To his relief, the driver also seemed disturbed by the unusual behavior of the fae. "Did you all get breakfast yet?" she asked, rearranging her wings into a motherly stance.

A questioning look was exchanged between the travelers.

While they figure out how to answer...

"Excuse me, Lase, are the Gorgons set to arrive on the next bus?"

The driver opened her beak to answer—but was interrupted by the lone human among the fae, turning on her heel to face him with the fury of a tornado.

"The Gorgon's already here!"

"WHAT?!" Mercurio squawked. Hours' worth of plans—past and expected—flew apart in his head. "How do you know?"

"Lisa..." went one of the fae in an undertone.

"I know because they took over the house we were staying in last night. *And* stole our money!"

"Are they still there?"

"Probably. They can't do anything to *you* because you're Osidern."

Mercurio popped his screen out of its sleeve. "Where they at?"

The Netron girl's mobi seemed to magically appear in her hand. "Here, I'll send the address."

The devices announced the successful transfer of information with two distinct *bling!*s. He tapped a key to open the map.

"*No me digas!* All the way out there? Did you fly?" Oh, wait, yes, they did. They actually *could* fly with those wings. His own, beautiful but useless, flapped fruitlessly.

"You'd better hurry if you want to catch them—the actual owner of where we were staying is Osidern; he'll be able to kick them out."

Mercurio squawked again. He turned, halfway in a run, then remembered himself, wheeled back in a circle that threw up mud.

"Thank you!" He tried an awkward bow. "Consider joining my feed, MercurioMaxFilms!" They were too far to throw business cards at, but now that he had her mobi number he could send her a link later.

"Don't mention us!" screamed one of the fae after him, but he was already off and away, his cameras zooming in formation above him.

7

MERCURIO

MERCURIO SLID TO A stop at the address. At last. His once-white puttees were the color of chocolate milk, thanks to the mud he'd run a marathon through, but he was here.

He bulldozed open the gate with one hand, began dialing in shot algorithms to cameras two and three on his screen while passing under the tall palms that lined the path up to the white-painted house. He should've been narrating, but he was still out of breath from tearing through the jungle.

I can come back and film establishing shots later, when there's no time crunch.

He cleaned his wrapped feet off as best he could with the scrubber at the bottom of the lanai stairs, then jogged up the landing.

He winked at the door, marking it as camera one's focus (he thought of it as MaxCam), double-checked his screen that number two (Wideshot) was getting a mid shot of the house, that number three (Angel) was set over his shoulder, and that all were recording smoothly to the armada of memory sticks on his bandolier.

He dropped his screen back into its holster, then rang the bell. He imbibed all kinds of informative scents just standing there catching his breath. The covered porch somewhat preserved the perfumes of the fae who had sat in the rockers that lined the porch (and smelled happier here, not mopey like they had at the bus stop), but the bristly ochre welcome mat had soaked up *something*...here. Something living, though it reminded him of decay...and also of back home, the dry heat of summer, but it also smelled like...maybe sealant? Sealant on mud? Who knew? He was no bear nose.

His claw went to the recorder, but he stopped himself. *Wouldn't do to have them open the door on me working. This is a business proposition, after all.*

Okay, it'd been long enough. He rang twice, then knocked an insistent tattoo on the door.

He waited as long as his patience allowed. Then an idea came to him. He pulled out his screen, navigated out of the cam controls and into the messaging program.

"Hey," he typed. "By chance did the owner leave a spare house key somewhere? Or is there a code to get in?"

The Netron girl replied a moment later. Mercurio left the doorstep to find the dragonfly-painted rock sitting next to the scrubber at the bottom of the lanai stairs. It was light when he held it in his claw.

"Cattycorner," he said to it, and the enchantment disappeared, leaving him with a metal house key in his claw. He trilled in amazement, smile pulling at his beak until he remembered that camera one was still staring at the front door.

Shoot, wish I'd gotten that on MaxCam! Angel, over his shoulder, wasn't close enough to've seen the cool stuff in detail. Maybe he could do a reenactment later.

He skipped up the lanai stairs again. "Housekeeping!" he called, before unlocking the door.

He stepped inside.

"Kind of cool," he said to himself/his audience, pausing both to take in the front sitting room (kind of mysterious with the curtain pulled), and loft balcony overhead, and to give the cams a sec to adjust their apertures.

The outside looked more luxurious to him than this dove-brown painted interior. Though the mat he stood on was thick and squashy, not sisal-y, that was nice.

A door opened upstairs.

Mercurio's nostrils twitched. The scent hadn't carried yet, but it was them, HAD to be!

Of course, if it wasn't, he'd arguably just committed breaking and entering on a fellow squar. Oops. Well, it'd make for an exciting headline on his feed!

Creaks above helped Mercurio track the Gorgon's position.

"I know you're not the owner, because the owner wouldn't have knocked."

Mercurio followed the creaks until the human, Icarii, stepped into view, dressed all in tan like a safari tourist, looking down on him from the loft, one hand on the banister. Good mercy, he was tall!

Mercurio winked, putting the male Gorgon into focus.

"I don't suppose you're Lane Ho'okano, are you? And turn those cameras off, we haven't given any permission to film!"

Oooh, but how his mismatched eyes SPARKED! How could he tell Mercurio not to film such a compelling, infamous, new-follower-attracting face? He wouldn't, not if he knew.

Mercurio drew himself up.

"I am Mercurio Maximino Macoya, creator and content director of MercurioMaxFilms."

He awaited a flash of recognition from those eyes; got...nothing?! "...And I have a business proposition for you."

"Cameras off *now*, Lane Macoya, or you'll get nothing from us."

"If you insist."

Mercurio slid the remote out, brought the cams to him in "rest" formation so they stacked into a vertical column behind his wings, lenses facing straight down. He left the audio recording on, though. Wouldn't be broadcast quality, but might be good for ADR or reenactment later.

He put the remote away, held his palms out, *whaddya say?* style.

Icarii rested his elbows on the banister, began leaning forward, but the wood gave a worrying creak and he stood again.

Here goes nothing. "What I'm proposing is—"

"You wouldn't happen to have something to eat in one of those pouches of yours, would you?"

"Yeah, sure." *Weird request*, thought Mercurio as Icarii came down the steps three at a time.

And then, he was RIGHT THERE, smelling of dustbath powder and human deodorant that did nothing to cover up that strange sweet decay mixed with a dash of desert heat.

Mercurio cranked his head up just to see the patient face—with hungry eyes.

He quickly flipped open his snack pouch (good for bribing squabs for info, and wildlife for B-roll), pulled out the first package he felt. He held it up, discovered a meal bar dangling from his claws, but it didn't get to swing an inch before it was pulled from his claws with a quintessential Netron bow.

"Thank you, cousin," he said as it was being ripped open.

Icarii took a bite that made his eyes roll back. "Oh, that's *terrific*," he said, hand over his mouth. He examined the package, chewing, chewing.

"It's just a Wikibar," said Mercurio. "Oatmeal cranberry peanut butter."

A hard gulp. His odd eyes searched Mercurio again. Icarii opened his mouth—Mercurio would have sworn in court he was about to say, "Got any more?" but instead he said, "It's great. Never had this flavor before."

Mercurio preened his wing. "That's because it hasn't been released to the gen-pub yet. I did an unbiased review of it. Sponsored vid. I used to do a lot of food reviews. Perhaps you've seen a few?"

Icarii's grin twisted funny. "Probably not, Lane. The past few years of my life were consumed with more pressing matters, in case you haven't seen the news."

Mercurio's teal comb bobbed with his nod. "Oh, I saw! You're notorious!"

Another funny look. "...Thank you?"

"That's what I'm here to talk to you about! See—"

"Speaking of which, how'd you find us? Only the hotelier...motelier? knew we were heading out here."

Upon mentioning *us*, Mercurio's gaze flickered to the upstairs, where Icarii had come from. *She's up there somewhere. I wonder if he negotiates for the both of them, or if I have to sway her, too.*

"Some fae girls at Crooked Neck's glamorous bus stop told me."

Icarii went strangely still.

Mercurio guttered, worried. *Did I tick him off? Why does it look like nobody's home? No, that's not quite it—*

"Surely no fae talked to you," said Icarii, suddenly reanimated.

Mercurio clucked, surprised. "You're right, actually—"

"The Netron girl with them. She told you where to find the house key, too? Nevermind. I'd invite you to sit down, but it isn't my place to. So say what you're going to say. We need to be off soon."

"Okay, okay, listen. You two are considered the most evil people in the galaxy right now, aren't you?"

"It doesn't seem prudent for me to answer that."

"Yeah, yeah. Anyway, I'm offering you a chance to tell your side of the story. On my feed!"

"I've told my story to Warfather Alwitz."

"But was a camera present? No, there wasn't, or else it'd be out by now. You'll be visiting everyone on Osider and their first impressions of you are all rumors. You need a platform—and I'm here to offer mine! A partnership!"

"Lane Macoya, we don't want a platform, we don't want a feed. We want to be fed, and thanks to the generosity of Warfather Alwitz and the administration which he serves, we are."

Except the Netron girl said they stole their money. And..."took over" this house? Come to think, why weren't they at the motel? Or staying with someone? Maybe that Ho'okano guy he'd asked Mercurio about?

The local peeps knew they were coming...but they had to take over a place to stay? Were they guests of the town or not?

"How long are you staying here? In this house, I mean."

"This is the end of our stay. There was—nevermind. So if that's all, we will be leaving for our workday. If you give me the spare key"—his huge hand was already out—"we'll make sure the owner gets it."

He's not telling me everything. There's got to be a way to get them on my feed!

Mercurio handed the key over with a smile. "I understand. Thanks for your time, cousin."

He kept his tail jaunty and his walk steady until he was off the porch and back on the ground. Then he ran. There was a way to get what he wanted—but the answer was back in town. With Lane Hoʻokano.

8

KEONAONA

Squargling families were already gathering in the plaza down in the bowl, but no real line had formed yet. From this distance, they looked like a beach of colored pebbles under the wan grey sky. They were packed more densely towards the opposite end of the plaza—where the lodge and chapel stood—but on this side of the soaking pool that marked the plaza's midpoint, the crowd was more spread out, with actual breathing room between each body.

Keonaona pulled the cold cart behind him, towards the more loosely-spaced customers. If he'd had his way, he'd be at home, trying to sleep through these particular few days. Though, looking at the plaza (which he'd never seen this crowded before, packed wing-to-wing from the squares' side to the hens') he wondered with dread if the Gorgon's visit wouldn't extend out into *weeks*.

But long before everything had gone wrong, his friend Analū had asked if Keonaona would run the fruit cart while he stayed behind at Nibbles, Crooked Neck's own general store. It would be good for business—Mother knew the town could use the jen—and, at the time, they both thought it would help Keonaona gather...open-minded guests for the dinners he'd be in charge of. Show the Gorgon the kind of hospitality a little community like Crooked Neck was capable of.

Now, Keonaona just wanted to get through the day without seeing the Gorgon, or anyone else he knew. By the size of the crowd, he'd be too busy ferrying an empty cart back to Analū's and restocking. Most of these squarglings were city wings, and if they had enough money to take the one bus all the way out here and pay for rented rooms (or the motel's newly-raised rates), they'd have money for a sweet, juicy treat while they were—

Keonaona flushed with rage, warmth making his head feel tingly

—waiting their turn.

He shook his claw out. He'd been strangling the pull handles. Who had he turned into?

He was glad these people were strangers; he knew everyone in town by scent and sight; he could avoid them easily just by serving the newcomers.

Despite his plodding pace, he had inevitably arrived the edge of the plaza. He started looking the strangers over—but there were too many families with hatchlings in arms...worse yet, he saw squares without their mates, surrounded by their squabs...Families with oddly-shaped holes in them, the absences screaming out at your eyes like someone missing a wing or an eye or an arm.

Mother, if you're there—please be there!—I can't do this. It will last forever. I can't even handle this moment of seeing them, but there are so many of them, and I can't—

He did not even know what he was praying. Incoherency. He used to bless his home from the floor to the boards from the head of the table, making those who stayed at his home feel blessing-touched—not a brag; many had told him or his wife this on their own, in private—and now he didn't even know what he was praying for, couldn't even get out a coherent petition, and would She even bother with a request whose components were scattered like discarded nut shells spat out on the floor?

He began singing the fruit seller's song, trundling into the crowd. But Keonaona kept his eyes down. There were no competitors here. Those city sellers hadn't come. Business would come to him.

He sang the song but kept his beak alert for any scent of his neighbors. Though, he seemed to recall—again, from before the awful time—that village residents would be first in line at the chapel. He imagined they'd be crowded over on opposite side of the plaza, where Lono and his wife would be queuing everyone before they were summoned to his house—or at least, that had been the plan when he was housing the Gorgon. So perhaps he wouldn't meet any out here if he stayed on this side.

Two squabs interrupted him. They left with a packing box full of fruit cups and an extra-large envelope of Zing! to sprinkle on it.

He paused to feed their money into the slots of the lockbox. That family must be huge. Unless they planned to resell it? None of his business, as long as Analū got paid.

Not long after the squabs left, Keonaona kept getting stopped every few steps to sell. All strangers, thank Mother. But maybe it was time to find a place to settle in for the day, pull out the awning and let them come to him. He knew he didn't like having to track down the nomadic vendors working the colossal city plazas, back when he'd worked in Kapekolo. He looked about for a landmark—the spiky red bromeliads in front of the bank would make a good one, but it might get too crowded with everyone going in and out of the bank. Plus, it was a little too far out, inconvenient.

(The wise, he supposed, would push their carts up and down the line when it formed, but if Analū wanted him to do that...well, Analū could do it, and *he* would see to the store! Only he couldn't, because Analū would never let him; that store was his very own nest and egg.)

He'd stay away from the chapel and the lodge—too great a chance of seeing *them*. And neighbors, who would ask questions.

Stay on the opposite side. That left the old café, the new café—if it was still open—and—ah, that would work.

The thick rubber tires of the cold cart made the uneven crackles and splucks of mud spattering almost comforting as he pressed his way through to Nika's repair shop on the squares' side of the plaza. After scanning the dizzying number of electronics posters in the window, he spotted the "closed" sign—then under it, a sign in Nika's favorite font saying the shop would be closed for the duration of the Gorgon's visit.

Safe.

He parked the cart in between the giant buttressed roots of a ceiba tree and cranked the scented awning upright. Normally, the melon, white, and green stripes would catch the sunlight and color the ground around the cart, but in today's rainlight, they only served as a bright accent amid the browns and greens of the plaza. A good little landmark, and he'd be out of the way, and out of the rain when it came, but still easily visible.

He was debating starting the song again when a portion of the crowd traveling towards the lodge-and-chapel end of the plaza broke off to surround his stand. He served up pre-carved cantaloupe bowls, glistening ruby cubes of jubal fruit, and wedges of juicy pineapple, slid all the money away, and wondered where Analū kept the "be back soon—re-stocking" sign. At this rate, he'd have to run back to the general store before the hour was up.

It was a relief to be busy.

Keonaona had had to scramble between orders to dig up the sign; he wound up putting it up just after fifteen minutes or so after the first hour (or so it felt; in Crooked Neck nobody cared too much about exact time, which was one thing he hadn't liked about city life).

He whistled the fruit seller's song of *be back soon* before he dashed off, was pleased to note that despite some groans, most of the new group milling around the cart did not turn away to hunt for available food, but began chatting with their neighbors instead. Analū would be pleased.

Maybe he should take Analū's electric driving cart, tow some coolers behind him this time—if Analū'd thought ahead enough to be chopping while he took care of the undoubtably quiet store. Sure, old Mo'o and Kahele normally dropped by to peck the shells with him, but all the action was in the plaza today, and probably would be for the next few days, so all Keonaona could picture was Analū yawning behind the peanut barrels.

Keonaona's breathing grew heavy as he made his way up the bowl of earth that the plaza was nestled in.

He'd better not be standing there preening his wings. If all he does is chop fruit while I'm gone, I'll make him rich as a mint by the time all this is over!

Out of the bowl and down the cone, he took the forest path to the general store practically on instinct. Even wading through the calf-high stream newly swollen with rain was done with the practiced ease of a Crooked Neck native. It was like his time working in the city had never happened at all.

But it did. Maybe I never should have left.

He splashed out the other side, puttees washed lighter from the stream surging past.

If I hadn't gone away, nothing bad would ever have happened.

He shook himself from comb to tail, water whipping off him at every angle. The sound of his wings slapping against his sides echoed around him—more importantly, the violent sensation stung the downward-spiral thoughts out of him for the moment.

"Just get to Analū's," he said, and trudged forward.

Thinking of the awaiting crowd back in the plaza, he forced himself to run the final leg up to the store.

It wasn't long before the sunny tip of Nibbles' steeply pitched roof came into view. As the A-shaped store grew more prominent, so did its trademark scent, a distinct sweetness that reminded Keonaona of jelly beans, only lighter, not at all cloying.

Keonaona jogged up the steep concrete stairs built into the hill the store was perched on top of. The flat clearing at the top of the stair let Keonaona's claws get a better grip as he approached the store's lanai with its glider benches, empty today due to all the fuss back in town. He dodged around the gliders and burst through the door a little too fast, causing it to slam and Analū to shriek in surprise.

He *was* standing over the peanut barrel.

"Sorry," said Keonaona. "But your fruit's a big hit in town. I left an auditorium's worth of city wings waiting in front of the cart."

Analū flapped his banana-colored wings. "Empty already?"

"You just stand back there and chop fruit. I'll fill the coolers and take your driving cart back, if you don't mind. And you may as well send along any spare Zing! you got."

Analū whistled, impressed. "Even the city wings can't resist the old Ho'okano hospitality!"

The compliment struck Keonaona like a spear; somehow leaving him feeling both pain and emptiness.

Hospitality. Since when had that saved anyone?

Analū stopped heading for the back. "Hey—you okay? You got a little grey suddenly."

"Just worn out," said Keonaona quickly. "It's been a jaunt."

"Got it, brah. I'll give you the keys to my drivee."

Keonaona didn't have to face any questions while they chopped, loaded, and hitched up the wagon for the trip back. But outside in the driving cart, just before he put his foot down on the pedal to descend the hill, Analū stuck his head under the roof.

"Hey...you know anyone named Mercurio? Got a bite to his scent like cherry soda, green, blue head? Maybe from the city?"

Keonaona burbled impatiently, thinking of the restaurants opening back in the plaza.

"No."

"Well...he was here, asking after you. Bought an orange Jukee, too."

Keonaona whistled acknowledgment, but his thoughts were down the road and the stream. He might have to unload the coolers to get them across...

"Okay," said Analū. "Well, thanks for making me the red stuff."

Keonaona snapped back to the store, looked his friend in the eye. "Thank *you* for letting me."

9

KEONAONA

THE PLAZA WAS LOCATED in a natural bowl located at the top of the hill—well, a long-extinct cinder cone, but no one around here called it that—whose slope only looked gentle. This slope quickly proved to be too much for the drivee, so Keonaona parked it on the side of the road up. Some young city squares heading up the hill saw him pulling out the first cooler and quickly offered their help. Keonaona accepted it gratefully.

They refused to hear of him carrying anything of his up, and since there were five of them and five heavy, fruit-laden coolers, Keonaona didn't argue. Ever since...what had happened, much of his usual vigor had left him. Due at least in part to that, running up the hill to Analū's had taken more out of him than usual. He'd be only too happy to let them cut the line at the stand and give them each a cantaloupe for their trouble.

They made it to the top with only one of them almost taking a fall on the treacherous trail (an anise-smelling, grey fellow with red stripes, who'd laughed it off), then carefully picked their way down into the bowl.

The looser conglomerate of squarglings standing at this end of the bowl kept up their congenial chatting, parting only when Keonaona began singing the fruit seller's song. Then the little bunches and circles of gatherers hopped aside, freeing up space for Keonaona lead his short train of city helpers through to his spot outside Nika's darkened shop.

Hearing him come, the crowd he'd left behind formed back into a slightly more linear queue. Keonaona heard a little grumbling when he presented a fruit to each of the load-bearing squares (four cantaloupes and a honeydew; they all refused the Zing!, though), but that was to be expected.

Soon he was open again, taking orders in a steady stream that demanded all of his attention. It tired the body, sure, but it blessedly numbed the mind.

Maybe this is the answer to my prayer.

Even that thought came only in little sips between tutus shuffling away from the counter with their sweets and bachelors speaking their orders as they bounced up to replace them—a thought like a quick fish flashing in pondlight before disappearing into liquid black.

The five coolers lasted some three hours. The customers were nonstop. Keonaona was panting by the time he put the "be back soon" sign up, wings sagging from fatigue.

He crushed the last order's bills against his palm, left the coolers where they were (but open, so all could see they were empty) and decided to risk heading towards the center of the plaza, where the squares' café was.

His gaze swept the crowd left!, right!, left!, right!, like a sugarcane switch as he approached the soaking pool at the center of the plaza, but he saw no one he recognized. *If* the Sweet Land Café were still open, probably Firmino would be there, but he could play everything off to being tired—if the newcomer even noticed anything off about him.

Tails hugged tight to their owners as he wove his way through. But the café was as dark as Nika's place. Keonaona raised his wings to block out the rainlight shining into the plaza and peered into the glass.

All emptied out. No chairs, no nothing.

Well, that wasn't much surprise. This poor little spot never could keep a proprietor long. New businesses rotated in and out of this particular unit within months. If he believed in such things, he'd say it was cursed. The Crooked Neck Café, on the other claw, had stood on the hens' side of the plaza since before the lodge had been built; in this town, it was an institution.

Keonaona turned around, got on tiptoe and leaned to try and see around the palmettos and artfully stacked rocks that contained the soaking pool. No use; he couldn't see to the hens' side. He'd have to fight the crowd to get to the café.

"Anybody know when they're 'sposed to show up?"

"...no local Kōkoʻolua in charge of this thing. Shouldn't be surprised with that blueberry in off—"

"...if you have to register at the lodge first?"

"...in town yet?"

Voices came in and out of focus in the starts and stops that Keonaona had to take to cross to the hens' side of the plaza. He kept his head down and tried not to step on any feet.

The Crooked Neck Café was lit up—but a sandwich board stood guarding the front doors. *Be back soon*, in the same bubbly writing that Lani had been writing the daily specials in for thirty years.

Forced to stop, the little mosquitoes of warning landed on Keonaona again. He could've fooled that newcomer about how he was feeling, but Keonaona and his wife were friends with Lani—she'd lent a claw with catering more times than he could count. She would know something was bothering him. And he didn't want to talk. Not ready.

He backed up, thinking to sit on the rock wall that contoured the soaking pool—but any seats available were already taken by the various city tutus. (The widow ʻEwalani—the lovely old hen—was nowhere to be seen, yet her sore old bones forced her to practically live in the water, "like a lilac-scented petrel" as she liked to joke. That she wasn't here for a soak must mean the townsfolk were all at the lodge side of the plaza, if not waiting in the chapel itself. Now Keonaona felt certain of it.)

He scurried to a tree within sight of the café and pressed himself to it, thinking over his options. Del's place would be a good choice—the restaurant stood opposite the chapel, about as far away as you could get from it while still being in the plaza—but—

But I don't belong there anymore.

Quickly, before the horror could set in, he pulled a replacement thought into his mind and focused on it firmly: *But Del's is a sit-down place. And I don't want to linger.*

The jen was still in his hand. He could pay someone to carry the empty coolers down, drive back, cadge a lunch from Analū instead. He turned around to do just that when an alarm shriek cascading through the crowd made him (and three dozen others) look up.

Some squab's ball was whizzing through the air over-head—but already a following call told him it wasn't dangerous. He quit shielding himself with his wings just as the ball slowed in midair—and now, as it turned a black glossy spot towards him, Keonaona recognized the ball for what it really was—a camera.

A camera! Here in Crooked Neck! He never thought he'd see the day!

His marveling, however, quickly turned to unease when another floating ball descended beside it...and then another.

All three shiny black eyes were pinned on him.

It's just cameras, Keonaona. They can't hurt you.

But the way those black spots held him, unblinking, in their view...no, no, he didn't want to be seen. It was one thing to be part of "the awaiting crowd at Crooked Neck" (or whatever the reporters were casting this scene as), it was entirely another to be singled out.

Are my feelings that plain on my face that they'd pick me out of this crowd? Or do they know I shirked my—

No, hosting the Gorgon wasn't a duty; the Kōko'olua had repeated that, too.

—that I changed my mind?

The middle ball slowly—*intently*, Keonaona thought—began advancing on him.

The red square turned and ran. So sudden was his panic that he didn't realize he was heading away from the fruit stand, deeper into the crowd, closer to the end of the plaza he had until that moment so successfully avoided.

He glanced up behind him. The silly balls kept pace effort-lessly, black eyes still staring down upon him. An extended croak leaked out of him, edging from anxiety into terror.

And now, familiar scents were swiftly passing by him in the air.

"Keonaona!"

"Keonaona, why you running?"

"Where you been?"

Oh, no. Oh no no no! There was Mo'o and Kahele and Auntie Melia and Pali and his other neighbors he didn't want seeing him.

He ran blindly, swerving only when he saw the lava rock face of the chapel, changing course towards the hens' apothecary, the nearest building. He could circle around back—

But before he could make it even into the shadow of the building, a figure leaped in front of him.

Keonaona shrieked, tried to throw himself out of the way so he wouldn't collide with him, but to his astonishment, the figure mirrored him, wings spread and claws out, as though trying to catch him.

He's crazy! thought Keonaona a second before impact.

The other square was younger and outweighed him by a few kilos, so after the initial thud, when they went tumbling together in a jumble of tails and scales, they rolled back into the plaza.

He lay there a moment, panting while the blue-headed stranger hopped back up to his feet.

Scents swirled around him again. Keonaona knew without opening his eyes that his neighbors had them surrounded.

"What'd you do that for??"

It was Lani. Must have left the café to check the news on the Gorgon's arrival. Keonaona could picture her facing down the stranger, large wings spread.

"Is he Lane Ho'okano? Can any of you tell me?"

Keonaona'd never heard that voice before. Keeping his eyes closed and his breathing shallow, he tried scenting his—well, attacker? All he got was the familiar scents of the plaza, his neighbors, and the acrid smell of puttee dip.

"You knocked him out cold, you shell-eater! See if I ever sell you a mango again!"

"Sorry, Auntie, sorry, sheesh! I promise I didn't mean to clobber him, I just wanted to talk!"

Funny, this square almost sounded like he was...smiling.

No, Keonaona. You just got your beans tossed, you're not thinking straight.

"So—*is* he Lane Ho'okano?"

"Who wants to know?"

"Mercurio Maximino Macoya, creator and content director of the feed MercurioMaxFilms."

So he's not with the news?

"My card," added the new square.

In the pause that followed, Keonaona considered peeling an eye open, to get a better look, but thought better of it; maybe he could find out more if no one thought he was listening.

"Okay. That still don't explain—"

"I'm a great-nephew of 'Ewalani Marcos. I'm staying at her place while I interview peeps for my feed. A-and when Lane Ho'okano didn't show for our interview, I thought I'd try and find him myself."

Do *I know him?* Now Keonaona couldn't resist a look.

Keeping his eyes squinched as narrow as possible, he dared a blurry peek at the young voice.

Green body, navy lavalava, blue head, rakish teal comb, looked like he'd seen a couple seasons at the mating grounds, but no more. Nobody he'd met before. The dashing square happened to glance down. When he saw Keonaona, he winked.

Utter confusion (*should I know him? Is he someone important? Is he someone I forgot?*) at this gesture of confederacy made Keonaona's stomach tumble—until one of the silver cameras rose over the square's shoulder and fixed its beady eye on him. He was in control of the cameras.

The square knelt and offered him his claw. The jig was up.

"Sorry, brah," said the blue-and-green, pulling Keonaona up. "I thought you said to meet you at the opposite end of the plaza. When you didn't show, I got worried. Now we can begin the interview." He pulled some piece of equipment off his vest.

Lani bristled again. The orange-creme insides of her wings were raised so high, they reminded Keonaona of a sailboat on the sea. "If he's okay, you mean!"

"I'm fine, Lani, I'm fine," Keonaona said quickly.

"Good, 'cause Lono's been looking for y—"

Lono? No, I don't want to see him, either.

"Great!" said the young square. "This location will do, let's get you set—"

Keonaona shot the new square a significant look, hoping Lani wouldn't notice. "But I was looking forward to seeing that enchanted backdrop you said you set up behind your great-aunt's house."

"Backdrop?"

Keonaona flashed his eyes.

"Oh, right! Well, I think it's in the wrong place. Might need moving."

"I'll help you. We'd better get going now—don't want to get caught in the rain."

"Sure, sure!"

The fellow—Mercurio, was it?—whistled cheerfully and gripped his shoulder in a chummy way. Then he pointed at Keonaona's neighbors. "I'll be back to interview you all later. And while you're waiting around, consider joining my feed, MercurioMaxFilms!"

10
MERCURIO

SURE GLAD MAXCAM'S LOCKED onto this guy. If I didn't know any better, I'd say he's trying to ditch me!

The awesome-smelling red square with the gold comb, Ho'okano, hadn't even waited for Mercurio to finish plugging his channel before he turned and practically sprinted into the plaza crowd. So Mercurio had to rely on MaxCam, floating high above the crowd, to follow his subject. Even then, the cam followed at a distance, its algorithm trying to keep him within its cone of vision. Plus, with so many different wings jumbled in here, it *was* technically possible for the cam to mistake a similarly-colored squargling for him and lock onto her instead—but Mercurio felt confident that wouldn't happen. MaxCam had never let him down, not when he was tracking street food vendors in Osider's Embassy Plaza or recording him taking on the tallest water slide in Las Palmas.

He only wished he had time and space to get Wideshot and Angel back in "rest" formation at least, to conserve the batteries. The enchantment he'd paid a wing for killed the noise the propellers made, but flying around still drained the batteries quick, especially in auto-follow mode.

"S'cuze me—sorry, Auntie—outta the way, kiddos..." Couldn't this guy've gone round to the squares' side? At least directly in front of the shops the crowd wasn't so, well, crowded.

Come to think...Maybe that's the ticket, thought Mercurio. He unhooked his eyes from MaxCam and began sidling his way towards the squares' shops.

Sure enough, the walkway was far clearer. He ducked out from beneath the awnings from time to time to track MaxCam, but made better time without pushing through all the waiting people.

When he finally caught up with the square, he found him directing a small group of wings to pick up a set of empty coolers in front of a friendly-looking little vending cart. A twitch of his nostrils brought the aroma of melon—and was that jellybeans?—to him, confirming the cart's purpose.

*Lane Ho'okano, the humble fruit merchant...*he mentally narrated. No...*What connection could the nefarious Gorgons of Hriana possibly have with humble fruit merchant Ho'okano?* Ooh!

He could see the title card now, complete with a still of the red square fleeing in the crowd, hunted look on his face. MaxCam got a shot of that, he was sure of it!

The red was closing up the cart now, the striped canopy producing another candy-sweet breeze as it was folded back down into the body of the cart. Some squarglings nearby (*waiting for the cart to reopen, I guess*) whistled sadly as it did, but they only dispersed when Mercurio's subject whistled the "day is over" song. But the melody stopped short of where Mercurio expected.

No "see you tomorrow"? That's it, this guy knows something.

The red went around and took hold of the cart's pull handles.

He's setting off. Can't let that happen!

Mercurio stepped out from under the walkway.

"Hey, you're fast!"

Ho'okano jumped in the air with a startled cluck.

Mercurio took up a place next to the red, leaned on the top of the cart. "You even got me winded!"

The squares carrying the coolers looked to the red—he quickly waved them away, out the plaza. "I'll meet you down there," he told them. Then he turned to Mercurio. "Lane, you and I both know I didn't agree to an interview with you. I've never *met* you. And I'm too busy now to talk. So I wish you well on your videos—"

The square was interrupted by the gurgle of his own belly. His tail lashed.

Mercurio's claw was already in his snack pouch. This time, though, he checked the packaging before handing the goodie over.

The red accepted it with a wary "thanks". But he tore into it like a starving piglet, and the peanut butter kept him from talking.

"Good, huh? Wikibar sent me a box for a review vid. Complimentary. That flavor ain't even out yet. You like? So did the Gorgon."

Mercurio had expected a response, yes. But more along the lines of going grey, or maybe freezing in fear.

What Mercurio did not expect was the square puffing up and—*snap!*—unfurling his wings, spitting the partly-chewed bar at his feet, then screeching like he was going to chase him up the nearest roof.

Instinct made Mercurio hop away, cawing in alarm. He collided with an onlooker, and while he was apologizing, the red hauled his cart away and out of sight like his tail was on fire.

Thank Mother for MaxCam!

Mercurio ran in the general direction the square had left in. Between the ruts of the cart's wheels in the mud, the sweet smell of its canopy, and the occasional glimpse of MaxCam whirring overhead, catching up wasn't at all hard. But getting to him down this crazy hill, well, that was another thing.

A broken leg might grab a lot of views, but he didn't have the cash right now to hire a faerie healer and he didn't have time to waste recuperating. He'd promised his viewers a Very Special Event premiering at the end of next month...Barely enough time to film *and* edit, and that was only for one episode...

So Mercurio crouched and carefully eased sideways down the cinder cone, while the crazy bird—halfway down the hill already, for morning screeching!—slalomed the cart this way and that along the path, somehow keeping them both upright.

Mercurio finally gave up watching the square and focused on his footing.

When he caught up with Ho'okano again on level ground, the square was handing out jen to his assistants who'd borne the coolers down the hillside (three of them, Mercurio noticed, had mud staining the backsides of their lavalavas). Now, in addition to the vending cart and the coolers, there was a drivee with thick jungle-ready tires and a simple flatbed trailer attached.

Gotcha, thought Mercurio. He waited until the help left back up the hill, then sauntered up to the square as if nothing had happened. He received a dark glance for his trouble. Mercurio shrugged it off.

"Help you load the trailer?"

The help, for some reason, had placed them next to the trailer instead of putting them in—a clinch opportunity for Mercurio.

"NO," said the red.

Mercurio hefted a cooler up anyway.

Once again, the square surprised him—he didn't sullenly let Mercurio help, but crowded him and screeched again in his face. "What part of 'no' don't you understand? I don't want anything to do with you, I don't want anything to do with your videos, and I don't want anything to do with the Gorgon! Stay out of my life!"

Mercurio resisted the urge to drop the cooler and run.

"Whoa, whoa, easy, sunset! I'm just here to help!"

"I bet you are."

But he didn't run Mercurio off. Mercurio set the cooler in the trailer, turned around for the next, found the red loading one up himself, wings held stiffly, mouth a stubborn line. That still left three more. Mercurio loaded another. Then stood by.

He'll figure it out. He hadn't seen a hitch on the front of the vendor's cart. He'd have to make two trips to get all his equipment—or let Mercurio help.

And by then, I should be able to get him to talk. Everybody talks to Mercurio in the end.

Sure enough, when all was packed and ready to go, the red square stopped between the drivee and the vending cart, looking back and forth at each, puzzling out the situation.

"I could follow you in the drivee," Mercurio said in his ear.

Ho'okano turned his head, stared right into Mercurio's face. Again, the reaction wasn't anything like he'd expected: though his red scales hadn't dulled one bit, the fire had gone out of his honey-colored eyes. He looked ragged, suddenly—*like he's homeless*, thought Mercurio, *only that's not right, he smells clean, his lavalava looks brand new...*

His thoughts cut off entirely when the square turned from him and slumped down on the drivee's seat. His tail curved tight around his body and his head bowed into his wings, face hidden.

Mercurio cringed. *This isn't what I'm looking for! People want action, not moping!* If it was a breakdown, it wasn't a compelling or photogenic one; his subject sat in the drivee, boring and still as a statue. A waste of battery! A waste of memory sticks!

He slapped his remote out of its pocket, called the cams to rest, shut them off for the first time that day.

"What's the matter with you! Can't accept any help? Well, good luck getting all your junk back without me! All I want are a few lousy answers!"

The square muttered something then—"*So do I*"? What the heck did that mean?

The square raised his head. He still looked like a wreck. "Fine. Ask me something."

Mercurio held in his peep of surprise. "Really?" Mercurio's thumb worked on his remote, releasing Angel into the air.

The red square's head dropped in a simple nod.

"Okay! All right! Do you know why the Gorgons had to take over someone's house last night?"

A flash in Ho'okano's eyes—Mercurio couldn't quite tell what it was.

"Yes. Yes, I suppose I do."

Mercurio waited for more.

Ugh, no, he's not gonna be one of those guys you gotta drag the story out of, is he?

"So..." said Mercurio. "Why did the Gorgons have to find their own place to stay last night?"

"Because I'm supposed to be hosting them. Keep them in my own home, feed them, make them comfortable in while they...do their thing. In Crooked Neck. But I don't want to anymore."

"Well, why not?!"

The red square swung his feet all the away into the drivee.

Then the stubborn crow jammed his knuckle onto the key-plate.

"Hey! Hey!" Mercurio screeched.

The headlights shone on the ground.

"You helped load up two coolers," said the red. "So I only owe you two answers."

And then the jerk drove off, leaving Mercurio alone with the empty fruit stand.

He stood there a second, looking after where the cart had zoomed into the thick jungle. The electric motor's hum had already vanished into the general noise of the forest.

"Son of a stoat!" he cursed.

Then he grabbed the fruit cart.

Now he *had* to track him down.

11

GORGON

THE FAERIE HOUSE WAS over an hour behind them. The sky overhead was grey as an anvil and felt about as heavy, poised to fall on their heads with the same pleasant sensation, whenever the rain decided it was ready.

And now, before them, rose up this...sweet little hill, something he'd be able to run straight up with no problem...if he'd been caught up on his sleep...and not forced to carry this load on his back like a pack mule on jungle roads that seemed insistent on never lying straight for more than a few meters. If he'd had the option, he'd curl up right now—on the road, not even on the shoulder!—and nap.

/Excellent way to gain worms digging in your face,/ sent his Queen, not without a dusting of sympathy and affection.

Jerimin sighed. They weren't getting out of this, and the packs weren't getting any lighter.

She bent forward, looking like a bull ready to charge, but moved slowly, planting each foot with a pause, as though to let it anchor her to the hill before she proceeded up it. Within a few of these determined steps, she was ahead of him. He crooked himself over and followed.

Weird!

Whatever she was doing to add weight to her feet, she now deigned to do to his own; the sensation was strange. The only thing he could compare it to was lifting oneself out of bath water; body parts in the air moved with less resistance than those still under the water.

/This hill is a liar,/ she sent. /It only looks sweet, but the earth here delights in us falling./

/Evil hill?/

/Not evil. More.../ A feeling of superiority, the ghost of crossing his arms and smiling, of daring someone to best him.

/A sort of 'prove your worth, mortals' thing?/

/Hm. Yes-no. More mischief than pride. It is...good-natured, this hill's challenge. An echo of its former self, but awake to today's reality./ She sent this first with an image of roaring volcano under a black sky, which then brightened to the hill before them under a sunny sky. Now that she'd made him aware of its past, like magic, he became aware of the occasional lava rocks strewn among the grass off the path.

"I thought you said Osider wasn't a good fit for your element. Too much—" he began to pant, /water./

/Eat no mistake, my Jerimin. This place is too wet for us both./ She overlaid the memory of him dumping half that morning's dust bath into their clothing, makeshift anti-chafing treatment for the day. /But we are inland enough that...things aren't yet as draining as I feared./

/Good to hear,/ he sent as they took another switchback. He could hear the parrot-house commotion of squarglings on the top of the hill, but wondered at the lack of travelers on the hill itself. He didn't think they were late—he'd memorized the first day's itinerary, long before his mobi had drowned—in the two towns before, once they'd arrived, a host had taken them in and had made sure they were where they needed to be when they needed to be.

They paused for a drink of water at the top of the hill.

He'd filled up from the house sink before they left and he was regretting it; though it was clear, the tap water put a funk in his nose, like he was drinking distilled *eau de swamp*. He knew it had no taste, not really, but that smell really fooled you!

He chugged as much down as he could stand, then took a look over the top of the hill.

The trees here had been cut away, so now he was given back one of the advantages of his height—long sight lines.

They stood now partway behind a smooth cream-colored building—maybe made of rammed earth? Elegant terra cotta-colored patterns were painted on all the marshmallow-round corners. It was the largest building he'd seen since coming into

70

town, at least as wide as one of the buildings that had made up that three-pronged motel. Compared to the skyscrapers of his home city, it was a shrimp—even with the tall tower rising up from the back of the building—it still only rose up three stories. But for being made of mud, he supposed it was beautiful.

/Many beautiful things can be made from earth. Our *home* was made of earth./

Now looking at the thing made him sick for the smooth walls of the subterranean home they'd been forced out of.

/All to do...this. Over and over again.../

He shouldered off as much of her homesickness as he could, tried to stuff some of his own in with it for her to handle. They tussled over it a while, shoving the feelings back and forth until he finally agreed to bear his share.

He shouldered his pack.

"Come on. Let's go find out who's in charge."

The closer they got to the front of the building, the louder the squargling voices got.

/So many./ The words were tinged yellow with anxiety. He tried sending reassuring feelings back, but his private, suspicious thought was *Too many.* The population count was only four hundred; had everyone in town turned up to see them? They couldn't have killed that many from here, the numbers didn't sort out right in his head. In the past towns, there hadn't been many requesting a session—

/audience/

/*session*/ with them; most the crowd were looky-loos, or merchants cashing in on the opportunity to sell food to the hungry looky-loos. It was the Osidern way.

They were about to turn the corner into full view of the crowd when she stopped.

/Let's ghost./

He couldn't blame her for not wanting to be mobbed. Screamed at or wept over with joy, so much emotion from so many people was especially overwhelming for her supersenses. He was also a little relieved; he was so hungry, he figured she was running on fumes. But if she wanted to spend the energy ghosting, she must not be as badly off as he'd thought.

He didn't have to assent and she didn't wait for it; they walked together into the crowd looking like two random squarglings to anyone who saw them—so long as no one caught a whiff of their scent (his scentmod was almost empty—he'd have to mention that to Lyle in the next mobi message—gah, what he wouldn't do for a working mobi!)...and as long as he kept his mouth shut. Even coming out of the guise of a squargling, his voice was probably too well-known by now, unless he spoke Native, and even then, he didn't trust his accent not to betray him.

So when they approached the little bubble of squarglings out in front of the cream-colored building, she took the lead.

"Who's in charge of this thing?"

He almost jumped; she was speaking in a Standard-accented voice pitched much higher than he was used to hearing come out of her mouth.

The conversation within the group went dead and they all stared at them.

/Next time, start with "hello."/

/Too late now./

"I don't mean to be rude"—he could feel the words being sucked right out of his mouth; she would never come up with such a courteous phrase on her own—"I'm just wondering where we go to dig up some information."

The squarglings warbled doubtfully at each other, but a taller hen wearing a white apron and colored in blushing oranges and soft vanilla yellows—*like a citrus cream cake—oh, that sounds* DIVINE—answered.

"That'd be Lono—I mean, Mayor Likeke."

"Lono Likeke." His Queen murmured the name, but he, too, felt the pleasant way it rolled off his tongue.

The citrus-colored hen nodded. "He's in the lodge now"—she raised a wing towards the low-slung, wooden building next door to the earthen scrollwork building—"but I can tell you right now he don't know when the Gorgon's gonna get here any more than you or I do. I just asked."

"Hm. Good. That's all I needed to know," said his Queen before walking away towards the lodge. He followed, fighting down the urge to turn back and bow in apology.

But heavy footsteps quickly caught up with them. Citrus Hen.

She began walking alongside them. "You gonna go in and talk to Lo—the mayor? After I just told you I did it?"

"Yes."

"Lase, I got done talking to him not ten minutes ago...nothing's changed between then and now."

His Queen didn't break stride. "I know."

The hen tuttled—Jerimin couldn't tell if she was alarmed or exasperated. "But you'll just be wasting your time. He's not seeing outsiders! I'm a resident, I know him."

They were approaching the threshold of the lodge grounds. "Youdo—you live here?"

"Yes!"

"Are you in charge? Of anything?"

The hen clucked, looking bewildered. "I...run the hens' café."

"Then come in with us."

"You serious?"

"Do I look un-serious?"

Now the Citrus Hen threw a look at Jerimin, as if to ask, *Are you seeing this?*

He smiled apologetically and shrugged.

His Queen continued. "Give me—what do you—" She jabbed a hand into his brain, yanked out the proper phrase. "What's your name?"

"'Alohilani. —My friends call me Lani."

"'Alohilani. Is your café open?"

Jerimin tried not to grin at the expression on Citrus Hen's—Lani's—face, a face that said she didn't know how she got pulled into this strange conversation.

She might even be asking herself why she's still walking with us.

It reminded him of when he'd first met his Queen. Sometimes, just going along with her weirdness was the easiest way.

"Yes...I'm out to lunch now, but we're open."

"When can we eat there?"

They were off the main plaza now, walking between two high lava rock walls that funneled a street-wide path up to the lodge's lanai. He liked the way the fanlike ferns planted along the tops of the walls bobbed; he could picture lemonade carts (*Ooh, lemon ice!*) and squargling merchants hawking their wares beneath; if the sun was out, this path would still be shaded.

"After Lonooo...the mayor's assistant kicks you out, I guess. Though if you wanna eat together, the family café is on the opposite end of the plaza."

"No. We will eat together at your café."

Now the hen was absolutely goggling at him, like his Queen had suggested they all dance in their underwear together, or something.

Luckily, they'd reached the lodge entrance.

He hurried to open the door for his Queen, gestured Lani in after. He brought up the rear, closing the door behind them. The veil sight delineated a quick sketch of the space while his eyes adjusted, blue shadows and white sparkling shapes outlining carved wooden support beams and clay-smooth walls arcing up to a constructed arch that was like a "D" flattened on its side. The materials looked/felt more modern than he'd expected from the outside, just like the lodges in the last two towns; and just like the last two lodges, the pocket doors in the outer walls that were normally kept open for the cross ventilation were shut tight for privacy. That made the lodge—to him and her—cozily dim (for the various bas-reliefs carved into the walls were spotlighted only by tiny picture lights), but also ratcheted up the humidity by volumes. He swiped the sweat from his upper lip and squatted to unload the pack in front of the door.

Lani whirled around and clacked her beak at him. "You're blocking the exit!"

"That's the point," said his Queen, accent and pitch back in place.

The hen whirled back, saw his Queen sans ghosting disguise, and shrieked.

Out of the far corner of the lodge came the sound of feet barreling towards them.

Lani turned again to flee for the door, but stumbled to a stop, neck cranked to see Jerimin where the silent square had just been.

He bowed, winced from the sensation of a fork jabbing deep into his brain, recovered. "Our apologies, Lase. We didn't want to be mobbed outside."

She blinked a few times, but nodded quickly, seeming to get a hold of herself. While she resettled her wings, he stepped around her and helped his Queen remove her pack.

She was rolling her shoulders out when the two lodge occupants reached them.

"You're here!" said the male, neck wreathed in leis. His coloring—a strange mix of earthy purple, cheery red-pink, and berry blue—reminded Jerimin of the Fruity Frazzles cereal he ate as a child.

"But how?" asked the hen who'd run up with him, whose toasty golds and browns put him in the mind of crème brûlée—

—*no, it's your STOMACH doing that,* he chided.

Crème Brûlée continued. "I haven't been able to get ahold of Keonaona at all!"

"Is that Lane Ho'okano?" asked Jerimin.

"That one refused us entry last night," said his Queen.

"We had to take a house to the south," he finished.

"With Griffon? Griffon Cortez?"

"We don't know," said Jerimin. "Fae were staying there, so they let us in." He felt the ghost of a nasty grin below the surface of his lips.

/Close enough./

"Those girls came in the café for takeout a couple times," said Lani.

"Did you make the fries?" they both asked at once.

Lani looked into both their faces and the little ruff of fur on the side of her face puffed.

He blinked hard. /Cool it—we're probably staring at her like hungry sharks./

"I don't make fries at my place. Must've been The Lunch Box—that's the restaurant for couples I was telling you about."

/I'd kill for a potato./

A peanut butter jar floated in his vision. /You'd kill for much less!/

/I'd rank peanut butter higher than a potato. More protein./

The jar disappeared, and the squarglings before them—meaty roundbeaks all—pulsed warm in his vision. His tongue caught a taste of meat only she'd eaten...

/Absolutely NOT./

The squarglings twittered, confused.

"Absolutely not, what?" asked Crème Brûlée.

Shoot, said it out loud!

/You eat anybody here and we'll be back where we were before. They'll separate us./

/I know, I know. Only ki—/

She caught the sharpness in his look, changed her word. /...remembering./

"Lase—Lani, we didn't have much of a breakfast today. Could you please bring us something? Lunch is fine, too, it's been a long few days, you see, and we've been eating out of our packs all that time."

"Sure thing. Be right back."

She slid his pack out of the doorway.

"Put it on my tab," said Fruity Frazzles. "And don't tell—"

"I know, Lono, believe me! I'll keep quiet. I'll just say you two decided on lunch."

She ducked outside, letting in a slice of light that disappeared when the door closed.

Crème Brûlée and Fruity Frazzles conferred with each other in undertones—but he caught the Native words for "house" and (he thought) "guide."

"Sorry for the excitement earlier," said the colorful square. "We were expecting you earlier with Lane Ho'okano. I'm Mayor Likeke, and this is my wife and assistant Rosaura."

"Pleasure to meet you both," said Jerimin. He began inching forward, but jolted out of his bow, wincing a little as a painful shock zipped through his spine.

/The Gorgon does not bow!/

/You're right, you're right./

"Welcome to Crooked Neck," said the mayor.

Looks passed between the two squarglings in the awkward silence that followed. The muscles in their cheeks worked, but their beaks never opened to twitter or burble.

"So...how does this work? And—what should we call you?" said the mayor.

"Call me what you want," answered his Queen automatically.

He put a hand on his wife's shoulder. "The Warfather called her Mahina."

The mayor whistled, a rhythmic piping. "Mahina it is, then. All right." More looks exchanged. "So...will she be starting now, or...?"

She remained stone-faced, but her jolt of *no!* hit him in the gut and made his shoulders hitch.

"In the previous towns, we were taken around the first day—given the nickel tour, so to speak," said Jerimin.

"There was a dinner," said his Queen.

"In the first town, yes."

"Okay, okay," said Lase Likeke. "That's a little different than what we had planned."

When the hen didn't say anything more, Jerimin said, "Oh?"

"Yeah..." said the major. "We assumed you'd lodge...and eat...and hold your seances at Keonaona's...It's the nicest place in town to stay, and he knows how to treat a guest!"

At this, his Queen coughed. But he was fairly certainly only he heard the contempt in it.

Lase Likeke spoke. "We've been waiting for him to call all morning."

"The plan was to meet you over there during a lunch break this afternoon, then start sending our people over in the afternoon. But if he hasn't taken you in, we'll have to find somewhere else for you to set up."

The mayor's wife turned to him. "I guess I could take them on a tour—"

"It doesn't bother us to skip the tour," said Jerimin, "but we're concerned about where we'll be staying, especially given the rain." *Please don't make us camp. Please don't make us camp.* "The proprietress of the motel said there was no vacancy, and that everyone else was full up as well."

"Yes, those 'Ehanuanites swamped us overnight," said the mayor with a satisfied-sounding chuckle.

"What stops us from staying in last night's house?" asked his Queen. "The owner is back today, yes?"

Another look passed between the squargling pair, this one with a heaping dose of skepticism. "I'll call Griffon and see," she finally said. "'Scuze me, I left my mobi back in my office," she said before leaving for the back corner again. The mayor watched her go.

She opened a door that was almost hidden among the wood paneling and shut it behind her.

The mayor turned to them. "I wouldn't count on staying at Griffon's."

"Why not?" asked Jerimin.

The mayor shrugged his wings. "It's a long story. Some of it's bad blood—the way I heard it, he thinks I 'stole' Rosie from him—some of it's he got rich for a while there and thinks he's better than everyone...Built that big nest out there as a big 'I'll show you!' But now I hear he has to rent it out just so's he can keep traveling..."

"You heard?" Jerimin heard himself say with a meaningful tone.

He threw a look at his Queen. It wasn't the first time she'd used him as a ventriloquist's dummy this trip. But her expression didn't change, and if the proxy comment had exposed any noteworthy insight about the mayor, well, she wasn't sharing.

The mayor waved a claw dismissively. "He keeps to himself mostly. You know how far outside town he wound up! Wouldn't surprise me if he said no just to be a pain in my tail."

Their inner weather clouded over beneath the green shadow of their tent.

Behind them, the lodge door opened again, casting light on the floor in a wedge briefly before Lani the orange café hen stepped in, bulging canvas tote bags hanging from each fist. The mayor hurried over to help her in, then locked the door behind her.

"I don't think we need anybody else walking in on this, do you?"

"You're the mayor."

A table and folding wooden chairs were unhooked from their pegs on the walls and set up farther into the lodge. As far as lodges went, Jerimin still didn't feel he had them figured out. He'd assumed at first they were for housing squares; then, after the first town, for makeshift banquet halls...until the second town, where they had held most their sessions right inside one. Now his theory veered towards designating them community multipurpose rooms.

Lani set out the brown takeout containers.

/You know I'm getting desperate to eat when the idea of poi makes my mouth water./

/She brought fries./

/WHAT?! YES!!/

He almost laughed to see his Queen straighten up, up, fighting to keep his triumphant smile off her face.

/You're adorable./ He did his best to make a picture of a giant pink heart floating over to her in the air.

"Hmph." But she let him bestow the silly heart upon her head, took control of the image from him and placed it over her shoulders. For a moment she wore his affection around her shoulders like a stole.

"Sorry it took a bit," said Lani. "I ran down to Del's to pick you up an order of fries." She set a black takeout container down in between them. "Fresh from da fryer."

Jerimin gave her puppy eyes. "Bless you, cousin."

She gave him a funny look, but it was somewhat amused. "Haha. That'll be..." she swept two paper receipts out of the bottom of the bag, held them up to her face to read, "Forty-seven oh-one."

Jerimin's hand slid towards the wad of jen in his pocket, but the mayor flapped his wings and said, "I said, put it on the mayor's tab, Lani. We don't want to look stingy next to the other towns."

"All right. I'll let Del know. Rosie, you want these receipts?"

The toasty-gold hen, back from the office, held out her claw to take them. "*Mahalo.*"

Jerimin and his Queen began lifting lids on the food.

/Tleh. You take the seed-cards,/ she sent along with the sensation of itchy, piercing seeds stuck between her teeth. He grabbed several of them and began eating, the first bite shattering satisfyingly in his mouth. He didn't mind the crackers so much—they reminded him of eating papadum from his favorite Eastern restaurants back home—but would it kill them to lay off the fennel?

Opening the takeout boxes—like most their Osidern meals so far—was like a disappointing Pāheahea day where he wanted to immediately exchange everything he opened: bland poi, plain carrots and other raw vegetables, more seeds mixed with something that hardened into half-inch cakes that made him feel like he ought to be perched on a feeder hanging outside someone's window box...

Now, okay, corn chips and mango salsa, that he could get behind...and here, a vinegary chopped vegetable salad, she could eat that safely...He set it close to her, along with a fork.

He'd eat till the last crumb was a memory, but it was purely in service to her voracious powers than for any love of the cuisine.

Seeing nothing else her carnivorous digestion could handle, she took the entire box of fries and set it before her.

He had no illusions of his getting more than a scant pinch of those crispy, golden beauties—but when she gave him his nibble, it would come with that lovely floaty-humming feeling along with it, the feeling that said he was hers, and she was his, and they would take care of each other. And that was worth more to him than anything in all of Paxis.

"Everything look good?" said Lani.

"Yes, Lase. We thank you."

"Well, if that's all, I'll be heading back now," said Lani. "Gotta run. Enjoy your meal, cousins."

She waved a wing in the direction of the mayor and his wife and let herself out. The mayor was hot on her heels to lock back up.

/Is it just me,/ Jerimin sent, /or did she seem to be in a hurry to get out of here?/

/Agreed./ But no more information came.

Jerimin frowned. *Her power must be low.* He shoveled chips into his mouth as quickly as he could.

"Griffon isn't back yet," said the mayor's wife. "I left a message, but...I wouldn't hold my breath. He may have the room, but he's an odd fox, that one..." The corner of her beak curled in disgust as Jerimin drank the dregs of the salsa out of the serving bowl.

"Perhaps we could stay under here for the night," said his Queen.

"Oh, no, no!" said the mayor before his wife had the chance to reply. "We wouldn't dream of it—unless...did any of the other towns you were in put you up in their lodge?"

Eeegh. "No—excuse me," Jerimin daubed salsa juice off his mouth with a napkin. "The first put us up in a hotel—"

"Their *best* hotel," added his Queen. He nudged her under the table with his foot.

"—and the second had us camping outside. But there wasn't any rain, then."

"*Himmel sei dank,*" muttered his Queen. He nudged her again.

"Well—we'll find you accommodations before tonight, even if we have to take you in ourselves," said the mayor, frowning at the outraged look his wife was blasting him.

"We wouldn't want to impose," said Jerimin quickly. "Any-place dry would be appreciated."

/*Dry and private,*/ she sent, along with the sensation of a cloud of warm breath against his neck.

He shivered with pleasure, had to duck his head to hide his grin, though the blush would still be obvious.

/Quit it! I'm sure they can smell.../

/...Arousal?/

He could feel her lining up some other sensation to tease him with; he had to derail it.

/First sleep, then.../

/Sex?/

/I was going to say intimacy./

She coughed at his primness. He tuned back in to the mayor's voice.

"—No, we're not going to make the Gorgon of Everlush sleep in the cursed café!"

"But Lono-love, it's completely vacant! After they leave, we can probably charge twice our asking price!—You know, 'the Gorgon slept here'?"

"Cursed?" said his Queen, eyes bright with interest.

The mayor chuckled strangely, three little *hic-hic-hic*s. "Just a joke, Your...Gorgonliness. There's a suite in the plaza that can't seem to keep an owner."

"If it's empty and dry, we don't mind taking it," said Jerimin.

"No no, I won't hear of it!"

The mayor's wife brushed him with an oversized wing. "Let's just sit on this decision for now. Griffon could call back and solve all this for us. In the meantime...do you feel ready to start?"

The question hung in the clammy air.

/Well, what do you think?/ he sent. He could feel her hesitations and considerations rolling around like rubber balls on a tilting plate. One was in the shape of her ritual robes, folded neatly in her pack; another, the shape of her head, overheavy with weariness, weighed against the empty food containers, enough to sustain her for a while...He caught the warm snuggly relief imbued in the memory of this morning's stolen bed dueling with the desire to simply be done with her task and into the jungle, away from the bustling masses of people with their thoughts and feelings and desires all blatting against her consciousness like a cloud of drunken insects.

The thoughts swirled and struck each other and never came to a standstill.

The squarglings' stares began pressing upon Jerimin.

/Maybe...If you get some of the out-of-towners knocked out today, they'll leave, and we can take their rooms?/

The balls of thought stopped rolling; frozen, they lit up with wary hope.

She held in her sigh so the squarglings wouldn't see it.

"I could see a few today. But first I must to—must change."

The mayor trilled, wings flapping.

/You just made his day./

/Mm./

"Rosie, let her use your office—"
"Right this way," said the hen, gesturing.
"I'll bring you your pack," said Jerimin, standing.
/Idohope we do not regret this./
Privately, he hoped so, too.

12

KEONAONA

Keonaona squeezed his face tighter into the corner of the bed. In the week since it had happened, this plain box from the extras room had become his sole retreat. It was one of the few objects in the house free of history. So even though every bench and sofa was still in the house, covered in white dust covers from before they'd left, he'd dragged the forgotten old thing into a spare room and had dug in there.

He didn't want to go upstairs.

He didn't even want to think about upstairs. He just wanted—*dear Mother, please!*—blessed unconsciousness.

Actually, he wanted to be dead. But he didn't think he deserved it.

But for now, sleep would do, sleep would let him escape...

Radda-thunk!

Someone at the door.

"No, no!" he moaned, flattening his tail and wings to his body, trying to hide his face. He should have left—re-packed his suitcase and walked to the airport. It was one thing to play the anonymous fruit seller for strangers from the city. But to stand around and be grilled by that...feed reporter, or whatever he was...no. No no no no—

Keonaona's thoughts froze at a familiar sound. A key turning in the back door.

He held his breath, trying to discern if the sound was real, his guilt, or the rain starting up again.

There. The creaky step outside the kitchen. Someone was in the house. Someone who had a key.

Couldn't be that blue-headed leech. But if it wasn't him, who was it?

"Hey, Keonaona!"

Lani!

Right, his wife had given her a copy of the house key so she could come in on her own anytime before a dinner or party and set up. But why would she come here now? She'd already delivered the food meant for Hriana's Gorgon; it was stashed away in his refrigerators in easy-to-reheat containers. If he stayed quiet, would she leave?

She'll have to! She can't keep the café closed for long! The walk out here wasn't some quick jaunt. If he just lay low, she'd realize she was burning up time...time better spent on the road back to her business, while all those new customers were still in town.

Unless...someone else was with her. Had driven her, maybe?

He listened for a second set of footsteps. He hoped that feedster kid hadn't convinced her to find him, take a camera along. He shuddered at the thought.

But no—it sounded like she was alone. But she was moving swiftly now, footsteps beating a dogged rhythm above as she swept the kitchen, the living room, the parlor, the music room, the extras room...she even returned to the kitchen to check the pantry!

Her nails left off clicking on the kitchen tile and turned into muffled taps as she went around to the entryway, where his wife had had the notion to lay out the rain mat before leaving.

Tap, tap, tap.

He waited, wondering what she'd do next. She hadn't checked the private wing of the house yet. The guest rooms—including his hidey hole—were all laid out in a row. She'd find him.

Then, the stairs upstairs began to creak.

He didn't know whether to be astonished by her nosiness or impressed with her boldness. That was their level, his family's level! Private, no one allowed!

As he heard her opening and shutting the various doors above, he was struck with the impulse to race up there and drag her back down. But...if he got up, he could move his bed to the bathroom attached to this room, shut the door behind, and wait it out—after he smoothed the rug, of course, and doused the room in Scent-Klear. Should be some in the bathroom, in fact.

He heard her say something—maybe his name.

Muffled. Good, she was still up there. Keonaona backed out of the box bed and carried it with him into the bathroom. Past the sink, he ignored the closed door leading to the toilet and opened the one leading to the dust bath. Fresh, unscented sand covered the floor like sugar...oh well, the bed would clean.

He slid the bed in, careful not to get any of the scrub on him—a fine thing that'd be, to leave white tracks like he'd been baking human bread!—then turned to the cabinet beneath the sink.

His beak told him his misfortune before his eyes knew it; the cabinet's stale air had none of the reek of cleaning supplies or rags—there was nothing in there at all, just pipes and blackness.

The footsteps above were coming back downstairs.

The jig was up. Next she'd search the guest rooms, and even if he shut the bathroom door and if she wasn't nosy enough to open that door, just to check, his scent was too fresh. It would jump out at her, his perfume bright (well, distinctive; he didn't think he'd ever feel bright, not ever again) against the walls of the house from the years he and his family had lived in it.

He closed the dust bath door. He'd get the bed later.

He sat on the actual guest bed—cushioned and clean—and waited. Footsteps down the stairs. Now turning to the quiet side of the house. The first bedroom door, opened, called into. The second. The third. The fourth.

He closed his eyes.

And now...

She peeped in surprise when she saw him—jumped, too.

"Keonaona! What's wrong with you?"

He opened his eyes. "What do you mean?"

Her wings buzzed in outrage. "Whadya mean, 'what do you mean'? Lono and Rosie've been trying to get a hold of you all morning and I just brought lunch to the Gorgons at the lodge—and you with four freezers' worth of meals I cooked special for them! Why ain't they here? And where's Hana and Kaimana?"

He had been inhaling to answer her—but her final question stole the breath from him. His cool reply stuck in his chest; he could do nothing more than gape at her.

She saw him.

And it was just as he'd feared; somehow she knew instantly. "They *wen mahke*! Oh, Keonaona!"

She rushed him and enveloped him in her wings. For one second within that unexpected shelter, he felt truly hidden from reality.

Then the pain that he'd been fighting flooded back in, forcing his paralyzed breath out in a wheeze.

"Oh, honeysuckle, I'm so sorry."

Keonaona drew away, hiding in his wings, forcing the pain back inside.

She allowed him this space, stepping back. "What happened?"

He waited until he could take a breath without it catching before he answered.

"I don't want to talk about it. And I don't want everyone in town to know," he said, cutting her with a fierce glare, but seeing only concern in her eyes, he dropped his head, ashamed and tired all at once. "And I can't have *them* in the parlor making peace for war widowers when I..." He shut his beak with a snap.

"When you didn't lose them that way," she finished softly. "But Keonaona, you're—you'd be hosting...I'm sure you could ask!"

"I don't deserve any favors."

She tutted; he could see her ready to ask what he meant, so he blundered on. "They have their assignment. But I can refuse mine."

"I—you can, but I guess they stayed at Griffon Cortez's place last night?"

"Good for them."

"And Keonaona, the town's full up, couldn't you at least let them bunk here?"

"I don't want to and I don't have to. They've got tents."

He caught her puzzled look. "I watched them coming up the walk last night. They're Lono's problem, now. I think I'm going

87

to get out of here." He raised his thumb to his beak, chewed the claw slowly...*pok*...*pok.*

"Where will you go?"

"Their—" A surge of pain flashed through him. He fought to get the next words out without panting. "Their bodies are in Pillars Beach. They're gonna ship them here, for...but I can call, cancel that. Go up there, have them...you know. Up there."

"Buried there instead of here?! Keonaona, they were in that city for a month. They lived here all their lives! They should be resting here in Crooked Neck!"

"I KNOW THAT! Don't you think I know that? I just can't han—handle it right now!"

"Oh, honeysuckle, I'm so sorry." She fell silent a moment. "Is there anything I can do?"

Her silence had given him time to master himself. "Just don't tell. And...leave me be. I'll be gone soon anyway—to Pillars Beach, I mean. You can take the meals back, if you want. I'm not hungry."

He caught her watching him in the dresser mirror, frowning. He didn't like that look. It was too examining; a look that was hunting for answers like a coati looking for a way into a trash can.

She'd discover his guilt.

He stood. The chair slid back.

"I'm going to make that call. Bye, Lani."

He left the room, ignoring the old-fashioned telephone sitting on the table next to the door.

13

MERCURIO

It had been easy for Mercurio to follow this guy's scent to the incredibly-colored general store. (What would you call that color? *Goldenrod*, Mercurio decided.) He was, honestly, one of the best-smelling squarglings he'd ever met, like jasmine and honeysuckle and relaxation all in one, and at just the right intensity—*though with a name like Keonaona, I guess he'd better smell amazing!*

Mercurio dropped the handles of the fruit seller's cart on the property's rubberized track and flew up the stairs. He burst into the store, startling the apple-smelling clerk into dropping a peanut shell into the barrel in front of him. The scents of dried apple rings and poppy seed cakes, of jelly beans and laundry soap crashed into his face like an ocean wave. Behind him, his three cameras floated parallel to his back, turned off to save precious battery.

"Where's Ho'okano?"

The shopkeeper bristled, and his wings spread.

"So you're the reason he ran out on me! My braddah come in here and threw the cash box at me—couldn't get my uniform off him fast enough! Then he split!"

Mercurio danced in place. "Where to?"

"Who knows! He didn't say—and even if he did, I don't see why I oughta help the rattlebrain who just cut my cash flow off at the neck!" He flapped his wings back with three sharp snaps. "Unless you gonna replace him?"

"Sorry, too busy. Hey, can I get another orange Jukee? Same size as before." He pulled his wad out from one of this pouches.

The shopkeeper huffed, but walked back to the coolbox to get him his drink.

89

While his back was to him, Mercurio's brain churned. *How can I get him to give up the goods?* Everybody wanted something. Especially this guy, standing around in this dingy-lit *palheiro* out in the middle of nowhere. He had to want something Mercurio had—or could get him.

Or make for him...

The shopkeeper was glaring at him now from behind the only register in the shop. The soft drink stood on the counter before him, orange aluminum sweating gently.

"That'll be fifty cents."

Mercurio came forward, tossed his money on the counter, then popped the top. After the liquid hissing calmed, he started to take a drink—but then stopped himself.

"Mind if I look around a little more?"

The shopkeeper huffed again. "It's a free country."

Mercurio began strolling the aisles—not much here in the middle that was fun, lot of canned nuts and dried fruit mixes in outdated brands he last saw in his tutu's pantry...

He turned the corner. Oh, school supplies, including power chargers, prepaid mibis...not much selection, he guessed school was out now? This place seemed like a town for oldsters, though, so maybe there weren't many schoolbies...

He turned the corner again, tapped his tallboy against his beak tip when he saw nothing but white sacks of bathing powder stuffing the shelves like fat grubs...Then he caught sight of the back wall, gleaming like a tapestry of gems.

This ought to be the first thing you see when you walk in here! Why the heck doesn't he move it out front?!

It was a wall full of binned candy—from common sweets like Hokka-Chokkas and Dulcitoz and Spicy-'Onos to exotic ones he'd never heard of. (Bamananas?! With a name like that, how could he not try some??) Plastic scoops stuck out next to the clear bins so you could put your sugary booty into little netted sacks or paper bags with clear windows in them.

And now Mercurio had a plan. But it'd only work if the shopkeeper was a little more modern than he looked.

Gotta get him talkin' to me first.

He whistled low, to get the guy's attention. "Whoa! 'Tsa heckuva candy wall you got there! You gotta have the biggest collection this side of the river!"

He heard the shopkeeper shuffle out from behind the counter. Mercurio kept "admiring" the wall, took a sip to hide his grin.

"Yeah, had a sweet beak since I was a squab." The shopkeeper stood next to him, arms akimbo, looking up and down the wall before stepping forward to dig into the Foxtails with a scoop a few times, like he was aerating them.

"I woulda packed some up to sell with the fruit today," said Mercurio over the rattling candy.

This earned him an annoyed glare. Mercurio shrugged his wings modestly. "But whadda I know?"

Seemingly appeased, the shopkeeper finished tending the Foxtails and stepped back.

"Bins seem full. You sell a lot?"

"Sell enough."

"I guess it's hard to turn a profit on anything out here. Numbers just aren't there, you know?"

The shopkeeper clucked noncommittally.

"But you seem to be doin' all right. You sell online at all?"

"Actually, yeah."

Bingo!

The shopkeeper went on. "My niece set me up a net store a couple years back. I send out a few orders here and there. Easy to do, not too much fuss. Got a little boost during the war—families sending box hugs to their kids out fighting."

"Cool, cool. You ever done any advertising? Not just banner ads, I mean, but, like, on the feeds? Video?"

"Uhhh..." The shopkeeper's tail swept back and forth like a cat's. "I guess I never thought about it, no."

"Tell you what. I've got nine point nine thousand active followers on my channel, MercurioMaxFilms. There's, what, a thousand people living in the town?"

The shopkeeper's frown looked less like a *buzz off* frown and more like a considering one. Which would make sense, because Mercurio had deliberately guessed too high.

"Loyal customers, don't get me wrong," said Mercurio, "but...in the feed biz, it's all about numbers. Get your product before more eyeballs, you start to convert a few—boom, revenue!"

"Think I been selling a little longer than you, little braddah."

Mercurio chuckled. "Okay, okay, you got me! But hear me out: if I whistled about your candy store to my feed's followers, even if just one percent convert, that's a hundred more customers you got for nothing!—And if ten percent convert..."

"For nothing?" The golden tail was sweeping the floor again.

"For nothing. Hey, you got candy here I ain't never seen! And if rare candy don't get bought, the manufacturer goes belly up, and then—no more Firebitz or SlimSlams for anybody, EVER."

Mercurio watched the square's eyes. *Yeah, that hit a nerve. Guy must be an aficionado. Probably remembering old junk food he used to gobble down.*

"I'd be happy to video this wall, post a photo of your most exotic candies all set out on a plate, link to your site, talk it up...I'll do that, for free, for the next two months on my feed—"

"Six months."

"Three."

"Five."

"Four, and I get a bag of Bamananas to go..." Mercurio pointed at the shopkeeper with his claw, fingers still wrapped around the Jukee can, "and you give me your single best guess as to where Lane Hoʻokano went. Best guess."

"You're kind of a louse, aren't you!"

"Maybe, but a popular one! Picture it! Nine point nine thousand pairs of eyes and ears learning about your store for the first time ever. Imagine if five percent order from you, even just once!"

The shopkeeper's tail went berserk against his ankle, as though urging him to take the deal. Mercurio finished his Jukee, waited him out.

Finally, the square grabbed a paper bag and stomped to the Bamananas bin. Two scoops of lime green candy went in the bag and then the top was rolled tight before he tossed it at Mercurio's face.

"Four months. I'd guess he went home."

"Where's that?"

The yellow scowled. "West of here. Down the fire-ash path, turn left at the carpet-shampoo sign. Got crossed palm trees in the front, can't miss it. But even *if* you find him, Keonaona can handle you. My bet is he won't even talk to a kid like you. More likely you'll get the door shut on your beak, hotshot! And it'd serve you right."

"That's fine. I'll be back tomorrow morning to film the wall—gives you time to dust it—you send the info and the pic of the rare candy to the addy on the card I gave you by the end of the week, or the deal's off. Thanks for the sweets!"

He was out the door before the sucker could make another peep.

14
MERCURIO

THE STEELY SKY—BRIGHT AND sharp as a nickel shining out from mud—looked so dang cool! (*no...majestic! Important!*) behind the two crossed palm trees that arced over the entry to the Hoʻokano estate that Mercurio actually stopped and let the cams out, getting the shot from every angle possible.

You can't buy lighting like that! Mother knows I've tried.

Luckily the weather was still holding out, he didn't have the money yet to buy an anti-wet enchantment for all three lenses. The shot of him approaching said crossed trees in silhouette against the bright sky, with that mansion (three-tiered like a cake; the bottom stack split in half by a sweeping stair that landed you on the lanai, with the second-story balcony landing looking over the front grounds and the third story narrowest, almost a tower) looming in the background—that'd make a cheap and easy gift for his BFF-level subscribers—mobi wallpaper or a self-printable poster. Maybe toss a quote on it—something profound, or maybe just some slammin' narration he'd come up with later or maybe a quote from one of the Gorgons...

Speak of the popsicle hen, he could smell the Gorgons on the gate—Icarii, at any rate. And the mango-café hen. Hopefully she was gone. What a hassle!

Mercurio lifted the latch to let himself in, winced at the way the gate banged after him. So much for the element of surprise.

He could smell the red—he'd been here recently—and the mango-selling hen...but Mercurio relaxed when her scent left the gravel path leading up to the lanai. He kept on forward, breathing in the rich, floral perfume of his quarry.

His claw reached for his recorder, hungry to narrate, but he decided against it. —Aloud, anyway.

I thought the house that sheltered the Gorgons the night before was big, but this humble fruit seller's home is like a resort hotel dropped in the middle of the jungle...and everything about it, from the undulating curves of the porch rail (stylized to look like river waves) to the solidness of the stairs beneath my feet invites the weary guest to stay, rest, and recuperate...

Dah! He hoped he would remember that later!

Mercurio rang the bell. Another waiting game. Ugh, he was wasting valuable editing time—

The door opened. It was Ho'okano. He really looked ragged now, like some newbie feedsters he'd seen at ScrobCon, foregoing sleep to edit vids that had to go up before sunup hit for their main follower base, with staring eyes and the editing suite interface practically embossed on the surface of their corneas.

Yeah, he looks like that. Only worse.

His hands hung limply at his sides, and the fuchsia-tinted maroon of his hide seemed three shades paler—*though it could be the lighting? I guess?*

"It's you. Of course."

Mercurio had never thought a phrase could be said with zero emotion, but this...this was absolute zero, like, *what's even making this bird speak, it's like the lines from his heart to his songbox have been cut...*Mercurio's wings shivered.

Ho'okano turned his back, but he didn't go anywhere, didn't touch the door, and didn't say anything.

Ugh! What is his problem?

Mercurio opened his mouth to kick the red into gear, but then the red turned around again and walked out the front door like Mercurio wasn't there. Mercurio had to jump out of the way.

"Hey! What's the idea?"

Ho'okano walked to the lanai's balcony, stared out over the front yard. Mercurio glanced through the still-open front door, the portal to polished hardwood and a curved staircase so old but well cared for that it could've been a set piece in a movie, then back at the broken square, staring his no-sleep stare out into the silver nickel light.

Mercurio croaked, feeling strange and uneasy at the sight. The red's hands were still at his sides.

"Pull up a seat. If you want."

Mercurio's ruff splintered in disgust at the robotic tone—but then, Ho'okano suddenly jerked about and took a seat at a coffee break-sized berry-blue wicker table topped with a circular wafer of seafoam glass. Mercurio hurried to the chair opposite.

The red square continued staring.

Mercurio's hand went to his bandolier...then hesitated.

Are you kidding? This is as compelling as a cobra dancing before a spiny gerbil!

He was right, of course. But he'd have to conserve battery. He let out MaxCam and winked at the red, setting the focus. The wooden slats of the lanai made a classy background for the red.

The smell of waterproofing stain and rain hung thick around them.

Ho'okano stared glassily through him.

Slowly, like he was clicking a questionable link in an email, Mercurio hit "record."

"So...what's going on, here?"

The square took a moment to answer.

"You had questions. Why don't you ask them."

Mercurio's thumb lingered on the MIKE SENSE ADJUST dial. Ho'okano sounded like he was in a different room, he was talking so softly now. He decided to risk too much ambient noise and upped the mike sensitivity by two degrees. If that still wasn't enough, he'd add captions later. He'd remember.

"You told me you were supposed to host the Gorgon but changed your mind. You never said why."

Dead air.

My battery, my battery!

Then:

"You ever have a chickadee, Lane Macoya? Someone you loved?"

"Naw, not yet."

"What about a friend? A sister? A brother?"

Just play along with the crazy coot.

"Sure." He had to stop himself from adding, "Why not?"

96

"Good. Then you understand love makes things complicated. Love is wonderful, makes the good times so fantastic, makes you feel like you could fly..."

Well, this was weird. But weird was clickable. So Mercurio made himself wait.

"But when it ends...abruptly...love makes everything complicated. It's simple, but it complicates things. Take me, right now, for instance."

Mercurio leaned forward. *Now we're getting somewhere!*

"This is my home, and I love it. It's been in my family for generations. Beautiful. It's...I've hosted most the town here. And their friends, and their families. Strangers passing through stay at the Canopy. But if you're connected, you stay with me and my family. It's who I am."

Mercurio nodded like a woodpecker.

"It's full of everything I love, everything that's c—..."

Dead air again. Maybe he could overlay some music in. It'd all depend on the volume of the audio he caught.

"That's comforting to me. It's a part of who I am, this place.

"And right now, because of love, I would rather be ANYPLACE but here."

A puzzled gurgle escaped Mercurio. He was glad he was filming this, because right now, he couldn't fathom the mania—or was it anger?—gleaming in the red's eyes.

His voice dropped again. "If it wasn't for love, I'd walk straight into that forest"—he pointed a claw out to the side, towards the jungle, glowing almost acid green against the burgeoning grey sky—"and never return.

"But I'm stuck here, because I waited too late to call, and they're already shipping my wife and child's bodies back here."

WHAT THE—?

"They're dead?" The question fell out of Mercurio's mouth like a coconut dropping out of a tree, and landed just as heavily.

"Yes. And it's because of me."

Mercurio's mind flew to ancient legends of squares chopping up their mates for imaginary offenses. "WHAT?"

"Because of me, they're dead, and because of love, I'm stuck here. Stuck here for two more days, when all I want to do is go. *I want to go*! But love is keeping me from doing the things I want to do."

His voice, which had pulled taut and strengthened in the course of this outburst, fell again.

"But you know what?"

"What?" Mercurio's throat had gone dry as paper; the word came out a rasp.

"I don't love you. So nothing you do or say is going to get me to tell you how my family died, so you can root around somewhere else for your clickbait, you ice-blooded vulture."

Mercurio jumped to his feet, wings spread, scream of rage rushing to his throat. But Ho'okano held up a hand.

"No, no, I forget myself."

He swallowed the scream. *An apology! That's more like it!*

"At least when a vulture's tearing the eyeballs out of some poor beast's face, it's clearing away disease—doing something useful. Not just whoring for attention."

Mercurio dove at him, screeching. Most of him belly flopped onto the table. While he was clawing through the air at the red, Ho'okano kicked over the table and Mercurio found himself flung sideways, wings flapping helplessly for balance.

Ho'okano took hold of the equipment bandolier around Mercurio's body.

"Leave...me...ALONE!!!"

He swung the blue-headed square off the lanai.

Mercurio found himself surfing the cubbat-quality grass with his face, slid to a stop in a muddy heap next to the gravel walk.

Mercurio flipped himself over. His palm came down hard on a stone at the wrong angle, but he wouldn't notice the twang of his bone until later.

MaxCam hung in the air, its eye faithfully pointed at the red, now braced, wings wide, at the top of the lanai stairs, trumpeting calls to warn Mercurio off his territory. Mercurio replied in kind with infuriated cawing. They stopped only when a clap of thunder interrupted them both. Ho'okano glanced up, and so did Mercurio. Now that they weren't fighting, the smell of impending rain was obvious as a street sign. Mercurio cawed back a final time.

Ho'okano swung a wing at him dismissively and went inside his house.

Mercurio stared at the door as if he could set it on fire.

Lousy, no-good jerk! Insult my work, will he? I'll make the next two days of his life a living misery! He'll wish he'd died with them!

That was it. He'd have the Gorgons here on his front porch tomorrow. Those two'd make mincemeat out of that sunburnt turkey!

Mercurio would get his story.

Mercurio got to his feet and stomped down the gravel road off the estate. He slammed the gate behind him.

And the rain came down like a hammer...

15

GORGON

JERIMIN SAT RAMROD STRAIGHT on the carved chapel bench, watching the old hen shuffle down the ramp towards the chapel exit. Overcast light beamed into the dark chapel through clerestory windows like a spotlight on his Queen, wrapped in the blood-red robes of her occupation. Her face was partly hidden by the hood that covered her eyes (the better to ignore the world of the living and see the dead), but the heaviness in his shoulders and the tense strain on her lips told him she was tiring. This had been her third session—the ancient hen had lost her great-nephew in the Lanakila Massacre, and though she said he hadn't kept in touch as he'd grown older, she felt it only right to make sure he didn't have any unfinished wishes she could help with.

As far as sessions went, it really couldn't have gone more smoothly: upon bringing her great-nephew's soul into the visible spectrum, the ancient hen had nodded to herself, as though she'd known all along there was a functioning after-life, then proceeded to ask her kin questions so evenly and pleasantly, you would have thought they were on a video call.

Zero histrionics. Not that the two before her had gone hysterical—but there was hatred in them for his Queen, and having to come to her for these final farewells, and you didn't need *nensha* to spot that.

The ancient hen paused at the door and sprinkled the contents of...was that a packet?—he leaned forward—some sort of wax envelope into a tube bolted to the clayen wall; the contents drifted into a glass bowl heated by a low flame, and in a moment, a musty perfume entered the air with a puff of bluish smoke.

She muttered some words, then left the chapel. The smoke of the strange perfume rolled through the air. Jerimin resisted the urge to lick the taste out of his mouth.

An elderly teal square came out from one of the four round bays that petaled off from the main—and largest—bay. Jerimin hadn't been able to see inside any of these bays, but he assumed there were seats?

/Tell them this next one is my last./

The spark of urgency underlying those words sent him to his feet. He stepped sideways off the dais (too grand a word for the little step-up platform hugging the back wall) and hurried towards the mayor's wife, who was at the teal's elbow speaking instructions softly in his ear.

No one seemed to cut across the middle of the giant round bay—every squargling he'd seen today had hugged the wall, going around the long way to the dais at the back, so Jerimin did likewise as he approached the pair. No sense offending if he could help it.

The old one held Jerimin in a wary look while he waited for Lase Likeke to finish.

The toasty-gold hen patted the teal on the arm. "Go on up, it's okay."

A lunge towards Jerimin and a quick rise of his wings seemed to Jerimin more a protective gesture than actual aggression—maybe a warning not to give her any trouble.

The mayor's wife clucked reassuringly and the teal continued his slow progress towards his Queen without a second look back.

"He lost his granddaughter," said Lase Likeke, voice a touch icy. Now that she was seeing them in-session, she was remembering how much pain they had caused. "Drowned at Fermata."

He fought the urge to look back at his wife. *That won't be a friendly session.* Grandparents losing their grandchildren seemed to go the worst.

"I'm sorry," he said. "Is he a local, then?"

Her tail lashed. "Yes, just like the other three! Why?"

He had no desire to answer her. "I'm only here to tell you that this is her last session for the night."

"The night?! It's only six o' clock!"

He reined his reply in, stuffing as much patience as he could into his words before he released them.

"Yes, and the first two sessions took over three hours each. This next one could take twenty minutes"—like the calm old hen who'd just left, Hera bless her—"or two hours."

"But there are others waiting!"

How many others from your town?

"We'll stay in your town as long as it takes. But after this...gentleman, we end for today."

"But—"

He rose to his full height, but kept his voice down. "I am informing you, not negotiating."

"Jerimin." His Queen, calling.

He stopped himself from bowing. "Excuse me." He hugged the curved wall, returning to his Queen's side. She couldn't start without him.

The teal square glared at him as he took his seat in the shadow beside her.

"You two in here, sitting up here like you queen and king. It ain't right."

She offered her wrist for the teal to take. Her raised hood, covered eyes, hid all expression from the square. But Jerimin felt her burgeoning exhaustion.

The old square glared at her—then grabbed her wrist.

Jerimin sighed as his gravity left him again.

Another soul was called.

An hour and a half later, they watched the remainder of the squarglings file out of the alcoves and out the chapel door. He was relieved to see the back of them; his knees and limbs all had tremors. This was new. And unwelcome. Normally, going weightless (which somehow made his Queen more comfortable in-session) felt so good he felt guilty about it—enjoying himself while she dealt with the messiness of their victims' emotions.

When she finished, and his gravity pooled back into his body, it was like coming off some wonderful theme park ride.

But today he just felt cold and a little sick. How much of this feeling belonged to her and how much to him, he couldn't tell. Some moments of some days the boundary between their two mind-spaces was especially porous.

He curled his fingers under the bench seat, *Press, two...three...four...*a little trick to help him settle back into his body.

It was working, but it didn't make him feel any better; if anything, it forced him to feel how deep the chill in him really was, and now he felt trapped in his skin. He formed a box around the feeling—one that highlighted, not one that contained.

/Can you stop this? I don't feel so good./

He felt something like the shutting of a window; she had cut off some of their connection

—battening down the hatches

which gave him a bite of loneliness until he took a second. His perception adjusted like vision in a dark room: the shining wire embedded in his head was still there, and her feelings still pulsed through it, albeit muffled. Odd, how this muted bond felt like a great separation now, when just a year ago he'd been actually alone in his head like the rest of the human race, without her or her shining-wire *nensha* hookup.

But maybe it's time I stop thinking of myself as human. The thought brought a wry smile to his lips, which the mayor's wife—now before them after seeing off the crowd—frowned disapprovingly at.

He wiped the offending expression from his face. "Yes, ma'am?"

"Since you're 'done for the day'"—he could hear air quotes around the phrase—"we should go back to the lodge and see about your overnighting situation."

In the course of speaking, her gaze had migrated from his face to his Queen's, only she hadn't taken her hood off yet. The hen's toasted tail lashed before she shot him a quick glance, annoyed (he thought) at his Queen's unresponsiveness. He reached out from his mind to prod hers, but since she'd narrowed most the link between them, it felt like it had before their connection had formed—like he was calling out to a void. He had no idea if she'd picked up his gesture.

He took a slow breath, reexamining the stability of his limbs. The tremors seemed under control. He stood, put a hand on his Queen's shoulder. She gave her own quiet sigh before finally lifting her hood. She looked like someone coming out of a dream, not quite awake yet.

"Lead the way, Lase," he said to the mayor's wife.

He must be tired; he didn't remember following the hen around the curves of the large bay, nor arriving at the strange bubbling smoke-maker and the chapel door next to that.

"Lono's waiting for us next door. I suppose we'll have to figure you out some dinner." She pushed the sun-carved door open—

A terrible harsh light speared into them, joined by a flood of voices. The mayor's wife squawked. He ducked, threw his arms up instinctively to protect himself from the stones screeing through the air at him, only to realize at the last moment that they weren't stones, but cameras!

He growled at the memory of that blue-headed idiot who'd tracked them down—until he picked a voice out over the general clamor.

"Harold-miss Euphegenia, Netron World News Association! We'd like a word with you, Gorgon-sir!"

Netron news? I thought that square was a feedster.

"No comment," he said. Then, in an undertone to Likeke, *"Get us out of here!"*

Without the veil sight, he was completely blinded—each one of those nasty little cameras had an obnoxious floodlight on it and seemed intent on keeping the beams jammed into their eyes. His Queen's own pain pounded dully through the lines, making him feel like the snare in his head was biting into his brain.

"Gorgon-sir, what can you tell us about your treatment of one Plattman-miss Lysandra?"

PLATTMAN.

Though his eyes were slammed shut, he saw red for a moment—though that could have been the result of some camera light penetrating his eyelids, sheeze!

He flinched when Lase Likeke gave a mighty two-note honk. "The Gorgon has no comment at this time," she added. The rapid-fire beating of her wings followed, and then he felt her three-fingered claw on his hand.

He took his Queen by the wrist.

"Go, go," he hissed to the hen, and he bent himself almost double to keep his tall frame from interfering with their getaway.

Thunder crashed above them.

He dared peer his eyes open—and met the gaze of some sound tech with a fuzzy thing on a boom keeping pace with them while the rest of his pack—and the cameras—lagged behind.

Lightning flashed as they left the chapel's narrow path and rounded the corner back onto the main plaza walk. Hundreds of squarglings in the quad gabbled and shouted from beneath wings tented to shield them from the darkening sky, and whatever might fall out of it. Lase Likeke didn't hesitate but kept swerving—they'd be in the funnel of the lodge's walled walkway soon, but he didn't think that would stop the crews from following them clear up to the lodge doors.

The hen kept a steady barrage of cuckoo-sounding honks as she moved—he didn't look behind him, but thought he heard some of the squargling-squawking moving to cover their flight.

Their interference seemed to slow the crews down enough so that their trio was alone when they ran up the lodge's entryway.

He hauled his Queen up the final steps onto the lanai (he'd been half-dragging her the entire way anyway; fleeing was an instinct her body was entirely devoid of) while Lase Likeke bombed into the door.

It exploded inward and the group of squarglings waiting within squawked in ear-splitting cries of surprise.

The hen released his hand and Jerimin swept his Queen into an unoccupied corner.

Ka-THOOM!!!

Jerimin ducked, cradling his Queen, certain the roof was about to cave in on all their heads, but only a ferocious shower of rain followed, slapping at every surface outside.

The mayor ran up to his wife.

"Lock the door!" she screamed at him, and he veered around her to do just that.

He threw the bolt.

"A boar?"

The room held its breath.

"Worse! Paparazzi!"

"Media!" said the mayor, face suddenly bright. Jerimin's spine chilled.

"*Netron* media," said Lase Likeke. "Your—G—you two, in my office, now!"

He kept his grip on his Queen's arm as he walked them through the squarglings filling the lodge. They'd pulled down extra tables and chairs and were waiting in clusters. It was easy to imagine them all at a wedding reception. Some of them watched them pass by with open curiosity; others, complete loathing. He could have taken them the long way around, hugging the side walls instead of cutting across, but it didn't seem right for the Gorgon to be seen avoiding their "adoptive family."

Lase Likeke's little office would have been crowded enough with two squarglings, her desk, and her screen and keyboard, but now that he and his Queen were in it, along with their packs (stored away earlier, before they left for the chapel) and the Likekes, he felt positively ironed into the walls.

On the other hand, seeing as Lase Likeke practically had to wear the mayor in her lap made her a little less intimidating when she asked (with all the no-nonsense gravity of a hardened school principal), "What was that about, Lane Icarii?"

He thought he'd stay silent, see what her strongest complaint was about.

"Your itinerary isn't shared with Paxis at large. Our media aren't even in the know. So why are there Netron reporters chasing us down?"

"They chased you? Really?" said the mayor. His wife's wing waved him silent.

Jerimin tried prodding through the lines, asking for a read on the hen, but got no response. He glanced at his Queen. Staring off into space, exhausted.

Damn reporters blinding her! Chasing her! And after eight hours in session!

"And who's this...Platt...'Platter-miss' they brought up? A faerie?"

One last glance at his Queen. He'd have to field this one alone. Eegh, where to start, where to start?

"First, we apologize for the clamor. Those reporters were a complete surprise, believe me." *But they shouldn't have been, not with her* nensha. Her power made detecting living people—through walls or anything else solid—a non-issue, normally. But if she'd contracted the eye of her awareness down so narrowly that she couldn't see through walls, then she must be close to complete depletion.

She needed—*they needed*, the weariness in his bones moaned—food and a bed.

"...Lane Icarii. Lane Icarii!"

He came to at the sound of the mayor's claws tapping on the desk.

"I beg your pardon?" came his automatic response. *I must be tireder than I thought. More tired?*

"How did they find you?" repeated the berry-colored square.

"I...suspect the Netron girl who was with the fae at Lane...Griffon's house tipped them off."

"Why would she do that?" Principal Likeke again.

"I don't know," he lied. "Perhaps we can figure it out over dinner? Please?"

He hated hearing that plaintive note in his voice—the only thing he hated worse was not hearing his Queen's reprimand—/The Gorgon does not beg!/—just how tired was she?—but the mayor putted in a concerned-sounding way and said, "You guys have been gone awhile." He picked up a nearby mobi. "Dearest, what can I order you?"

Lase Likeke's hard stare at Jerimin broke.

"Fruit salad. I had some seed cakes on me but I didn't want to eat them in the chapel." She began working her claw through her comb. The mayor tapped away at the recessed keyboard.

"And for you two?"

"Uh..." He racked his brain for memories of the fattiest, most caloric foods they'd been served so far. "Peanut butter. A few peanut butter sandwiches for me, if they've got 'em...Else, ah, just put it with some apples...Fries? Are you messaging the place with fries?"

The mayor nodded. "*Ae.*"

"Like, four orders of those. And maybe..." He almost asked for mayo to dip them in, but caught himself in time. Egg products were a no-no in a society who hatched their future generations. No pizza here. Pasta was iffy, rice about the same. MEAT, flesh would be a big help now! "Do you guys have a boar hunter here?"

Little puzzled crackles from both squarglings. "There haven't been nuisance pigs in Crooked Neck since my mother was hatched," said the wife. "What's that got to do with dinner?"

"Then...corn chips?"

"With the mango salsa?" said the mayor.

"Sure."

"Anything else?"

Well, nothing ventured..."This place doesn't have any cheese, does it?"

The mayor whistled. "No, that's an import—too rich for our blood way out here!"

"Never mind," he said quickly. "I guess that will do for now. Maybe...we could be brought a menu? For next time?"

"Oh yeah, sure," said the mayor.

"How is Del going to deliver it?" asked Lase Likeke. "Those reporters would mob him just to get a word about these two!"

The mayor stopped clacking on the mobi and set it down with a final-sounding *tunk.* "I told him to sneak in the back way. And if these reporters make any trouble, I'll get Adanna to run 'em off. Loitering on city property without a permit. If they want to try their luck at camping, they can battle it out with the 'Ehuananites in the plaza."

"All full up then?" she said.

"Even the rain isn't stopping them from setting up tents." The mayor looked at Jerimin, leis rustling. "You two are incredibly popular. Best thing that ever happened to this town's economy."

"Griffon got back to you yet?" asked Lase Likeke.

The mayor's bright smile fell right off. "No. I've had your mobi with me all day. And the lodge filled up," he lifted his beak at the door behind them. "Nobody wants to get out of line."

"Lono!" exclaimed his wife, scandalized. Jerimin was confused until the mayor said, "Relax, hun! I got the squares here and the hens and pairs in the cursed café. I already got a folding screen set up for them."

Jerimin ticked the last remaining sleeping spots off his mental list.

Maybe we can hang our sleeping bags off the rafters....Sleep like bats.

"Any word at all from Keonaona?" asked Lase Likeke.

"Not a one. Mobi goes straight to messages, and his landline's off the hook."

"Did you send someone over?"

"Rosie, we've been slammed since everyone found out they were starting today."

"Call Analū. He might know."

"I did. He's not picking up, either. *We might have to take them in ourselves,*" he added in Native, with a glance at Jerimin. He carefully made his face go puzzled, like a dog's. Word must not have gotten out that he knew their language—or that if he did, he only knew nest talk.

"*No. I don't want them at home. Think of Elmer.*"

Elmer? If only his Queen weren't resting—but all he felt through the lines now was a distant feeling of hers: an irresistible yearning to lean against him. Probably to fall asleep. But outwardly, she was still and stone-faced, blinking with too much regularity.

It reminded him uncomfortably of the catatonia she'd fallen into before. She'd been starving then. His heart quickened. *Can't that food get here any faster?*

He cast an eye over the courtesy bowl of fruit on the hen's desk. Just a few wrinkly grapes, but food was food. He reached for them—only to have the mayor slide the bowl away. "I couldn't let our guest eat fruit this old! Nothing but the best for you two!"

He wanted to strangle him—but was too tired. Jerimin laid his hand back on the desk.

He'd missed further talk of this "Elmer." The mayor had turned to his Queen. "So, how did the first batch go?"

"As well as can be expected," Jerimin answered.

"It's kind of weird," the mayor's wife added in Native. *"Did you know I saw TonoTono for the first time in years? Guess it was the last time, too, till Mother takes us."*

The mayor whistled sadly, nibbled her shoulder a brief moment.

"Maybe I'll be able to sit in tomorrow, give you a break, Rosie dear."

"Maybe I should go looking for Keonaona. Even if he'd just let them sleep there!" Her tail knocked against a nearby hard drive. She winced.

"Now, now, dearest, no need to trouble yourself. It'll all work out."

"It took a long time, Lono. The whole time she was there, she only got through four."

"Only four? Analū had better put up signs. He'll rake in the jen!"

Lase Likeke frowned at him. But before she could go on, the office door opened. It only made it three-quarters of the way open before Jerimin's pack, stuffed in the corner, stopped it. Jerimin leaned his elbow casually across the desk, blocking his Queen from the new squargling's view.

He (from the smaller size of the wings) looked like a caramel turtle dessert on two legs: tan with cola-brown stripes and a white belly, topped with a caramel-colored comb atop his broad face. A black paper takeout bag dangled from his claws, still rain-wet (much like the square).

"Howzit, Rosie, Lono?"

"Griffon!" they exclaimed.

"In living color. Got your Del-ivery."

He leaned in and set it on the corner of the desk. Jerimin went straight for it but got a claw stuck in his face.

"You must be the Gorgon's better half. Griffon Cortez."

Jerimin took his wrist and shook it the Osidern way. "Icarii-sir Jerimin." He debated informing the burly square regarding his equal status as Gorgon, but the greasy smell of fries urged him not to bother.

He was ready for this handshake to be over, but the square kept his grip firm, his smirk intent, and Jerimin didn't think a Gorgon would be seen yanking herself from a handshake as though she were a fox in a trap ready to gnaw her own limb off. While he was thus trapped, his Queen leaned over and pulled a paper bucket from the Del's bag. She popped the lid off (it flew somewhere between the desk and the wall, slid down, and disappeared) and began feeding fistfuls of fries into her mouth steadily. Already the lines in his head felt better. Help was on the way. He hoped.

"You were in my house yesterday," said the big square. His orange gaze drilled intently into Jerimin's. An intimidation tactic?

"We were." *Let go of me, jock!* "I trust your vacation was satisfactory?"

"Yeah, yeah. Got to tell you, braddah, the last leg of my off-world trips is usually the worst—space sickness, you know? And the travel meds put me out like a tranquilized hog, so I'm always groggy when I get back. But your new teleportal's so cheap, I gave it a whirl. No need for the travel tranqs—so I skipped home like a swamp buck! And I wasn't groggy at all when one of my vacationers messaged me the news."

"Glad to hear it." *Let go, let go.*

"My place was in good condition, too. And now that I meet you," he tapped the side of his beak with his free claw, "I know who put the keys out on my desk, *mahalo nui loa.*"

Jerimin watched him warily. This was the windup, but what aim to the pitch?

Cortez's head cocked to the side. "You get a good look at all the rooms I got? I try to make them really nice for my guests. Got a designer and everything."

"It was very late, Lane Cortez."

"Must've been. Otherwise I like to think you two woulda taken one of the guest rooms, insteada stinking up my personal bed like dead—dead—moles?? Bats??"

"Griffon! Cool it!" hissed the mayor, over a clap of thunder.

"It was the room your guests offered us," said Jerimin, levelly. Speaking of room, there wasn't any in here to really let the square have it. Right between the eyes, that would be good.

"Yeah, well, they shoulda offered you one on the porch. Three bottles of Scent-Klear and I can still smell you gremlins on it! You're payin' for the next three, and if that don't work—"

"I'm sure we all together can come up with an arrangement that's fair, Griff," said the mayor's wife.

At last, the burly square turned away, charm emerging on his face in a smile that seemed to have no effect on the toasty-skinned hen. With this gesture, the too-friendly grip relaxed enough that Jerimin felt he could slide his wrist through the square's hand—smoothly, now, no jerking—with aplomb and without risk of being caught in the trap again. When he was free, he rummaged through the takeout bag without ever taking his eyes off Cortez. Squarglings weren't known to be violent, but Lase Likeke had called him an odd fox, and Jerimin wondered if he was actually something worse.

"Rosie, looking beautiful as ever."

The mayor's hackles rose, making his bristling purple cheek fur look like two spiny sea urchins sticking out of either side of his face.

He'd found his sandwiches—foil-wrapped and warm. From the hot fries? He didn't think it wise to glue his mouth shut with peanut butter as long as Cortez was here. He dug deeper in the bag, hoping for chips.

"So I take it, Griff, you wouldn't be open to letting these two stay at your place while they're here."

"I might've, for you, Rosie—but I already got a full house."

"Already?" said Mayor Likeke. "Let me guess, 'Ehuananites.'"

"Nope! All Netron—like him. They're a news crew," he said with a grin aimed at Jerimin. "I just picked up dinner for them, and since Del was sending Frankie out your way, I offered to bring your stuff, too."

"The film crews are staying with you?" said the mayor.

"Yup. Paid a nice lump sum up front. There's more if they stay past three days. So don't you two," he waggled a claw in Jerimin's direction, "be rushing through your voodoo sessions."

Jerimin found he had a lot he wanted to say to this jackass about their "voodoo sessions"—*how'd you like to see one from the ghost's point of view?*—but he busied himself with opening his box of chips and salsa without reply.

"Come to think, with what they've paid me already, I can buy a new bed. Forget what I said about owing me, Lane Icarii..."

If I paid you, would you go away? Jerimin bit down on his reply using a chip as a proxy. It was black, dry, and heavily seeded, a little too healthy tasting for his liking right now. The bucket of fries was almost gone now. Her hand reached in again, pulled out another handful. She loved him more than life itself, he knew, but he wouldn't be getting a bite of those angel potatoes. Not tonight.

"Of course, if you'd just confess to them how low you treated my guest last night, they'd go back to their studios—and then I might have room for you!"

"What guest? How low? What did you two do?" The mayor's voice was tight with panic; his wife began a low warbling that heralded the beginnings of squargling mass hysteria—even Cortez's ruff was breaking apart in alarm. Jerimin swallowed his mouthful in a hurry. A pointed chip scraped his esophagus as it went down.

"No harm came to any of the occupants of the Cortez home last night."

"She alleges that you terrorized them—threatened to kill her—"

"Terrorized?" said the mayor, colors fading.

"Her pride may have been bruised, but that's the end of it."

"She said you tied her up."

The mayor and his wife turned horrified gazes on Jerimin.

He ignored them both to plant a cool look at the brawny square. "She's lying."

He began unwrapping the foil from one of his sandwiches—both for something to do and to get time to think. Think,

think, uuugh, a thought was heavy to manage alone when one was this burnt! Like dragging a concrete block around by your teeth!

"She doesn't have any reason to lie," said Cortez.

"No? You said the camera crew paid you to stay at your place, correct?"

Cortez crossed his arms. "Yes."

"Did you ask how much they paid for her story?"

A muscle in the square's heavy jaw worked. *Score.*

"The Gorgon isn't someone a lot of people are bound to en-counter—especially Netron people. Any sordid story involving us would be valuable—but untrue. A fine way for a young girl with an overinflated sense of importance to get revenge for a perceived slight. You're playing right into her hands."

Cortez opened his mouth, but Jerimin shut it with a sharp look. "You'll look like a fool when this is over." And now, Jerimin knew they wouldn't stay under this squargling's roof for all the jen on Osider.

Cortez's brow was furrowed now, his tail working as he thought through what Jerimin had said. Rain continued to beat down on the roof, which wasn't helping his thinking any.

"Mayor, I'm sure my wife could like to eat the rest of her dinner in peace."

As if signaled—although this time it wasn't—his Queen *thock*ed the empty fry bucket on the desk and reached a hand into the delivery bag.

"What? Oh—yes, yes! Thanks for the delivery, Griff, I'm sure we'll be hearing from you again soon."

While Cortez was bustled out the door, Jerimin unwrapped his sandwiches. Exhaustion allowed a sigh of disappointment to escape.

Who puts peanut butter on a baguette? And then grills it?

A squargling line cook cooking for a human, that's who.

He took a bite. Ugh, sugarless peanut butter...

The Likekes had started up again in Native. He was saying that taking them in was the right thing to do especially now, and she was refusing on the grounds that...something something...hurt Elmer? His sagging brain waved the white flag.

"We'll just put up a tent for tonight. I'll do it after I'm finished eating."

Lase Likeke asked her husband something about the office...he said no...

Nope, said Jerimin's brain, *I'm done.*

And with that thought, his thinking shut off for the night.

The Native regressed to complete babble, accented by the rumble of thunder and the steely plinking of rain.

16

KEONAONA

KEONAONA HAD NEVER SEEN a sight more beautiful than Hana pointing out tiny crab lairs to Kaimana on the sunlit beach. From beneath, the light from the golden sand brought out the sheen in his wife's copper and emerald green body. She had made a visit to the dye shop around the corner from his condominium to add in a little iridescence to her greens, and it suited her. If she wanted, maybe it could be a regular thing back home.

When she warmed Kaimana in the egg (well, after enough time passed that dreaming about his future was safe), they speculated about his coloring, imagining a squab red-bronze with perhaps the golden comb of his father. Instead, Keonaona's comb had melted down his son's body and blended with Hana's copper genes and lightened her emerald, so the lad was all teals and golds. ("A regular little kingfisher," the widow 'Ewalani had called him.)

Now Kaimana looked like he belonged to the ocean, his golds reflecting the warmth of the sand; his teals, the ocean and cerulean skies surrounding him.

He squatted down, and his mother followed. Even from here, Keonaona could see Kai's beak a-sniffin' at a little critter on the sand. A second later, it zipped towards Kai and his mother. They shrieked in equal parts terror and delight before almost collapsing into laughter at their absurd cowardice in the face of a crustacean not even a hundredth of their size.

Keonaona grinned around his pineapple mango lassi. Then checked his watch.

He whistled at his family out on the beach, *twee-hee, twee-hee, twee-hee!*

They looked up, still laughing. Kai came running, throwing up propellers of sand beneath his feet. His mother followed languidly, drawing a serpentining line in the sand behind her with the tip of her tail. Keonaona's smile widened.

Wish we could take some of this back home with us.

Kai was here, happy and panting. *How'd he get so big so fast?* Seemed every time Keonaona turned around, the kid was another year closer to visiting the mating grounds.

Keonaona stood from the café table. What a fun little place—eating out under the shadow of an umbrella, toes in the sand, right there on the beach. They'd have to come back when he could do this as a serious vacationer, not just before and after the day's panels. At least Hana and Kai'd had fun this past month, playing tourist.

"I gotta go, sunny-K. Can't miss the closing ceremonies."

"You got foam, Papa." Kaimana tapped the tip of his own beak, as though he were his father's mirror. Keonaona dashed it away with a napkin before weighing it down beneath his empty glass.

Hana arrived, popping her wings at him. Keonaona returned the gesture.

"Aw, gross!" Kai buried his face in his wings. Guess the mating grounds were still a few years away.

Hana chuckled. "Sorry, *ipo*. I lost track of time."

"Don't be sorry! If I wasn't flying out to help Maui Ladeira, I'd skip it all myself and stay with you, but he said he'd help move my luggage to his shuttle afterwards, and I wanted to wanted to take him up on the offer. If I could get his trip down to two days, I'd feel a lot better about The Visit."

"But we're still staying at your condo, right, Papa?"

"Just for a few days more, Pinks," said his mother.

Keonaona's smile faded. "You sure I can't convince you to go home instead?"

"What, and miss out on four more days of sun and fun?" The ocean twinkled behind her.

"That was the original plan, pigeon. The only thing that's changed is I'll be helping Maui with a few pointers at his hotel before dashing back home fast as a rabbit."

"Can't you stay with us?" Kai asked. "We got the house ready once in just a day—for Uncle Nika's sister's surprise visit, remember? And Uncle Likeke said he'd help us this time if we needed it."

Keonaona and Hana exchanged a glance. Lono's help was not as rock steady a thing as their son believed it to be.

"And I bet Auntie Lani will have the meals all delivered before we even get home," his son went on. "We could do the boardwalk together!"

"Sounds like fun, Kai-in-the-sky, I really wish I could stay, but if you wanna come back for another visit, your Papa's got to make the red stuff. And what Lane Ladeira's paying will fund our return trip, one where I'll be with you, all the time, instead of herded around to a bunch of meetings. We can do the boardwalk all day, then. Sound good?"

His son trilled happily at the thought. "Okay, Papa."

Keonaona turned his attention back to his wife. "I really wish you'd go home like we planned."

"Cheapskate. I already told you I'd pay the daily rate for the days Kai and I stay."

"It's not that."

"Then what is it?"

Keonaona's tail twisted around in the sand.

"I guess I'm just...I don't know. Nervous isn't the right word, but...this isn't like hosting friends of the village. You know, controversial guests, special dietary needs...and who knows what else could come up? Before, we had a week to deal with any complications; now, we're cutting it down to what, three days to reopen a house that's been closed up a month? On top of everything else? I don't know, pigeon. It'd sure help me sleep better if I knew you and my number one wingman"—he nibbled Kai affectionately—"were at home already taking care of things."

His wife, her greens sheening like a mallard's neck, even in the shade of the café umbrella, looked deeply into his eyes.

The ocean exhaled behind her.

"You're really worried about The Visit, aren't you, *ipo*?"

"Yeah."

She held him in her eyes, saw everything Keonaona really was when he wasn't *Keonaona, holder of the Ho'okano estate, the best host in Crooked Neck*. Saw the regular square he really was.

"Okay," she said.

He putted in surprise. "Okay?"

"Okay. We'll go home early." A quick glance at Kai to cut off any protest before it started. "Then, after The Visit, we can all be on vacation together the next time. But your Papa's right. There's lots to do at home, so we should be there."

She whistled a question, offered Kai her hand. Kai looked back over his wing at the ocean. But when he turned back, he whistled his agreement and took her hand.

"It's settled. We'll go home today."

Smiling, she held out her hand to Keonaona.

He reached out to take it—

Then the world dissolved.

His eyes opened in the dark of his guest room.

The bright, salty smells of ocean and sunlight hadn't been in his beak, but all in his head. Now the air tasted like emptiness and damp. The boom of the surf melted into the fall of thunder; the hush of waves revealed itself to be the hiss of Crooked Neck rain. The pain of the dream grabbed his chest like crocodile's jaws. Keonaona cried out in sorrow.

If only it had gone that way! But she wouldn't listen! Why couldn't she have listened? But she didn't deserve to die for not listening. If only he hadn't gone for the extra money. If only he had convinced her.

If only...If only...

17

MERCURIO

AMID THE SQUARES COILED up on their sleeping pads atop the wooden lanai floors of the Crooked Neck Canopy Motel, Mercurio wrapped his wings even tighter around his screen. The pelting rain had devolved into a smoky mist sometime around 4 AM, but his screen—out of all his equipment—wasn't ruggedized, so he cradled it in both wings and had thrown his own sleeping pad on over top of it in the early dark of the morning to protect it from the wet blowing in from the occasional gust of wind. He'd never imagined himself chopping vid in the great (*not!*) outdoors; popping it in and out of its weatherproof pouch was about as much abuse he'd ever imagined it taking.

But here he was, tail numb from cushioning him on the rock-hard floorboards, back and neck screaming for him to pull out of the nerdy C-curve he was hunched into. But it blocked the light and kept the glare off his dark-themed editing suite, and this vid needed to go out, like, an hour ago, so frozen like a gargoyle he would stay. He was eating through his backlog a lot quicker than he'd expected, and the drama with Ho'okano had put him further behind schedule.

Next to him, some oaf let out a window-rattling snore so loud Mercurio could hear it over his prerecorded voice in his editing earphones. And now that it had started, it showed no sign of letting up.

The very tip of his tail—the only part of his tail he wasn't seated on—twitched irritably.

Aw, screw it. He saved his work and tucked his screen away in its pouch. *It'll go faster after breakfast.* He slid the screen out an inch real quick to check the time—he'd caught a few hours' sleep last night, after his dinner of Bamananas, but had been editing this vid since 2 AM. Now it was 6:20. He'd paid a few bucks extra for the cold breakfast, but that started at seven, according to the slip of paper with the net password on it.

Still—who could say no to a hardworking guy like him asking for a humble mango? Besides, he was just a few minutes early!

He rolled out his stiffened shoulders and wings—excruciating!—shifted around to get off his tail, then gathered up his empty Jukee cans on his knees while the feeling returned to it.

A quick stop at the group washroom for a brisk dust-off and change of clothes, then Mercurio headed to the motel's dining room, dropping his sleeping mat into the laundry bin he found on the way.

The purple clock on the wall read 6:35 AM. Beneath it, a drab square and a posse of squabs—related somehow, from the scent of 'em, but not, like, a father and his clutch—were unfolding cheap rectangular card tables that had a light whiff of mold to them. A few had already been stuck between nicer, more permanent-smelling round tables. One table had nothing but pit buckets and napkins waiting to be placed on the other tables. The buffet hadn't been set out yet, but you could see the folding, L-shaped shelves hugging the walls where the spread would go.

The working square shuffled between the buffet shelf and the new table, wincing when his tail got pinched going through the narrow gap.

This place is going to be jammed wing-to-wing later. Glad I'm getting out early!

Mercurio pulled his breakfast punch card out of his ID pouch and whistled a greeting. "Hey, I got an early day, can I grab some chow to go?"

"Ask the boss," said the drab as the odor of mint and melon entered behind Mercurio. He turned to see the purple hen who'd been checking people in earlier, followed by...

"Eyy, if it ain't Lane Nibbles himself!"

The banana-yellow shopkeeper lifted his wings in acknowledgment but kept walking.

And no wonder! That crate of apples looks like it weighs a ton!

"Just set it anywhere, 'Lū," said the purple. She spoke to the drab. "What's he wanna ask the boss, dovey?"

Mercurio held up his meal card. "Lookin' for some breakfast to go, La'," he said. "Early day, yanno."

"Okay." She felt around in her work apron, lashed her tail once. "Gotta go get my dang puncher, hang on." She hustled back the way she came. Mercurio turned to the shopkeeper, still recovering from the haul.

When he'd caught his breath, the yellow said, "Canopy's got more folks in than she reckoned for. Needed summore food, so she ordered it up from me. Just hope she don't wipe me out!"

"You got the pics of the candy yet?"

"Not as such, not yet. You comin' to film now?"

Peach pits! He'd told him this morning, hadn't he? But he still had that vid to post!

"How 'bout you just text me when you get those pics done? You have my card."

The shopkeeper bristled. "How 'bout you just come now? You beddah not be backin' out on me, braddah!"

The square and the squabs looked up from their table setup. Mercurio held his palms up.

"Relax, relax! I just thought it'd be more economical to film everything in one go."

The shopkeeper gave him a skeptical glare. But his ruff went down. "Speaking of our deal, how'd that go? You find Keonaona?"

Mercurio fought to keep his own ruff tamed. "Yeah."

The shopkeeper grinned. "He throw you out?"

"None of your business."

"Ha, haaa!" The yellow's tail thumped the floor in delight. "I knew he'd know what to do with a pushy little barker like you!"

"Yeah, well...he ain't doin' so well himself."

The purple hen suddenly loomed in front of him. The metal hole punch in her hand now looked like a cudgel. "That s'posed to be a threat, cuz?"

"Nono! You misunderstand! He just wants to move—"

The innkeeper and the shopkeeper exchanged bewildered *quelp*s.

"Keonaona move? I'd be able to fly first—that land has been in his family generations!" said the shopkeeper.

Mercurio shrugged. "Just tellin' you what he said, cousins!"

"Why would he say that?" said the innkeeper. "The house is his blood, like this motel's mine. How could he say that? How could he?"

The purple innkeeper's mate began chirping, to calm her.

Mercurio thought fast. Now wasn't the time to play all his cards. "I don't know, cousin, but I'll look into it today while I'm out and about. I'm sure you'll be busy." Hungry-looking faces began poking their beaks around the corner. The innkeeper glanced at the clock and squawked. "*Ki-yee-yee!* Here, give me your punch card. Kids, get the clunkets out on the tables—" Her orders came in a steady stream even as she punched Mercurio's breakfast card without looking.

"*Mahalo,*" he said before grabbing two apples out of the crate. Not much, but it'd get him through till his next meal—or Jukee. He began skipping out the dining room.

"Hey, wait, we had a deal!" said the shopkeeper.

Mercurio would've run out the Canopy, but the incoming couples and hens en route to the dining room kept him from building any speed, and the banana shopkeeper grabbed him by the wing just outside the Canopy's front door.

"Easy, easy! That's a wing, not a handle!"

"You running from me, camerawing?"

"No!"

"Good. That apple crate was my last delivery. We can get that filmin' out of the way."

"You sure you don't want to—"

"Ooh, I'll set it up while you get the wall. Already dusted it and everything!" He finished with a squeeze of his claws into Mercurio's shoulder.

Scowling, Mercurio let the old rube walk him down the motel stairs.

It was two hours before Mercurio left the general store—about a half-hour to film (true to his word, the shopkeeper made up the plate of candy for the shot—but then he made Mercurio use his equipment to capture the still—*which is probably a good thing, seeing as his photo would've turned out under-exposed or had his ugly mug reflected in the plate or something*) and a brain-busting hour-and-a-half to finish that day's feed video. Somewhere around the hour-and-fifteen-minute mark, the old shopkeeper came out on the lanai and comped Mercurio a Jukee, so maybe the old coot wasn't so bad after all.

Now Mercurio crested the top of the hill overlooking the town plaza. His gaze swept the dully-lit scene before him. His fist was wrapped around the cam-controller, but he hesitated, tasting the air. *Something's different here. Something new.* Not the Gorgons, either—all that stuff was supposed to happen at the chapel side. Not the restaurants, either—though some new recipe was on the heat, that his beak was sure of. No, but it was something different.

Mercurio let Wideshot fly. Freshly charged, he was quick off the line and soaring high over the milling folk below. He switched over to his digital recorder.

"It's the first day of the Gorgons' gloomy services in the village of Crooked Neck, and something different hangs in the air, a scent that doesn't fit among the grilled peach breakfasts, the dank morning mist, or the hordes of mourners packed in to await their turn with the butchers of Everlush..."

Yeah, but what is it?

He clicked off his voice track, pulled out his screen, and switched to the display of Wideshot's live recording. He sent the cam on a slow flight dead over the middle of the plaza. His eyes darted over the screen, searching for any clue to the new thing he was scenting.

Hundreds of squarglings jumbled and muttered in the plaza, although at this hour, most of the groups had stationed them-selves outside the two main restaurants. One of the mango-seller's employees called a name, and a group broke off from the masses to enter the hens' restaurant. Huh, no squares' café. And Mercurio bet a lot of people were missing Ho'okano the mansion-dwelling fruit seller.

A strange shape in a familiar goldenrod hue caught the filmmaker's eye. He took control of Wideshot and zoomed in.

"C'mon, c'mon, move!" he said futilely to the big blue hen blocking the shot. Finally, he managed to angle Wideshot just right to see around her. The shopkeeper, apparently, had sent someone up with some blazing signs advertising his store off the hill. *Glad I got outta that job.*

Come to think, hadn't he noticed someone leaving the shop while he chopped his vid? And he could kind of remember passing by some little yellow sandwich boards on the way here...

"Mneh," he said, and let Wideshot resume his regularly scheduled programming.

Mercurio scanned the screen again. In the central soaking pool sat a leaf green hen—ancient-looking, even from this far away. She was the only one in the water feature but the people she chatted with seemed to be eying the water with a promise to return and indulge themselves.

Wideshot proceeded down the plaza. On this end, tents of all sizes and colors seemed to have sprouted up overnight like nylon mushrooms. A few were in the process of being packed up by their owners; some were still unoccupied (or were their owners sleeping in?); others had handfuls of squarglings congregating outside their flaps. One group was passing around some object everyone was looking at. Mercurio zoomed in.

Oh. A photo slip of some squar, in dress uniform, in front of what had to be the blue flag of Osider.

That's the fellow they'll be saying goodbye to.

Strangely, Mercurio's thoughts flew to the moment yesterday when red Ho'okano had trashed the table Mercurio was at. A notion hummed at the edge of Mercurio's awareness, but Mercurio shook it off like an annoying fly.

He released Wideshot back on his route. There was the old-fashioned chapel...and there, next to it, the equally dated-looking lodge—it really was a miracle anyplace here had net access, wasn't it?—and...there!

Mercurio squawked. *No! What?! No way!!* No es cierto*!*

Standing around just off the village lodge were—one-twothreefourfivesix...a dozen Netrons—with men carrying mikes on booms...some lugging full box cameras on shoulders—and both men and women with hair coiffed like a square heading to the mating grounds.

"News crews!" he spat. "How'd they get—"

No...Not news crews. Netron news crews. *Only* Netron news crews.

He switched out of the filming screen and into his messenger. The Plattman girl was still on top. Mercurio's claws scrabbled furiously into the sunken keyboard.

MercurioMax

> **Did u tip off these reporters??**

He waited half a second, then added,

MercurioMax

> **U coulda warned me!**

He further punctuated this with an animated pop—a stick of dynamite, fuse sparking. He wished these machines could emit smell, so she'd get a whiff of the outrage he felt.

She took her sweet time replying.

L. Plattman-miss

> **Warned you? Why?**

Mercurio stabbed the keyboard.

MercurioMax

> **Hello, MercurioMaxFILMS? I wanted N exclusive with the Gs. Now gotta battle through a dzn chumps just 2 pitch my idea!**

L. Plattman-miss

> I apologize. I never meant to get in your way. I only want my story to be told. But if you want an exclusive with them, you had better not talk to me. He hates my guts.

There's something we have in common!

What story u trying to tell, NEway?

He tied me up, you know.

WHAT?! He hurt U?

No.

Mercurio's sigh of exasperation propelled his face heaven-ward.

So what??? My czins tied me up 4 half a day when i was 6. Left me on an anthill. I survived!

He paused before adding,

He could've gutted u, but he didn't.

Don't U think that's interesting? he typed, then deleted.

Don't u think that says something?

Are you defending him??

No. But u coulda asked me! I coulda told ur story!!

You wouldn't tell it right. You'd have to be Netron to understand.

What wouldn't i understand? Mercurio was in the middle of typing when her next message popped up.

> Sorry, I have to get ready for my interview. Good luck to you, Max-sir.

Interview!! Of all the—

Although, maybe he could watch it and do a quick reaction vid. As an apology to his followers for today's late post.

Mercurio texted himself this idea as a reminder, then switched back to Wideshot's view. A big tiger-striped brown square was making the rounds among the human news crews, yukkin' it up and passing out expensive-looking coffee that only some of the Netrons were brave enough to try.

That's it, I'm going over there. Obviously that's where all the action is.

Mercurio shoved his screen in his pouch, unholstered his cam controls, and unleashed MaxCam and Angel. A complicated blink pattern set MaxCam's focus on the brown's face, and then he was off, dashing around back of the plaza buildings on the squares' side. Maybe the brown could be his way into the camera crews' good graces. Or maybe he was an employee—he was good-looking enough to be an anchor, Mercurio thought with a *hmph!*

Whatever. Mercurio just couldn't let these crews get the drop on him.

He swung his tail sideways to scooch between two groups of chit-chatters outside their tents.

Maybe there was a way to direct all these crews to the opposite end of the village...After all, if Ho'okano'd just been a good host, the Gorgons wouldn't have had to have been so nasty to that poor (annoying) girl...

Having finally made it to the reporters' camp, Mercurio ignored all the humans and tracked down the big brown square by his cinnamon-cayenne scent; He stood out like a rock on top of a sand dune, especially among the soapy, sunscreen-heavy scents of the humans.

He's the only one who smells like he belongs here!

Mercurio cawed a greeting. The orange-eyed square gave him a funny look, raised his wings in reply. "You from E-city?" he asked.

"No! I'm Mercurio Maximino Macoya, and I am here to film my *exclusive* interview with the Gorgons. *Exclusive*, as in, no outside media allowed!"

"Oh really." A smirk surfaced on the brown's face. "They didn't mention it to me."

"Who, the Gorgons? You spoke to them?"

"Him, any bananas. She was too busy stuffing her face to participate in the convo. Coffee?" He bobbed the tray at Mercurio.

He took a cup. "Thanks." It was strong—and thick as mud, but that was fine. The semi-solid state of the caffeine should release slowly in his bloodstream throughout the day—that was his theory, anyway. Besides, being smoothie-thick, it'd help him to skip lunch easy.

The brown spoke while Mercurio was licking his beak clean. "When did you get a chance to talk to them?"

"Yesterday. At the big house south of here."

The big brown puffed his chest in pride. "My place."

"Where the Netron *chica* stayed."

The smirk again—this time aimed at Angel, over Mercurio's shoulder. "Very generous for her to send so much business my way. And she left me a top-notch review on the net."

"Good for you. So what are you doing with the humans?"

"Just being a good host. Though I don't think they trust the coffee. Most of them are dumping it out beneath a palm over there, but I can smell it. *Palermas*. Which news crew are you with, again?"

"I'm not. I run a feed channel."

"What topic?"

"Varies."

"Eh." The sound was disdain and dismissal all at once.

"I have ten thousand followers, you know!"

"You see these crews?"

"Sure."

"They each represent the biggest Netron news networks. Not just vid feeds, but written feeds and audcasts. Hundreds of millions of *active* followers, each—their people can't imagine them not being around. You've got to be missed to be important, and to be missed, you have to be seen in the first place. Your numbers may sound impressive to the rubes out here—present company excluded" (it took Mercurio a second to realize the brown was referring to himself) "but in comparison to these pros, you're invisible."

Hatred seethed through Mercurio.

"But if you wanna hang around, pick up some tips, I won't stop you. Tell you what, I'll even let you call yourself my assistant."

"I'm NOT your assistant!"

Mercurio's hackles raised, electrified, when he realized that that little sprinkle of LOUD had made every Netron's head flip up from whatever they were doing to look at him.

At him!

He repressed a smirk of his own and turned to them all, spreading his wings and arms and keeping the volume turned up for them all to hear.

"Your host here is trying to keep the REAL story from you. See, I've talked to the girl *and* the Gorgons, and I know the reason it happened!"

All those beakless faces were rapt, guzzling in Mercurio's words. Some of the boom mikes were raised. Aimed at him!

"On the south side of town, there's a huge mansion. A wealthy red square by the name of Lane Ho'okano owns it. He was assigned to take the Gorgon in that night, but he refused—at the last minute. That's right, he shirked his duty! And do you know why?"

The brown's eyes were shooting around, watching the Netrons watch Mercurio.

Mercurio milked the moment a little longer.

"Truth is, I'm not sure. But if I were you...I'd ask the fellow why he moved back into town without his wife and squab."

There. Just enough mystery to intrigue, just enough hint to scandalize. Mobis were being pulled, satnav maps consulted. Within minutes, producers began leading their teams into the plaza—hustling their gear *away* from the chapel.

Mercurio grinned up at the brown.

"Hmph. Doesn't put a hole in my money pouch. And I'm not the one they'll shun once they come back from that snipe hunt you just sent them on."

"Won't matter—I'll have my exclusive then."

"*If* you can beat this crew," said the brown, pointing to the lone foursome of humans who'd stayed behind. Their producer had her cameraman aimed at the entryway of the village lodge.

He caught the moment the door opened. He'd caught it on film.

The tall man was ducking under the doorframe.

Mercurio blinked furiously, training focuses, his other camera controls in hand, setting parameters. The old queen was ushered out.

The brown spoke in Mercurio's ear. "Some wisdom, *mijo*. Nobody ever remembers who came in second."

Mercurio raced forward.

18

GORGON

JERIMIN WASN'T SURE WHAT he should do when he saw the news cameras aimed at them from the doorway of the lodge. Glare them down, or ignore them? He'd sneaked himself and his Queen out of their tent much too early in the dark of morning and made it to the lodge for a fry-free breakfast (they'd eaten through this Del's entire stash, apparently) unaccosted by the media or the still-snoozing squarglings—but this! They'd lain in wait for them, as though they were prey.

The Gorgon was not to be treated as prey. He didn't need his Queen to be absolutely bone-deep certain of that—but she wasn't saying much this morning.

Hand gently pressing her shoulder, he guided his Queen out the lodge door. From a few yards away, a bright light from a camera winked on, shone in his eye.

Her only words, in fact, had been a single sentence to the mayor's wife, interrupting the hen as she ran down the day's itinerary with names they, of course, didn't recognize, and—at last!—a more explicit rundown of chapel-appropriate behavior. She hadn't gotten far on the topic when his Queen lifted her head and said, "I don't want to be in your chapel."

This simple phrase had left the cramped little office stunned.

/Why?/ he sent. But there was no reply.

By his estimation, four full seconds of silence passed before the mayor over-jovially insisted that there was no nicer and roomier—and peaceful!—place in the plaza to hold their sessions.

"Where else would you hold them?" The square chuckled. "At Nika's Electronics?"

Her head had bowed—without a single clear signal through the wires—and she had said nothing more.

Now, as they left the lodge's paved walkway to cross over to the chapel, the news crew began to migrate towards them, like filings catching up to a magnet. For the moment, Jerimin opted for silence, and ignoring them. But looking straight ahead made it harder to make out their numbers. Out of the corner of his eye it seemed like there were many fewer—*wake up, wake up!*—noticeably fewer invaders. With his Queen's veil sight, he could've assessed their number easily, without having to look at all, but she must be conserving power for their sessions. He hoped.

The news crew splashed alongside them as they rushed up the rain-darkened walk to the chapel. He let the reporter's questions turn to white noise and kept his hand at his Queen's back, propelling her against her instincts. The Likekes surrounded them with wings as they moved, the wife saying "no comment" over and over like a mantra.

They made it to the chapel doors. A sort of architectural visor put them in shadow while they scrubbed their feet on the already soggy welcome mat. Jerimin outlined the awning's shape mentally, sent it in her direction. /Must be to keep the rain off. Clever./

No response. Behind them came the clumping of the camera crew's feet. Jerimin turned sideways so they wouldn't be at their backs.

"'Scuze me," said Mayor Likeke before leaning forwards and rapping on the chapel door.

The door opened immediately. There was a square inside the darkened bay, blue and yellow. For one instant, Jerimin's heart leapt in joy, and tension seemed to spring off of his shoulders. *Lyle!* When Jerimin didn't reply to his weekly email right away, he must have known something was wrong and come down. Ez would have given him the info—genteel Lyle was the epitome of calm and reason; if anyone could get Ho'okano to budge, it'd be him!

Then the square stepped into the light, and the disappointment—*ow!*—landed back on Jerimin at twice the weight. His squargling friend Lyle was aqua and yellow, with an indigo comb and diamondback pattern on his body; this square was colored wild greenish turquoise and acid yellow, and was a round-beak besides (Lyle's own hookbeak made him resemble a toucan—a little anyway). This new squargling's lavalava matched the chapel's exterior colors, and his shell lei click-clicked as he looked from face to face to face, stopping first at the Likekes, then at Jerimin, then to the film crew. He pushed past the Likekes and Jerimin and his Queen to put himself between them and the reporters.

"No filming is allowed in the chapel," he said. "If you wish to come back without your equipment, we would welcome you inside to sit in contemplation during the farewells."

Jerimin cast another look at this new square. Now that he was out of the shadows, he didn't resemble Lyle much at all. For one, this square was shorter and squatter, like he enjoyed an extra meal or two. And from the way his wings sort of slowly twiddled themselves behind his back, he was no expert in handling Netrons.

At least he seems to be on our side, he thought, but the thought didn't soothe the pain—like homesickness—friend-sickness?—of Lyle not being there. And with his mobi dead, he couldn't even reread his friend's letters at night—the letters that made it a little easier to continue on with their penance, kind words from someone who understood Jerimin hadn't intended to blow up his life (or anyone else's) so thoroughly. His kindness was so kind, it was painful.

A woman—a producer, maybe?—was aiming her screen, full of intimidating small-print documents, at the chapel official like it was a weapon—and it was working, the square chutting deep in his throat with anxiety as she recited principles of interworld cooperation, information freedom and goodwill. The turquoise official looked behind each of his wings while (probably) silently praying for backup.

That was another beautiful thing about Lyle: he'd been raised on Netron and seemed to know how to gracefully outmaneuver difficult people.

What would Lyle do?

Jerimin stepped forward, ducked down a little to be nearer the chapel official's ear. But he spoke loudly enough for all to hear.

"I believe it was mentioned to me that this no filming policy is a *standard regulation* of this religion."

The turquoise's bewildered stare held on Jerimin's face a little too long, so he added, "Isn't it so?" with a quick but meaningful raise of his eyebrow.

"Oh!" The turquoise turned back to the producer. "Yes, it's a hard-and-fast rule for everyone, Osidern or not."

While the producer's mouth was closed, he pushed her screen out of his way, and Jerimin couldn't resist a nod of approval. *Attaboy!*

"*Inside*," said the chapel official in Native out of the corner of his mouth, and then the Likekes were herding Jerimin and his Queen inside the dim building. The door closed on the turquoise official and the Netrons.

The smoke issuing from the bubbling glass bowl on the wall had a minty, almost-but-not-quite medicinal aroma to it today.

/Smells like they're boiling lozenges,/ he sent to his Queen, to no response.

They hurried before the Likekes around the edges of the large central bay—where sacred dances were held, Jerimin now knew from this morning's briefing. It would offend their goddess if these areas were merely walked across; so when not in use, they were either avoided or gamboled across. On their way to the dais at the rear of the chapel, they passed the two smaller circular bays on the side. Benches were set up in them for the mourners to wait in. How the squarglings normally used these areas during worship had not been explained to him, nor the ones across the way.

Another thing it would have been nice to look up on my mobi.

Each of the four bays off the central chapel were empty for now, including the two across the dance bay.

They stepped onto the raised platform. Their benches were right where they had left them yesterday, and the same tired light shone in from above.

His Queen slumped into her place, face a distant mask. Unease got its teeth into Jerimin, but before it could take a serious bite, Mayor Likeke was off and running.

"Rosie, you think you could hold the fort outside for Nika? That'd give him some quiet time here before his visit. I'll watch a few sessions after, then we can trade off."

So...the chapel official was their first session today? Nika sounded like a familiar name...but...wasn't that the owner of the electronics shop? Jerimin normally wasn't too bad with the details, and could even hold some of the the longer Osidern names in his head comfortably, but the lack of sleep paired with the screaming hunger in his innards made him inclined to let little details like that slide clean through his ears.

"Good idea," said Lase Likeke, and Jerimin appreciated that she hustled her way around the big bay, to the official's aid.

"Please, sit, sit!" The mayor waved him towards his bench with vigorous wing flapping.

Jerimin folded his hands behind his back and molded his wince into a smile.

"The hospitality is appreciated, Mayor, but since I'll be sitting most the day, you'll understand if I wish to remain standing now."

The mayor tutted solicitously. "Oh. Oh. Of course!"

"Thank you. Now, could you tell me a little more about our first mourner? Is it to be the good square we met just now, outside?"

"Yes, yes. That's Nika, the Chapelfather. He lost a good friend to...in the war."

"I see. Is he the same Nika who runs the electronics shop? Or did I get my names crossed?"

The mayor whistled cheerfully. "He's the very same! Good catch!"

"So...He has two occupations?"

"Oh, no. Mother's Brood has lay clergy at the local level."

"Huh!" It wasn't like an Osidern to do a job for no pay—but perhaps it was different in the religious sphere. In any case, it was good to know. If things went well, maybe Jerimin could get him to repair his mobi.

The mayor was nodding with enthusiasm. "Yes. My Rosie's the dance leader here, for the hens, of course, and I'm assigned to schedule building cleanings. You could say that in here, Nika outranks me."

"Interesting..." And it was, but the door at the far end of the chapel had opened, and a good hundred or so squarglings had entered, led by boldly-colored Nika. The smell in the chapel changed as individuals dropped things in the boiler near the entrance. The sight of so many, and the long, hungry day in session they promised took any lightness the mayor's small talk had generated and squelched it. That would have been enough to put Jerimin down in the dumps, but then he saw that blue-headed feedster squargling again. Like many in the crowd, he had a loud striped blanket thrown over his shoulders and wings to ward off any chill.

Or to hide his cameras.

"Mayor, what can you tell me about the square who just came in—blue head, green body, uh...teal comb?"

The mayor about-faced in the direction Jerimin had indicated with the lift of his chin.

The mayor began shaking his head. Toss another load of misery onto the pile.

"Sorry, don't know him. Must be an out-of-towner. Do you want me to go—"

"No, thank you."

The bays seemed to have filled up—though from this angle, Jerimin couldn't see into any of them—and now the blue-headed auteur took his place leaning against the wall of the main bay with the rest of the overflowing crowd.

We're going to have an audience? Great. Given a choice, his Queen would always prefer to do these sessions in private—with (at minimum) a closed door between her, the mourners, and those waiting—but it looked like she didn't get a choice today. He checked her face, and the lines in his head. If she was bothered, nothing indicated it.

Unease gnawed at him as Nika the Chapelfather approached their seats.

The mayor got him into place, then stood off against a nearby wall to watch. Before Jerimin could settle Nika in with a little small talk, the turquoise spoke.

"Is it true, Lase, that you can help me say goodbye to my friend Rai?"

The unease let off a little when she raised her outstretched hand. The band of quiet chatter along the walls dried up instantly.

"We shall see," she said.

Jerimin took his seat on his bench in the shadow. At this angle, he couldn't see her face, and the lines remained stubbornly dark.

The turquoise gingerly—or hesitantly, maybe—took her wrist.

What was she feeling?

How was she doing, really?

But it was too late to ask. She raised her hood.

I'll tell the mayor we need a break after this. Something's not—

He stopped the thought cold—she had tossed the hood off and was glaring over her shoulder at him (arm still being held by Nika the Chapelfather, Nika of Nika's Electronics), burning Jerimin with a look that told him it was time to shut up, even in his head.

He closed his eyes, wishing he could doze; knowing he wouldn't until he really found out how his Queen was holding up.

19

GORGON

JERIMIN SHIVERED AS HIS weight returned to him, skin erupting in goosebumps. *Cold again!*

The mishmash-smelling smoke in the air hit his nose and turned his stomach. He grabbed the underside of the bench. *Maybe I'm coming down with something.*

He missed whatever the Chapelfather said to his Queen just now—the session hadn't been bad; after some initial emotion, the soft-spoken turquoise and his friend had swapped war stories together, laughing often. Apparently they'd been comrades in arms, sent to different regions, and friends long before that—but the Chapelfather was courteous—probably out of respect to his countrymen—countrywings?—waiting along the walls, but it had felt respectful to Jerimin, too. Just because you *could* use a Hriannen's power to visit with your dead at length didn't meant you *should*. She wasn't a damn modem!

As the Chapelfather left the dais, the mayor came forward to replace him. He cupped his claws, face far too perky for Jerimin's condition (though at least his body temperature seemed to be regulating).

"That was really something. You sure made Nika happy! I never see him talk that much—here or at his shop!" he said, cheerful face faltering briefly when he realized the hood wasn't coming off his Queen. He began addressing Jerimin exclusively. "That makes the last of us Crooked Neckians."

"Is that so!" In just the little time the mayor had been prattling, the nausea had dissipated entirely. Well, maybe it was there a little—hunger nausea. But if they could get just one out-of-towner out of the way before lunch, it'd make them both feel a whole lot better. *Just one more session and we might get a vacant room.*

A room all to ourselves...! It sounded like just the cure for what ailed them.

"Is there any way..." *we could prioritize people staying at the motel?* He was going to ask, but the mayor had turned away, towards a growing gabbling echoing along the walls. Someone was coming down the line.

Jerimin stood, ostensibly to stretch his back (though from the rice cereal cacophony, it needed it), but mostly to get a better look.

His stomach groaned at the sight of the orange--cream-cake-colored hen. Lani the Lunch Hen walked up the p ath between the walled crowd and dancing bay and came up to the dais. She ignored the mayor to stand between Jerimin and his Queen. Her head went back and forth between them.

"Fries?" he almost asked, but the not-joke flew out of his brain when the hen did a clumsy little dip with her wings out—an imitation curtsey?!

That's new.

"Your, um...Lase and Lane Gorgon, I have a question for you."

"...Okay," said Jerimin, and, like the mayor, the lunch hen stopped switching her head back and forth and pinned her attention on him.

"I have..." She chittered softly. "I recently lost someone. —But it wasn't in the war. Would you be willing to do goodbyes for me? I can pay."

At last, the lines in his head came alive—and they were jittering and screaming *NO!!!!*, making his skull feel like it was being broken open by a jackhammer intent on pulping his brain. He quickly sent agreement and the apocalypse in his head disappeared as abruptly as it had arrived.

After a second to touch his head and reassure himself that it was really still in one piece, he gathered his hands in front of him—but stopped the bow before it could go any further. He measured his words carefully; offending people who had fed them was the last thing he wanted to do. But it'd be bad—no, disastrous—precedent, fulfilling her request, payment or no.

"Miss—Lani—if I may call you that?"

She nodded.

"We're sorry for your loss, of course. Death is difficult to face under any circumstance. However, your request is outside the scope of our duty." He watched her face carefully. There was no sign of impending breakdown—but also no sign of fighting one, either.

But she'd said it happened recently. Something's up here.

But why should he care? He glanced over the crowded chapel, saw some leaning out of the smaller bays. The longer he spent thinking about it, the longer the day would be.

"We are honored that you..." *Thought of us? For all your posthumous communication needs?* Who else could she go to? They were the only ones who could do this! "...felt comfortable enough with us to make your request."

Now her wings slumped.

She's not a mourner. You're missing something!

/C'mon, tell me what's going on with her really. Please?/

But his Queen was not interested in exerting herself right now.

"I'm sorry," he said again. "*We're* sorry."

"Well...it was worth a shot," she said, more to herself than him, and left the dais without so much as a nod, let alone a curtsey.

After an awkward moment of watching the lunch hen thread her way between the dance bay and the wallflowers, the mayor piped twice. "I'll bring the next one up." He zipped along the other curved wall (the awaiting squarglings—including the blue-headed feedster—looking bored) and disappeared into one of the bays. By the time he exited it, the lunch hen had left the building, her exit marked by grim grey light slicing into the chapel as the doors opened, then retreating as the doors fell shut behind her.

And then, before the needed break could be asked for, the next collection of mourners was there before them. Jerimin's throat tightened with tension, but he managed to keep the dread off his face as he asked them to introduce themselves: a widower, his parents, his in-laws, his two sisters, the deceased's brother and sister, and one tiny squab, all come today to say goodbye to the soldier they'd lost at the Lanakila Massacre.

They'd brought a picture of her, of course. He'd already seen so many in the past months. He made sure to study it for a few moments after they handed the screen over.

He would forget the details soon after the session was through, but he thought it important they should see...what, he didn't know. That he cared? Maybe regret? Whatever they were looking for, he imagined that what he had for them was too little, too late.

He offered the screen back, but none in the family reached for it; his arm, outstretched, began to tremor. He pulled it back. *Need more sleep!*

The squab squirmed to get down out of its grandmother's arms. The old hen lifted a wing at his Queen. "She gonna look?" she asked him, bouncing the raspberry-hued babe.

"She'll see her in a minute, along with the rest of you," he said smoothly. Once sessions started, she seemed oddly determined to keep the hood up. Maybe to help her concentration? He'd never asked, only made sure he had some kind of answer for the mourners. That seemed the more important part of his duties.

He offered the screen back again, and this time a sister took it.

The family stared at him—except for the squirmy tod-dler-child. He found he was too burnt to even entertain the thought of small talk, or explanations of what was going to happen. They had seen—or maybe had just heard—what happened with Nika. Surely they could extrapolate.

He put his hand on his Queen's shoulder. "Ready?"

A hesitation, before a slow nod.

Wish I'd gotten her that break.

He stood straight again and beckoned to the widower. His call, he was certain, would be the strongest.

The widower moved like he was underwater, but held out his salmon-colored hand out when Jerimin prompted him to.

Another hesitation—as minute as the one he'd seen when he'd asked her if she was ready—and then his Queen took the widower's wrist.

Jerimin sat back on his bench. He closed his eyes.

"Give me your name," said his Queen.

He did—Daimon or Daijon or something—he couldn't hear him clearly, he spoke too softly.

"Daimon," (or whatever), "call your wife by her name. Call her to us."

Two long, deep breaths passed.

"Wait, I want—"

Jerimin opened his eyes; the squab was being passed into the widower's arms. The widower bounced the baby a couple times until it settled.

"Yes," he said, voice thick. "Okay."

Jerimin closed his eyes again. A pang of hunger struck his body like a gong before he went weightless.

That's never happened before.

The dead mother's name was called. Jerimin opened his eyes.

The hen in the photo stood before her family, in vibrant chocolate browns and raspberry pinks. Her husband's eyes lit up. The squab reached both tiny hands out to her.

Then Jerimin's pulse began throbbing in his ear. *Ugh! What is this?*

The zero-gee floatiness left like someone had flicked it off—he felt his weight filling him up in great clumps, like someone emptying a bag of powdered cement in great—hefting—shakes—

"Shit!" he heard his Queen say.

The world tipped forward, like it was dumping him out of a pail.

Then everything went black.

She shoved the mourner away, into his family's

(*o, Mother, what's she doing? no, our baby! she's gone AGAIN!*)

arms with just enough time to spare before the last enchantment slipped entirely from her grasp and and unraveled—the enchantment that kept her contained in a two-legged, flat-toothed human body

screaming, razor screaming, but no a siren's attack, they're only bird-throated

she fell forward wearing her whiskers, catching herself on grey arms, bone and muscle coils spilling out off the dais—

(is that???)

still quick enough, though, to swerve around on those coils and catch her Jerimin

dead air. unconscious

before he hit the floor.

The screaming filled the clayen walls till she was drowning in it, clutching her Jerimin, flattening her oversized ears to her head

(get to the exit! she'll kill us all!)

The squarglings flowed out the main door, colors reminding her of the way her vision had gone colorful and spotty the last time *she* had attempted to drown her

white, smooth, sliding, and those green, mad eyes staring into her own

"No, no, I'm here, not then."

She ran her fingers through her husband's hair as she muttered. They were all out now—all but the resident spirits; they glared at her disapprovingly from the chapel edges (she was now grounded in the center of the worship-floor, where they had been watching her all lasterday) their tails lashing and their colors just as bright to her as any living.

But no, here was one, one standing along the wall, heart drumming the air like a rabbit's. She *thought* he was alive. She could hear the piercing scree of something electronic coming off him. It was somewhere under the blanket he wore.

Must to be alive; ghosts do not keen electric.

So he held a machine. She couldn't use machines; they broke a while or died forever in her hands. She needed her Jerimin to handle such things. Or the owner.

The space above the square's blue head was yellow-sharded fear. But only faintly.

And now that all the thinkingbreathingfeelingbodies were outside...it was like they had vanished. Ceased to exist.

She thought she felt a stirring in her husband's side of their mind...object...permanence?

But where his presence normally sat in (or perhaps, next to) her mind, there was nothing but a dark room. Things were still in it, but reaching for them, she reached through them.

She couldn't energize him now.

She clutched him closer.

She needed meat.

"I know you," she said to the trembling (alive?) squargling. His faded verdantseatropical colors now began blotching the same sand color as the wall terror had pinned him to. Like bruises coming into being before her four eyes, bruises trying to hide him.

He panted, beak parted.

But the fear-yellow above his head was disappearing—not being replaced by new thoughtcolors of emotion, but fading from her perception.

Her lips pulled tighter around her bared teeth, *ANXIOUS ANXIOUS ANXIOUS*. It was like when she was with Kolar and his kind, when she was finally escaped out of the attic. The Orlock were unreadable by their natures. Everything, everyone else, she'd always been able to read. Her anxiety-grin stretched even tighter. So her *nensha* was gone, her power was fading, and she would have to stumble through this alone. She squeezed her husband's limp body.

Terrible. No comfort. Like when *she* had murdered her poor kitten Char-lot and left it with her...

She lifted her gaze from her husband's form and bit herself, sharp teeth solid and immediate.

I'm here, not then!

That squargling was a decent morsel of meat. But she would not do that anymore. Her own purr started up, to soothe her, but now the squargling's eye bulged and he looked ready to screamfaintdie so she halted herself.

The chapel spirits watched her silently.

/help/

But if they heard her plea, they did nothing.

She swiveled her ears back to the squargling on the wall.

She needed this one's help.

She tried to think of what her Jerimin would say.

145

He would tell me to put my nerves away off my face. She forced her terror-grin away, tried relaxing her ears. The squargling's eyes stopped bulging, and two of the wall-bruisings were reversing themselves back to his hide's right colors.

"You are Mercury. Mercurial."

An eddy stirred faintly in her husband's mind, glowing only for a moment.

"Mercurio! You are the Mercurio. From the house. You will help me."

His colors were revibranting—but now his gaze slid towards the door.

No.

can't let him see

he MUST help

but I can't let him see our need.

We are the Gorgon

She glanced over the squargling's head.

still unreadable.

Must stumble through.

She bolted forward.

20
MERCURIO

MERCURIO HAD ONLY GLANCED at the chapel door when there was a blur and the grey, four-eyed monster was suddenly there, in front of him, tiger-big—no, bigger! Huge! Big enough to cradle that lanky palm tree Icarii in her arms like a doll. Big enough to crush him with her arm-length teeth and eat him, like she had so many in the war. She smelled like the promise of death, and faintly of the desert; a fuller, richer, more overwhelming version of the scent he'd encountered at Cortez's house.

"You will not leave," said the grey Gorgon.

Her voice reminded him of a sound effect he'd messed with once, like two voices piled on top of one another, one just a little off from the other. It had been for a horror-themed vid and he'd ultimately scrapped it and gone with different effects, but that's all he could come up with right now. The horror that sound filter hadn't inspired, her (apparently natural??) speaking voice evoked in him with zero trouble.

"You will use your mobi-thing and call the mayor."

"I—I—" The words kept getting caught. He could see his own terrified reflection in all four eyes. They seemed to be looking into his soul.

C'mon, Merc, c'mon! Get that sentence out, wouldn't wanna make her mad!

"I don't have a mobi."

Her jaw clenched, and Mercurio prayed to Mother she wouldn't snarl again—he really couldn't handle seeing the teeth, he'd decided. Instead, she lifted her arm covering Icarii and pointed at Mercurio.

"You do," she said. "There."

He looked where she was pointing.

147

Somehow, despite the *serape* covering it, she'd sussed out the exact hiding spot of MaxCam, currently strapped to his bandoliers and recording.

He recalled how the anger had flashed in Icarii's eyes back at Cortez's house. What would SHE do to him if she didn't want to be filmed?!

"Oh. Oh! You mean this! My screen!" He pivoted on his heel, letting the blanket sweep around so she couldn't see anything beneath while he pulled the larger, rectangular device out. "It can't videocall, but maybe I can message someone for you? Idunno anybody here…"

Batlike ears flattened, and Mercurio felt himself go grey again.

"No, that is not it!" She pointed again, right at MaxCam.

Mercurio felt like a block of ice had lodged itself in his throat.

Fumbling beneath the *serape*, he unhooked MaxCam and held it out in his palm.

"It's not recording."

"Liar," she said.

Mercurio closed his eyes. Never thought it'd end this way. He hoped it would be quick.

Then, instead of biting him in half, she took MaxCam from him.

The icy fear dropped into the bottom of his stomach and turned to lead.

"Hey! That cost money, you know!"

Her big pair of eyes—yellow, and slitted like a fox's—glanced at him, but she didn't answer. Spidery fingers rotated the sphere around in one hand. The black eye of the camera turned, disappeared like an image on a rotating sign.

Then, raising up on those weird bone-and-muscle bio-bellows that seemed to make up her strange, legless body, she stuck it between two bony rings. They looked strong enough to crack it like a nut. He had hundreds of jen invested in that one piece of equipment, and that wasn't even counting the price of the enchantment on it.

But today's video is all on storage…

Storage he was wearing. And he still had Angel and Wideshot on his back, under the blanket. If he could just get out of here, he wouldn't need the Gorgon's cooperation any-more...footage of the séance or whatever falling apart...no one could ignore that! —But first, he had to escape.

She watched him silently, for so long—*like, waaay longer than anyone's ever waited when I was in trouble*—that it unnerved him again.

Her scent, though, it didn't...well, he didn't *think* he smelled anger on her. And her face didn't look angry, though with features that strange, he honestly couldn't tell.

It made him want to narrate.

The giant form of the Gorgon of Hriana stands (stands? What do you call it if there's no legs?) *before me, golden eyes weirdly staring out at nothing...but then I spot smaller eyes, lower on her face: black and red, that hold me paralyzed...*

No. Paralyzed? That wouldn't do. That's not cinematic!

"Hey." His voice squidged like he'd barely gotten out of nest talk. Her ear twitched, and he thought he saw annoy-ance in the red eyes. He swallowed quickly. "Hey." That was better. He nodded at Icarii, who hadn't moved this whole time. "Did he faint?"

No answer. Under the *serape*, his wings slid forward, hug-ging the fronts of his shoulders, but they couldn't cape around because his screen was in his claws.

His screen!

"You want me to call someone for him, right? But Idunno anyone here, like I told you. I'm an out-of-towner."

Her gaze—he thought—turned inward a sec. He thought.

"Do you keep a room?" she asked.

"...Keep?"

"Do you...where do you stay, now?"

"Uh, at the motel."

Her bio-bellows elevated her and then extended her for-ward. Now that gigantic head was so close he could see the wiry whiskers on her face move when he chuffed in panic. "B—but I don't got a room, I swear, I'm out on the lanai!"

Her bio-bellows contracted (reminding him of optical zoom lenses he'd handled), taking her head away from him.

The head didn't look happy.

"Yeah, it—yeah—it was raining most the night. Wind'd blow in and get me wet, it really wouldn't do for you, your...Gorgonliness."

The yellow eyes rolled!

What? But somehow it felt safe to Mercurio to keep talking. *Just pretend you're streaming live.* Even if he started out broadcasting to an empty chatroom, the longer he spent talking, the more people usually dropped into his channel for a look...on the net, that was. The longer he kept talking here, the more likely it was someone would come through the chapel doors, and then these two wouldn't be his problem anymore.

He hoped.

"So, how you likin' it here in Crooked Neck?"

The look she gave him seemed to shoot the sentence dead in midair.

"That much, huh? I hear that. Listen, we both wanna get out of here, so if you just move aside or whatever, I'll go find somebod—"

"No."

"*Wahk!* Lady, then how dya expect me to go get him help?"

The air darkened and the walls shuddered. Mercurio flinched, thinking he'd enraged her—but then the patter of rain above made him look up. A storm had come in—you could see it through the chapel's skylight. The clouds were so dark and close they made him feel like an egg being sat on.

Satisfied, he looked down before she did and caught the expression on her face.

Doesn't look like she's a fan of the rain. Curious, he took a whiff of the air.

Could that be fear? Maybe? Besides her being a freakin' monster, there were a lot of other wings' fear stinking up the air. He just couldn't be sure.

She wormed herself lower, hugging the hard concrete floor like a cat settling in. Her free arm was over Icarii again.

"Message the mayor. With your screen thing. Tell him to bring us a big lunch."

"Sure, sure."

He pulled up the messaging program, told it to locate him and compile a directory based on location.

He waited. And waited. He waited a long time for him.

"Scorpion hairs! I can't get a signal!" The chapel went white under the lightning's flash. "Gotta be the storm." He lifted his screen at Icarii. "Does he have...?"

She waited for him...apparently incomplete sentences were not allowed.

"You know, his own mobi?"

Those big ugly bat ears jumped, as though surprised.

"Drowned," she said. "The rain."

"Oh. Too bad. Guess..."

Her expression darkened the longer he held out the word. "I'll have to run out, then. Lodge is next door, right? The mayor's bound to be there, I'll grab her for you easy-treesy! Whaddya say?"

Nothing, it wound up. She just kept watching him. Watching him and holding her pet human...despite his cozy *serape*, Mercurio shivered.

Then: a clunk. From *behind* her. From the door!

Her ears turned first, then the rest of that weird body followed, curving upwards like a living spiral staircase—but Mercurio was still trapped. She was like a snake—naturally replacing her body with more body when repositioning herself.

Like, right now, he was seeing her ribby back? But also more rows (and rows and rows) of those bio-bellows.

Some moments passed. He could hear clunking and shuffling.

C'mon, what's going on? He was tempted to release Angel to get a better view...

Then: "Haa...Haa...Harold-miss Eu—Euphegenia, Netron World News Association." Another long pause. "How...d—do you do?"

Glad to see I'm not the only one overwhelmed by the grey Gorgon!

"You are not to record in here," came the layered horror-voice.

"We're streaming with permission to the mayor's office through the landline. He wanted to know what happened. Why did all the squarglings run out?"

No answer.

"Is anyone hurt?"

"No."

What about Icarii? Can't they see him?

"Is anyone here?"

"No," said the grey Gorgon, and Mercurio felt the room spin.

What?! She can't keep me trapped here!!

He cawed, loud and brash. "I'M HERE!"

The world righted itself. When it did, the grey Gorgon was shooting him a dirty, four-eyed look over her shoulder. Mercurio felt himself go colorless again—but forced bravado into his voice.

"Yeah, go on, show 'em. The jig's up." Mercurio began walking forward towards the bio-bellows blocking him in. "You caught us, guys," he said in a voice pitched for the camera crew, but with a *follow my dance* look aimed right at the grey Gorgon. "But you're too late. They've already agreed to an exclusive interview with me."

He'd nearly reached the bio-bellows when they lifted up, forming an arch over his head. Now he could see the Netron camera crew—camera operator, sound man, producer, and talent—and a thick cable trailing out through a gap in the exit doors behind them.

Thunder rumbled.

Mercurio walked through the coils, stopped between the grey Gorgon and the Netron news crew. The boom mic swiveled to follow him.

"In fact, I'm their sole videographer for the remainder of their stay here."

"Once he gains permission for us to room with Lane..." Four eyebrows raised expectantly at Mercurio.

"Ho'okano," Mercurio finished for her with a plastic smile.

"Yes, him."

Mercurio turned a grin on the film crew. "Lighting's better there, anyway."

"While Lane Mercurio accomplishes this," said the grey Gorgon, "we shall remain here and lunch. Tell the mayor that."

Rain drummed on the chapel roof. Mercurio was just a few yards from the door. He'd never been so eager to run out into a flood.

But the talent (who reeked of fake vanilla) just had to open her mouth.

"So, just to be clear...Gorgon-miss..." said the reporter, "You'll grant an exclusive interview to whoever can get you housed at the Ho'okano residence?"

There was a pause. Mercurio looked up at the grey Gorgon. To his horror, it looked like she was seriously considering this.

Oh no! No! This deal's between us! Don't you—

"Yes," she said, dark eyes flickering towards Mercurio just for a moment. "Yes, that is the contest."

The reporter spun her finger in the air, and the rest of her crew about-faced with the gesture. They were out the door before Mercurio could say boo.

He squawked at the grey Gorgon. "What's the idea?! I just saved your tails gettin' grilled over that Netron girl! If they come back with a room for you at Ho'okano's, they won't go easy on you!"

She raised up on her bio-bellows, seemed to fill the entirety of the chapel. Her teeth grew in her mouth. "Which is why it would be wisest for YOU to make Ho'okano cooperate before they do!"

Mercurio paled a moment—then cawed again. "Fine! I will!"

He spun on his heel towards the door.

With the disaster footage I got, all I have to do is get out of here. Once it's uploaded, I won't have to dicker with that rockhead Ho'okano or worry about an interview. I'll have all the views I need. And I'll never have to see this sorry mudhole ever again!

"Mercurio."

He spun back again. Icarii was nowhere to be seen, but the grey Gorgon's bio-bellows were bent in a funny way—maybe she was hiding him in the bend. "What?!"

Huge hands scooped him up under his *serape*, under his arms, then a single hand crushed him against a curve of bio-bellows. With her free hand, she swiftly began tearing his equipment off him. Mercurio screeched and screeched, wings battering uselessly at her. Within seconds, his chest was bare: no mem cards, no screen, no control stick, no Angel or Wideshot.

And no séance footage.

The bandoliers swung from her hand like giant, dead worms.

He thrashed against her grip, but the bio-bellows (and the one arm pinning him against them) were python-strong. "At least gimme my screen—" His voice cracked. "I need it to help you!"

"No," she said.

She lowered him safely to the ground—then tucked all his equipment behind the curve of her body, which opened a little, revealing Icarii, still out cold. "Your things will return to you upon our receipt of the room."

Mercurio gawped at her.

"But—but—"

She hissed at him, eyes rolling back in her head. She looked like a demon out of a nightmare.

"GO!"

Mercurio turned tail and fled out into the storm.

21

KEONAONA

ALONE IN HIS KITCHEN, Keonaona sipped listlessly at his pineapple *atole*, long gone lukewarm. A dish on the well-patina'd table was covered with three slices of crouton-loaf, but only one had been broken in half by his beak—and that half lay on the plate next to the other, untasted.

He eyed the fractured cracker wearily, resentfully. He had a heart that was shattered, a mind that was exhausted and numb, craving the sleep that would make these hours disappear in one gulp. But he also had a stomach, which, traitorously, refused to let him sleep until it was filled. But the sight of this, the most plain and basic of foods, the sort of food...

The sort of food they'd make Kai eat when he was sick, the sort of food the boy now reached for himself when he stomach wasn't right—

Used to reach for.

The realization gouged into his heart, a merciless shard of stone. He gulped his mouthful of *atole* quickly and wheezed another sob that reached the highest corners of the empty house.

Tomorrow. After tomorrow, I'll sell it all. Move to the north—or even Netron, maybe. Someplace where there would be no reminders, no history. A place to be invisible, alone.

He couldn't comprehend the future. Fleeing this place, that was the last thing that had made sense. So that's what he was going to do.

The rain had passed over earlier in the morning—he'd listened to it drifting across the roof towards the plaza that morning, after the nightmare. So there were only the faintest drips plucking at his ears (inconsequential, and therefore white noise

155

after a lifetime of living here; he knew the rainy season like a good friend) when the boards outside the house creaked and clunked.

He groaned silently, pulling his wings over his face. No, no more people!

But as the people came nearer, the boards reported something new: these people wore shoes—no puttees. Even freshly treated puttees never clacked; dipping only added an extra edge to the thuds, was all.

Beak working, Keonaona slid off his stool.

All the wooden shutters were shut tight, but he still felt safer pressing his wings tight to his body and slinking about, nearly on all fours. He lifted the claws of his toes as he sneaked into the foyer, relaxing them back down only when he safely stood on the rubber rain mat.

Even if he hadn't heard the excess of footsteps outside, the great jumble of foreign scents on the other side of the front door, just barely whiffable here, made it certain: this wasn't the feed vulture. And it wasn't the Gorgon. No, this was a mishmash of human colognes and deodorants, sweat, rain, mud, and...determination?

Keonaona's stomach groggled again, sending nausea along with its announcement of hunger. He grimaced.

The doorbell rang.

Perhaps they were lost—new vacationers looking for Griffon's place. Their respective houses were on opposite ends of town, so a local never mixed them up, but this wouldn't be the first time a group of human tourists had gotten turned around on the jungle roads. They were always instructed to look for a big house with palm trees in front, and his and Griffon's were the only "big houses" in town.

Now (after a courteously-timed pause), a knock.

The quicker I give them directions, the quicker they'll leave.

Keonaona scrubbed his face with his wings. Being human, they'd be unable to scent any sorrow or upset on him. Directions, and he could go back to his loaf. Or maybe find something else to eat, something he actually could bear to swallow. Banana chips, maybe.

One deep breath. Wings back.

He reached for the door.

Still expecting lost tourists, he opened it freely so all of him was revealed in the doorway. Even the bright light shining in his face didn't faze him; the jungle formed a ceiling of leaves so dense in some places that some of the roads crisscrossing Crooked Neck were always night-dark; it wouldn't be strange for a traveler to carry a flashlight in the middle of the day.

But when a microphone appeared under his face, his stomach did another turn that had nothing to do with what he had or hadn't ate.

A voice came out of the light. "Canningsley-sir Perseus, Kosmopoulis Standard. Sir, why did you abandon your duty to host Hriana's Gorgon here in Crooked Neck?"

"Green-sir Herman, New Delphi Review-Journal. Do you feel, sir, that you are at least in part to blame for the psychological torture of Plattman-miss Lisa, due to the negligence of your duty?"

"Varma-miss Thais, Inquiry News. Sir, what happened to your wife and child?"

Keonaona was past thinking now. He shielded his face with his wings and blindly shut the door on the barrage of introductions and questions aimed at him.

Footsteps immediately spread out over the lanai. They called "Sir! Sir!" over and over, polite as the tall Gorgon. The wooden shutters were shut so tight that none of their awful blaring light invaded the house, but just hearing them out there...he was surrounded. Or soon to be, if he didn't move fast.

Analū's.

Keonaona pictured the cot in his friend's office. There.

Keonaona raced for the room he had been sleeping in. Precious minutes were wasted while Keonaona ransacked the room for his mobi. It was dead now, but once plugged in, Keonaona could pay for Analū's food he'd be eating. He couldn't leave without it.

Once it was in his hand, Keonaona bolted for the side exit. They probably had the back door leading to the kitchen covered by now, but there was a chance they hadn't made it around this

157

wing of the house, which stuck out longer in the back than the other half of the house, on account of his forefathers expanding on the house whenever their growing clutches (or their clutches' clutches) seemed to need it.

Doorway after doorway blurred by. Up ahead, silvery light shone through a round window in a door, bright as an exit sign. Escape.

Keonaona found himself hurtling towards it at breakneck speed. He blinked and the two six-foot-long panoramic landscape paintings on the wall were already gone.

Two steps and he was upon the door.

Maybe I should have snuck out, he thought, colliding with the door with a THUD. He rebounded back, unlocked the door.

Should have been quieter.

But no one was back here on the smokers' porch. Keonaona banged into the glider bench, leaped over the stairs down into the yard. His knees twanged on the landing.

Ow! That never hurt when I was younger.

"Sir—excuse us! Sir!"

Shoesteps knocked across the lanai.

Spotted.

Keonaona didn't look back, but swerved towards the clubhouse—a place where his father had played, and then him, and then Kai—a wooden structure set just out of the way of the picturesque backyard, convenient to some enchanting mud piles—but easy enough to spot with its painted red roof.

A hundred feet of manicured lawn stretched before him. He pelted across it as fast as he could. Camera lights shone at his back, throwing his shadow in front of his feet, making him feel like a prisoner fleeing out from under the beam of a guard tower.

But there was no wall behind the clubhouse, only jungles he had been playing in since his youth, terrain as familiar to him as the scent of his mother. Once he was in it, they wouldn't be able to find him. From there, he'd make his way to Analū's, through the back roads.

It was a perfect plan, so he shut his brain off and let his feet do the thinking. They brought him to the clubhouse's doorstep in no time. But upon spotting a Quopple toy souped up to its neck in the mud in the clubhouse's front yard, another dagger of loss pierced his heart and exploded (*that's the last toy my Kai ever played with out here; it will be his last forever*).

For a moment, he saw blackness—*going blind with grief, is that even possible?*—misstepped and staggered, felt himself toppling too far to one side. He shoved the razorous thought of the toy away from him, but though his wings and tail both flailed, they couldn't keep him upright and he fell on his side in the clubhouse mud with an impact that both bruised his ribs and knocked the sight back into him.

He was almost there. If he cared to, he could have counted the fingers on the fronds of the two bottle palms, planted side by side, an excellent adventurer's entrance into the jungle to play. His doorway to escape.

His breath filled his ears as he sat there in the mud, panting. But he pushed himself up (twinge in the meat of his palm, elbow, where he'd tried to stop the fall) and forced himself forward, ducking between the little shorties.

The faint scent of his Kai on the path made him want to scream—but the faster he ran, the more the smells of rain and mud buried it (*no! I don't want to forget him!*), until he could shut his brain off again.

Analū's.

He ran.

It was...well, he didn't know how long. But Keonaona had been running through the forest for some time, the pungent-smelling green foliage turning his red hide sickly shades, when his pace slackened, turning churning legs into slumping falls forward. His forward progress slowed like a boat whose engine had cut out.

But I haven't done anything! I've been sleeping, I should be rested!

His toes dragged furrows in the mud. There was a stump around the next twist in the trail. Tongue lolling, he forced himself forward until he reached it. There, he collapsed on it, palms on his knees, belly swelling and shrinking with air.

But when his breath returned to normal, the hum didn't leave his ears.

He looked around, sniffing. Rain still dripped from the trees, but there was no wind...It sounded like a leaf blower, or like something down at Zorin's garage. Mechanical, not natural. He even smelled metal, now that he wasn't racing around like a panicked quail.

His gaze followed his beak towards a dark shape hidden in the canopy's shadow. Up high. Beak still gaping, he peered at it, willing the odd shape to pop out against the hazy green.

No. Nothing. Keonaona peered harder, but the shape remained obscured.

He forgot about rest and stood up, facing the growling thing in the treetops.

He took a few steps towards it (distantly, he noticed that he hadn't bothered with wrapping puttees this morning, so his legs were mud-brown up past his knees, and the mud was sticky between his toes)—and the shape retreated.

He warbled with worry, dropped low and crabbed to the side, like he was trying to corral someone's pet pig.

He could hear it moving in sync with him. Matching his—

He flashed on the other day in the plaza. Chased by the camera orb of that blue-headed jackal.

He was being hunted again.

To test his theory, he hopped a few steps away from the shape, keeping his eye on it. Sure enough, it came towards him into the light, and even bounced after him, mostly in sync.

A flying camera. Its propellers whirred in their casings.

Keonaona grew cold. Now what? With that, they could track him anywhere; it was bound to have a geolocator on it.

Was one of those news crews traveling to him even now, or would they wait until he holed up somewhere and tree him there? How did it know to follow *him*, and not, say, a coati blundering across its path? Was it piloted? Could it see? What was it tracking on him?

At this thought, Keonaona turned in every direction at once, slapping at himself like it was mosquito season. He stopped a minute later, realizing there was no way they could have planted a tracker on him. There'd been no opportunity; they'd never touched him.

He smoothed down his lavalava with grim dignity. If only it would rain—that might short it out (or make its pilot shelter it somewhere); then Keonaona could hightail it to Analū's. After all, it was only following him; it couldn't read his mind, nor his intentions. He didn't have his sling, or his gun, else he might have taken it down from here. If it weren't so afar off, he might've been able to lead it to the river and drown—

...

—submerge it there.

He watched the camera. How could he throw them off his trail?

A monkey howled in the distance.

Well, don't take it to Analū's.

Keonaona stalked into the forest, his metallic ghost doggedly following behind.

22

GORGON

SHE HEARD THE RAINDROPS, but could not feel their spiritbod-
iesstructures falling and then striking the solid clayen shield of
the chapel ceiling before oozing harmlessly down the walls to
be soaked into the ground, not as solidly as usual. She, who cou
ld, of late, leave her body unattended and visit far off dens and no
oks and fields, found this dampening of her perception disturbi
ng. Cause and effect all worked the same, but with her veil sight
and senses so fatigued, the world was flat and distant.

She frowned at the unconscious form of her husband, draped
carefully across her coils. Before him, she'd had her sight—but
almost never at full strength. Since him, she'd felt the electric
vitality of it roar alive—could feel the smallest thing, or feel only
the big things, if she wanted. At last, she controlled her power;
its demands no longer made her a slave.

Until now. Was freedom always so fleeting?

The chapel door croaked open, swollen wood protesting. Her
coils seized—it had been a long time since anyone caught her
unawares.

But they didn't see.

She turned to face the newcomers, lowered her arms to the
floor like a sphinx. It was the idiot mayor and his married supervision. They carried a food-Del-bag. Brownpaper. But fryless it
was—she knew that from this morning. It would be all birds'
food, to pierce and stick in her gums, or sweet fruits whose
sugars dizzied her. Not a problem when she could feed them to
her other mouth...

No. She'd imparted all her exhaustion into him; he held it for
her now. But until he was well again, he couldn't contribute to
her energies. Now he only accumulated her exhaustions.

162

The two alive squarglings saw how she filled the center of the place and made those troubled little *gzrrk!* sounds. Well, the dancealtarfloor was the only place her whiskered body would fit. Even the spirits here understood that, though they still muttered darkly from the edges of the pit.

"That will not be enough," she told the alive squarglings. Crème Brûlée (those names he chose!) held out the bag anyway, doing them no favors.

She wished she could see inside it—to know for sure. But—this was no ambush, so why wait around to tell them?

"I need flesh to eat."

The mayor warbled, but his dessert-wife didn't move. Both their hearts drummed.

"Is that what happened?" The dessert-wife's lizard tail switched to and fro behind her ankles. "Is that why you're...this way now? You didn't get enough to eat?"

She thought about the answer, bending her ear away from the ghostly peanut gallery heckling her.

"Not enough of the right things. To eat. And not enough rest."

Her Jerimin had passed out in the tent last night—probably the only reason they had lasted as long as they had today, but she'd stared at the underroof of the tent, dozing fitfully, lightly?, hearing every little thing, even snatches of conversations in tents around them. Not what she needed.

Her coils scraped at the chapel floor. How rapturous it sounded: dig a grave in the earth, crawl in, sleep like the dead.

Only the earth here was half-water—a drain on her power—and she was...Well, instinct and power told her sleep was unwise, now. After all, a half of her already wouldn't wake up. For a Still-child like her, sleep was the last step before death.

"I need flesh to eat."

"Well...get started on these chips." The dessert-wife shook the bag. "I've seen you eat those."

She took the tiny thing from the hen, who trembled only a little when she approached on her coils. The bag rustled in its friendly way as she dug through it, but even with the rain and the muttering ghosts, it was easy for her to overhear the alive squarglings whispering to each other.

"Flesh?? Where are we gonna get that?" The candy-cereal mayor.

"He asked about hogs—"

"Where is he, anyhow? He's definitely the better one to talk to."

Chips. Dry. Blue. Seed-covered. She pulled the sleeve of them out. They were absurdly small in her whiskered mouth.

The first bite. Loud in the chapel, a crisp, a snap.

They turned, looked at her, froze.

Then they turned back to each other and began speaking again—in their own tongue. And her translator, limp across her coils. Her depleted *nensha* couldn't even show her shades of their thoughts anymore. She growled in frustration, and the two alive squarglings went silent again.

She tried pushing some vitality into her Jerimin—/awaken, I need you!/—but felt only empty currents. No glow of response.

Chips gone, she ate the paper sleeve. Because why not? If her power couldn't burn good fuel, it would burn anything she gave it, and poor fuel was better than none. She slipped her grey hands in the Del bag again.

The alive squarglings restarted their conversation.

Fruits. Nuts. Nuts weren't bad—very earth-directioned, some nuts—but on this world they always seemed to be mixed with pointy seeds. She pulled this second sleeve out and began plucking the large, rounder juvi nuts out, one by one.

An odd image ghosted into being from her Jerimin's side of their head. She tried to grasp it, but it faded almost immediately...a twig being thrown into a fire-lighted place. A furnace? She wished he were awake to elaborate.

She missed him.

She turned, desiring to nuzzle him, but the alive squarglings—and the dead ones—were watching her again. She curled herself more tightly around the sleeve of nuts.

She ate, sad and mindless. This food was no joy. Her power was a burden again. And no one knew how to help her...

She was the Gorgon. This was only their third town. She couldn't be seen brought so low, so fast.

Nuts gone. Tiny black seeds piled at the bottom of the bag like dead beetles. She couldn't eat a bag full of seeds.

She was about to pick her way through the rest of the Del-bag when the mayor spoke to her.

"Your...Lase Gorgon. You must know we here are all vegetarians."

She rolled her eyes.

"We really don't have supplies like that around here! The only, well, prey you'll find would be the alligators living in the 'Ehuana."

Water-directioned animals. Like fish, ingesting them would do her more harm than good.

She watched him over the bag with one set of eyes, kept searching the lunch bag. So far the contents were all off-limits.

"Sheepherding died out a generation or two ago—easier to just import our clothes, see?—no one's really keeping animals in Crooked Neck nowadays, you uh, understand?"

She gave him her drollest look. "Yes, mayor, I do think my four years of economics in the royal academy may help me understand the fate of your little town's gasping economy." Hriannens were flighty—but did people truly think they handed out royal titles without any prior preparation?

It's your face. You look like a beast—

She cut off the thought—in *her* voice, of course—returned instead to a memory of her and her Jerimin discussing the deeper meanings in one of their favorite books.

He sees who I really am.

The mayor's mirthful berryshades demoted themselves to pastels. "Uh...uh...oh. Right." He gulped. "Well, what I'm trying to say is—we don't have any meat."

She stared at him.

So tired.

A nightmare.

Have to rely on idiots.

Wish I could eat them.

Even in his detached state, the thought made her husband's mind blossom angry, disapproving crimson. Her ears pinned back, chagrined.

Now the dessert-wife spoke.

"Maybe you can come up with a list of alternative foods...Granted, supplies are a little low now, but if we just know—"

"Animal shelters?" she asked.

They made confused sounds—then stared at her in horror.

"If they're only strays..." She stopped herself. A word had stirred, bright in her Jerimin's mind.

No, not a word. A name. Elmer.

"What about Elmer?" she asked the alive squarglings.

The hen's wings flared open with a snap. "What about him?!" Her eyes were fierce with challenge. Protectiveness.

Her ears twitched back and forth between the two alive squarglings. Whatever she had asked, it was not going over well.

/What trouble have you fed me now?/ she sent. To her surprise, a new shape went alight—but it only confused her more, and was faded-gone before she could examine it the way she needed.

Dig forward. No way to undig.

"What...What is an 'Elmer'?"

Now they were looking at her like she was insane.

She wrestled every coil she had down to that hard-baked clayen floor, fighting her impulse to rise up, tower above them, and scream at them until the walls shook, until they did something useful instead of gawking at her.

"They're our cousins, now." Her Jerimin pulled the back of her hand to his lips and kissed it. This had been in between the first town and second, when the ground was flat, the hunt good, the nights *sanft* and lonely. Just the two of them, no want.

"We have to treat them like 'ohana. Or at least friends."

"What is a cousin—Idomean, what is a cousin-one treated like? You do keep none, do you?"

"Egh, no...I come from a long line of only children. But a cousin is like..."

"How do you know this, then?"

"I read a lot."

"Mm."

"They're like"—and he'd sent feelings and images along with his words: ally-feelings, strangers-almost; but ones who felt favorably towards you, though they didn't know you. Mixed in were vivid exceptions—brats who tormented (this a picture of one cousin rubbing a black stylus with charcoal, to stain the hero's hand) and the shy and useless or the self-absorbed. She had separated those away and mulled over what he'd shown her.

"So cousins are like the Orlock, to one another."

He stopped nuzzling her hair. Abruptly.

/?!/, he sent.

"The way they treated one another. I saw, when they were at court."

And civilizing me, she didn't have to mention.

She'd sent sunken-eyed, rat-toothed faces greeting others like them warmly (well, as warmly as an undead one could) even when they were only rare visitors...or human agents of Kolar's, unknown (and often unaware) "family members" in training.

"They may not have lived together, or seen each other oft...but they could always presume...aid? Friendliness?"

"Yeah, that's about it."

And so she hummed to herself in the clayen chapel, ignoring the now-terrified looks on the alive squarglings' faces, until she was able to say softly and calmly, "Please—cousins." The word sat between them, heavy and squat. "I receive much information outside the usual...channels. I don't always know its meaning. So, again...what is an 'Elmer'?"

Their bright eyes met one another's while they made nervous little bird tuttering. More language she didn't speak. She waited.

Finally, Supervision answered.

"Elmer is our pet fox."

She sent this information into the dark room that was her husband's mindspace—no response. *Why feed me that clue?*

She reviewed the last few minutes in her mind. What had unearthed this name? Talk of eating animals. Strays. But he would never suggest she eat a named pet—she was was fairly sure.

But then there had been the second shape—small, silver? Simple. It had felt like correctionclarification.

The name was the first part. The shape, that was, she thought, what she was intended to inquire about.

A troubled sound, short but distinct, escaped her as she looked at the empty spaces above the alive squarglings' heads. The edible-to-her contents of the Del-bag were not enough for her *nensha* to reawaken—damn it. Otherwise she could have simply reached into their heads with the shape, evoked Elmer, see what dusted to the surface.

Tleh. How did anyone stand not being able to read others? Kolar, father-one to the Orlock, had told her it was the norm. But she'd seen how quickly her Jerimin had asked for the extra information only she could glean. Like a child with a new toy, one he was joyousgreedyeager to use and keep always in his hand.

She shook out her ears. You couldn't hunt what didn't stand there before you.

"Tell me about your Elmer fox."

The professional air abandoned the dessert hen entirely—she shimmied her wings, making an intriguing, whispered rustle-rattle that pricked her ears and her interest.

"Why should we? We'd never give him to you to eat!!"

She scoffed, rolled her eyes. "When do you say I asked for that? Please remind me."

"Wi—you—what else could you be asking for?"

"INFORMATIONNNN." The end of the word turned into a thrum that made their pupils shrink to pinpricks while they clutched each other.

She halted the sound quickly but they didn't recover until she retracted herself from their space. Yes, of course, she frightened them...so now she had frightened, stupid...people (*not* prey) to work with.

"What color is it?"

The idiot mayor finally answered. "Grey."

"Favorite...toy?" She thought of their old rabbit. "Does it chew?"

"He's got little toy monkeys. There's a sound box in them that chitters when you drop it. We've had to buy crateloads of them, he loves them. Chews 'em to pieces!"

/Are you eating this?/ she sent to her Jerimin along with the words, but all blackness, no movement.

"He, uh, got sick last year when he got into a box of chocolates widow 'Ewalani brought us for Pāheahea. Had to have his stomach pumped."

"Poor thing," Dessert-wife added.

Stomachs. Foxes. Predators. Like her! She kept her voice calm. "What do you feed it in its days?"

"He gets two cans of wet food daily, treats at night in his kennel..." The idiot mayor looked to his married supervision.

"What lies in the 'wet' food?"

"Well...oh." Realization showed up on the idiot mayor's face, and then his wife's.

Dingdingdingding.

"Yeah...would that—work for you?" asked Dessert-wife.

Before she could answer, the little dweeb interrupted, scandalized. "Rosie! We can't feed the Gorgon of Hriana fox chow! What will everyone think?"

She could taste the satisfaction she would gain if she could only flip the little half-wit into the clayen wall (*would his hide stain it berry colors?*), but his married supervision seemed to sense danger, like an elk catching her scent on the wind, and she dug her tan claws into the foolish creature's arm. "*Lono...*" she said under her breath. He looked at her—and seemed to comprehend.

"Yes. Bring me your fox's meat-food. All of it. You will only win the praise of the Gorgon, Mayor, since that is the thing you seem to desire."

"Yes, right away!" said the supervision, and she dragged her idiot husband out into the rain before he could speak another word.

But alone in the chapel, she had time to think. She should have demanded all pet food for carnivores in the town. Any and all. Perhaps their supply on hand wasn't enough. What then?

She curled her coils around tightly, placing her face close to her Jerimin.

At least I didn't have to beg.

"The Gorgon does not beg," she said to herself.

One of the chapel ghosts leaned out from the seating bays, cackling with glee. "No. But apparently she has to eat Happy Paws!"

23

MERCURIO

MERCURIO SLID TO A stop on the rise overlooking the Ho'okano mansion. After a solid five minutes bent over braced on his knees, his aching lungs stopped burning.

When that evil—no, despicable!—robber-bat had chased him out of the chapel, he'd fled straightway down the hill. He'd tripped three times, almost turning his flight into a headlong pinwheel down the hill, but his fright, somehow, kept him upright and on his feet long past the treacherous descent. He'd never run that fast before in his life, not even when Emerald Kahananui had set her security dogs on him for trying to film her and her family eating dinner.

At first he'd run in mortal fear for his life; then, somewhere around the churning stream on the way back to the shopkeeper's place, he'd run in fear of losing his equipment. He could picture his precious cameras, his trusty screen, all being crushed between those huge, pointy teeth, like autokinets sent to a scrapyard. Worse yet, his brain kept replaying that particular torture show, recutting the horror from different angles every time.

He didn't stop running until he was was in Ho'okano's neighborhood.

He looked out over the street. Though brighter than the stormy skies currently sitting on the Gorgon, the light here seemed to bleach the scene of color; the dark cinnamon red of the mansion walls had a ghostly cast to it, and the trunks of the entrance's crossed palm trees were bonewashed white somehow.

(*Bonewashed!* He reached for his voice recorder, patted only his empty chest. He let out a sinking whistle of sorrow. *I'll never remember that.*)

Netron camera crews stood intent around the gate leading onto Ho'okano's land. Mercurio panicked at first, thinking that the team from the chapel had beat him to the peanuts. But the black uniforms of that team were missing.

Thank you, Mother!

He began descending the rise towards them. As he got closer, he realized that the crews had surrounded a familiar-looking hen. The mango-café hen. He couldn't scent her from here, but from the stiff way she held her wings, she wasn't happy.

What do they want with her?

If they were all out here (though he thought one of the crews could be missing—it was hard to tell, since three out of the five teams wore navy-colored uniforms—so unimaginative!), maybe they'd missed Ho'okano, or maybe Mango-mama was running interference for him again.

Mercurio jogged the rest of the way down to join the group.

The humans were so intent on her—*hey, give her a little space, huh?*—that they didn't see him until he pushed his way through the humans.

"Hey, uh...uh...Lena, right?"

Her face—which had opened up in surprise upon spotting him, dropped into a scowl. "It's Lani."

"Lani, right, sure. What's going on? Where's Lane Redbeak?"

Now the cam crews all turned to him.

"You mean Ho'okano-sir, correct? He fled his house," said a human producer with a silver patch on his navy chest that said in an important-looking font, "STANDARD." "The New Delphians managed to get a tracking camera on him, but we were thinking one of you might use your, uh, heightened olfactory scenes to lead us to him."

"He's my friend," said the big hen, anger turning her fried-plantains-and-pomegranate scent a touch sour, "and I won't track him for you like he's some prize butterfly escaped from your net." Then she flared her wings at Mercurio, "And if you know what's good for you, you won't help them either."

"We're offering fifty jen to anyone who can take us to him."

Fifty! Not much, but it'd help replace that cam the big Gorgon stole! "Well..."

The big hen growled at him, sounding like an angry blender. Mercurio fought back a grin—what a weird sound!

"You're a real creep, you know that? Fouler than gator breath. You got no idea what Keonaona's been through—"

Mercurio crossed his arms. "I might know more than you think!"

Every human head shuttled towards him, but if Mercurio thought the hen was angry before, now she was livid. Her wings stretched completely vertical, adding another foot and a half to her already imposing stature. "You know what happened, and you're still messing with him? Mother make your comb fall out, you...you...son of a weasel!"

Mercurio flared his own wings right back at her. Insult him, would she?

She revved her blender-howl at him. The humans started backing away.

"Go on," she said, "I'd like to see you—" Her angry glare fell on his chest, turned puzzled. "Where'd all your *pono hana wikio* go?"

Mercurio slammed his wings over his body, his missing equipment. "None of your business!" What was he doing, arguing with her, bargaining with his competition? All would be lost if Harold's crew found Ho'okano first! His channel, gone! Followers—wandered off to other channels! Watching feedsters without even half his talent! He glanced over his shoulder, half-expecting to see the fake vanilla-scented woman leading her pack over the rise.

Ho'okano fled. I don't know which direction, though—and I bet if I ask the Netrons, they'll set a cam on me when I do go looking and use me to get to him.

But there was one crew that already had a cam tracking him. Maybe he could track *them*? Where would the red go, though? He had that huge mansion, why not just hole up there? A Netron was as likely to break down a door as a wild hog was to serve tea—totally impossible!

Last time I was with him, he said the bodies were coming in two days. That's tomorrow. What's around here? Dangit! Without my screen, I can't look anything up. Bet Mango-mama here would know what's around here, where he woulda gone. Maybe if I follow her?

But...the house was empty now, right? And it had plenty of room—well, if the grey Gorgon could be put back in her human container, there'd be plenty of room. *I mean, I know the deal was to get Ho'okano to agree to take them in—but what he don't know won't hurt him. Heck, the mansion's so big you could pro'lly hide 'em away in one wing and never see the red for a whole month!*

Except for her stink...no scentmod could change that.

Still. It'd keep him from having to chase the red all over the map. If he met Harold's team at the door, deal "sealed" (as far as they knew), they'd give up and go home, right?

But what if they ran into team New Dolphins (or whatever)—and tracked down Ho'okano with them? And then, when they found him, did a *real* deal with him, directly?

But they wouldn't team up with another crew—they're supposed to be competing...right?

Mercurio looked over the mansion again. Would he bet all his equipment on it?

No. Get Ho'okano, secure the deal with him. That was the only sure way to get his stuff back.

Mercurio examined Mango-mama up and down again. *She's my best bet. She wants the crews off of him.*

Mercurio took a quick look at the humans. Time for another bet: did any of these humans speak the language? He'd always heard it was hard on human throats, but then, if it existed, animal, vegetable, or mineral, some Netron somewhere was bound to study it.

"They wanna hunt down your friend and put him on video, right?" he asked her in Mother's Tongue. He punctuated the question with a snootful of air. The scent of confused human was strong. Good.

Mango-mama was testing the air, too. After a sec, she replied in the affirmative, a single *putt*.

"Well, my goal ain't to get your friend on camera. I just wanna talk to him. Even if I wanted to, I can't film him." He flashed his empty chest again.

"He wants to be left alone," she replied.

"Do you think anybanana would bother him if the Gorgon was roosting in his nest?"

"The Gorgon's part of the problem. I'm tellin' you, he wants to be left ALONE." She stretched the last word out, stamped, and flapped her wings, for absolute emphasis.

Mercurio thought of the weird, broken way the red had talked. *"Do you think he should be alone?"*

Now, this! This made her ruff puff, her startled song twitter.

"Right, that's what I thought. Listen, Auntie, we want the same things—find him and keep the cams off him. Let's ditch these fleas and get to him before they do!"

She snuffled towards the ground, shaking out her comb and wings.

She might not do this, he thought. *But I'm not making a deal, here—I'm just pointing out the obvious.*

She finally settled with a call of agreement.

"Well that's—" he started in Standard, only to be interrupted by her grabbing his wing roughly in her coconut-sized fist.

He shrieked. "HEY!"

"'Scuze us, folks. In the course of chatting with my cousin here, I remembered he owes me for the breakfast I gave him yesterday."

"What, you—!"

"Follow my dance!" A mere two-note cry in Mother's Tongue, it silenced him immediately. "I have to get him back to my restaurant for some dishwashing," she said, and left the group, dragging Mercurio along by the wing. The humans watched, dumbfounded, but they didn't follow.

She hustled him up over the rise and a ways farther before she released him behind the shelter of a banyan tree. Even the shadows beneath it smelled green.

"Think they bought it?" she asked.

"Yeah. You know any shortcuts? Or where he'd go?"

"Analū's store, Nibbles. There's a back way..." She looked off the road, towards the manor's side of the forest. "Maybe he's already there."

"Maybe. But they said the Dolphins got a cam on him. So that's a crew we might bump into out there."

"Speaking of cams, what happened to your"—she mimed tossing a hovercam into the air.

"Tell ya when we're off the road. There's one last crew lookin' for Ho'okano, and I don't wanna be on the road when they come down here."

She rolled her eyes. "Now you tell me." With that, she nosed her way through the thick ferns off the well-trodden path. Mercurio hurried after, making sure he had a good beakful of her scent in case he lost sight of her. Vines draped dry atop Mercurio's head, weighted just like a snake, startling him—and alternately, feathery ferns tickled his knees as he followed his wide-winged guide into the jungle. No matter where he looked, there was only green—and no Angel to send above the treetops to help him get his bearings. Alarm suddenly washed through Mercurio.

"You *do* know where we're going, right? 'Cause all I'm seeing is scenery copy-pasted straight outta *Doom Island*."

"Cuz, my 'ohana's lived in Crooked Neck going back ten generations." Her head was on a swivel, her nostrils rhythmically flaring in time to her sniffing. "This is my backyard, *ahee?* So don't you worry your handsome little head, you'll make it to the mating grounds this seas', promise."

Mercurio cawed softly, nerves making it impossible to voice agreement any louder.

The well-treaded travel paths of Crooked Neck will connect you to Nibbles, the town's cheerful yellow general store; the lately bustling plaza with its traditional baked chapel and split streets; and to the opulent homes of some of its most notable residents. But mere feet off these forest by ways lies a jungle thicker and deeper than any imagined by the movie moguls in Las Rojas. To the residents, it's merely their backyard. But to those whose lives are centered around the brighter, more civilized asphalt jungle, there is terror lurking in every step off the trail...

A branch raked his neck, and he jumped with a screech.

She screeched too—until she saw nothing wrong with him. She cuffed him with her wing. "What you doin' screamin' like that?! I thought a jag got you! You watch too many movies! Just stick by me and you'll be fine. And keep your break high; Keonaona's scent can blend in 'round here if you ain't awake." She cracked the end of her tail for emphasis.

"Really?" Mercurio sampled the air. *Guess there's some florals out here he'd blend with—hard to smell 'em over the rainwash.* "You don't forget a scent like his. I'm surprised some Incensario hasn't come out here and dried to dupe it in a bottle."

"Oh, they tried—but that was years ago, with his great-grandfather."

"Serious?"

"Mmhmm. Guess they got some inspo out of it—'Sugared Crooked Gardenia Number five-oh-three' was inspired by him, they say—but, you know—can't dupe the snoot."

"Well, the tech's better now. I bet someone could."

"If you scented as much as you talked, we mighta found him ten minutes ago."

"Yeah, yeah." Mercurio shook off an errant raindrop, bombed right into his eye. Rainwater had been dripping onto him this whole time. He missed his *serape*—but it had flown off him in his flight from the Gorgon and was probably frosted with mud by now. He could imagine the original seller blundering upon it when things dried out a little, popping it in the wash, and selling it for a second time. And why not? Mercurio wouldn't be around to claim it, nosiree.

"Okay," said the hen. "We're off the road. What happened to your stuff?"

"Big Gorgon took it."

She putted *and* gave him a lemon-twisted look of skepticism. "That don't sound like him. Unless you were—"

"No, not the tall Gorgon, the BIG"—he flapped his outstretched wings to illustrate her terrible size—"Gorgon."

"What are you talking about? I was at the chapel today—she was human, he was human. —*He* was the big one."

"Yeah, well, after you left—I was there, too—Idunno, something went haywire and..." he felt himself paling at the memory, "she was...*big*. Four eyes, flappy bat ears, the whole deal. BIG teeth, too. Probably the way they saw her at Lanakila..."

Mango-mama stopped her clambering over a thick root and looked into his eyes. The intensity unsettled Mercurio, but before he could rise to his defense, she looked stricken. "My soul," she said. "You ain't lyin'."

His cheek ruff went down. "Nope."

She stood there a moment, just...looking at him.

This is taking too long.

He checked over his shoulder, but caught no fake-vanilla whiff. When he turned back, Mango-mama shook herself and finished crossing over the belly-high root. She waited on the other side for him, which was good, because it took him a couple attempts before he could scramble over. *Maybe I'm not the first city wing she's dragged out here before.*

"So she got big. What happened next?"

"The chapel emptied out like"—he snapped his fingers. "I was filming at the time—"

She scolded him—*eh*-eh-*eh*-eh-*eh*-eh! "Shame on you. You know there's no vid allowed in there!"

"So...at first, when things went crazy, I just thought, 'hey, keep filming!' But then...you know, she got big, and people ran and I couldn't move—then *she* started talking to me!"

"She?! I don't think she said boo when I served 'em lunch the other day. He did all the talkin'."

"They went to your café?" He couldn't picture them holding menus; it was too weird.

She ducked under a dripping, low-hanging branch. "No, at the lodge, with Lono—that's the mayor. I brought 'em takeout."

"Lucky you. He fainted or got knocked out or something. So it was just me and her in the chapel, alone. She had me boxed in with her weird body...I don't think she has legs...couldn't see any..." He shook himself. "Anyway, at first she wouldn't let me leave. She wanted me to message the mayor for her, but

I couldn't get a signal. Then the Netron news crew showed up, their hard line let 'em stream to the mayor's place, at any rate...and I made a deal with her, that I could film them—the Gorgons—exclusively, if I got 'em a room at Ho'okano's. Except those idiot Netrons horned in on the deal too, so first one to get the Gorgons housed wins filming rights, and that's why I gotta get to Red first, see?"

"That still don't explain why your stuff's gone."

"RIGHT! Well, after the Netrons jetted, it was just me and her again, see? And she...she stole my equipment! Yanked it right off my body! Said I'd get it back when I got 'em roomed with the red."

"So winner takes all..."

"Whatever! She wants me to win—the Netrons plan on grillin' her...them...whatever—about some Netron girl they tied up the first night they were here—"

"They tied a girl up?"

"He did, anyway."

"...And?!"

"Nothin'—I've messaged with her, nothin' happened, she's pretty annoying, I can see where..." Smelling the outrage coming off the hen, Mercurio cut the thought loose and went on. "Anyway, that's why I'm here in the jungle with you, cameraless, and that's why you gotta help me convince Ho'okano to keep 'em."

Mango-mama shook her head. "All this trouble for want of a hotel room."

"And lunch."

A funny expression grew on the hen's face, but Mercurio ignored it. "She kept telling anyone who'd listen she wanted lunch." *Wonder if the grey Gorgon found my snack pouch yet.*

"Hope everyone back in town's okay," said Mango-mama.

"I don't see why not. Thanks to the Netrons, the mayor got the message. She's probably munchin' away in the chapel, cozy as a coati in a dumpster."

"Hope you're right."

"Sure I am! They're prob'ly feasting on mango cups and seed crisps."

179

"...They don't eat the same things we do."

"So?"

"Keonaona had me cook up a menu special for them. They're all in his freezer now...Not stuff any squargling would normally make. And I know he bought bread and things direct from Netron."

"Seriously?"

"Yeah...he's a good host. He can make anybody feel comfortable."

Mercurio scoffed, rubbing his cheek. It was still tender where the red had thrown him out on the turf. "Yeah, right."

"He's not himself right now. You should know that, you heartless crocodile. Still..." She shook her head, went silent a long while. "Maybe it *is* better if Keonaona takes them in."

They continued farther into the jungle, ignoring game trails and sometimes passing under trees grown so thick that they blocked out all light, and he could only follow Mango-mama by scent. Luckily, there weren't too many of those places.

Wherever we are, thought Mercurio, slipping and jamming the side of his foot against a giant scrapey rock, *we have to be closer to Ho'okano than the Harold woman.*

A low sound jetted through the air. Merc got small and froze every muscle in his body before he consciously identified the sound: Mango-mama had grunted the nest talk command to freeze.

Breathing shallowly, he tried to suction a clue from the air about the danger, watching Mango-mama's back the entire time.

It seemed like twenty minutes before she finally stood upright again. All Mercurio had gotten was a possibly imaginary tang, hanging nebulously in their general region. She beckoned him over with a wing and wordlessly indicated the ground.

The tang was there—like a housecat on steroids. But also...milk?

"Big Jenny's had her cubs."

An itchy feeling crawled up between Mercurio's wings. "What's a 'Big Jenny'?"

"Crooked Neck's resident jaguar. I think she's left here—but we don't want to get between her and her nestlings. We'll go slower."

"Slower?!"

"Yeah, so Jenny doesn't get a chance to chomp your city-wing head open and suck out your brains like melon cooler! I didn't bring my nuisance gun with me—I was planning to visit a friend at his house, not go galumphing through the jun—"

Her complaint was interrupted by a chorus of high-pitched screams. To Mercurio's horror, Mango-mama ran *towards* the noise.

He stood his ground. "Are you coconuts?!" he shouted after her—but the screaming continued, and she didn't reply and now Mercurio was standing out here in the jungle *alone*. He cawed in protest, then swam through the bush after her scent.

He pulled up short behind her big wings, spread like a creamy orange billboard. He ducked under them to see what all that screaming was about.

Aw, man. Aw, man. Of all the times not to have my cameras!

A jaguar stood just a few yards off, milk-smelling, round-shouldered, huge; head switching between Mango-mama and a now-silent, fear-reeking pile of humans—the camera crew it'd cornered against a three-autokinet-tall rock in the clearing.

Was it his imagination, or did Mercurio smell blood?

"Psst, Blueberry! Follow me. SLOWLY." Mango-mama whispered at him. He was temporarily dumbfounded until she began sidling towards the film crew. "Easy, Jenny, easy..." she spoke in a low, shaking voice as they maneuvered their way closer to the humans while keeping their distance from the bulky cat. "Nobody wants in your nest, baby, we just all wanna go home and leave you be..."

Were *they* filming? Mercurio wished he could see the crew to check, but found he couldn't tear his gaze away from the blood-breathed toothy cat, though its attention seemed entirely pinned on Mango-mama. Its eyes were wild, its ears pinned back, and the white teeth gleamed from its gaping jaws.

Few terrors in life come close to the monumental realization that you are alone in a room with the grey Gorgon...except realizing you're within pouncing range of a real live jaguaress.

I might be the only person to know this firsthand, Mercurio realized. *And I might be the last.*

Their slow sidestepping had taken them in an arc across the clearing—the jag growling in the center of it. They were halfway to the pile of humans when the panting jaguar took a step towards them.

Mango-mama stepped back so suddenly that Mercurio was nearly knocked back onto his tail. Luckily, he kept his footing.

Now it was advancing on them, taking a step, pausing, taking a step...Mercurio was alarmed to note they were backpedaling at the same pace, but no faster.

"Now, Jenny. Jenny, ease up, babe. We're goin', see? *Blueberry, be ready to screech your fool head off. Can you find a rock? Blueberry!*" she hissed.

"What?" the word hardly had any of Mercurio's voice behind it. More like a puff of air.

"*Rock?*"

Mercurio unstuck his attention from the advancing beast and gave a quick glance around their feet. Nothing but mud and leaves, from what he could see. His gaze snapped back to the cat. Its tongue lolled. Angry? Or hungry?

"No."

"*Oh, boy.* Jenny!"

The jag dropped into a crouch, gathering itself.

Great Mother. Its going to pounce.

"JENNY, NO!"

The jaguar charged straight for them.

24

GORGON

J<small>ERIMIN</small> <small>AWOKE</small> <small>WITH</small> <small>A</small> strange taste in his mouth. Something new. Not...entirely unfamiliar...

His tongue slid back and forth in his mouth. Nothing was in it.

Empty mouth. Weird taste. Tumblers fell in his head, unlocked understanding.

And now the warm, cozy grey walls surrounding him—and the view of a tan-colored ceiling—made sense.

Well, at least a little! The almost black skylight seemed odd.

He pushed himself upright, tapped the soft inner coil muscle nearest to him. The living fainting couch he was sitting on rearranged itself. Now he looked into the grey-faced visage of his Queen, wearing her whiskers. Her yellow eyes found his and bulged in relief. She swallowed whatever was in her mouth. The odd taste receded.

"*Himmel sei Dank*." She butted her head against him, purring. "You're awake."

"Yeah...what happened? A session. Did...?"

Shame pulsed through the wires—she threw a loop of coils over her head and snugged into it, as if to hide. "It all unraveled. I wasn't strong enough to hold—" *Everything*, came the unvoiced descriptor, a wordless feeling that encompassed their exhaustion, the hate and desperate want of the squargling mourners, the scorn of the ghosts-in-residence (/Ghosts-in-residence? Here in the chapel? Why didn't you tell me earlier?!/), the shape-spell containing her, and the inexorable drain of her power. All this was uploaded straight into his head, along with an insistence that he send some sort of feedback—good, bad, or otherwise.

She wants to feel you're okay.

He sent back loving, relieved reassurances—*it's not your fault, we set too many plates spinning, without enough rest*—but he couldn't hide the fact that he was still run down.

"So how am I awake now? Did they find extra fries?"

She held up something small in her hand.

He rubbed his eyes—things were still a little muzzy, and responding to waves of her relief and affection rolling in on his mental plain was making it hard to focus—then reached for the object.

A can, with a red label: *Happy Paws Gourmet Chicken Foxy Feast with Meaty Chunks in a Savory Gravy.*

"'Foxy feast'?"

A dry twist to her grin. "Vulpine vittles."

Nose wrinkled, he asked, "Is it any good?" He'd only recently been introduced to the joys of eating meat, and his encounters with such meals had been brief. None of it, to his knowledge, had come from a can.

Her large head tilted left right, left right. "I have chewed worse." She took the can back from him and popped the top. She knocked it back like she was drinking a shot. The odd taste came back, then disappeared again. She turned away, and the familiar *thock* of an empty can being set down echoed through the chapel.

"It was your idea. Floated up from your head. Useful prattle from the dark."

He shook his head. "Sorry, can't remember."

He pushed himself off the gentle hill of her coil, found his knees a little wobbly. He looked down while steadying himself and saw a screen and some other stuff on the floor at his feet. "How many cans have you had?"

She sidewindered her coils to one side, revealing stacks and stacks of the little tins.

What is that, four flat packs? Five?

"They"—images shared indicated the Likekes—"are finding us more."

"They'd better, if they want you to stop wearing your whiskers." Keeping a hand on a coil to steady himself, he knelt and picked up the screen. "You didn't eat anyone, did you?"

"No." More petulant than defensive. "But that one was tempting. The Mercurio."

"That feedster? That explains these." He toed a nearby camera. It rolled until it reached the flattened cutout of its casing, designed for the camera to look out of. He shook his head wonderingly. "He's got a lot of nerve. A chapelfather tells humans not to record, but he goes ahead and breaks regulations anyway."

"Ididmust to touch them, to take them off the Mercurio. Are they dead?"

Actually, no. His screen started right up. But it was password protected. Kind of surprising; few people anywhere pass-locked their personal screens. There wasn't any real reason to; people were honest. But perhaps the auteur was paranoid about the competition. The feed game was a vigorous—some might even say vicious—one. Jerimin reached into his pocket for a spare boot drive and (after some searching) plugged it into the proper slot on the side of the screen. One reboot later, he was on a portable operating system.

Hold up a sec. He'd launched a mail handler and a net browser purely on autopilot. *Let's be smart about this. I'm a feedster illicitly filming my countrymen's farewells. What did I catch—or hope to catch—on film? And where would I keep it?*

He opened an obscure-but-well-loved (by him, at least) search utility. After a long ten seconds to scan (must be a lot of data here!), an index of the feedster's files lay open before him.

His wife craned her huge whiskered head over his shoulder; four eyes reflected in the shadow on the screen. He opened the three most recent videos.

The earliest filmed was darkness and noise—the distinctive liquid *plonk!* of things being dropped into the smoke bowl at the front of the chapel—the camera's clandestine entrance. Near the end, a teal-claw-tipped hand had appeared and the lens was better aimed; now Jerimin and his Queen were visible in the gap of the feedster's blanket, sitting up on the dais. That file ended there, but, from the timestamp, picked up right afterwards in the next file. He'd captured the entirety of Nika the Chapelfather's session. While Jerimin scrobbed through, she turned away. Three cans *click-pffi*ed open in succession.

"The ghosts show up well," he said, hoping moving his tongue in speech would distract from the phantom Happy Paws chicken taste coating his mouth again.

Her head returned to watch. /You are surprised? They are not Orlock./

He sent thanks for not speaking aloud and therefore sparing him a warm cloud of meat stink right into his face.

"Guess I—" They both flung themselves into each other at the cannon blast of thunder overhead.

/How long has it been doing THAT for?/

/Since I lost my grip./

/They do have a lightning rod on this place, RIGHT?/ He'd once seen her struck by lightning three times within three seconds in a storm, not three feet away from him—granted, they'd both been on a roof at the time, and the storm had been supernaturally sourced, but still...Her direction was her direction.

/*Ja*. And the chapel is earth. It is used to this. And I do not/—he strained the essence of the images and feelings she sent to mean, "I don't stand out from the chapel."

But when the thunder crashed for a second time over their heads, he wasn't sure he believed it. When his ears stopped ringing, he turned to her with his sternest look. "You're not leaving this chapel till the storm is over."

She growled. "The spirits—we cannot stay here!"

"Promise me."

"Mmm." But she nodded. He doubted she really wanted to go out in the water anyway.

After a moment to resettle (and frown at the skylight), he skipped to the end of the video, which ended with the chapelfather's descent from the dais. Jerimin pulled up the last thing recorded. It started with restless shuffling—the effect a little nauseating, to be honest—that continued through Lani the Lunch Hen's entreaty to them. It couldn't be heard clearly in the recording, but his instinct elbowed him. He paused her with a tap of his finger. She froze, mid-gesture.

"Something was off there." He pointed to the orangey hen. "Did you feel it?"

"I kept much tiredness then; I did not care to raise my eyes or ears or attention at anything or anyone."

"Right. Well, I think she was lying. I just don't know what about. It was a strange conversation."

"You, familiar with strange conversations?" she teased.

"If we see her again, if you can, will you get a read on her for us?"

"Mm." The affirmative came with a brief purr and press in his neck. He sighed, listening to the raindrops. How could one person feel so tired, yet so happy all at once?

"That's another thing." He lowered the screen, looked up into her face. "I'm sorry I didn't ask them for a break. No—I should have made them give you a break. I meant to...then the family came up, and I thought if we got rid of them..."

Her face softened. "You do not eat any blame, not in my eyes."

"I'm your husband. I'm supposed to take care of you."

"Wedotake care of each other. Now, do you want to see the rest of the video or not? The idiot and his married supervision"—he almost choked on his snort of laughter—"could be back any time. I'm not seeing out far right now. Things past the chapel walls"—she lifted some coils in a flippant wave towards the door—"are disappeared to me."

"No object permanence," he muttered, raising the screen.

He felt his back snap into a C-shape, like an angry cat's, matching her sudden arching of coils.

"You and your babble!"

He straightened himself out, but the sensation of being puffed up in shock persisted. "Agh! What?"

"You muttered the same thing when you were..." *asleepabsentoutofcommissioninanimate*—the not-quite-suitable words flew through his head like she was tossing them over her back. "Unenergied" was the made-up word she decided on.

"Well, it's relevant, isn't it? Come on, let's see what else he got."

He dragged the video slider till the big family walked up.

Aaah. Oooh. That *did* look bad. And creepy, especially watching his own eyes go absolutely empty before he went down like an axed tree.

She turned away at the sight of herself losing her human shape, shaking her head. He was glad she'd had the foresight to push the mourners out of the way; crushing them would have made for an inauspicious start to their forgiveness campaign.

"Every enchantment I had—slipped!"

He muted the screaming. "Don't be so hard on yourself. You've gone your whole life maintaining, what, just a spell or two at a time, right?"

A grumpy *mmm.*

"Right! You're still learning!"

"A Gorgon is a mast—"

"A Gorgon is what *WE* are now, so...whatever we are, that's what a Gorgon is, got it?"

Her ears metronomed left and right.

"And now, *this* Gorgon is interested in how you wound up with Lane Macoya's equipment. So hush." He unmuted the video and watched intently as his recorded Queen tried to get the feedster's help without looking desperate. The square's panicked screeching—and the video—cut off unceremoniously after being grabbed by her grey fists.

"Hm...I bet if you hadn't stripped him of his gear, the little fink would have posted this and left you here. In fact..." He started a new utility, designed not so much to delete data as it was, via multiple, furious overwrites, to pulverize every bit and byte into so much digital dust. He aimed it at the disturbing video and fired. The processor chugged almost to a halt as the cybergears began to grind. "Now he'll have no dirt on you—except for the spoken deal you made—although without the film, I guess it's just a case of 'he said, she said.'"

"The deal does not hold. With no vow name, neither of them have an arrangement we will honor."

"News team's gonna *love* that."

She chatterboxed her jaws in his face while a fierce bolt of hot color shot into his head. "I do not care what they love or do not. I care you stay awakeable the rest of this stay." He heard the chapel door open somewhere behind her coils. "And if I have to crush a thousand foxes in my jaws to make that so, I will do it!"

The door clunked shut.

He saw a shudder pass through her coils, felt his own surprise and urge to jump twinge. His Queen turned, then rearranged her coils so he, too, could see the Likekes standing at the front of the chapel, dripping wet and holding flat packs of dog (or whatever) food in their arms. He caught the horrified looks on the squargling couple's faces and pinched himself hard to fight the laughter that wanted to bloom on his own face.

/Apparently they caught the last half of your sentence./

/Yes—how did you know what their Elmer was? It was another thing you babbled—but a useful one./

He shook his head. /I don't remember. Just a hunch, I guess. They mentioned him the other night in Native./

"Hello! —Hello!" In the time their mental discussion had taken place, Lase Likeke had marched up to him and begun waving her wing back and forth in his face so it snapped like a flag in an angry wind. "Did she really mean that?"

"Dearest!" hissed the mayor, staring up at Jerimin's Queen. "Lane—Lase Gorgon, if you'll please excuse—"

"No! I don't want her even joking about eating pets anywhere in my vicinity!" The toasty hen threw the flat packs of food she had been carrying on the floor, not an inch away from Jerimin's feet. Only the sudden and deliberate fist-grip of his Queen's be-still instinct around his own kept him from jumping out of the way to save his poor toes.

Wrath surged through him. He fixed the hen with a look. She mantled her wings.

"Pick it up," he said, not quite able to remove the anger from his voice.

Her wings spread even wider.

"Rosie!!" The mayor was already stooped to gather the boxes, but Lase Likeke pushed him back with her arm, bangles cracking. "No. We can't let them say awful things like—"

"Don't you worry about your precious kitties and puppies," said Jerimin. "Just keep the meat coming and there won't be any problems."

"Any problems?? We've got hundreds of terrified people out there in the storm, no place to put 'em, we're running out of supplies, and the river's high so no shipment's getting through until it's settled again, and this"—she gestured from the flat packs in the mayor's arms to the offending boxes at Jerimin's feet—"is *all* the pet food left in town. Once she eats it, that's it. It's gone. Along with the fries, and three-quarters of Del's menu. You ate it all! Lani can't feed you anymore—she can't, or we won't have anything left for the 'Ehuananites."

"Then we need time alone," said Jerimin. "Here in the chapel. For a day or two. For a break." He couldn't believe he was seriously planning on defiling a church (even if these weren't his gods) but as long as she was stuck here, this is where the problem would have to be solved—and quickly, before one of them went unconscious again. But first, they'd have to ditch Nanny Lono. And after that, he'd need a bed and about forty-eight hours to be unconscious. Only after that could he even begin to think about fixing things. Maybe.

"Nuh-uh. The 'Ehuananites are ready to riot as it is."

Jerimin's fists clenched. "We don't have an obligation to that town's residents. They can go home, we'll get to their city later!"

"You go out there and tell them that!" said Lase Likeke, pointing to the plaza at the same time her husband said, "No no, we can't send them away!"

"Why not?" said his Queen.

"We're a small town—we're making it, but...you know, mostly we're a vacation town, a quick trip, for the E-cityers. If we show 'em a good time, they'll keep coming! But if you don't perform—"

Jerimin's hackles rose. "'Perform'?"

A coil pushed him firmly aside, and his Queen extended further into the conversational circle. "If I don't 'perform', as you name it, youdothink that's the end of your little town. Yes?" she asked.

A thick gulp, then the mayor nodded.

His Queen turned to Lase Likeke. "Do you agree?"

So confronted, the hen's wings tremored a little. "Vi-visitors already have plenty of reasons to choose other places over us. And our clutches are moving away."

"Do you *agree?*" she repeated, voice making the floor shake as well as any peal of thunder.

Lase Likeke's voice was a little thin when she spoke. "Yes, I do. But it's a moot point with the river high. They can't leave, and they won't, not till they've got what they came here for."

Lightning flashed again. The rain clatsched into the chapel walls, a constant hiss even through the thunder that followed.

Jerimin and his Queen exchanged looks. Now was the time for fast, thorough thinking, but he already felt the gears of his cognition grinding with fatigue. He ran down a list in his mind—what did they have now, what did they need, and in what order of importance did they need it?

She needed to get back into human shape as soon as possible; even if she wasn't actively using her power, simply wearing her whiskers burned through it quicker by default. Being small would buy them some time before...what, total unconsciousness for him? Followed by a coma for her? That sounded about right. So she needed to stuff her maw.

What should *he* do in the meantime? Go to the motel and beg for a room? *The Gorgon really shouldn't beg*—But she could trade. He had the cash on him from the fae...

The chapel interior strobed a few times before the thunder dropped on top of them.

The squarglings flinched, but during the lightning his Queen had pressed her be-still instinct into them both, so they appeared unbothered by it.

Who's gonna want to trade their nice cozy motel spot for a fistful of lousy jen? He didn't think any of the town's residents would board them—but he supposed it couldn't hurt to ask.

Ho'okano, Ho'okano! Why couldn't you just have let us in? Indeed. Why hadn't he done his duty? He'd never met the square. To him, this owner of the manor house, Jerimin and his Queen were perhaps some boogeymen from TV. Not real people. Maybe if Jerimin could talk to him...face to face...maybe he could convince him? To give them a spot, just for a couple nights...That was really all they needed...

He turned on the mayor. "Did you ever track down Ho'okano? Send someone over personally to talk with him?"

"N-n-no. We've been too—"

"Too busy. Right." Jerimin stepped away from the flat packs on the floor and began heading for the chapel doors.

/You keep eating. Take off your whiskers as soon as you can. I'm going to go do this clown's job for him./

A faint pulse of assent and approval warmed his head, and then her presence removed itself entirely. He'd be on his own, again, out in the town and in the storm.

"*PICK IT UP.*" he heard his Queen snap behind him, her voice making his bones itch. Panicked cheeps followed, along with the scrabbling of claws on the chapel floor, followed by *click-pfft!, click-pfft!, click-pfft!*

Well, that was one thing on the list getting taken care of.

Thunder boomed as Jerimin reached the doors. He tried opening one like he was exiting an office building, but it was so heavy it barely moved an inch. That one-inch gap, though, was still enough to let the rain to blow in. He jerked away from the spray suddenly in his face, letting the door fall shut again.

"Mayor!" He didn't bother turning around—didn't have to; the children's-cereal-colored square came running like a dog.

His useless purple-berry face simpered up at him. "Yes, Lane Gorgon?"

"You got an umbrella in that lodge of yours?"

The mayor gawped at him a minute, then tucked himself under raised wings in a practiced move, probably natural to all squarglings in this region.

"Of course. Yours are built in." He pushed roughly past the fool and touched his palm to the heavy doors.

"Ah-um—Lane Gorgon?"

Jerimin was sorely tempted to ignore him. But instead, he turned to the square.

"Yes, Mayor?"

"Ah...is that...screen yours, sir? You didn't come in with one."

Jerimin looked down at the equipment cradled in his arm. Lightning flashed again. He scowled. This incompetent shouldn't be questioning the Gorgon.

While the mayor flinched at the thunder, Jerimin yanked his spare drive free. Had the videos been completely deleted? Now there'd be no way of knowing, unless he somehow got the screen back again.

That didn't seem likely.

The thunder faded away.

"Someone left it behind," Jerimin said to the mayor. His beak opened, but before he could say anything, Jerimin said, "Catch," and tossed him the screen. *Would've been useless wet anyhow.*

Jerimin pocketed his spare drive and bulled the chapel door open.

Before the heavy door closed behind him, he saw the awaiting shapes of the mourners, standing in the rain. Some, watching the chapel, had seen him already, and their rain-shielding wings seemed to stiffen as they stalked forward.

He stepped out from under the chapel's awning. Instantly soaked. But that didn't matter. He pulled the fistful of red bills out of his pocket and held it high in the air.

He approached the mourners.

"Two hundred jen for anyone who can take me to one Lane Ho'okano!" he called over the rain.

It didn't matter who he had to fight through, snap at, or push aside; he would find Ho'okano and make him take them in.

25

KEONAONA

KEONAONA COULD SEE NOTHING, smelled only heavy greenery licked clean by rain and the mud beneath his bare feet, an odor both musty with decay and tangy-rich in nutrients. But in this blacked-out, canopy-made cave in the jungle, he could still hear the dull roar of the mechanical specter hovering just outside the dark refuge. It had followed him down the rabbit paths so far into the darkness that he'd feared the thing actually had infrared on him and that he'd never lose it. But a few yards into Smuggler's Grove (as it was fancifully named—it had been generations since any smuggling had taken place in Crooked Neck; and when it had, you could bet the hidey holes would've been nearer the river than this, but it'd made for a marvelous bad guy outpost when he was a squab, playing Merchants and Mayhem with Lono and Analū and the others) the whine of the fans had stopped advancing on him. He'd looked back to find the thing doing an absurd little halftime show in midair: rising, jerking left, slowly sinking, rotating around; rising, jerking, sinking, rotating again, movements silhouetted against the brighter haze of trees outside the grove. In other circumstances its dumb dance would have made him smile. But he felt (more than knew; he wasn't familiar with video tech past shooting gift-opening reactions on Pāheahea morning) that the automated calisthenics were the thing's way of trying to find him again. So he'd turned his back on it and blindly felt his way into the back of the grove.

The smell of rubber and mildew led him to the four or five folding stools set up around the pit for the electric lantern set into a shallow ring of stones (Hana had painted the lantern glass green once without telling anyone; when it had been switched on for the annual telling of the summer scare stories the effect had been electrifying). He carefully felt his way around the lantern-pit, hoping not to tear his unwrapped feet up any more than he already had today, and took a seat.

There he sat, losing his vision to the grove, listening to the baffled machine going up and down in the distance. He couldn't even see it now, he was so far in. He could simply crawl out the back way, if he really wanted. But somewhere on the rabbit path, or maybe somewhere here in Smuggler's Grove, he'd lost his heart. With nothing to see, it was all too easy to invent pictures, awful mental photos, of what Hana and Kai's final moments must have been like, and if he pushed those self-made nightmares away (*only they're not self-made; they're* WHAT REALLY HAPPENED TO THEM), the memory of the moment he found out the terrible news rushed in to fill the empty space.

To be smiling and joking one minute with Ladeira, a new friend; to be face to face with a Whistle City Incensario and a law officer the next, and having his world fall out from beneath him...

Why, it made the idea of going to Analū's absurd. Better to just walk into the river.

He blinked, shivered, but not from cold. Had he just said that out loud? Keonaona thought maybe he had.

The blades of the camera chopped the air, distantly.

He felt like he was tumbling. Even his tail, tip touching the ground, was no anchor. Adrift, that's what he was. Adrift, hunted. He could go to the river or he could go elsewhere and be hunted—maybe not by this camera, but by any of the others brought in by the Gorgon or that feedster. *Who knows? Maybe there are reporters on their way in from Pillars Beach.*

The thought made him go cold. Was nowhere safe? Out of the public eye?

The river.

No. No. They're coming home. Then, maybe, I can think about the river. But it's not fair to leave them in-between. Not when I can bring them home. It's what I have to do for them. I can't fail them again. I won't!

195

The sleeping mats still here were squab-sized; some smelled moldered past usability. The rubber straps of the stool he sat upon were already growing uncomfortable.

Analū's. I'll go there.

Keeping an ear on the camera's whirring, Keonaona slowly pawed his way to the back of Smuggler's Grove. Crawling through the exit tunnel out was an uncomfortable exercise in getting his wings and ears snagged by nasty overgrown branches, but gradually the dark left his eyes and he could start seeing the shapes of the forest again.

Which was nice, but not as good as when the tunnel ended and he could start walking upright again.

But maybe I deserve to crawl. If crawling through the overgrown wilds of Crooked Neck would bring them back, he would drop to his knees right then and there and nose around in the mud for as long as it took.

But crawling would do nothing, so he didn't.

Sharp-fingered fronds clawed at his calves; prickly pods and sharp stones bit into his feet. The leaves were a ceiling of green, with occasional gaps showing the sky growing darker the closer he got to Analū's, though whether it was because he was catching back up to the storm or because of the lateness of the hour, he couldn't tell.

He trod the back paths robotically. The canopy above him condensed and thinned, so that he walked in blackness sometimes, or sometimes in misty luminance that touched the creeping orchids and vines and turned them into skeletal shapes.

If anything, his unwrapped feet made it easier to feel the path when the dark came.

It was here, in one of the dark parts he licked the scent of Big Jenny off the roof of his mouth. She hadn't been here in a while—she'd lived long enough in this territory to know how to live adjacent to the squarglings, her wild paths rarely crossing their civilized ones—but it was a second option, besides the river. He'd be helping Jenny grow her cubs, in a way. He liked the thought of that. Had she had them yet? When Adanna had smelled the change in Jenny's scent, she'd put the town on alert. Jenny'd be slowed by her belly swollen with unborn cubs, but

196

once she had them, everyone would be wise to give her a wide berth...But he'd been out of town so long, he'd lost track of the big cat's pregnancy. Maybe the notice was still up at Analū's.

Anyway, it was another option.

He plodded forward, and the smells that made up the wilds of Crooked Neck didn't care. He passed through them a stranger.

At last, the trees above began thinning. He was approaching the base of the hill Nibbles stood upon. Any time now the glaring yellow A-frame would rise into view at the top, in between the widening gaps of the treetops. A glance up still didn't tell him whether the sky was dark due to time or storm, but that quick lift of his beak did tell him that there were wings at Analū's. A lot of wings. It wasn't just the storm blurring the scents together, either; they still had a distinct edge to their shapes that said they were standing around nearby. Probably around the other side of the hill, where the front of the store faced and where the main street was now hidden from Keonaona's view. Most likely outsiders, most of them. Analū might even have his hands too full to inquire after Keonaona; that would suit him just fine.

Keonaona faced the stone stair built into the back of the hillside. At the top stood Nibbles, the sharp peak of the building defiant against the dark sky. Not far now. He stiffened his tail, took a breath, then began the trudge upwards. It felt odd to feel the textured concrete directly molared against his toes and spur. It still held the damp of the monsoon rains, but it was otherwise warm as skin, though unyielding.

He reached the top of the stair. The door to Nibbles' loading dock was open, but the inside gaped, dark and empty as the mouth to Smuggler's Grove. What day was it again? Was a shipment due in? But the river...even if one were scheduled, nothing was coming into town if the river was high...

He stopped. Nothing coming in. His...his family, they would be held up, wouldn't they?

He rubbed his face with his palm, behind folded wings. River was up, river was down. The fact was that he didn't know what the river was doing and the other fact was that it didn't matter. He was stuck until they came, tonight or two weeks or two months.

Two months?

His wings turned leaden.

No, can't think that far ahead. Right now, he just had to get to the cot in the office.

He entered the loading bay. Cardboard perfumed the air; by now the smell was embedded in the walls, maybe even sunk in the cool flooring beneath Keonaona's bare feet. Nibbles was another Crooked Neck institution.

Now that his eyes had adjusted, Keonaona realized that there were hardly any boxes here. The wheeled carts Analū used to unload were bare. Keonaona held no illusions—Nibbles was no big outfit like Sun Mart (darn Lynn owned everything), and it wasn't like he was here often...but he was used to seeing more stock in. Much more stock. And the teleportal was off—it was one of the now-obsolete Cavanaugh models, and it'd never done well in storms. Once, during one, it'd thrown off sparks and almost burnt all of Nibbles down. Now Analū kept it off during storms—and nothing short of a commandment from Mother Herself could get him to turn it back on before the rain was well and clear.

Keonaona looked around, tail curling with unease. The wheeled carts were all lined up tight like books in a shelf, but the one hoverdolly—Analū's prized tool for working back here—was gone, so the square must be working now—maybe stocking the front.

Keonaona began making his way towards the front of the store. Loaded carts were pushed through a private connecting hall to the front of the store for stocking. Just off this hall was the break room, through which you could access both the office and Analū's bibs-and-bobs room. Right now, the hoverdolly stood in the hall. Keonaona wove around it and pushed open the break room door.

Several people were seated around the break room table. Their very human heads popped up upon Keonaona's entrance. So did Griffon Cortez's and Analū's. They stood in the back, and from the billfold in Griff's claw, were in the middle of negotiating something.

Then Griff saw him. A big grin moved the tiger stripes on his face, and the billfold was surreptitiously put away. Analū's tail lashed.

"If it isn't the square of the hour!" said Griffon in his loud voice. "Everyone, meet Keonaona Ho'okano."

The humans whispered behind their hands among themselves, glancing at Griff and looking impressed. Griffon went on. "Keonaona, meet Lase Harold and her news crew. They're from the Netron press. They want to talk to you."

Keonaona paled. He shot Analū a silent look of *what is going on here?!* Which was returned with a *how should I know?* shrug.

A woman—she smelled of vanilla musk perfume, not very much, but he knew immediately it was a foreign-formulated smell; one made without considering a beak's tastes—rose and bowed. "Ho-oh-kah-no-sir," she pronounced his name carefully, "we need to talk."

"I—I don't...want to talk."

The eyes of her crew seemed glued to him—a man cradling a shoulder camera, one who held a furry microphone on a long neck like a spear, another woman with a screen who began sweeping her fingers across it furiously. Their sweat smelled tense, and a little eager, and suddenly Keonaona felt like meat hung out for a dog.

Behind them, Griff crossed his arms and looked on, smug as a crocodile hidden among river logs.

"It's very important that we do," said the woman.

"I'm not interested."

Analū shot him a look that said, *are you crazy?*

"You haven't heard our proposal."

Proposal!

Griffon and Analū were watching him...Griff coolly, pretending, as he so often did, to be bored and above it all; Analū with confusion.

The vanilla woman suddenly bent over, pulled out a stool, gestured to it. "Please forgive my manners. I'm Harold-miss Euphegenia of the Netron World News Association. Please, have a seat."

He should never have come for the cot. Maybe he should have never left the house. He seemed to be running straight into trouble instead of away from it.

Keonaona's tail went limp. Maybe there was no escape. Maybe this was his punishment. Maybe he should just give up. Tell them everything. The thought of it made him sick—these people were no different than the feedster, trading misery for play counts—and pained him all at the same time. Simply existing without his family felt like being stabbed; talking about it would be like sawing the blade deeper.

And now Analū was coming around the table, towards him. He leaned in till they were beak-to-beak, then curtained them together with a lift of his yellow wings.

In this little bubble of privacy, he whispered in a voice barely audible, "Brah, what you doing? Listen to them, you could make a good buck!"

Annoyance warmed Keonaona. This close, the stress and misery pouring off him had to be obvious. Couldn't Analū sniff it?

"I don't want to talk to anyone," he whispered back.

Analū guttered, troubled. Maybe his snoot was awake after all. "Why not? Whaddap? I heard a rumor...you wanna move?"

Keonaona shut his eyes, suddenly weary. How many times did he have to say it? "I don't. Want. To talk."

Analū jolted back, hurt flashing across his face. His wings dropped and and now Griff and the humans could see them.

"Not even to me, brah?"

Keonaona raised a wing, blocking the room from view again. "I just came for your cot."

"What? There ain't enough beds in that house of yours?"

"No." Keonaona lowered his voice again. "I came to stay here. On your cot."

Analū looked completely lost. "But you're hosting the Gorgons, you can't—"

"I'm not hosting them. I turned them away, okay?"

Analū's jaw dropped. He sputtered a few moments, eventually spitting out, "You—the Gorgons—refuse?"

"Not...beak-to-beak!" Keonaona groaned, dropping his wing, holding his head in his hands. He didn't want to be thinking about this, let alone explaining it...he was—so—tired!

"Is he all right?"

Keonaona looked up. The newswoman had stepped towards them, reaching for him.

He studied the features of her human face, the blonde hair and the way it had been wrapped up like a bread bun high on the back of her head, and how some bits—strands, that was the word—of it lay sticky across her brow. She didn't seem to be money-hungry. Her face was pleasant. Compassionate, even. Maybe.

"Ho-oh-kah-no-sir?" she asked uneasily.

He wasn't sure how long he'd been staring.

Fighting. Fighting was making him tired. Fighting and running...

He went past Analū and slumped into the proffered stool. He sighed.

"All right. What do you want?"

The woman hurried to take the stool across from him. After adjusting her lavalava—no, it was called a skirt over there when women wore it, wasn't it? And those were pleats. After smoothing them flat over her knees, she spoke. "We'd like to make an arrange—a deal. Nine hundred jen for a room for the Gorgon."

So they didn't want to buy his misery. Just his decision.

"No," he said.

"Twelve hundred jen."

"Lase, I know what you think of my kind, but I'm not haggling with you or trying to drive up the price. I already made the decision. It's done."

"Very well. Is there anything—anything at all—we could give you that would change your mind?"

My wife and Kai back.

"No. Nothing you could give me."

He rose from the stool. Headed for the exit—he didn't want the cot anymore. He didn't know what he wanted anymore.

But before he made the door, Griff put himself in front of it.

"Don't rush off, Keonaona. You hardly listened to them. I don't know what worm got in your apple, but I think they've traveled a long way out to talk to you. Wouldn't entertaining them a little longer be the hospitable thing to do?"

"I'm not entertainment."

"'Course you ain't, rosebud. But you're also not doin' so hot. Your comb's not on straight. One...hospitality expert to another, let me help you out."

Keonaona sighed again. "Griff—"

He cocked his head in a challenging way. The steady orange gaze, the dark striped wings held broadly, uprightly, smile confident. Here was a square with all the fight in him at his clawtips. But that was Griff—always had been. Back in school, he'd argue with teachers till his ruff fell out—argue with anyone, really. As far as he was concerned, his opinion was factually correct one hundred percent of the time. When he left Crooked Neck to become a big-time lawyer, everyone Keonaona knew said, "Good riddance," but Keonaona himself thought, *good for him; maybe he's finally found where he fits*. But no one else's opinion of Griffon had been changed in all the time Keonaona discussed this with his fellow Crooked Neckians (not even Hana's), and he supposed when Griff came back a hotshot lawyer showing off a new, custom-built house to everyone, rubbing their beaks in it, he had been forced to admit that Griffon Cortez had earned his reputation as a pot-stirrer fairly. But he could never fully side against the ornery cuss—because (maybe due to his family's wealth, or because Keonaona had always tried to treat him courteously and sincerely believed the square wasn't as bad as everyone had decided him to be) he and Griff had always been on semi-friendly terms.

He's going to air his arguments a dozen bananas or none. Fighting him will just make the path there longer—and unpleasant.

"Okay. Let's hear it," Keonaona said softly.

Griff brightened. He gestured to Analū's office door. "Step into my office," he said. Keonaona trudged inside the dusty room and Griff closed the door behind them, trapping Keonaona in the room with him, Analū's desk clutter to his back. Keonaona stared at his dirty, mud-dried toes. Still, the grin in Griff's voice was clear as he laid out his case. Truly, lawyering fit him like scales on a fish. "First: if you accept now, you'll be getting paid for a job you already agreed to do for free."

It's not about the money. It never was.

"Second: you'll be promoting interplanetary relations, *dada-da*, bananas, bananas...but that could mean more visitors to the town. And I know you know how desperate ol' Lono is for more income. Imagine if this human news crew tells their friends, and then we get visitors from *Netron*. Our friends could keep their jobs, grow their businesses! You'd be the town hero!"

Who cares? One way or another, I'm leaving Crooked Neck forever.

"Third: it's not like you have to *be* there."

Keonaona looked up. Griff's smile broadened. "All they're bargaining for is a room—nobody said anything about requiring you to play tea party with 'em—though I'd bet my tail stripes you're set up to do it in style. You've seen how well I do renting out my second house to vacationers—and I don't ever meet 'em beak-to-beak! I just have a little info binder. It's easy money, my friend! Just say 'yes' and get out of the way."

Say "yes" and get out of the way. In other words...if I say yes, I don't have to deal with this anymore?

He could receive his family. Then leave, if he wanted.

"Look at it another way: even if you ran out the door right now and holed up in the chapel—if you could hole up in the chapel, which you can't—not right now, at any rate—they could all still follow you in. Every human news crew. They just can't film ya. So why not give these humans what they want, and get 'em off your back once and for all?"

One word would stop the hunt for him. He could go any-where. No more skulking through the jungle trying to hide from cameras. No more dodging the blue-headed feedster; he'd have given up his cards. Wouldn't be accountable to anyone but Kai and Hana. And perhaps that was more important than holding fast to his earlier decision.

I should really think about this some more. There's a lot of angles here. Lots to consider.

But he was tired and considering things felt worthless.

"I strongly advise you to take the deal," said Griff, professional manner coming to the fore.

"I think you're right," Keonaona said.

"Of course I am." Griff stepped aside. "Thanks for giving me the chance to change your mind," he said, opening the door.

"Wait," said Keonaona. "Before we go out..."

Griffin closed the door.

"Is the river high tonight?"

"Sure is. Breaking records left and right."

"Thanks."

So they won't come in tonight! Oh! Keonaona's wings drooped. He'd have to face another night alone before he could make arrangements.

Griff opened the door again. Keonaona stepped out into the sallow light of the break room. Analū flexed his wings, question on his face. The humans rose.

Keonaona went to the vanilla-perfumed woman.

"Okay," he said. "I'll take your deal. One room for the Gorgon at my place."

Analū's frown of confusion deepened, before he shot a glare at Griff. The humans exchanged hopeful looks. Keonaona went on. "There's a condition, though."

"Sir?" said the vanilla woman.

"I will not be providing any hosting services while they're in. I have other places I need to be."

"But you'll give us a key."

"Yes. Though I think the back of the southeastern wing is open. I left in a hurry. Anyway, I just need a charge for my mobi."

The screen-woman reached into a bag of hers and produced a charger plate almost immediately.

Keonaona pulled his mobi from his mud stained and jungle-roughened lavalava and passed it over.

Within a few minutes of being set on the plate (during which the humans bowed and thanked him profusely, calling him "honorable" and such), the mobi was ready. Keonaona transferred a keycode to the vanilla woman's mobi. His mobi alerted him of a twelve hundred jen increase to his bank account. He felt nothing. He slipped his mobi back in his pocket.

Almost as soon as he had done that, screen woman shoved her screen in front of his beak. "And, sir, would you please sign this? Verifying the authenticity of your permission?"

He scribbled his name with a knuckle.

"It's done, then?" he said. "You know how to get to my place?"

"Analū can take them there," said Griff, who'd stepped to the humans' side during the charging.

The yellow storekeeper screeched. "Some of us have a store to mind, thanks!"

"Oh, right. Then I'll lead the way."

Human fear sweat jumped into Keonaona's beak. "Actually, it would be most helpful, Cortez-sir, if you would go back to the chapel and notify the Gorgon of this development," said the vanilla woman. The others around her nodded wildly.

"It would give us more time to set up," added another.

Griff's tail whipped about, sending his own anger-and-fear scent into all corners of the cramped breakroom.

What's that about? Even if they're frightened of the Gorgon, they'd be breaking good news to them.

"It'll cost you. One-fifty."

The crew looked to the woman with the screen, desperation in their eyes. After scrolling on her screen a minute, she shook her head. "Sorry, budget," was all she said.

Griffon sniffed. "Then one of you can go."

The screen woman nodded to herself. "Here." She wiped through her screen. "To make it fair..."

Keonaona gave a half-hearted preen of a muddy wing, listening to the virtual wheel of chance spinning on the screen woman's screen. It stopped spinning with a single cold chime, different than the rattling maracas and clanging bells you'd actually hear at a genuine Osidern casino.

"Sorry, Stevenson-sir. We can buy you an umbrella here, assuming, sir, you have one?" she asked Analū.

"Actually, I do," he said, and turned his yellow back to enter his bibs-and-bobs room. While his friend was distracted, Keonaona edged out of the room. In the connection hall, he turned towards the front of the store, pushed his way out of the swinging double doors, and was met by a wave of strangers' scents. Wings packed the aisles and the line zig-zagged to the single register where young Julio stood ringing up orders, claws tapping on the screen fast as an accountant's. And you could bet with this crowd, Mariana was scrambling across the candy wall like a capuchin. But Keonaona ducked his head and plowed into the crowd without looking. He didn't want to be here when the Netrons left; Analū could ask questions.

"Hey, Uncle, you work here?" asked a young voice.

"Sorry, no," said Keonaona without stopping. He made it through and stepped onto the lanai; the cool wood and air refreshing after the cramped capybara pen of Nibbles' break room. Keonaona never stopped moving but clapped down the stairs and into the street. Gabbling clusters of out-of-towners were shooting up the main thoroughfare towards the golden sanctuary of the store.

No one noticed the dry mud on his naked legs, the low feeling in his scent, nor the dullness in his eyes as he trudged against the crowd.

No one noticed, either, when the cloud cover parted, just for a moment, and his newly-charged mobi, in the brief seconds it had a connection, downloaded a single message and beeped—*kuwee-wheh!, kuwee-wheh!*—to notify its master.

Keonaona dragged it from his pocket. That sound was too chipper for the way he was feeling now. Then, with a surge of pain, he remembered: *I let Kai pick it out.*

He was about to enter the mobi's settings to silence it when his eyes scanned the message's subject line.

With the push of a button, he pulled it up. He read the first line.

His heart dropped.

Crushing the mobi, the message, against his heart, Keonaona changed direction and ran away from the chapel.

This changes nothing.

This changes everything.

26

MERCURIO

IN THE DRIPPING GREEN clearing that stank of big cat, fear sweat, and human panic pee, Mercurio's brain had frozen, unable even to narrate as the sunset orange monster cat bore down upon him and Mango-mama.

It leapt the last few feet towards them, soared into the air and then (it seemed to him) hung there—*like it's in ultra slo-mo.* He could have counted the rosettes on its pelt, if he hadn't been so terrified.

Golden eyes grew and grew, filling Mercurio's vision. *The last shot I'll ever see. Extreme close-up.*

And then the golden eyes snapped shut. An awful snarl made Mercurio's chest rumble. Time resumed normally. Freed from the spell of the jaguar's killing stare, Mercurio could suddenly see everything again—an inactive silver hovercamera ricocheting off the side of the cat's skull, falling to the forest floor, followed swiftly by two noisy drone cameras that wheeled around in the air to face the cat and—*BLAMM!!*—snapped on their lights. The jaguar snarled again, a sound like water gurgling down a deep drain, mud and wet leaves spattering in every direction as it whirled around. Was it confused? Or maybe trying to smash the lights out with its meaty paws?

"QUICK, QUICK, THIS WAY! RUN! FOLLOW ME!" Mango-mama was screaming, and the humans were running, but only when she gave the great ululating nest talk scream for *killer, run!* did Mercurio find his feet carrying him out of the clearing, away from the tormented big cat.

The humans made an easy scent to follow, their tweed clothes and foreign deodorants distinctly out-of-place in the wilds. Mercurio had to remind himself that Mango-mama was the only one who knew where the heck they were going and forced his beak to whiff through the human scents eddying past his face and focus on hers.

He could definitely smell blood. Two kinds, now. The blood-scents kept his legs pumping, sharpened his awareness to the point where he could dodge ankle-turning rocks, duck beneath noggin-crushing branches, and leap come-outta-nowhere tree roots smoothly even as he kept in view the muddied grey suits and bouncing equipment cases on the backs of the news crew.

It wasn't long before he made it to the front of the pack, neck and neck with the sound guy, following Mango-mama's pale orange tail and wings. The other two men seemed to be hanging back to make sure their producer, a woman, didn't get left behind. Good for them.

Whiffing blood more strongly now, Mercurio put on speed, almost made even with Mango-mama, fear and warning screeches pouring out of her with enough intensity to pull this strange un-flock after her. She juked to one side and Mercurio followed automatically—that was all squargling instinct—but the fervored panting behind him told him, unbelievably, that the humans were just as in sync. He'd be amazed if he wasn't still convinced the jaguar was somewhere behind and gaining.

It seemed like they ran through melting green glass for an eternity. Nothing changed.

And then, they burst out of a line of trees onto the hard-packed road, into a crowd! Cheek ruffs bristled and alarm shrieks were taken up instantly—*and who can blame 'em? We probably smell like we've been running from the Death Jackal himself!*—but Mango-mama (who'd put on the brakes) turned around and cheeped a nest call to gather at the humans before shaking herself. "Are we—all here?" She was still breathing hard. "Blueberry—is this them all?"

Sweat-smelling faces were all a-huffing and puffing—but all four were there: cam operator, sound guy, talent, and producer.

"Yeah—Auntie—the gang's—all—here."

"Who was at the back? You?" she asked Mercurio.

"No"—he took a couple seconds to hang over his knees and breathe—"them." He pointed with his tail-tip and at the men he'd seen at the back of the pack. Mango-mama pointed a claw at them. "You see Jenny—the jag—following us?"

The men were panting, too, and grabbing at their sides. One of them managed, "No—didn't see—it."

"Good. Must have—stayed behind—with her nestlings."

By this time the street crowd were pelting her with questions. She whistled "all clear" in reply and the protective circle the crowd was forming around them dissolved. But a paper-smelling square and a couple who smelled of oily-olive pressed in on Mango-mama.

"You're hurt," said the square.

"No, she's not," Mercurio said automatically. She couldn't be!

"Yes, I am," Mango-mama said calmly as the paper square (a chalky color beige, like dust) said, "Then what's this?" and the oily-olive couple yowled their disbelief at him. It was then Mercurio took a real look at Mango-mama and realized the additional blood he'd scented during the getaway had been hers. The cat, somehow, had raked its claws into her forearm, which she—come to think—had been cradling with her other hand this entire time. Based on the flap of orange skin flopped over her thumb like a cooked noodle, and the blood pooling down her forearm to drip off her elbow, she wouldn't be letting go of it anytime soon.

"He's hurt, too," said Mango-mama, lifting her beak at the cameraman.

"Just a scrape," he said, though his eyes were round as coins, fixed on the blood coming off Mango-mama. And was it the jungle leaves playing tricks on him, or were the humans starting to tinge green? Could humans do that? It didn't look right on 'em.

"She needs a doctor," said paper-dust square.

"No signal," said the oily-olive square, looking at his mobi. Alarm and concern filled his eyes, and for the billionth time, Mercurio cursed his lack of cams, that face was so...*oonf!* So much in it, and it was flying by, never to be experienced again, the moment lost to ever-scrolling time.

"It's okay," said Mango-mama. "She just tagged me. I live here, I know where to go." She clucked reassurance to all three of the onlookers. "You go on with what you doing."

While Mango-mama shooed her would-be-rescuers off, Mercurio patted himself down. Still no cams. No big scratches, just a few scrapes where the particularly prickly jungle flora had nabbed him during their flight. He did a quick preen to soothe his battered wings, then crept over to the Dolphin crew, who were now surrounding the producer with her screen.

"—lost him," he caught her saying. "The cam's been stuck on 'acquire' for over twenty minutes now. He's long gone. So it doesn't matter. We're all going to the doctor with you, Gideon, and after the doctor's made sure your leg isn't infected, we're getting out of here."

Gideon—the cameraman, apparently—made a sound of disgust. Now that there wasn't a big cat around commanding all his attention, Mercurio could see the nasty-looking scrape that had tore up the entire side of his calf, turning the smooth, normal surface of his skin angry and red and bumpy (and was that rocks mixed in there? Is that what those dark flecks were? Ewww). Beads of blood oozed from it, the unusual, coppery smell making Mercurio grimace. Now that he'd seen where this blood scent was coming from, he couldn't un-smell it. He turned away.

Mango-mama's fans were gone, and now she was heading this way—against the flow of the crowd, who all seemed to be headed in one direction.

Mercurio stood on tiptoe and scented the air, but couldn't get his bearings. They wouldn't be heading back to the chapel, would they?

"Everybody okay?" Mango-mama called to them. Nods all around, and the producer stepped forward to confer with Mango-mama.

The Dolphin news team had lost Ho'okano. Mercurio had zero idea where the red was, and he doubted Mango-mama would feel inclined to take him through the jungle again, not when she needed stitching up. And no way he'd go back in alone!

His equipment was good as gone.

His wings drooped and he let his tail-tip drop onto the muddy street. Back to reviewing mediocre snacks, performing stupid stunts, and commenting on movies he didn't care about.

And that was only *if* the big Gorgon let him take back his equipment and slink back home. If she didn't...He shuddered. He'd have two flavors of hell to pick from: either another tour of duty in the Lynn Enterprises customer service call center mines, or sending his scanty resume to any business currently running. He'd done both before. He didn't want to do either of them ever—and he meant *ever!*—again.

"Blueberry? What's wrong?" Mango-mama was wincing, still holding her arm.

"Oh—nothing. Just...thinking."

"I ain't going back out after Doc Fern stitches me up. You gotta know that."

"Uh-huh."

"But you could still go to Nibbles and find Keonaona. It's not far." She gave a wry chuckle. "We ran half the way there."

"Yeah?" A grain of hope fell into Mercurio's heart.

Mango-mama lifted her beak in the direction of the street travelers. "I reckon you head the way they're going, you'll hit the stream."

"Yeah—yeah—I know where to go from there—and he put up signs this morning!"

"Yeah, well—careful out there; the stream'll be high, so watch your step. And make sure you get to Keonaona first. I don't want him fighting off these news people—no offense," she finished with a cluck at the producer.

The human woman bowed. "None taken."

"Yes, ma'am!" said Mercurio, and skipped into the crowd before she could whistle another note. Guilt made his chest prickle—if his tutu saw him running off instead of walking an injured hen to the doctor, she'd caw him deaf!

But Tutu, I'm doing something she wants me to do! I'm practically running an errand for her!

The prickling went away, and Mercurio put on speed, keeping his beak alert for the sweet scent of the yellow general store.

The rediscovered fear of losing his equipment to the Gorgon made Mercurio fleet of foot again; he passed the amblers on the road like they were standing still. Little scraps of conversation caught in his ears, then flowed past, much like the shapeless green scents of the forest around him. His bruised wings were grateful the trees along the road were trimmed back.

It wasn't too long before the street began to resemble the one he'd traveled before. He was somewhere between the plaza hill and the stream. *She must've run us across the little street that leads to Ho'okano's neighborhood—it's only a drivee wide anyway. If there hadn't been any people, would she have run us all the way up to the plaza?*

He fell into a rhythm that lulled his anxiety enough that his inner narrator stuck its head back out.

Countless mourners shake the storm water off their wings and descend the hilltop plaza of Crooked Neck, their hopes of speaking with their deceased (yech) *loved ones crushed by the strange incident in the chapel. In the intermission, like all good audiences—and funeral attendees—they seek food to weigh down their bellies, a weight that assures them they're alive—*

Oh, great, now *he* was hungry! Well, the coffee couldn't last forever. Probably burned up all the caffeine running from "Jenny." Jenny! What a *stupid* name for a killing machine! Too much time out here in the mud had made these Crooked Neckers go mealy in the head.

A smell like a freshly-opened bottle of water teased Mercurio's beak.

The stream! Within moments, he was on its banks. It *had* risen, up to chest height, and was running fast, sound less like a gentle shushing and closer to a serious roar.

He ignored the city wings hemming and hawing at the edge (well, he cawed at them to get out of his way—which they, for once, did) and plunged in, slashing his tail side-to-side in the water to propel him farther, faster.

The swift current meant he climbed up the other bank a few yards down from where the road actually was, but squarglings on both banks cheered and whistled while he shook himself dry. He grinned widely and waved back at them, their brave trailbreaker, ever wishing he had some cards to give out.

Some of the squarglings hesitating on this side seemed to find their resolve, looking to him and chirping thanks before entering the stream themselves; and he thought he heard splashing from the bank he'd just left, too, though he didn't turn around to check. As soon as his feet found the road again, he was off at full speed.

There. The sweet smell of...well, okay, it wasn't victory, not for sure, but the sweet smell of hope. A single word from Ho'okano could reverse Mercurio's fortunes.

C'mon, Red. Be there!

The candied scent was getting stronger—and now Mercurio could make out the golden sides of the store shining out from among the trees. He raced past the dawdling lookee-loos and up the hill to the store. The sugary smell grew stronger as Mercurio followed the curving road up to the base of the green mound where the store perched, glowing like a golden beacon against the monotonous green backdrop of the jungle. The stair up the front of the hill was crowded with people coming down (arms loaded down with snacks—what, no bags, shopkeeper?) and going up, chatting to members of their groups or calling up the stair in loud cries of Mother's Tongue to find out if the place was any good. Unlike the last few times he'd been here, the lanai was stuffed with tutus in glider chairs, squares pointing off the balcony, mothers surrounding the barrels set out, turning them into makeshift tables, dividing spoils among their broods. Maybe there were still some peeps camped out in front of the chapel, but this place looked like party central. Would Red really want to come here?

Well, while Mercurio checked on that, he could buy another Jukee. Assuming they weren't sold out.

Chukking and croaking for people to make way on the stair (the idiots here weren't near as quick to move as the wings back at the river), Mercurio battled his way up to the store's lanai. Now the only thing blocking him from the store's entrance—and possibly Ho'okano—and a desperately-needed Jukee—were about three dozen lanai loiterers, who, this close, and this stupidly blocking the door, weren't as charming as they'd seemed at the bottom of the hill. Mercurio drew himself up, winged his elbows, and dove in.

Getting to the door involved a lot of pushing and shoving and stepping on toes, and scolding calls after him told him he hadn't made any friends, but at last, he made it.

He was just about to enter when the door opened of its own accord, revealing the tall Gorgon—Icarii—arms overflowing with junk food.

Mercurio froze. The lanai chatter plummeted.

Whatever mod he was wearing when I first met him must've washed off. Because now all those desert and sweet decay scents, though still there, were squelched under some horror-show mulch-up of human, big Gorgon, and death—straight up death—*if you made me close my eyes and scent this, I'd never guess it belonged to a human, not in six years!*

On top of all that, sweat, rain-smell, and faded anger were new, alarming additions to his freaky scent.

Mercurio finally choked the word out. "You!"

"Afternoon, Lane Macoya." His pleasant voice stood in stark contrast to his ghoulish scent. "I hope you have good news. Step aside, please?"

Mercurio hopped to and the tall Gorgon stepped out. An avocado escaped from the man's arms and fell to the lanai. Mercurio dropped down and picked it up immediately. It was hard as a stone, nowhere near ripe.

Extremely bottom-of-the-barrel.

"Thank you," said the tall Gorgon. He ducked under the doorway and proceeded towards the stair. Mute, the lanai occupiers parted before the grotesque scent like butter before a hot knife.

That extra space made it easy for Mercurio to keep to Icarii's side, but joining up with the man meant going down the steps and away from the store. And possibly Ho'okano. And definitely a desperately-needed Jukee. Though Mercurio could scent aluminum cradled in the tall man's elbow. Mercurio had fed him once—maybe he could get a drink in trade?

The gang on the stair likewise parted before him (Mercurio could hear dark murmurs behind, though, after he passed) and the tall man carefully picked his way down to street level.

Icarii looked both ways, slowly. Taking in the scene?

A new rainbow of colors appeared as wings opened so people gawping at him could talk behind them. Some shot the human wary looks.

Deep within the crowd, someone shouted, "KILLER!"

There was a hitch in the smooth movement of the tall Gorgon's scan of the street.

Not exactly a flinch...Would've been nice if MaxCam had picked that up. I could have played it back later.

"Do you know any benches or picnic tables around here, Lane Macoya?"

"No, sir."

Icarii stopped scanning the street and examined Mercurio. Seconds passed without him saying anything. Mercurio couldn't tell what he was thinking. *Does he know I don't have a room for them?* The square's heart began to pick up.

When the tall man finally spoke, all he said was, "'Sir'? That's new." And then he set off onto the street, turning in the direction of Ho'okano's place. A few more screams followed him.

Is he gonna do the deal with Ho'okano himself??

"You're not going up to Ho'okano's, are you? I just been there, he's a no-show."

A bag of veggie puffs dropped out of Icarii's arms and into the muddy road. He stopped. "Grab those for me, will you?"

Mercurio bent over and added the bag of puffs to the stony avocado wedged in the crook of his own elbow.

"Right now," said Icarii, "I'm just trying to find someplace to sit down and eat. Although...Lane Ho'okano had a table out on his lanai...Hm."

Oh no, was he seriously thinking about going down and eating his lunch on Ho'okano's porch? No, no, no!

"All the news humans are there, too—camped out on his lanai! But I know—"

"Lane Macoya?"

"Yeah?"

"Shut up and look for a place to sit."

"Yes, sir."

The farther they got from Nibbles, the sparser the crowds got; maybe everyone had gone to the plaza that morning. The few who did drift past them kept their distance from Icarii, like he bore a killer plague.

They passed the foxleg that led up to the Canopy Motel and kept going. Soon, nobody was on the road, and Mercurio realized he was walking alone with this man-who-wasn't-a-human...

C'mon, Merc! He can't eat you—he doesn't have the teeth for it!

But if he closed his eyes, Mercurio never would have believed that...He smelled freakier than any of the monster scents they'd cooked up for Redd Razor's movies, and that guy was the *king* of horror.

"Oh, finally!"

Mercurio stopped short as Icarii darted across his path like a cat. He stopped in front of a taller-than-normal tree stump and carefully leaned himself down to sit. A box of Foxtails fell from the pile in his arms. This time, he shook all the bags loose from the pile (or tried to, anyway, there were some caught up by the avocados and Jukee can that wouldn't go) to join the candied nuts on the ground.

There was no stump for Mercurio. He walked up, tossed the bagged veggie puffs on the ground with its friends.

He offered the avocado he'd been in charge of. "Where d'ya want this?"

Tossing the puffs to the ground had earned Mercurio a glare as Icarii gulped from his cucumber-melon Jukee. But when he finished his swig, he extended his hand and said, "Give it here."

Once he had it, he wedged his tallboy carefully into the soft ground and proceeded to cut the 'cado in half with a folding knife he had in one of his safari pockets.

Mercurio didn't like seeing him with a knife. No, not at all.

"I can cut the others for you," said Mercurio, pointing to the line of (likely also rock hard) avocados now lined up against the stump like little ancient idols.

"Thanks," said Icarii, before biting into the pitless half of his fruit.

Mercurio's claws and beak made short work of them and their pits—but Icarii took and ate them as fast as Mercurio prepared them.

"You know those are better with salt on 'em, right?" As soon as he said it, Mercurio slapped his shin with his tail. *Couldja wait till he puts the knife away? Besides, if I stay on his good side, keep doing him favors, maybe he'll give me my equipment back! Or at least give me a new deal!*

"Yes, and they could use a few more months on the tree, couldn't they?"

Mercurio nodded, feeling the way his leg smarted.

He stood there watching the man(-thing) eat—*no, devour!*—until the mound of snacks, nuts, and candy was gone, save for the wrappers and skins. After patting his mouth clean with a handkerchief from his breast pocket, Icarii gathered up the wrappers and began folding them into crisp squares, even running his nail along the folds to make sharp creases. "I take it you don't have a room for us."

"I never said that!"

"True, but I get the feeling you wouldn't be able to stop crowing about it if you did."

"Okay. Got me there. But look—"

"Do you really know Ho'okano isn't home? Or is he just holed up inside?"

"No—he's not there—the Dolphins news crew had a cam on him—"

"Dolphin news—? Oh, New Delphians. Got it. Go on, sor—go on."

"Yeah—they had a cam tracking him in the jungle—but it lost him and there was a jaguar, so the crew gave up and I lost my guide."

Icarii looked confused. "Are you saying a jaguar got Ho'okano, or your guide?"

"Neither! Me and my guide and the Delphians got cornered by the cat—Mango-mama said it'd just had cubs—"

"Mango-mama?"

"She runs the hens' café."

"Wait—Lnnn...Lani? Orangeish hen? Light orange and yellow? Lani was your guide?"

Funny how humans always described by color and never smell. "Yeah, her."

"Is she all right?"

"Yeah, she made it out, but the thing got her with its claws. She's up at some doctor's now, getting stitches."

"And the New Delphians left."

"Well, they said they were gonna after they got their cameraman checked out."

"He was attacked, too?"

"Yeah"—Mercurio croaked with dry amusement—"by the jungle. Big scrape down here." He presented his putee'd calf with a game-show wave of his tail.

"Ah. I see." Icarii slid a batch of the folded snack bags into one of his pants pockets and buttoned the flap over. He started folding the next batch. "What were you doing at Nibbles?"

"Mango-mama said he'd probably head there. I was going in to check, but then you came out."

"I see," said Icarii, looking back the way they came. He was quiet a long time.

Though the Gorgon Icarii looks like a regular—if freakishly tall—human, the scent that emanates from him when his scent-mod is gone is the stuff of nightmares. Your humble correspondent could hardly stand to, well, stand by him (that'd need a rewrite), *and every minute in his presence made my skin want to crawl away. Truly, long-term exposure to the former queen of Hriana has turned him into a monster—albeit one with all his manners intact.*

"Where were you going to look for him? At the general store, I mean?"

"Oh, uh—if I didn't scent or see 'im in the store, I was gonna ask the shopkeeper. I think they work together or something."

"Do you know Ho'okano's scent?"

"Yeah, sure!"

Odd-colored eyes bored into Mercurio's face. Nervous twitters escaped the square. *So intense!*

"You're not telling me some slick lie just to keep me from knocking on Ho'okano's door myself, are you? Think carefully before you answer, Lane Macoya. My wife would find your equipment very satisfying to hurl into a wall. This town has put her in that kind of mood."

Mercurio's wings popped out in panic. "Nono, I swear! I've talked with him beak-to-beak, he smells, like, amazing" (*unlike you*) "and his granddad or something's even the basis for some Incensario stuff..."

"So even if he were hiding in the back of the store, you would be able to find him?"

"Yeah, sure! You, uh, might have to stay back in another room, though."

In the flick of a tail, Icarii's professorial demeanor vanished, replaced with rage. His huge hand shot forward, fingers digging into Mercurio's shoulder. Mercurio flinched, his wings curling forward to try and protect his face.

"*If you think you can*—oh," said Icarii, and he let go just as quickly as he had struck. Now he didn't sound angry at all —maybe just annoyed. "My mod's washed off, hasn't it?"

Mercurio emerged from his shelter. "Uh-huh."

Icarii scoffed. "Perfect." He stuffed the remaining wrappers into his pockets (both folded and unfolded got crushed in his fists beforehand) and stood up. "Let's go."

"Back to the store?"

"Back to the store." Icarii set off without looking back. Mercurio lunged to his feet and threw himself after the long-legged Gorgon.

Sheesh! Guy takes two steps and he's halfway into the next county!

But Mercurio was by Icarii's side soon enough. The thick rubber soles of his hiking boots hitting the trail made a steady rhythm against the quicker *pad-pad-pad* of Mercurio's treated puttee soles. The canopy above was thinner, but the eerie glare of the cloud-cover above made it impossible to tell the time of afternoon. Mercurio searched for a break in them, to see the true sky, but no dice. *May as well be a matte painting up there.*

From time to time, Mercurio aimed his snoot at the thick greens that hedged in the road, but not once did he smell the jaguar. *All those flashbulbs going off in its face probably scared it back into its nest with a headache. Stupid cat!*

"Keep up, please, Lane Macoya."

In his whiffing for the big cat, Mercurio had fallen behind Icarii's two-mile stride. He hurried back to his side. In a little while, they passed the foxleg to the motel again. Now wings were beginning to appear on the road again, mostly ones and threes, traveling up motel way. Maybe going to their rooms for the evening? Like before, they gave Icarii (and by extension, Mercurio—*ugh, I hope his stink ain't catchy—I hate tomato baths!*) plenty of space.

"What were you planning on doing with that film you took in the chapel?"

Mercurio shot back the first thing that loaded into his beak. "I didn't film that!"

Then, hearing what he had just said to this safari-guide-dressed monstrosity walking next to him, he gulped hard. But the tall Gorgon only threw back his head and barked a single laugh.

"Ha! You'll have to do better than that." He flashed Mercurio a crooked—but...not...unfriendly?—smile. Mercurio didn't know; it was hard to trust your eyes when your beak was screaming DANGER.

Still smiling. "Want to try again?"

Mercurio glowered. "It was my ticket out of here without having to chase down Red—Ho'okano, I mean. My tutu died two years back—"

"What's a 'tutu'?"

"Grandmother. Anyway, she left me some money and a note to take a shot at my dreams. I'd always wanted to make movies—I mean, I did some silly stuff as a squab, with a grown-up mobi I saved up and paid for myself...Urima, Coval, Machado, Redd Razor, those directors were my heroes growing up. Then, you know, I started career training..."

"For which career, now?"

"Hospice counseling. Kinda like a palliative Incensario, but you don't have to go to school for the perfume...What?"

Icarii was staring at him, looking mortified. But he quickly shook his head. "Nothing. Please go on."

Mercurio drew himself up. "I did okay at my training! For the first few weeks, anyway. Then I dropped out. Did some other stuff. But, you know, the filmmaking itch was still there. I couldn't do anything about it, though, till Tutu's gift. So I quit, grabbed up some equipment and started a feed. But short films weren't working for me, even when I put 'em on the net, so I started the feed thing seriously—you know, for the cash. But it ain't bringing in the red stuff like I need. Tutu's cash runs out at the end of next month.

"But if I shoot you two—on film, I mean!—I could have the start of my documentary series out in two weeks. Everyone wants to know about you. I'd have what they want, they'd have to come to my feed! With the views, and the revenue, I could shoot real movies, the ones *I* wanna make, not just slog at stuff I don't care about! You'd bring me enough eyeballs to carve out an audience. Or...or even if that didn't happen, you'd make me enough cash to at least keep doing the feeds."

"So, one way or another, you see us as your ticket to the big time."

Mercurio didn't answer right away. Something small rustled in the ferns lining the road, but he didn't even lift his beak.

"Yeah. Guess that's it."

A spotted pink hen clutched herself as she passed them, her wide eyes glued to Icarii.

"Here's a question for you, Macoya."

"...Okaaay..."

"What if there were no Gorgon? I mean, if we weren't around to exploit, how would you make it to the top of the charts?"

"That's the—I already tried—there's no other way!"

Icarii peered at Mercurio like he was a very puzzling creature. "You really can't come up with a plan B?"

"I don't *want* a plan B! YOU are plan B! Vids are what I'm meant to do. If I can't do the ones I want, I don't know what the point is!"

Icarii's look softened. But he looked away when he said, "Be careful when you're feeling desperate, Lane Macoya. I myself was feeling *very* desperate when I got mixed up in the war."

A big group—big enough to be family, though they didn't smell or even look much alike—had appeared down the road and was passing them now. They were piled with snacks from Nibbles, and a few takeout bags to boot. Mercurio sniffed eagerly, trying to get a bead on where he could go later.

Then, from the back, or somewhere, someone screeched, then screamed, "MURDERER!"

Mercurio jumped, shocked at the venom in the accuser's voice.

Icarii just kept going. But once the family had gone past, he gave Mercurio a look. "See what I mean?"

"Doesn't it bother you? People calling you 'killer' and stuff like that?"

Icarii looked at him. "They're not wrong."

Mercurio couldn't make beaks or tails of that expression. But it was dramatic and perfect and—

He croaked in exasperation. "If you could just see yourself! You'd know exactly why I need to film you two!"

"And fattening your wallet would have nothing to do with it."

"Money wouldn't come out of your pockets."

"I suppose that's true. But—and correct me if I'm wrong—you seem to want to show a...softer side to the Gorgon. But we have an image to consider. Don't think portraying us as warm and fuzzy is doing us any favors."

"So you want people to meet you thinking, 'Here's that jackal who tied up that Plattman chick'?"

He scoffed again. "Not you, too."

"Hey, I don't care! She's annoying. But I'm just sayin'..." Mercurio trailed off.

Icarii stopped. "What exactly are you 'just saying', Lane Macoya?"

Mercurio's brain scrambled for a reply. Icarii's gaze bored into his the entire time.

"Just...that...if you...gotta manage an image...you gotta, you know, uh, step up to the tee. Actually *manage* it."

The answer hung in the air a moment. Then the tall man stopped staring at Mercurio and began walking again.

Thank you, Mother! With a scent like that, Mercurio was convinced (for a second, anyway) that Icarii was going to take a bite out of him.

They continued down the road without speaking.

Chatter dries up among the travelers who see the tall Gorgon stalking the road towards them, leaving the air bare save for the rustling of the jungle's leaves, the footsteps on the mucky rubberized road, and the scents of apprehension, the sweet general store, and—a normal human??!

NO!!! he wanted to scream. He ran ahead, the general store's sugary scent filling his head, but never fully expelling that vaguely familiar scent from the chapel.

It was true: over the next rise in the road, there stood one of the newsmen at the base of the stairs to Nibbles, holding out his mobi to every squab and square who passed by.

He was there—probably with the room—and Mercurio was here, leading the tall Gorgon right to him.

"Well, well, well," said Icarii, coming up behind him. "Isn't that your competition?"

27

GORGON

THE RUBBERIZED ROAD THAT made up this squargling street (which made Jerimin homesick for the running track at his old apartment) softened the sound of Lane Macoya suddenly galumphing ahead of him. The blue-headed loudmouth spun around, began talking and gesticulating wildly while walking backwards down the hill in front of him. Jerimin kept his eyes high.

The Netron World News Association crewman (from the insignia on his grey uniform) was busy showing his mobi around to any squargling nearby, but it'd only be a matter of time before some squargling caught wind of Jerimin's unmodded scent and pointed him out...Rivulets ran down his forehead from the newsman's close-cropped hair, and his clothes looked soaked through. *So, already been up to see my Queen.*

Every step Jerimin took made the hill's dark horizon drop lower, so that the blaring yellow general store rose into view like a nuclear sunrise. Yikes, that place was bright! Garish—but...he kind of liked it, too. Nothing back h—on Netron would dare be so loud.

Speaking of loud...

"Yeah—I know—listen," said Macoya, "If—if they got you the room, you gotta please give me back my equipment. It's my livelihood! My tutu's last gift to me! We—we can make some other deal, can't we? I could be your delivery wing! Gotta feed the missus, right?"

Jerimin kept advancing. If these reporters had gotten them the room, he wanted to be in it ASAP. "One thing at a time, Lane."

Finally, the auteur hopped aside, resumed scrabbling alongside Jerimin like a stubborn stray dog.

The jig was up: the newsman had spotted Jerimin, along with the dozens and dozens of squarglings picnicking on the sides of the road and the hill of the store. The closer Jerimin got, the straighter the man stood, and the tighter his fist clenched around the radioactive cherry umbrella at his side. On the one hand, Jerimin was taller and probably outweighed him. And he knew he was a fiercer and more experienced fighter. On the other hand, this guy's shoulders were broader than your usual workaday office drone's, and if he had any sense, he'd put that umbrella to use in a fight.

He was the first countryman (well, human countryman; Lyle was no doubt a Netron) Jerimin had seen since the war's end and he wasn't sure what the guy might try.

So he kept his senses sharp even as he walked past the sullen newsman to throw his wrappers in a nearby garbage bin. Then he turned around and genially approached the man, looking him right in the eyes.

Civil tone, civil tone. "Icarii-sir Jerimin, Gorgon of Hriana, Defender of the Realm of Hriana, Servant to Queen Jantessa Summersong of Everlush, how do you do."

The newsman seemed to gather up all his disgust and beamed it back into Jerimin's face.

A kitten could do better, but good effort, I guess.

"F—fine, thank you. Stevenson-sir, how do you do?"

Jerimin rolled his eyes. *Yep, already tired of this.* "Do you have a room for the Gorgon, or not?"

Jerimin had thrown the newsman off again. "Y—yes. At the Ho-oh-key-no—"

"Ho'okano," Jerimin corrected at the same time as Macoya, who'd been watching them both this whole time.

The man's mouth worked, annoyed; Jerimin fought back a grin. "Ho-oh-*kah*-no resi—"

"Good," said Jerimin.

The newsman jolted, visibly offended. That was one thing Jerimin didn't miss about Netron; if you interrupted a squargling, they didn't act like you'd just spit in their child's face.

"Let's go." Some of the squarglings around them were beginning to honk softly—they wanted them gone, and this was the first—and nicest—step in encouraging them to leave. But with so many seated in family groups it wouldn't be long, he was sure, before somebody got brave and decided to chase them out. Correction: chase *him* out.

He flicked a *get going* hand at the newsman, but the man said, "Wait. Your...the Gorgon...up at the chapel said to give this to you." He opened his coat and unshouldered an Osidern messenger bag—the pattern on it looked familiar, maybe it was Lase Likeke's?—and thrust it out at Jerimin like it was a dangerous creature he wanted off him as quickly as possible. So naturally, despite the honking escalating in his periphery, Jerimin took it from him slowly, deliberately. By the time he'd finally taken it out of his hands, the guy's jaw was clenched tighter than a stuck drawer.

Jerimin smiled at him.

A quick flip of the flap revealed Macoya's tech. He shut it quickly, hoping the little loudmouth hadn't gotten a whiff. Jerimin looked at the newsman. "Thank—"

"HEY!" Screamed by Macoya loud enough to turn every head on the hillside. "That's my stuff!"

The newsman jumped, seemed surprised to see the blue-headed square there. But then his gaze searched the square's chest.

"Is it? I didn't look inside."

"Yeah, yeah, it's my cams, it's my mem sticks! Show 'em, Lane!"

Jerimin slung the bag over his own chest and snugged it tight. Nice and out of reach. He gestured again to the newsman. "Let's go, shall we? Or do you like standing around looking like you just climbed out of a spittoon?"

The newsman shook himself—almost like he was coming awake—and, after a dirty look at Jerimin, started down the road towards Ho'okano's.

"But—" squawked the auteur.

"We can discuss it on the way, Lane Macoya."

"But—"

"GO."

The square hopped to, and now Jerimin could comfortably leave the area.

He tried to look at lots of things around him as he proceeded down the road. If either one of this traveling companions looked back at him, he wanted them to see an engaged predator alert to his surroundings, not a flagging man who (despite the earlier junk food binge) was fighting the urge to lie down and nap.

By his count, this would be the fifth time today he'd traversed over this particular rise: first, when he'd gone up to the motel to see the proprietress about Ho'okano's whereabouts. While he was there, he learned a vacancy had opened up—but the moment Jerimin mentioned having his Queen in there with him, the motelier had shot him down. Apparently they were very strict in these parts about segregation of the sexes, something he hadn't encountered before working with squarglings on Netron. Maybe it was a backwoods tradition? So unless a couples' room opened up (and that didn't seem likely, given the number of squargling groups glaring at him from every lanai in the place), they were out of luck.

The second trip had occurred after the purple motelier had refused him lunch (well, to be fair, she was refusing it to anyone not staying at the motel) and he'd legged it all the way back to the yellow general store; third, up the road again with motormouth Macoya to find a place to sit and eat; fourth, back again to see if Macoya could sniff out Ho'okano at the store. He was starting to wish he'd stayed back at the chapel.

The messenger bag swung gently against Jerimin's body, pressing in, pressing out, in rhythm to his footsteps, and that didn't help either. To keep himself awake, he started making a mental inventory of what was inside. He could remember the hovercameras and screen and memory sticks from the chapel—though he couldn't recall the exact number...he pictured Macoya at the faerie house while feeling the bag, trying to envision anything else the square had had...

THE SNACK BAR.

He'd undone the flap and wormed his arm into the pack before he remembered himself.

"Hey, Macoya."

The square had put a few yards' distance between them, but hurried back at Jerimin's call, like he'd been expecting to be summoned. The newsman, in the lead, turned to watch them. Macoya spotted the open flap on the bag and his blue nostrils flared. "Yeahyeah, *qué pasa?*"

"Do you have any more of those snack bars?"

Macoya's eyes dropped to the bag. "I...might."

"May I have them?"

"Uh..." There was a long pause. *Because he's somehow trying to wangle a deal out of me, or because my scent's got him flustered?*

The square's tail quit its dogged wagging. "Yeah, okay."

"Thanks."

"Do you want me to find you the pou—"

"Nope." *Nice try.*

Jerimin's hands went back to blindly feeling for the snacks. "Let's keep moving, shall we?"

The square *krekk-krekkd* in assent and galumphed away.

They kept moving.

It took some fumbling around, but soon he'd collected all the snack bars in the pouch among Macoya's equipment. The first one tasted great. The second one made him feel like his saliva had been replaced with glue. By the third and final one, he could feel the bars in his stomach melding together into a small wad of lead.

Ugh. The things I do for calories.

Hoping for a distraction from the way the equipment bag and the snack bar lump now collided against one another as he walked, he lifted his gaze again. Macoya had caught up with the newsman and was now talking with him.

The man—Stevenson-sir—glanced back at him.

It was the furtive look in his eye that snapped Jerimin's instincts awake.

The newsman turned away quickly. Now Macoya's wing was lifting, cutting off their faces from view.

Jerimin lengthened his stride until he was immediately behind the pair.

"Lane Macoya," he said brightly, and both newsman and squargling jumped like they'd been caught playing screen games in class.

"Keep walking. While we do, why don't you tell Stevenson-sir about your encounter with the jaguar today?"

Macoya smiled at the newsman, whose eyes had widened in alarm. He gestured with his tail, tamping the air down. What had they been planning?

"Oh, heh," said Macoya. "He wouldn't want to hear about that...It's really, uh, dull, when I—"

This little attention hog's refusing to tell his exciting escape from death to a perfect audience? He must *be planning something.*

"I didn't think so. Go on. It might be important for him to hear. Might save his life."

Macoya was all smiles now. "I—I really couldn't. Not my story tell, real—"

Jerimin put his hand on the squargling's shoulder. "Lane Macoya?"

"Yeah?"

Just a drop of steel.

"Tell him about the jaguar."

A drop was enough.

"Yes, sir!" Macoya faced the newsman, who, from the way his head swiveled about, wasn't sure if the bigger threat walked right behind him, or lay somewhere beyond the jungle grasses next to the road.

"So there I was, on the back roads of Crooked Neck, a jungle so dense with the scent of green that I could barely hold the scent of my local guide in my beak..."

Jerimin released the little weasel's shoulder. That should keep them both occupied. And hopefully he'd caught them before they'd gotten around to any real cahooting.

Cahooting? Well, it ought to be a word.

Being Gorgon was turning out to be more complicated than he'd expected. It seemed a powerful position, but little flubs like that made him feel so exposed, so vulnerable. He hadn't expected to feel this way.

229

And I suppose Crooked Neck's shown us one little inter-ruption in our supply—of food or privacy—could leave us dead in the water.

Or just plain dead.

The last Gorgon had made it look easy—everyone fell over themselves to keep that nasty granny happy. But then again, she'd been the royal boogeyman for over three centuries. Her reputation had done her intimidating for her.

They, on the other hand, had only been Gorgon three months. And all of it had been spent on a mission of penance—an idea the old Gorgon would have laughed out of the room, had anyone been brave enough to bring it up to her in the first place.

The penance made things so stupidly complicated: to Osider, they had to be like family—or approachable, at least. But to everyone else, they had to command fear and unquestioning obedience. But nosey parker Netrons like that girl and this pig-faced dullard ahead of him weren't falling into line. And that was a problem.

The more we're forced into cooperating with them, the weaker we look. And we can't afford to look weak.

He kept within earshot of his companions' conversation for the rest of the walk.

The Ho'okano estate looked like a heavenly sanctuary against the silver sky. The moon's discrete shape had vanished behind the solid dome of clouds but illuminated them like a flashlight behind a hanging sheet. The various edges of the house's roofline, banister, and lightning rod were all traced in silver, and now he could grasp the impressive size of the house in a way he hadn't when he'd first looked up at it in the pouring rain.

The clearer weather also let him enjoy the sweet smell of—what? Freesia? Jasmine? It was all heady and mixed up with the clean smell of rain—not that he was some floral expert anyway.

The sight, the smells, even the incessant *rakka-rakka* of the frogs hidden in the grass all served to help Jerimin forget about the heavy lump in his stomach that had been making the final leg of the journey one short step away from miserable. Now he was a mere block away from a blessed bed. Squargling bed, human bed, flower bed, what did he care? Someplace safe to go horizontal and unconscious. Done. That was all he wanted.

But first, the tiger-striped squargling—*Cortez*! his slowing mind supplied—was waiting at the gate. His head was bent over his mobi, and from the way the lights changed colors across his face, he was probably watching a movie.

To Jerimin's chagrin, Macoya raised his beak and cawed a loud Native greeting.

He had been hoping to...maybe not surprise, but make their presence known only after they'd gotten closer to him. Jerimin didn't like the self-satisfied look on the striped square's face as he watched them approach.

That loudmouth crow gave him too much time to study us.

Jerimin willed his feet to lift a little higher instead of drag, was careful to watch his step coming off the gentle hill of the street. Cortez didn't need to see him stumble. And when he got close enough, he met the brown squargling's gaze with one of his own, praying he couldn't tell how much effort Jerimin was putting into keeping his eyes actually focused. He could barely see straight.

I've got to sleep, I've got to sleep.

Cortez had his mobi lifted, frontside illumination strips turned on so it acted like a mini lamp. He looked them up and down.

He chirped a perfunctory-sounding greeting in Jerimin's direction, then turned his attention on Macoya. "*Mijo*, glad to see you. And surprised. You obviously didn't get your exclusive."

"I'm not your *mijo*. And thanks *so much* for helping me out."

Macoya's sarcasm made Jerimin do a double take at the auteur. *Guess Turtle Dessert has a talent for rubbing people the wrong way.*

"Helping you out didn't fill my purse. On the other hand, offering to drive this fellow"—he lifted a wing at the newsman—"back to my place earned me a twenty jen tip."

"Your team's staying with Cortez?" Jerimin asked the newsman in an undertone. He gave Jerimin a wary look, but eventually nodded.

Cortez cocked his head at Macoya. "You're staying, what, at the motel? For fifteen jen, you can ride along."

"No thanks," said Macoya flatly. "I still have business with—" Macoya jerked his thumb at Jerimin.

Cortez smiled nastily at Macoya. "Then I guess I better let you two in. The other Gorgon is waiting inside."

Jerimin's heart lifted. Macoya, on the other hand, made a strange series of strangled-sounding clicks.

Cortez shone the mobi overhead while he fiddled with the gate. It released with a smooth click; cloudlight raced along its edge as it swung open, the shine jade green.

Cortez gestured grandly down the gravel path leading up to the house.

"Your room awaits, O mighty one."

"Don't call me that," said Jerimin automatically. *But should I have let him?* On the other hand, he thought he had detected sarcasm.

UGH. I DON'T WANT TO THINK. I JUST WANT SOME SLEEP.

He stepped forward, gravel crunching beneath his boots. Macoya's footsteps joined his, and Cortez shut the gate behind them.

Ugh. Loudmouth's really coming with me. He should probably protest, or something, but the house was so close, his Queen was so close—they could deal with him inside, together, where they'd have two brains.

Hopefully she got a nap in. *I wonder how long she's been here.*

"Step this way, Lane Stevenson." Cortez had the umbrella-toting newsman bundled up in the back of his electric golf cart and humming up the road in seconds.

Jerimin trudged forward, head down, glad he didn't have the weight of his usual pack weighing him down. The gravel crunched double-time with Macoya's companion stride all the way up to the lanai. There, Macoya looked at a nearby wicker table. "Huh. Who put that back?"

A real paper note was stuck in the crack of the front door. Jerimin pulled it out. It was explained (in someone's tidy hand, not his wife's *nensha* etching) that, in the interest of expediting tomorrow's interview, the crew had set up in the front room of the house, and, in the interest of "preserving set integrity" were keeping the front door locked. A carefully drawn diagram and arrow indicated a back door off another bird-foot branch he was supposed to enter.

Oh, and he was to be up and ready for makeup at four AM.

Jerimin crushed the paper in his hand. He growled. "If they think..." *I'm going to interrupt my sleep so they can slander me in time for the evening news, they've got another thing coming,* he started to say, but the sight of Macoya watching him keenly made him go silent.

"Come on. We have to go in a back way." Jerimin gestured him ahead. They turned and proceeded down the lanai, which hugged the house's perimeter, followed its angles till they got to a comfortable-looking back porch, complete with glider swing and ash trays on tables, and a slate-blue painted door leading inside. It would have been very inviting in other, non-brain-fried circumstances. Jerimin tried the handle and the door swung easily open.

"After you, Lane."

When the square just stared down the already-lit hall (*yes, you will have the Gorgon behind you and in front of you. Didn't think of that when ol' Turtle Dessert shut the gate behind you, did you?*), Jerimin put his hand on his green shoulder and started walking. The squargling croaked in surprise, but got with the program.

Paintings and doors passed by on the walls, but Jerimin was too tired to be curious. His initial thought was to look for a light beneath one of the doors, but no, even if she weren't sleeping (*and why wouldn't she be???*) she didn't need light to see.

So he called and sent, "Dearest, I'm here, where are you?" *I brought dinner,* he was tempted to joke, but Macoya had already begun crackling to himself, sounding like a nervous Geiger counter.

His sing-song was rewarded by her messy-haired head poking out of a room a dozen doors down. Her bright expression quickly dropped into a bored cat stare upon spotting their blue-headed guest, but cheer rushed to Jerimin's heart anyway. He grinned and pushed Macoya a little faster. The squarglings' soft crackles turned to loudening (she had a better word for that, but she was still keeping their connection closed) croaks that sounded on the verge of hysterics.

He reached her. She kept in the doorway, let him put the crackling Macoya between them. Her expression did not change. He jabbed at the lines in his head, but nothing.

"The Mercurio," she said.

At his name, the square went dead silent.

She looked at Jerimin. "What is this one for, then?"

"He wants to make a new deal for his things." He patted the equipment bag against his belly.

She now addressed the square. "You failed the last deal. What do you offer us now for your things?"

The square's wings were shivering now. Uncontrollably, it looked like.

Was it their scents? It must be. In other circumstances, Jerimin might have laughed. Or he might have had an encouraging word for the square. But right now, he just wanted him *out of here*.

He shook the auteur by one shoulder. "Answer!" he hissed.

The square's beak worked almost as quickly as his shivering, closing with distinctive clicks—but no sound came out.

His eyes met his Queen's over the square's head. *Please*, he tried to tell her with his face. *Get rid of him, I WANT TO GO TO SLEEP!*

Her gaze dropped back to the square's. She reached out. With a squeeze of her hand, she shut his clattering beak. Macoya's colors found another shade of pale.

"No deal, no equipment. Goodbye."

She released the squargling's beak, and Jerimin wasted no time pushing him back down the hall from whence they came. Macoya stumbled along until they came alongside the superlong panoramic paintings just before the door to the outside. Then the dumb cluck tried digging in his heels.

"NO," Jerimin snapped. He dug his fingers as tightly as they'd go into Macoya's shoulder and changed his push into a haul. He turned the door handle with his free hand, but used Macoya's face to bash the door open the rest of the way before jettisoning the warbling auteur off the porch. Jerimin pulled the door shut quickly and threw the bolts, locking it.

Good riddance!

The deed done, he found he couldn't keep upright any longer. He slumped back down the hall (had it always been this long?) to his Queen's side, bent double. Was he really shaking? From exhaustion, like some poor overworked beast. He found her neck, nuzzled into it for comfort, and she bore him onto the bed inside. Maybe three-quarters of him fit on it, lying diagonally, but right now he didn't care one iota. Sleep was claiming him, pulling him under. He couldn't open his eyes, only felt her warm hands prising under the strap of the sling bag he still wore. He curled himself upward (eyes still weighted shut) in an attempt to help her wriggle it off him. His belly felt immediately cooler, and freer, when she finally lifted it off. He heard it being lowered to the floor on one side of the bed, a soft sound. She worked off his boots, and those clunked to the ground, too. Then he felt the warmth of her curling up against his side. Knowing where she was, he could finally release the final concern keeping him tethered to wakefulness.

He let go.

His brain drifted lower, into soft darkness...

Almost gone...

Almost...

Al...

...most...

.........gone.

...

...

KWAWWWNK!!!!!

Rage at this, the most abominable—no, hideous—no, *obnox-ious* noise ever heard by human ears, worse than any alarm clock or smoke detector, ripped through his system, popping his eyes open, rigoring his arms straight, throwing him out of the insufficiently long bed and launching him at the wood-shuttered window, where the sound—and now, a stream of cacophonous *BLATTS* and *WHU-WHUUPS* and parrot deathbed screams—was issuing from.

He tore the wooden slats open to see Macoya standing outside the window on the lanai. The scent-fear-stupor was gone from his eyes, and replaced with a sort of suicidal determination as he blared the calls into the window, a living megaphone Jerimin now wanted to kick the living shit out of.

Macoya looked Jerimin straight in the eye. And began emitting chalkboard squeals, even louder than before.

The next thing Jerimin knew, he found the shutters exploded open, the window raised, and the bag of video equipment crushed in his grip.

He pivoted like a champion discus thrower, and hurled Macoya's equipment directly at that screeching blue face. He heard a violent thud, a squawk, then a crash, but didn't bother looking upon his handiwork.

"CHOKE ON IT!" he screamed, and then the Gorgon of Hriana slammed the window shut.

28

KEONAONA

THE PLANTER-LINED PATH UP to Ria's shop was empty when Keonaona finally arrived, and all the glass front dark. Rose and pansy scents hung invisibly in dreamy clouds above their planters where the florist had stuck them, mixing Osidern favorites with off-world novelties to create enticing new perfumes. Keonaona strode through them all to go around to the basement entrance around back; a path that was wide, but screened from most approaches with tall grass, deliberately placed. Keonaona found the basement door, pushed it open, and descended the stairs, footsteps echoing, gripping the banister more tightly than he'd ever gripped anything before. Overhead, the sky rumbled, but the sound disappeared almost completely when the door finally shut behind him.

Only a dim light at the bottom lit the way now. It pulled Keonaona forward with an awful promise.

Ria, like her foremothers, was a florist, and when she came into ownership of this shop, she'd come to realize funerals made up the majority of her business in this village that was dying. Since the nearest funeral parlor was in 'Ehuana City, she'd gotten the license, and equipment, and could, from then on, store the bodies of Crooked Neck's dead next to the hibiscus and lilies that sold to husbands wanting to please their wives.

Could. But didn't always.

Now was not one of those times.

Flower leis, bouquets, and greenery stood like props in their glass-fronted refrigerated cases. Not many—one wall was almost entirely covered now in silk flowers, the first concession Ria's family had had to make as sales died.

But on the cold concrete wall deepest into the hill, next to the cold flower cases, there were four drawers, painted white except for their solid steel handles.

Yellow ribbons had been tied to two of them.

Keonaona saw them, stopped, took a breath, feeling like he might be dizzy. But he wasn't. He couldn't put a name to the strange feeling he felt: edginess that made him want to flee; a sort of...floaty apathy that kept him rooted to the base of the stairs; and an underlying dread of dread—a fear of the fear that something terrible was surely about to happen, but with zero evidence of the catastrophe's arrival.

They'd come in early while the river was still low. Ria had brought them here when she'd been told of it—she was the one the docks knew to call. And then she had messaged him, only he'd missed it because his mobi was off...

He'd left them waiting for him all day.

Keonaona stood in a stupor. He didn't think any thoughts for a while. Only stared at the drawers with the ribbons.

Imperceptibly slowly, his wings hugged around him against the chill.

Finally, he took the first step forward.

Once taken, he found there was no stopping.

Maybe that's why I hesitated so long, he thought as his body moved him towards the drawers like a twig on the current.

Here. The handles, right at hand. Drawers white like stones against the darker wall, like clean headstones revealed by rain.

A humming had grown louder in Keonaona's ears as he'd approached. He thought it was his madness—something only between his ears—until his palm brushed the icy handle of the drawer. Then he knew it was only the refrigeration units, thrumming in the walls and now up into his hand.

He closed his eyes.

Gently, he tugged the drawer loose.

Don't be Kai. Don't be Kai.

But of course, it was.

Even under the green sheet embroidered to look like woven leaves (*because the old ways are the only ways*, he thought nonsensically), he knew from size and scent it was his egg.

He stood another long while, fixed on the shadows and valleys his son's form made beneath the sheet.

He could shut the drawer again. Would that be best? What he saw could not be unseen. Of course he had identified him after the accident, but that had been at a distance. Here...

It'd be like tucking him into bed.

"He's not sleeping, though," said Keonaona aloud, though to his own ears it sounded slurred, unintelligible, like speaking through banana mash.

Maybe just a little.

His hand shook, but he managed to pinch the leaf-shroud between two fingers and pull just an inch of it back.

The familiar shape of his son's brilliant mint-blue comb was revealed.

This is real. It really happened. This isn't a bad dream.

Inexpressible horror grew out of the pit of Keonaona's throat, suffocated his body, obliterated his sight once more. His insides were screaming, splitting his closed-up throat, the scream beating against his bones *he did not want this to be real, someone come down and FIX IT*

but he blindly, silently, replaced the shroud, so that the offense was covered. As long as he couldn't see it, it couldn't be true. See?

His sight returned.

The screaming in his body subsided. He slid the drawer shut and stepped up to the next one. Hana's drawer.

This, he couldn't turn a blind eye to. They'd been through too much together. Barren nests. Dead eggs and dead parents. Why, they'd even hosted their parents' viewings, right there at the house. So many in Crooked Neck had known Hana's mother—she had been a school teacher...everyone had come, there had been food enough to make the tables creak...Of course Hana had missed her, but her mother had lived the long life of a turtle, so it was also a happy time...The most upsetting thing for Hana had been the blue tablecloths, but a mix-up at the laundry meant they'd had to make do—

He could see Hana shaking her head, eyes sad even while she smiled. *"Mama hated this shade blue—she'd come crawling out of that coffin if she knew..."*

When he came to from the reverie, he found himself swaying on his feet. Odd, to escape this with a memory of a funeral, of all things. But the house had been so warm, so lively! It wouldn't be like Hana's funeral.

So stupid.

Hana, you idiot, you gecko-brain.

No. He should blame himself. He shouldn't have split them up. Should have brought them all home.

Well, we're together now.

He pulled the drawer open, lifted the shroud.

Smells like they touched up her dye. Her greens look as iridescent as the day she got them done.

He laid his palm against the side of her face. It was cold and soft as orange pith.

Ipo. Sweetheart.

Something broke in him.

The cold in Hana unfurled its way up his palm, like a green shoot growing, only this was icy. It was numbing. It unfurled broad sheets of cold into his arm, then into his chest, put down roots in his legs and feet, raised limbs and branches into his head.

We aren't together. They are together. I am alone.

He removed his hand, stared at her face, beautiful like a statue's.

I am alone.

He shut the drawer.

I am alone.

He turned, faced the concrete corner a while. Then he turned some more, crossed the basement to the stair. He switched off the lights. Then he started up the stairwell, to where the lightning flashed beneath the cracks in the door.

I am alone. I can't go on alone.

I can't say goodbye.

I won't say goodbye.

I'll say hello, instead. At the river.

Keonaona opened the door and stepped out into the night.

29

GORGON

SHE LAY PRESSED AGAINST the bony side of her snoring Jerimin, staring up at (but not through) the ceiling. She had
already drawn her eyes along the dark room, taking in the
book-shapes cuddled on the shelf together (though the titles
were beyond the reach of her veil sight) across from the bed,
the claw-carved nightstands sentineling the bed-for-hu-
manoid-shapes on either side of them...Pity the misfit table
in here (just to the side of the sleepy window, which had
gotten a shock so great when her Jerimin threw it open, it had
almost shattered in surprise) was the wrong height to move
to the end of this bed. The way his legs dangled off awakened
soreness and strain in her own...borrowed pain for phantom
legs.

She was glad she had received enough meat cans to return
into her human shape, and gladder still when the storm had
abated enough that Married Supervision could transport her
down here in her little cart. Though she could have done
without Married Supervision making her crawl into a mail
sack for the trip.

The chapel spirits had laughed her to scorn—but between
the sack and the back roads Married Supervision had taken,
she had traveled to the estate unnoticed, unharrassed, and
she grudgingly decided to stop imagining what that idiot
mayor's body might feel like were she to grate him against
the nearest rough stone.

She sighed. She was discomfortable again; she flipped herself
for the tenth time that night. Entirely unheard of—her instincts
could keep her motionless for the ambush for hours at a time,
with no discomfort noticed. *Must be from you*, she thought,

looking at her husband. But if her eating his tossing and turning left him in a deeper sleep, she would gladly sup it all.

After the final prodding of her Jerimin by the Mercurio, her Jerimin had nearly been foaming, pacing the room while damnations and sadistic (she would say Gorgon-worthy) threats erupted forth out of his mouth in a weird (and, beneath other circumstances, BREATHCHOKINGLY HILARIOUS) mix of Standard, squargling language (both the spoken and the squawks), and guttural Earth language. She was talking language changes midsentence, sometimes mid*word.*

But she had needed him catatonic, not volcanic, so when he failed to come down on his own, she mustered up power enough to send him to sleep (after standing upon the bed and administering a firm whack on the forehead to set the power in motion, of course). He'd fallen into the bed like a puppet with strings sliced and hadn't moved since, save for the rise and fall of his chest.

Would that she could do the same. But she could not cross into sleep; the bridge was barred for some reason, had been for hours now.

She turned the other way on the bed. The sentinel night-stands held lamps. If she clicked one on, it would not work right away—her *nensha* ensured that—but some smaller electrics could come back alive a while after she had touched them. And with some light, she could read one of those books on the shelf...

"*Ko, ko.*" A muffled voice outside the door. Coming from the house. *Not* the Mercurio. She turned and looked at—but not through—it. The canned meat had helped, but keeping her perception narrowed was wisest, for now.

"*Ko, ko,*" came the soft call again. A child, it sounded like a child. She pushed herself upright a little more.

"Um...that means, could you please open the door?"

Oh. She supposed she could do that.

She caressed her Jerimin's hair (no response, only unbroken snoring), and then pushed herself off the bed. Her bare feet made sticky sounds when she passed over the underbed rug and onto the wooden floor in front of the door.

She pulled it open, leaned forward into the gap.

Here stood a squargling—smaller than her, though not by much—wreathed in fiery coppergolds and blues like the ocean's truth (she could not trust the ocean, of course, but it still told its own truths, nevertheless). She could think of artisans, both Orlock and faerie, who, upon seeing this one, would want to render him in their arts over and over and over again.

"Aloha," he said, after a soft, nervous bird-stutter. "My name's Kaimana. My mama wanted me to show you a few things to make your stay more comfortable."

He seemed a decent child. Forthright, not one who would snicker behind his hand at her later. And unafraid. A pleasant change.

He backed away to give her room as she stepped out of the door. She wanted to silence the door's shuttingclicks with her power, but since she had none to spare for such a frivolity, she turned back and pulled the whole apparatus shut as though it were made of glass.

There. Sleep on, my love.

She readjusted her cloak, then nodded for the...squab? to lead on.

She followed his gloriously *ombréd* wings through the hall and down two turns. The floor switched from the wood to a sort of gelled? plastic?? (she reached for her Jerimin's mind to find a better word, but halted herself, in case the intrusion would wake him) rug with tendrils which, though foreign, was not unpleasant on her feet. It squelched squeakily as they both walked on it.

Strongly fire-directioned. But not plastic. What could it be?

The young square stopped in front of a white double door, made of slats on both sides. She wanted to lean forward to peer through—how ridiculous a one like her looked when conserving her perception!

He gestured to the two pull knobs at the front.

"If you'll pull these, you can pick out your towels for morning, and any extra blankets. Please!"

She took the two smooth knobs in hand (odd they weren't faceted crystal, like at Everlush, but this was a house, not a palace) and tugged.

So it wasn't a room, but a linen closet, shallow-backed. Soft, poufy things stacked, sleepypurring and content, like litters of animal young. They had been sorted by type, then color. A few types she recognized—her Jerimin, ever meticulous, had gathered such things for use at the last two towns they'd worked at. Normally this task would belong to him alone (she had, after all, been queen, and he, not) but she wanted him to rest long...and to be pleased with her when he did arise, and see the good thing she had done.

So she pulled familiar things into her arms by twos—washrags, hand towels...no, no need for blankets, there were two quilts in a hinged trunk in the room—

"Do you keep..." The picture came clearly to her head, but the unfamiliar word was slippery. She'd have to settle. "Towels for bathingdrying that are overbig? Oversized? Very big."

"You mean bath sheets?"

The word snapped into place like a bone to its socket. She nodded.

He looked to the sides of the closest, seeming to search for something. Then his tail wrapped around his ankle. "They're on the top shelf." He rose on tiptoe and pointed; a ledge far beyond them both. "Sorry, I guess our grabber got moved."

"You kee—have them. That is good. I'll have the Gorgon retrieve them in the morning." *Or whenever he wakes up.*

The squab chirruped, a puzzled-cat sound. "The Gorgon? I thought you were the Gorgon, Lase."

"I am. And he is. Take us back, I do not care to carry these all night."

"Yes, Lase." And he led the way, but now he skipped sideways to talk to her and lead her at the same time. "But isn't he your husband?"

"Mmhmm." Gelly-tendrilled floor, again, *squelch-squelch.*

"Then why don't you call him that?"

She had to think a while. The explanation was a thing she knew, but had never put into words for anyone else. No one had ever asked.

They were back on the venerable wood floor and were coming up on the first turn when she answered.

245

"If the Osidern president marries, what is his wife?"

The squab answered promptly, like he was in school. "The first lady."

"Yes. Holding that title, can she recommend a Warmother to the Mothers in Council?"

"No."

"Lead an ousting vote against a corrupt governor?"

"No."

"Sign a bill in his stead?"

"No!"

They took the next turn. She remained silent, giving him time to digest her words.

"Yes, she said, "Because she is only his wife. But my Jerimin is not only my husband. He is fully the Gorgon, as much as I am. He is authorized to do all the things I can, for the protection of the realm of Hriana, and he takes—claims—the same protections that come with the title. Idothink if I named him to others 'my husband', they would think him 'only' the Gorgon's husband, without any power, which is a false thing."

"Oh! But—"

"Now, quiet." They had reached the hall where their room was. She crept to their door silently, then deposited the towels inside before closing the door again.

Her guide stood where she had silenced him, watching her, a brilliant statue in the stately hall. She returned to him.

"You were asking?"

"Do you miss not calling him your husband?"

"Idocall him that. Just not to others. He knows what he is. Now, is there a thing I can eat?"

He brightened, wings flapping. She glanced above his head, but the color of cheer was still missing. Yes, food was needed.

"Right this way." He did an about-face. She followed.

I eat gladness someone found a way for us to den here. Yes, the koa wood details in the nooks and crannies were carved expertly, the linens sumptuous, and the place settled but spotless. But for her, it was the actual space that brought her contentment—or at least the feeling, the expectation, that she could, if given time, really REST here. The narrow hallways with ceilings that were high enough for her Jerimin, but not too high, connecting greater, opener spaces like the parlor (where the soon-to-be disappointed news crew had set up their umbrella lights and flimsy backdrops) while cozier chambers lingered in the crisscrossing byways...Why, that alone reminded her of her burrow. And that it was a wooden, aboveground almost-burrow somehow only served to make it more pleasing. Like...

Her mindfingers itched to pluck the precise word from her Jerimin's mind. But she had seen him when she was planting the linens, and he had been sleeping so gently, like their old rabbit.

Like its differentness is here to delight me, not to irritate or intimidate me. She would not mind visiting more places like this; but from where they had stayed in the past towns, she did not think it was likely. The tent, the lodge, the inn—they kept differences that served only to carve the fact into their souls that they *were not in home.* For him, soap dishes and showerheads placed too low (if a rain-bath even stood there for him) twisted the knife; for her, the damn unending damp that sapped her power, day and night, even ruining the heat, when she used to bake herself in the dry sun that sheltered the Clatterdowns...But on this planet, the heat was no good, the chill was no good, all because of the wet in the air.

Her guide had stopped ahead of her, and was looking back, shy-shouldered, but an eager shine to his eye.

When she caught up to him, he pointed to a picture shining out of a digital frame. After whistling a cheerful arpeggio, he said, "This is my family."

Showing them off? She looked, to perform manners.

"There's Mama, Papa, and me," he said, pointing to a penny-and-felt-colored squargling hen, a golden-combed square (whose body color was something like pigeon's blood red, perhaps pinker), and himself, looking, she thought, younger than he stood now.

Making sure her electric-killing hands were tucked close to her, she leaned forward to study the father. Yes, this shape matched the one cowering behind the window the night they'd arrived. The one that had refused them.

That one didn't match this image, a happy, proud patriarch.

"Where is your mother?"

"Oh." A frazzled garble escaped the squab. "She's out looking for Papa. That's why she had me come look after you."

She let the mother hen in the frame fill her eyes, resisting the urge to open the eye of her perception further; a still image, there would be nothing—no...essence...of the hen for her to perceive, no matter how deeply she searched it. The most she could say? The hen was conscientious, she supposed, to make sure her offspring fulfilled a duty in her absence.

Her human stomach growled. The picture was of no importance.

She stood upright, and the son piped buoyantly before leading her onward into the kitchen.

A mug of something—an almost full mug of something—stood next to a plate of what looked like thick-sliced, rough-topped bread turned to crackers.

She picked one up, cracked a piece separate with her flat teeth, and held it in her mouth a moment. It was not sweet. A true surprise on this planet, where everything seemed a sugar-fruit or syrup. She could eat it safely.

The way the rest of the thumb-thick crackers broke brittle and dry against her teeth careened her back to the attic. When *she* did not keep any victims for her to eat, rough crackers like these, *tagein, tagaus*, were the only food given.

She gutted them all down, then looked up.

Her guide stood in the center of the stage-lit cooking arena, beaming at her from in front of two stainless steel fridges, like a banker proud of his vaults.

"We ordered lots of food special for you to eat, Lase! Things like macaroni *au gratin*, pita wraps, pizza...um..."

She began salivating. *Finally*.

The squab went on. "It's all heat-and-eat. Grab anything you want from inside." Both arm and wing lifted, presenting the refrigerators.

Her teeth chattered, cat-eager. "Open it. Bring it all out."

The squab's countenance faltered—his wings dipped briefly—then he recovered himself. "You can make yourself at home, Lase. Please don't feel—"

"You will open it for me."

Fluttering squeaks came out of the squab, like a rat struggling in her grip. His hands clambered over themselves as he asked, "I—why can't you do it?"

"Why can't you?" she shot back, and then, in a flash of insight, she looked at his feet. In the bright lights of the kitchen, the squargling son cast no shadow.

She swore. Loudly. "You're a spirit!"

He nodded, head turtled back into his wings.

She growled to herself. If her Jerimin had been awake, he would have told her she was speaking to things mortal eyes could not see, but since he wasn't—

She stopped at the nervous chatter of the squab. He was watching her the way a mouse watches a cat, all alarm-eyed and still.

"Do you keep fear of me?"

He nodded.

She considered him. He had not played a trick on her. And he had been polite. "Don't be," she said.

She went as close as she dared to one of the refrigerators and began examining its front. If the doors had handles like loops, she could make her own safe door-opening tail to pull with a dish towel—thread the thing through the loop, pull the ends, and *heissa hopsasa!*, an opened coldbox. But these were not built like that. No, they were straights-with-angles that made a ledge or a corner a one could claw her fingers around and tug.

Her stomach muttered. *So close.* Well, it would be good news for her Jerimin when he woke up.

"Youdoknow if you keep mashed potatoes in there, hm? Were they bought?" She would have looked herself with her veil sight if she weren't so worried about conserving her power.

He shrugged. "Sorry, Lase, I don't know. Papa and Auntie Lani took care of that stuff."

Yes, he was just a child, after all. Only some responsibility was fed him.

"Why?" he asked.

"No reason."

"Oh. Sorry I can't help." He ended with a cellophane crackle.

She turned away from the fridge. "It is not your fault. You will show me the pantry, yes?"

Relief opened his body up like a flower; the petals of his wings spread, confident again. "Yes, Lase, over here."

She followed him to a closet behind the refrigerators. She opened the door while the son watched. Unlike the other parts of the house, which had been walked through by the filmers, the lights inside were off. Her human eyes only turned the light behind her into shadow shapes. But this ate much importance, so she opened her perception just a bit, until veil lights outlined the contents of the food closet in twinkling blue. Mostly there were glass jars (with labels useless to her, just like the words in and on books. She could open her perception wider to sense past the glass and into their contents, but she would leave that her last option), crinkly bags, hand-sized cans...she recognized a rounded-rectangular cardboard box of shelf-stable milk, metallic tubes of mustard, and a double row of tea packets standing at attention in a paper tea box. Its lid was folded upon, but none of the tea was missing; the packets were a full complement, no gaps.

Without thinking, she sharpened her perception on it. It held the character of being new here, unusual, and...antsiness. A thing bought in anticipation?

"Does your family drink tea?" she asked.

"No, Lase. Papa bought it for your husband. Jubal-or-ange-raspberry. He let me open the box early—it's kind of neat, like these paper models I like to do. The back folds into a stand that helps prop all the little packets up—but it's round, like a bubble, see?"

"Mmm." So it was bought for them. Simply from the fee-lessencevibe of them...they were to be honored guests. So why reject them in the storm?

"Will he like it?" asked the squab.

Feeling a note of strain, she relaxed her perception. "*Ja*, very much." She pulled the milk, a small plastic jar, and a few promising boxes. These she carried out onto the cracker table. The light revealed unsweetened peanut butter (in a jar that was not even a quarter of the size of the ones her Jerimin bought at

Netron grocery stores, back before they were Gorgon), saltine crackers (she slid it behind her where her eyes didn't have to touch them), and "Cosmic Chew fruit snacks", which she simply set aside. She unscrewed the cap from the top of the milk—actually coconut milk, but unsweetened, and so, safe—box and began drinking. The milk was half gone when the squab gave a strangled peep. "That's for a curry for you one night, please don't—"

She slapped the empty carton on the table.

"...drink it all!" he finished, the words sighed in astonishment.

"I need it now," she said. She licked the cream off her lip.

"Well...if Mama gets mad...!"

"You will blame me. It is only right."

Gurgle-murmur. The squab, bouncing on his toes, gestured behind her. She didn't look. "You can have any of the fruit in the bowls around the house. Like this—oh. Papa left this one empty. That's funny."

Her Jerimin had told her about those. Fruit left out for guests, to be freely taken. Never did anyone here leave cheese out for her to take!

"Idothank you, but I cannot eat sweet fruits."

"Why not?"

"Allergies." Unaccurate, but an easy answer all understood. Her Jerimin had given her the word.

"Oh. Okay."

She unscrewed the tiny peanut butter lid. She reached in with her fingers, scooped out three-quarters of the jar, began licking it off.

"That was also for curry. Um! We have spoons. Over here!" he skipped over to a drawer he could no longer open.

She cleaned her stickied mouth enough to say, "In a moment." A spoon would help her get whatever she couldn't reach at the bottom. Already she felt a little better, less edgy and thin, though she knew if she used her power the new usual way, she would burn through it within minutes. But this snack should carry her over until her Jerimin awoke.

She got up and went to the drawer.

251

When the jar had been cleaned out, she tossed the spoon into it with a loud *clunk* and settled into her chair. She turned to the squab, who had watched her eat with goggling eyes.

"Is there anything else youdowish to show me?" The spirits the alive squarglings wished to goodbye had to be called by her—most accepted their deaths, were occupied in Heaven. With what, she did not know, and she felt it safest not to ask. So most spirits did not linger around the earthly plane unless they had business unfinished. This one was quite young to be dead...and if he was following his mother's orders, she must stand on that side of the veil as well. But the father-one not? Interesting...

"I could show you the television," he said. "I helped figure out how to get it to work with just one remote."

"Show the—show my husband later." Young and dead; a Gorgon's imagestationstatus bore no importance to him. "I can make you visible to him."

"That's what Mama and Papa told me, after we took the assignment. You'd be coming here and making ghosts alive again so their families could say goodbye."

"Not alive again. Only like-alive."

"Will you please make us like-alive so we can say goodbye to Papa? Please, Lase Gorgon?"

There.

She saw the clayen chapel again, the lunch-delivering hen asking to pay for non-war goodbyes with no hurt, no anger in her bearing. That was the missing piece, the lie whose presence gnawed at her Jerimin: the hen did not ask the boon for herself.

The host's son was still watching her.

"Idothink...that is a decision for your father-one."

He nodded, looked down, scratched some invisible stain off his lavalava. "Yeah. I guess we wouldn't wanna—"

An incredible BOOM interrupted, a thunderdrum that shook the house. She was working on ungritting her teeth when the son perked up and twittered. "Mama!"

She whipped around. It was the same copper-and-malachite hen as in the picture—only, the memory of water sheened her hide, and her cheek fur was wet and clambering against her face.

The spirit hen's eyes met hers. Desperate weight was in them. *A burden now to be unloaded onto me.*

"You have to help! You can see me, right?!"

A nod.

"My husband isn't in his daylight mind, he isn't thinking straight, he's...he's—"

The squab was at his mother's side. "Mama?"

His mother's wing curled over him; he snuggled close.

She did not delight in this new obligationweightduty being tossed onto her—especially not with her power so thin, a gruel—but their wide-eyed, panting alarm did not infect her. Instead, she felt the calmth of inevitability rejoin her. Aiding spirits, even when inconvenient, was an action as natural to her as waiting for prey. "How shall I help?"

The hen's eyes bulged. "Find him—bring him back!"

Thunder slammed into the roof again. The son twittered in alarm. His mother encircled him entirely in her wings and looked at her. Silent fears screamed through the mother's eyes, terrible thoughts she did not want her young to hear.

She rose from the table. "Be calm. I will wake the Gorgon."

30

MERCURIO

"Hur-ryyy...! C'mon, c'mon, you crippled snail!"

Mercurio urged the progress bar on his upload to fill. All he could smell was rain. The thunder was crashing above his head loud enough to make the wood of Ho'okano's lanai creak. He'd even glimpsed some yard furniture tumbling through the yard, but he ignored it. He had his wings curled around the screen to keep the gust-propelled rain out, but the sooner this Plattman reaction vid finished uploading, the sooner he could leg it back to the Canopy Motel, and a sleeping mat. The connection just had to hold out a few seconds more...

Mercurio's tail tip twitched as the final few percentages ticked up. *98%...99%...100%! Upload complete!*

He shut the screen down immediately and slid it into his chest pouch. Too bad he didn't have that *serape* to tuck in over it, but the flap would have to do.

BOOM!

Mercurio swallowed a shriek. Sure, he'd come around back to an entirely separate branch of the house, but he didn't want to risk ANY chance of the Gorgon finding him, not after getting walloped with his own stuff.

For the umpteenth time, Mercurio pushed away the niggling worry that a rib of his might be cracked. He'd just breathe a little less deeply for a while. Take it easy on the road back.

He pushed himself to his feet, staggering a little when unexpected pain shot through his chest and on the underside of the arm that was doing the pushing.

Nope, just ignore it.

He bent over and picked up the bag his equipment had bombed him in. He checked inside, where his cams gently clacked against one another like oversized billiard balls. Angel, Wideshot, and MaxCam were all still functioning (they'd been the first thing he'd checked—after fleeing from the unholy rant-ing had erupted from the room Icarii was still in—he was just glad the gangly monster hadn't crawled out the window after the bag and torn him apart.), but the vid of the séance disaster—and everything else he'd filmed since he got here—had somehow gotten deleted off his storage, and his Set-N-Forget hadn't been scheduled to run till after the deletion. No backup. No hope.

Stupid trip! What a waste. It was time to cut his losses and go home.

Aside from the chapel footage, all his stuff had been returned to him, including his Canopy breakfast card. After breakfast, he'd be on the first ride out of here—

Lightning flickered, then three bursts of thunder exploded overhead, one after the other, *bumbumBUMM!!*

—or at least in line for the first ride out. So long, Loserville!

Mercurio stared into the bag. Maybe he should put the screen in, too? The bag'd do a better job of keeping it dry, he bet, and if he kept it in its pouch, he didn't *think* the rolling cams could ruin the display any...Yeah. That made sense...

One shoulder strap shrugged off easy-breezy, but when he rolled his other shoulder back to finish the job, he shrieked in pain.

He clapped his beak shut immediately and froze. The Gor-gons wouldn't hear that over the storm, would they? It was loud enough, right?

Time to get out of here. His screen'd have to stay on his chest.

Gingerly, he reached across himself to put the first strap back over his shoulder. He was just scooching it back into place when, through the pelting rain, he heard the familiar rattle-squeak of a screen door opening behind him. He froze again.

The netherworldly stink of the tall Gorgon flooded Mercu-rio's beak.

"Macoya."

He raised his hands—*OW!* He raised one hand high in the air, and the other as far as his injury would let him and turned around. Yep, there was Icarii, leaning out the door, eyes planted on him. Nowhere to hide.

I guess I could run. But with those stilts for legs he'd be on me quick as a stoat.

"I can ex—"

Icarii crooked his finger twice, beckoning.

"Come inside. We need you."

Need me??

But you didn't argue with the scent of a madman. Mercurio marched forth like a prisoner, leaving his camera bag behind him on the lanai floor. At least they'd stay dry.

Icarii gestured him in first. He didn't seem rabid anymore—

Wow. This place was *swanky*. And smelled—not delicious, exactly, but how else was he supposed to describe it when a bargeful of rich wood soaked in multiple generations of wings who all had had scents as delectable as ol' Red's?

Man, these guys must've murdered at the mating grounds! Probably got any hen they wanted!

So overwhelming and relaxing was this house scent that Mercurio almost missed seeing the big Gorgon seated at the kitchen table, a human woman now with hair black as night. Her desert-decay scent was entirely muted in this form. Empty jars and boxes fanned out from where she sat—a quick whiff said they'd all had food in them until recently. A gold block of cheese was in her hand, the corner of it bitten off like a candy bar.

"You can put your hands down, Macoya."

Mercurio lowered his hands. Icarii went to the far side of the table and bent over, messing with something metal, from the smell of it. Then he picked it up and Mercurio saw it was a gun. Icarii turned away from them both and aimed it at a corner. *Clllick...clllick...clllick*, went the trigger, but nothing happened. Laser wasn't on.

Mercurio gulped. He looked *experienced* at pulling that trigger.

"Your beak is needed, Mercurio," said the big Gorgon at the table.

Mercurio twittered. "Who, me?"

"Ho'okano is out in the storm. You will track him alongside the Gorgon"—Icarii lifted his head briefly—"and return him here."

Mercurio cawed, outraged. "Why do you care if he's out there? You got your room, I got no vid of ya, can't you just leave me alone??"

"We cannot. We have been asked to find him—"

"By who? Nobody's out here!"

The Gorgons exchanged looks. Then she twisted in her chair and kind of...jabbed her head towards the hall leading towards the front of the house.

Mercurio looked where she seemed to be indicating—and saw two squarglings there, a copper hen and a blue-gold squab. He *rakkled*, startled—he hadn't scented them...And he couldn't scent them now! But how? What was going on?

"His family were the askers," said the big Gorgon.

Mercurio's gawked at the scentless squarglings. *No way.* "You're Red's wife and kid? The ones who died? How'd you die?"

The hen spread her wings and—well, he thought she was screeching at him, or something, but when she opened her beak, no sound came out. Like a show put on mute. But how could *reality* be put on mute?

"What?" Mercurio looked to Icarii, then to the big Gorgon for an explanation. Instead, the dead hen turned to the big Gorgon and said something to her. But again, Mercurio couldn't hear.

"I must preserve my power here if I am to help them out there," the big Gorgon replied. And then the wife and squab—just disappeared. Like someone clicked off a show.

The hall out of the kitchen looked empty again.

It was one thing to see it in a chapel, being done for other people, at a distance. It was entirely another thing to have it done just...RIGHT THERE.

Oh man, oh man, this is getting weird. And he wasn't getting any of it on film!

Icarii spoke. The gun was on his hip now, hanging in a holster on a belt cinched so tight to fit his palm tree bod that about a foot of one end dangled out of the buckle. "We need a squargling to track a squargling."

"Oh no! No! No!"

"If I had my wish, it would've been the lunch hen I found skulking around out back instead of you—"

"Ditto, I'll go get her!" Mercurio stepped towards the exit, was caught by Icarii on the arm—but firmly, not fiercely.

"There's no time. Apparently, Lane Ho'okano's not in his right mind. So you're it."

"No, I'm NOT!" Mercurio dove for the arm holding him, beak wide, preparing to bite down as hard as he could. Squargling beaks could crack through some of the toughest nuts without any problem; Icarii was scrawny enough—maybe he could break the bone?

Mercurio didn't find out, because the tall Gorgon released him and jumped back, quick as a fox on a hot stove. Mercurio's beak snapped down on air, but he didn't wait around. He ran for the hall the ghosts had been in, screaming all the way.

He didn't feel the long arm of the tall Gorgon catching him, and there weren't any boots thumping after him, either.

I'm gonna make it! I'm gonna make it! He could see the front door from here!

Clllick.

A scalding wave of heat flash-fried across his back—mostly on the side of the cracked (*no! Just tender!*) rib. Mercurio's scream thinned to a piteous whistle and he went down in a heap. The pain was changing—from near-boiling water to throbbing prickles.

Now he heard the boots, hurrying for him. Then Icarii had him—by his bad-side wing, no less!—before he could scuttle away. Where his five-fingered hand grabbed, the prickles turned back into stabbing heat again.

Mercurio tried to turn, could only see the him out of the corner of one eye.

"You SHOT me!"

"It's a nuisance gun. I saw a nuisance. I'd say my application of it was appropriate."

In the other room, the big Gorgon snorted—or choked, or something. Either way, she sounded amused.

Icarii hauled Mercurio to his feet. He wasn't letting go.

"That hurts!"

"Come on. The rain'll cool it off." He was taking Mercurio back to the kitchen.

If this guy thinks I'm gonna play bloodhound for him, he's got another thing coming! It'd be easy—just run him round the jungle till he wore out, then run—bing, bang, badoom! With the gift of his magic sniffer, Mercurio'd be back to Lousytown in no time!

Better yet, I could lead Icarii right to that dumb cat, then he'd really *see a nuisance!* From here, he kinda knew the direction of the beast's lair. Sorta. Even with the rain muzzying up all the scents, he bet its smell would be strong enough to pick out once he got close to its territory.

Yeah. That'll show 'im! He stopped struggling and walked with the man-thing, trying to look resigned.

Icarii opened the back door of the kitchen. Thick smells of rain, wood, and ozone rushed in. Mercurio had one foot planted out on the damp lanai when, behind him, the big Gorgon said, "No. Bring him back in."

He was gently pulled back inside by the wing, but Icarii's restraint didn't cut the feeling of doom squeezing around Mercurio's stomach.

Mercurio faced the same way as Icarii, towards the big Gorgon sitting at the table, but her head was turned away, towards Mercurio's failed escape route.

She's listening? That's sure what it looked like. Mercurio *squawwwed* nervously under his breath.

The big Gorgon faced Icarii. "She says the Mercurio needs a thing scented like her husband before he can track."

The air was still a moment, the swooshing of blowing rain outside the only sound.

It was a long moment.

The doom claw squeezed—and then Icarii's hand followed suit. Mercurio squealed in pain.

"Thought you were gonna give me the runaround out there, did you?"

"No, no! I wasn't—"

He shook Mercurio and the heat-pain and the rib-pain doubled, turning his words into a rasping shriek.

"I think you forget—she'd rather be chewing on *you* than some lousy brick of cheese, you got me?"

"We're 'ohana! You can't kill me, and I don't wanna do this, 'kay? I just wanna take my stuff and go home!"

The tall Gorgon's tone turned exasperated. "We're asking you to step up and help one of your own! Why are you fighting this? The longer you delay us, the worse his odds are."

Mercurio jutted his beak out. "Are of what?"

"Of injury—possibly death."

"So what? If he dies, great, isn't he back with his 'ohana?"

Icarii let go of Mercurio and stepped back. They were both staring at him, Icarii, bug-eyed, the big Gorgon with both eyebrows raised high.

"'So what'? 'If he dies, great'?" said Icarii. "Do you hear yourself?"

The doom claw around Mercurio disappeared, replaced with a terrible prickling in his chest.

"Are you really that callous? You're being asked by his *wife and child*, who can't do anything for him now. NO—you know what? I'll be right back."

Icarii walked away and opened the back door of the kitchen.

The rain-thickened scents of the outdoors rolled back in, lingered after the screen door banged shut.

The doom fist returned, slid higher, and squeezed Mercurio's throat almost shut.

He looked at the big Gorgon. "What's he gonna do? What's he gonna do?"

The big Gorgon stared at him with an unreadable face of stone.

The door out back opened again. The tall Gorgon stepped back inside. The sling bag swung from his fist.

He'll smash 'em. No, he'll hold them hostage again, force me to help.

Icarii walked right up to him. Mercurio cringed into his wings and shut his eyes tight, waiting for the first blow. *He's gonna beat me to death with my own equipment. What a way to go.*

But that didn't happen.

Instead, just a firm tap on his chest—over his screen pouch, in fact.

Mercurio peeked an eye open.

Icarii was holding the cam bag out. The bag hung right at Mercurio's belly, in fact.

Handing 'em over?

"Here."

"Really?"

The man-thing nodded. Mercurio took the bag from him.

He checked inside. Everything smelled okay. And the tall Gorgon hadn't been out long enough to sabotage anything.

The doom claw disappeared. Mercurio hugged the bag to himself as tightly as he dared, not wanting to crack his screen's display. He whistled cheerfully.

"Well, okay. So long!"

But they were staring at him with something like solemn disgust.

"What?!"

"You'd really run out on them?" said Icarii.

"They're dead, they're strangers!"

"They're dead strangers to us, too," said Icarii, "but we're the only ones that can help them now. And you're the only one who can help us."

"Yeah, well, you got your choices, I got mine!"

"We're going to go out and help them. You're going to abandon them. Do you think this is what your tutu wanted? For you to chase your dreams, everyone else be damned?"

Guilt crawled through Mercurio on the legs of a thousand centipedes.

"I—" started Mercurio.

"We do not have to guess at his grandmother's thoughts," said the big Gorgon. Still at the table, she offered her hand to him. Just like she had to the others at the chapel.

"Come here, Mercurio. Let us call your beloved dead and see what she thinks of your selfishness."

The guilt ran up the backsides of his wings now. Mercurio twittered higher than he ever had before. "Haha, no, that's not necessary—"

"It is not," said the Gorgons, in unison. "For if you leave now, you will hear from her on this, one way or the other."

The prickling mixed with the surreal-predator stinks and the true weirdness in stereo and the thunder outside.

Then, Mercurio threw it all aside. He shrieked once in Icarii's face. Both Gorgons winced. The big Gorgon actually threw her hands over her ears.

"Nice try! But I don't book guilt trips! Aloha forever, you creeps!"

He was out the back door in an instant. His initial impulse was to simply dash out into the yard, but the rain had turned absolutely torrential and he slid to a halt just a few steps from the kitchen door.

He stood beside a recently upended patio chair and hung the cam bag temporarily on his tail so he could fish his screen out with both hands.

Idunno, I just get the feeling it'll stay drier in the sling bag.

He was just nestling it in when the kitchen door opened. Icarii stepped out.

Mercurio flapped his wings and gave a long, piercing *I'm watching you!* whistle. But the tall Gorgon ignored him, jogged down the stairs and into the rain, which was pelting down so hard it was like a white sheet.

The rain blurred his scent the moment he left the lanai. The water turned his hair and his dumb safari clothes two shades darker and plastered them to his smooth skin.

Mercurio watched him leave.

Then he dug his hand into the bottom of the sling bag and fished out his digital recorder. He turned it on.

"At the request of two ghosts, not even war victims, the Gorgon, the most loathsome being in the galaxy, strikes out into the wilds of Crooked Neck in a furniture-wrecking storm to help them find the only surviving member of the little nest, lost somewhere out in the jungle."

The tall man seemed to grow smaller and smaller the farther out in the yard he went. He actually stopped a moment, holding something up close to his face. Mercurio continued on.

"Meanwhile, your humble correspondent stands by, watching from a safe distance..."

What? No, that didn't sound right.

He shut off the recorder. Then turned it on again.

"Not wanting to get caught up in this freaky ghost business, your humble correspondent turns tail and flees back to the safety of his motel."

He clicked the recorder off. Nono—that'd be authentic, but in the wrong way, the way that lost you viewers. *I don't wanna be* that *guy.*

Mercurio rewound and recorded the sound of rain over what he had just said.

The prickling had returned.

Icarii had disappeared from view entirely, turning the corner to go around to the front of the house.

Okay, then, let's tell it how it is!

Recorder on. "His precious equipment safe in hand, your humble correspondent abandons his pathetic red cousin to his stupidity and lets the galaxy's most hated beings be the hero instead!"

He snapped the recorder off a third time.

It's what Tutu wanted for me!

Thunder cracked like a giant wing. The sound rolled over the sky.

Don't you bring me into this!, he could imagine his grandmother saying. Cuervito, *you know better. You're that family's only hope of finding their papa!*

Mercurio looked out into the dark, rainy jungle.

Aw, crab apples. There was no way to spin it.

Mercurio turned around and went back inside. He needed something of Red's to scent.

31
KEONAONA

THE 'EHUANA RIVER HAD always held Crooked Neck close; when the river was high, the loop of the titular meander surrounding the town closed, cutting them off from all sides.

Won't be long before I reach it, thought Keonaona, pulling one foot out of the sucking mud after the other. Warm rain was sluicing off every branch and leaf, bringing canopy scents to the ground, making it smell like the world was melting around him. Mixed with the rain, it was both a peaceful smell and a disorienting one. But it didn't matter where, exactly, in town he was, just as long as he could find the river.

And be alone. No one needs to see this.

He sidestepped a few paces, found sturdier ground in the form of a raised lattice of tree roots. He steadied himself with one arm on the tree and leaned forward, letting his raised wings take a beating from the falling rain.

He was tired, but getting to the river was the only thing left to do. This way, there'd be no accounts to close, no school to notify, no headstones to pick out.

Perhaps no welcome in Mother's nest, either. Ending a life early—that was said to offend Her, except in cases of extreme suffering. Then it was said She understood.

Please understand! I'm sorry. I'm so sorry. Pain came off in soundless keens that rasped his throat raw. *I'm sorry, Mother, I'm sorry, Kai, I'm sorry, Hana, I'm sorry I was mad at you—*

Reality was swept away in the torrent of his pain. There was nothing left for him here.

Nothing but pain.

Thunder growled above him, the Great Jackal at his heels.

He forced himself forward off the roots. This was why he had to go. He could not bear this. How could anyone?

He put one foot in front of the other, fighting the sticky earth that seemed to want to trap him here.

In the rainfall, he would not scent the river.

In the thunder and in the urgent hiss of rain, he would not hear it.

He had only to go on.

When he saw it, he would know what to do.

And then this pain will be finished.

32

GORGON

THIS ISN'T HELPING THINGS one iota, is it?

Jerimin's instructions from the wife's ghost (via his Queen, of course) were to enter the jungle across from the house and to follow the path from there. It was a shortcut to the other side of town, where the hen had last seen her husband wandering.

Well, he had done that, and the path had been clear for a few minutes at least. But the nodding leaves and the water pouring off them seemed to have swept everything smooth...and he was no outdoorsman. All the mud (if there was any; sometimes the rainfall formed whitewater streams over the tops of his boots) was starting to look alike to him.

He paused a moment to check his magnetic compass. The moonlight that had greeted him earlier at the Ho'okano estate was gone entirely now. The only illumination left now was the occasional lightning flash overhead and that coming from the beam of his OsMil flashlight. It gave off an impressive amount of light, 1500 lumens. But in this storm, even it was struggling.

From time to time he sent at his Queen, requesting the veil sight (though with all the rain in motion over the jungle before him, he couldn't be sure if it'd be any help, either), but, save for the sight of Ho'okano's wife at the forest edge across the street, he'd been left to his own mortal senses.

He checked the compass again. He was facing west. He was supposed to be heading roughly northwest, and he'd been told the footpath wasn't a straight one. But though he was no outdoorsman, he'd spent his entire life walking the streets of Netron; he had a good sense of distance and direction.

This doesn't feel right. I don't think I'm on the path.

But he'd read that, in places like these, even expert woodsmen could get turned around. And those accounts hadn't even mentioned weather like this. Maybe he was still on the path. Maybe?

He lifted his head and shone the flashlight around, hoping for another glimpse of a spirit.

Incredible to think Ho'okano was willingly out in this. But then, his wife had explained he wasn't in his "daylight mind"—a squargling idiom that didn't quite mean being completely out of one's mind, but—more that one's actions were being dictated by fears...those little *what-ifs* and doubts that were manageable—maybe even laughable—during the day, but which grew large and serious and intimidating and all-too-likely-to-happen after dark.

He took three unsure steps forward and waited to see what his internal compass gave him.

This direction didn't feel right, either.

I don't know a thing about this fellow. Maybe if I knew what was specifically bothering him, I'd know where to go.

Thunder cracked overhead, but the following flash of light revealed nothing helpful.

This'd go a lot easier with Macoya. Macoya! He scoffed aloud. *And they call* me *a villain.* Jerimin had no doubt that hard-hearted little glory hound was long gone. Sure, he could have put the screws to the pest and forced him into helping...but every minute spent dealing with his obstinacy wasted precious time that could have been spent finding the family's father.

And oh, how that family needed help.

The desperation of the mother and the fear of the son had been palpable at the house, despite his only being with them a little while. The strain in her eyes, mostly. She'd kept a calm voice for her son, but her eyes betrayed her. That desperation clung to Jerimin like a strangling vine, made him want to hurry. He had to force himself to wait, to try a new direction and check his internal compass.

/Come on, can't you give me something? I'm not sure where I am anymore!/

Nothing. And his internal compass remained unsure. At least the rain was warm, though it amplified and reflected his own unwashed smell back to him.

He held the flashlight level and turned in a slow circle. He hoped he wouldn't see glowing cat eyes staring back. Macoya's tale of the jaguar encounter had seemed like an adventure tale during the day, but right now (*not in his daylight mind*) it struck him like a horror story. Would a big cat hunt in weather like this or would it hunker down to wait it out?

The gun on his hip was only modestly reassuring; though snug in the holster, the tail of the over-cinched belt flopped distractingly, no matter how he tried to tame it. And it still wasn't tight enough on him. It was all too easy to imagine the jaguar appearing, him attempting to draw the gun, and lifting the entire belt—holster and all—up his torso instead of drawing the weapon properly. And it wasn't like he was some expert shot, either, though he had put in his practice time at Setsor—

There! That shape was moving!

Parting the leaves of the jungle, heading directly for him. His heart seemed to flatten against the back of his ribcage.

Too high up to be a cat, though.

His hand was on the gun's grip anyway.

Should've practiced this draw.

The thing stepped out of the forest.

"*Waahk!* Put that thing down, you tryin' to blind me?!"

Macoya!

...Macoya?

"Yes, actually," said Jerimin, but he angled the flashlight beam lower so it wasn't blasting into the square's eyes. His memory sticks shone in the light where they peeked out from the sling bag his camera gear was in. "I heard there was a jaguar out here."

"You're not funny!"

"Why are you here?" He had to raise his voice to be heard over the rain. "I thought you were leaving."

"Couldn't let *you* be the hero!"

Ah, so his ego had brought him back in line. Naturally. But Jerimin wasn't going to turn down help, not in this storm.

Macoya went on. " I got"—he lifted up a plastic bag with something puffy in it—"the scent. Red's wife showed me. Now that I found you, we can try and see where he went."

"Am I on the trail?"

"No! Follow me."

Macoya's coloring did not make for an easy target to follow. And the rain made the dance of his weaker flashlight impossible to track. Even his blue head was just the right shade, dark enough to disappear into the night.

Wish I could paint some fluorescent orange dots on him...or wrap his wings in reflective tape.

Jerimin kept his own flashlight pinned to Macoya's green back and wings until he was close enough to put a hand on his shoulder. Macoya cawed in his face and pulled away. Jerimin reached out again, got screeched at.

"I'll lose you otherwise, you're camouflaged! I can't scent you, remember?"

Macoya *scree*'d. "Fine, but do the other shoulder! You wrecked this one!"

Jerimin rolled his eyes. "Fine. Take this." He gave the auteur his flashlight and, using his free hand, held the gun belt in place and drew the weapon.

"Don't shoot me again!"

Jerimin switched on the weapon light. *Hope it's at full charge. Who knows how long it'll have to last.* "I'm not, I just don't want to stumble." He aimed the light, mounted on the muzzle, just ahead of his feet, finger off the trigger, then laid his other palm on Macoya's safe shoulder. "Okay, let's go."

With Jerimin's stronger flashlight in hand, the square moved unhesitatingly ahead; in not too much time, the mud beneath their feet seemed smoother, less rock-strewn, and the plants at ground level seemed to be spaced out to form a border.

This must be the path. He must be scenting it—maybe it's been used so long by locals that its scent doesn't wash away entirely in the rain.

They stopped long enough for Macoya to stick his beak in the bag. He inhaled deeply, resealed the bag, then began swiveling his head, sniffing all the while.

"Nothing here. What about you?"

"What?"

"She said she'd help you see the family when she could. So, you see anything?"

A quick glimpse around proved he only had use of his eyes. "No, not yet."

They continued on down the path, Macoya sniffing continually. From time to time, Jerimin swept the jungle with the gun light, just to be sure nothing was sneaking up alongside them, but luckily, everything with teeth and fangs was saner than them, probably holed up away out of the rain.

If Ho'okano wants to die so badly, all he has to do is tilt his head and open his beak! It's like someone turned on a fire hose up there! And now he began to wonder if all this water was affecting her ability to send. Jamming their signal?

Macoya halted; Jerimin nearly stumbled. Before he could ask what was the matter, Macoya wiggled the flashlight in front of them, making the beam jump along the ground. "Path forks here. Which way we headin'?"

Jerimin peered through the rain. He guessed if it were daylight and if someone shut off the waterworks upstairs, he might have been able to see where the path split; but right now, it all looked like muck to him. He'd have to trust Macoya's nose.

Time to test my rain interference theory.

/Hey,/ he sent. /There's a fork in the road, do you know which side to take?/

Lightning winked overhead. As the thunder struck, the familiar mental weight of her coils landed in his head. With it came a change in his vision: the trees around them and a little beyond them were defined by the veil sight's sparkling edges, but the rain was also better defined; like static snow buzzing around an antique TV set.

Thermal vision might be better, he thought, just as Ho'okano's son stepped into view.

"Wait!" said Jerimin, tugging back on Macoya's shoulder.

"What?"

"It's the son, I see him!"

The little squab was swinging his arms around like he was ground crew directing a shuttle, urging them to the left.

Jerimin turned Macoya by the shoulder. "He wants us to go this way."

Macoya leaned in that direction, beak bobbing.

"You can really see him?"

"Yes!" said Jerimin, just as the spirit disappeared from view. The twinkling jungle went dark again; the veil sight was gone. "Come on." He pushed Macoya forward, but the auteur resisted. He looked back at Jerimin over his shoulder.

"You sure?"

"*He's* sure, and he's lived here longer than you. Go!"

Macoya croaked, but hopped into motion.

The sky flashed white as they traveled, but the booms of thunder that followed those flashes were delayed longer and longer. *Maybe we're finally getting out from under this storm.*

Sometime later, Macoya swanned his head upward, scenting the air. "Road's ahead."

Sure enough, a few feet later, their feet were on the rubberized thoroughfare. They both stopped in the middle of it, looking (and, in Macoya's case, sniffing) around. The rain here had eased to gentle plaps. It was nice not having to shout.

"Any sign of him?" asked Jerimin.

Macoya shook his head. "Uh-uh."

"Give me a sec," said Jerimin.

Macoya opened the bag again. While he dipped his beak in, Jerimin sent, /We're at the main road now, do we need to travel on it?/

The wire in his head seemed to flutter, and then the coil weight was there, bringing the veil sight with it. Across the road, the son waited, staring at them and hopping anxiously from one foot to the other.

/She has found her husband. He has stopped his wandering. She is with him./ An image of the copper-and-green hen in his head indicated the wife. /But he cannot hear her, of course. I did try to send to him, but my sendings clouded dead beneath his despair.

/Follow the son. I will give the sight to see him, but he does not know exactly where his father-one is, so tell the loud one to keep his beak high./

"Okay," he said. The substance of his Queen's voice departed his mind-space, but the coil weight and veil sight remained. When he had spoken, Macoya had looked up.

"'Okay' what? What? What is it?"

Jerimin switched off the weapon light; the veil sight was clear enough. "We're cutting across. We're following the son. Keep your beak up, though, okay? I don't think he knows the exact location. We should hurry."

"Right."

Jerimin approached the son, Macoya, by his side, still held the flashlight. The spirit urgently screeched. Macoya didn't react, but Jerimin heard the sound; the veil powers broadcast it straight into his head.

"Okay, lead on," Jerimin said to him. The bright little squab turned tail, and Jerimin and his companion stepped into the forest after him, leaves shaking water as they pushed them aside to go through.

But it wasn't the forest. A few feet later, they stepped out into a clearing, where the twinkling veil sight revealed a tired-looking fire pit, and the back side of a house. Jerimin was about to say something, but Macoya stopped of his own accord, beak bobbing.

"We're in a backyard," Jerimin informed him.

Ho'okano's squab, already at the other end of it where the forest grew thick again, was flapping his wings and crowing for them to hurry up.

"He wants us to cut through."

The square garbled, nervous. "Ooh...kaay..."

They broke across the yard and caught up with the squab. Mercurio, though, paused before they entered the jungle, looking back at the house.

The squab was flapping his wings and waving his arms. "Hurry, Lane Gorgon, *wiki-wiki*!"

But Jerimin turned to the auteur. "What's wrong?"

"I already been shot once tonight. If someone scents YOU crossing their yard in the dark, they're gonna shoot us!"

Jerimin frowned into the square's shimmering blue-edged face, puzzled. "Really? They'll probably just think I'm your jaguar passing through. From what you said earlier, I don't think they'd shoot it."

Macoya seemed to inflate a little. "You don't smell like no jaguar, *amigo!*"

Jerimin glanced over. The squab had quieted to let the grownups talk, but he was practically climbing up the trees in impatience.

"And do you have a solution to offer?" he asked Macoya. He supposed he could wear mud—but that'd just use up time. And it might not help much, given how...prominent his unmodded scent now seemed to be.

When Macoya didn't answer, Jerimin turned to the squab. "Sorry. Lead on."

The squab dove into the ferns.

The jungle itself seemed to be what divided the properties from one another. They emerged onto a small putting green; the practice hole was clear in the veil sight—and would have been clear to Macoya if he hadn't been shining the flashlight straight ahead of him to see and sniff towards some broken flower pots at the other side of the yard. Jerimin threw out an arm to bar the square from taking another step. "Watch it!" He didn't need his sole Ho'okano detector slowing them down on a sprained ankle.

But when Jerimin's arm hit, Mercurio grabbed his chest on that side and unleashed an ear-shattering shriek of pain.

"Sorry, sorry!" said Jerimin.

Suddenly, a barrage of Native alarm screams sounded. Jerimin jumped out of his skin—then a light went on, and he noticed the bevy of squarglings out on the house's back lanai, jumping from their sleeping mats, wings spread and cheek fur bristling.

Squarglings couldn't see well at night—certainly no better than a human could—so they probably hadn't seen him yet, maybe hadn't scented him, either. Jerimin slunk back a step until the ferns covered most of him, then took another look at this new company.

The veil sight showed...eight? squarglings standing, and a few squabs being smushed under their mothers, whose wings (he thought; the veil sight plus sprinkling rain was making things difficult to parse) were spread, as over a nest. The squabs had gone still like fawns. He scanned the group's waists and hands. No guns that he could make out.

No guns, but a lot of beaks.

Maybe he could widen the net.

Macoya was on his toes piping an *I'm-not-a-threat* call and shining the flashlight on himself. Away from the panicking squarglings, just past the back corner of the lanai, Hoʻokano's son swung his arm to follow him.

What would be best? Continuing on with just Macoya and himself, or recruiting these squarglings—or maybe even the neighborhood—to help with the search?

Colors in his head (such a normal occurrence these days that he hadn't noticed them slipping in among his own thoughts) roiled in, puffing shapes as his Queen considered the solution on her end. But before she could put in her two cents, the house door leading to the lanai was kicked open with a SLAM! and the (Jerimin was presuming) homeowner burst out, pistol at low ready, crowing a ferocious challenge into the yard. He was dark and broad-shouldered, with a burnt orange comb. More squarglings followed behind him as far as the threshold.

The lanai crowd jumped out of the line of fire, but one, light-colored (he thought), hurried to the homeowner's side and began talking quickly to him.

Hoʻokano's son left the corner to join the homeowner's other side.

"Yeah! Yeah!" said Macoya, coming into his Standard voice. "He's met me—I was with, uh...uh...plantains! —The café hen!"

"You mean Lani?" asked the homeowner.

"Yeah, her!"

"What you doin' in my yard, brah? It's after midnight!"

"I'm with the Gorgon."

Twitters of alarm broke out among the lanai crowd, but Homeowner gave a skeptical chuckle and said, "You are?"

Macoya whirled to look behind him. Seeing no one, he squawked in alarm. "Get out here!"

Jerimin holstered the nuisance gun and stepped into view, hands up and open.

Homeowner pivoted towards him instantly, amusement gone, dropping into a low stance as he trained the pistol's sights on him.

Jerimin heart froze. Then he saw that the square's finger wasn't on the trigger—yet.

He took a breath. "I'm not here to harm anyone. We've been sent to find one of your people, a Lane Ho'okano." He raised his voice to be heard over the hateful screeches that were now being launched at him.

The square lowered the pistol, suspicion in his eyes. "Keonaona? He'd be at his house."

"His wife says..." Yes, that was accurate enough, "he's lost somewhere out here. We need help scenting him out, and we have to hurry."

The imposing square scowled. "Lost? Keonaona's lived here long as I have—he's not lost!"

"Well, he's out here now. And his wife says he's not in his daylight mind."

Troubled chatter spread across the lanai.

Homeowner's olive-and-black mottled tail whipped to one side. "Why ain't Adanna with you? If there's trouble, she'd call Adanna first, she's the law here."

"We were closer—we're staying at the house. We—she couldn't get a call out, because of the storm." There, a nice, plausible lie that shouldn't lead to a thousand more questions. "Will you help us find him, or not?"

Ho'okano's son broke out of his frown and lit up. He nodded eagerly at Jerimin.

Jerimin turned to the crowd. "I'm asking all of you. He's got the scent here." At a gentle tap from Jerimin, Macoya held up his plastic bag. "The more scenters, the better."

Ho'okano's son was speaking quickly to Homeowner now.

/He can't hear him, can he?/ he sent, along with the scene before his eyes. The reply was distant, more hazy colors and feelings than words, but Jerimin took it to mean Homeowner might not hear a word, but could possibly feel the son's influence.

"I'm going with you," said Homeowner, straightening up and reholstering. The squab pumped his fist, *Yes!*

Homeowner spoke to his lanai crowd. "None you gotta, of course, you paid for sleep. But Keonaona's a friend, you dig? He would come for me."

Jerimin nodded encouragingly. But there was a not-quite-itchiness in the line in the back corner of his head, and then the coil weight, along with the veil sight, left. The squab disappeared along with the soul lights, and the night was dark to his eyes again.

Macoya and the homeowner were talking across the yard, and some of the lanai sleepers were stepping off the deck and onto the soggy grass, beaks aimed like magnets at the bag in Macoya's hand, but Jerimin was waiting, listening on the inside.

The coil weight returned with the veil sight—and a message.

He heard it, beckoned Ho'okano's squab down (Homeowner approached, but the ghost was faster), then tapped Macoya. The square and the squab both turned to him, pupils wide in the dark.

Jerimin lowered his voice. "I'm going to follow *our guide,*" he said with a meaningful tone as the crowd gathered, "since he'll be able to...track his mother by her calls." He looked at the son, who nodded. *Glad he understands the plan! I'm a little lost, to tell the truth.* "You get as many people together as you can, then follow my trail. You'll catch up with me soon or later, and then we can spread the search out. Understand?"

Macoya's eyes were darting all around. Good sign, bad sign? Was he overwhelmed, or trying to invent some deal?

"What if we find him before you do? You don't know our calls."

I know them better than you think. But if more than a few squarglings were searching and calling back and forth in the jungle, he didn't think he'd be able to distinguish the calls, let alone hone in on one's location. He glanced at Ho'okano's son. He'd be relying on the spirit, for the most part.

Yeah, but there's got to be a way to make this easier on you.

Jerimin turned to Macoya. "You'll have to make a call I can recognize, and one that'll travel far. What do you suggest?"

The auteur warbled, taken aback. Then he thought for a moment.

"I could—uh, make a jackpot sound. You know, like"—and then he let out a long musical jangle, a perfect imitation of an Osidern casino machine.

Distinctive, check.

"You can make it loud enough? —I *don't* need a demonstration," he snapped, as Macoya inhaled, gaping his beak.

The blue-headed square exhaled in a woosh. "Sure, sure!"

"Good. Let the others know," said Jerimin. Homeowner was just reaching their little circle. "I'm sure he'll help," Jerimin said, stopping himself from clapping the tough-looking squargling on the shoulder. The square had caught Jerimin's unmodded scent and bristling all over, ready to fight, though his eyes registered horror. So Jerimin turned to the squab, who was chirping and waving a hand at him as though Jerimin were a teacher he was trying to get the attention of.

"Yes?"

Ho'okano's squab spoke. "If I gotta hear Mama, we got to get out where it's quiet."

Jerimin nodded. "Lead on."

The squab turned immediately back for the corner of the house. Jerimin followed, his hand sliding towards the grip of the nuisance gun. *But I better not draw it here. I'll wait till we're in the jungle again.*

In Homeowner's front yard, Jerimin could see the loose circle of homes that made up this neighborhood. A loud cry followed them as they cut across the cul-de-sac. Lights began turning on in the houses, yellow blocks of light amid the sparkle-shapes of veil sight. But before anyone had come out of their home, Jerimin and the spirit had already returned to the jungle.

33

MERCURIO

MERCURIO WATCHED THE TALL Gorgon turn the corner around the house and disappear from view, the freaky scent hovering, stagnant in the air.

Wait, stagnant? Hey, there's no rain anymore! Mercurio looked straight upward, saw the sky was clear. He could get the cams out!

"Where's he going?" asked the big square with the gun. Up close he smelled like metals and concrete flooring. *Spend a lot of time in your garage, buddy?*

Mercurio handed him the bag, which the big square took automatically. "To, uh...meet up with our guide?"

The older square cocked an eyebrow at him. "You're not sure, brah?"

"It's complicated. Look, he wants us to gather up as many wings as we can, then follow his trail; when we get to him, we'll fan out and search. Whoever finds your friend hits the jackpot"—he jangled again—"easy."

Garage Hound whistled. "Followin' that palm tree will be easy—he smells *weliweli*, worse than a field of stink grass!"

"Tell me about it!"

"Okay, then, I'll get the neighbors," said Garage Hound. He sent his beak to the sky and screamed in nest talk, "*Lost squab, lost squab!*"

Mercurio and the big family renting out Garage Hound's house took up the cry and followed the mottled square around to the front of the house.

Oh, it's a whole subdivision out here, thought Mercurio as they collected into the center of the cul-de-sac. Lights were flipping on in each of the six shabby houses that surrounded the rubber-roaded center. The tall Gorgon was long gone, but his rank-sweet scent still hung in the air, leading off towards a house across the way.

How can a human follow a ghost? Well, maybe it came with the smell.

Doors opened and wings rushed out to surround the callers. Some twittered with worry, others warbled their confusion, while a few shrieked *killer!* at the tall Gorgon's unsettling stench.

Garage Hound shut them all up with a single *listen up!* crow. He spoke loud enough for all to hear.

"Keonaona's out in the jungle now, and he ain't in his daylight mind."

At the gasp that went up among some of the crowd, Mercurio's hand twitched for his remote before he remembered his cams were tucked away in the sling bag on his chest. If he activated them now, they'd just float in the bag, probably wouldn't even capture the audio. Instead, he pinched the zipper between his thumb and forefinger and ve-e-ery slowly began pulling it down. Hopefully Garage Hound's voice would drown out the noise—you could never mute a zipper!

"Hana wants us to find him," Garage Hound went on. "If you're visitors, he's no squab, he's about my age, a little older, and good wings, too, but if you wanna go back to sleep, I get it. But if you wanna help, dip your beak in here and catch his scent before we go. I gotta get something."

Mercurio squawked as the plastic bag with Ho'okano's bed cushion (well, the part of it Mercurio'd cut out earlier under the big Gorgon's direction) was shoved back in his claws. His sling bag's zipper gaped halfway open, and his cams clunked together uselessly in the bottom of his bag. Mercurio glanced up; you could actually see some stars.

C'mon! I can't waste this good dry weather—there's a Gorgon to be filmed out there! With the megawatt flashlight Icarii had given him, he wouldn't even need to worry (much) about lighting!

But first, he had to deal with all these wings. He opened the bag with Ho'okano's scent quick and held it out. The mob surged forward to get a whiff.

Mercurio cawed at the onslaught. "Hey, easy! Easy!" The crowd slowed up and came up two or three at a time instead. Within minutes, Mercurio's arms were tired. And the wing on his now-bad side drooped more than the other.

Then:

"Blueberry?"

Mercurio looked up. "Mango-mama!" The fried plantains-and-pomegranate scent on her was strong as ever, but mixed with the noxious smell of the orange antiseptic staining her stitched up forearm.

She buzzed her wings at him. "It's Lani."

"You can call me Blueberry, but I can't call you Mango-mama?"

"I ain't your mama. Though Mother know you probably need two of them. You still looking for Keonaona? He wasn't at Analū's?"

"No. I mean, yeah, he was at the store, but the news team got to him first—but I don't know where he went after, I found out from their cameraman."

Another pair of wings rushed up, dipped her beak in the bedding bag, then skipped out of line. Two came up next at the same time.

"Then why you wearing your *pono hana wikio*? I thought you said—"

"Long story. Listen, could you take over here?" He jounced the bag.

"What? No, you got that under control!"

"Yeah, but—you know my scent, Red's, and the tall Gorgon's—and even if you lose his trail" (*which'd be impossible*) "you know your way around. I gotta help the tall Gorgon."

She whirred, skeptical.

"It's true! They practically begged me to come out with him!"

"Who? The Gorgons?" asked the new hen at the bag. She smelled of grapes and lemon ice, bubbly and sweet. Mercurio puffed out his chest with a proud croak. "Yup! Sure did!"

"Whoa." The hen (who didn't look half-bad under the lone streetlamp) looked Mercurio up and down, sniffing, something like awe in her eyes.

Mango-mama, on the other hand, leaned back and screamed a hag-cat's laugh. "I bet they did, Blueberry. Right before they asked what flavor Jukee they could run out and get you."

"Well," said the sweet-smelling hen to Mercurio, "I could hold the bag." She held out her hands to receive it.

That'll work. Plus, it'll give me an excuse to talk to her later...

Mercurio began the handoff, only to have Mango-mama grab it out of his grip.

"Keonaona's *my* friend, thanks. Get out of here, you Ju-kee-swilling punk, and this time, FIND HIM!"

That'd work, too. Pity he was in a rush, or he would be handing out his card to the sweet-smelling hen right now. But compelling content waited for no director, so Mercurio dashed through the crowd, the monstrous scent smelling more and more like opportunity with every step.

The scent went around a house, into a nearby backyard. He vaulted over a planter, landed on a few flowers. Oops. Oh, well!

He paused where Icarii's trail entered the forest to get the cams out of the sling bag. He tossed them one by one into the air, controller in one hand, digital voice recorder in the other.

MaxCam reversed into the green ahead of him, lens loyally pinned on Mercurio's mug, and then Wideshot and Angel followed the square in.

I can still salvage this trip!

Three great—no, *unbelievably great!*—narrations later (the words were flowing to him in streams of inspiration—but he still knew he wasn't remembering all the cool stuff he'd come up with before, dang it!), Mercurio pulled up short and stopped his recorder.

To his left, the super flashlight showed level ground; a nice, easy-to-speed-across clearing under some very photogenic trees, whose white flowers studded them up and down, even on the bark! No, wait, those flowers belonged to the vines draped over the tree. Well, whatever!

It was clear, easy ground to cover. But it wasn't where Icarii's scent led. And the ground trail (a long-embedded airborne slurry of intertwined scents Mercurio bet could be matched up to each hick in this soggy town, if you could pull 'em apart) disappeared here, too. Instead, both trail scents jagged up and over a steep set of scrapey boulders. Might've been easy for that spider-legged freak to climb, but Mercurio would need all four limbs to scale it, and his right shoulder ached just looking at it.

And the thing was—just across the clearing, you could see right where the stupid trail markers picked up again, and Icarii's giant bootprints right between them!

Mercurio lashed his tail. What a stupid detour.

So stupid, in fact, that he wasn't going to take it.

He jogged straight across clearing, rejoining the tall Gorgon's scent on the other side.

There. Easy!

The Gorgon's eerie stench exactly followed the bends and curves of the trail scent for a time. Then, with a suddenness that reminded Mercurio of getting your arm jerked while filming with a handheld cam, Icarii's scent jumped the flattened-earth trail and blundered off into the bush.

He stood where the scents forked, tapping his recorder against his beak tip.

Click. "Up till now, the tall Gorgon's monstrous scent has mirrored the citizens' path through the jungle almost exactly. But here it splits, dashing off pell-mell into the jungle.

"Keep in mind when I first caught up with him earlier this stormy night, he was completely off the path. Now, friends, I step off the path to go save the poor lost human again."

He'd no sooner finished when someone cackled behind him.

Mercurio jumped, spinning around in midair, crowing a challenge as he landed.

A square ducked out from between two young palms. It was that cinnamon-cayenne jerk with the coffee! And right behind him came Vanilla Woman and her cam crew (including the cameraman, Steve-whatever, who'd filled him in on the making of the crew's deal with Ho'okano at the sweet shop), picking their way over the stones that lined the path. Their cams had been rigged to follow the brown, but their lights were aimed at the ground.

"You, save the Gorgon, *mijo*? I'm more likely to lay a clutch."

"It happened before, he was totally off the path—"

"Please excuse me"—it was Vanilla Woman, and some of her...bun? hair was spraying apart like a spooked ruff—"but, Cortez-sir, shouldn't we keep moving so we can rendezvous with the officials in charge of the search?"

"*I'm* in charge of the search!" said Mercurio. "Once they're all done getting Ho'okano's scent, they're gonna follow my trail to the tall Gorgon!"

The cam lights made the wave of surprise crashing on the newcomers' faces clear as day. Even the brown, Coffee Jerk, guttered in surprise.

"Keonaona?" he asked. "He's the one missing?"

"Yeah, we were sent out by his wife to come look for him."

Coffee Jerk's face twisted, confused. "You and Icarii?"

"There's a story here," said Vanilla Woman. She tapped a finger in the air, and then the cam was on Mercurio, lighting him up. He instinctively turned so the lens was looking at his good side.

"Yeah—me and Icarii are looking for Ho'okano! You need me to say it a third time?"

"Even though the Gorgon has the house, they're out looking for him?" asked Vanilla.

"Yeah, yeah, courtesy, or something!"

A search call, high and keening, rose up over the jungle, from the direction Mercurio had come. It was a lot closer than he thought it should be. Before Mercurio could stop him, Coffee Jerk screeched back the beacon calls. Then, to Mercurio's surprise, there came other beacon calls from almost all other directions.

Coffee Jerk spoke. "What, *mijo*? You didn't think the whole town would turn over and go back to sleep, not after a missing squab call, did you? They're all headed this way."

Mercurio looked around at the news crew. "Why're you here? What do you get out of it? 'Local squargling from small Osidern

jungle town missing' doesn't sound like something your audience would care about."

"Normally, no," said Vanilla, "but Lane Cortez said the
footage would be salable locally. And now that we know
the Gorgon is involved, we think the story could be very
interesting to a Netron audience."

Mercurio's tail lashed. How could they keep getting the
scoop on him? How could he stop them? Steve-the-cam-
era-guy had a *backpack* full of memory sticks, they had
thousands of jen...professional editors who could clean up
all their night footage and jungle sound noise...libraries of
pro music already paid for, better cameras...And what did he
have? A winning personality and some grit.

Next to what the pros had, it felt like nothing.

Before they'd shown up, he might've had a chance of
getting *something* amazing (or horrible, or whatever) on film,
something exclusive, something they didn't have. But now
that the pros were here, he couldn't see a way to salvage
things. Worse, he'd be leading his rivals right to the very
scenes he wanted for himself!

It just wasn't fair.

"Stevenson-sir, are you recording?" asked the producer.

"Haven't stopped since we left," said the man. "There's
plenty of battery."

But maybe he shouldn't worry...if he could get his face
seen on the Netron world news, that'd be cool enough to
share with his followers...but would *they* find it shareable
enough to bring new eyes in? And Mango-mama looked like
she'd throw boiling fryer oil on him if he didn't find Ho'okano
in a hurry. That last search call had been awful close, like
that neighborhood was already on the move. Mango-mama
would be with them, and if she caught Mercurio with a cam
crew, she might get mad again—just for doing his job!

He looked over the camera crew again.

*Even if I could...Idunno, forbid them from following me,
it's not like that cat Cortez couldn't just follow Icarii on his
own, not with that snoot-killing scent.*

Mercurio gruzzled in frustration. Looked like he was stuck with his rivals.

Well, better get a move on before Mango-mama shows up.

"He's gone this way." Mercurio lifted his non-injured wing to indicate the direction. The humans all nodded like they were fascinated or something, but Coffee Jerk just rolled his eyes. "I know, *mijo*, I scented that *hedor* long before you did! Let's go!"

Coffee Jerk made to step off the path first, but Mercurio rushed him, cawing in his face and battering him with his good wing. "The tall Gorgon put me in charge, so I'll go first! He doesn't wanna see your beak anyway."

Coffee Jerk snorted. "He probably doesn't even like you, *mijo*."

"Fine. You go first—have fun getting shot!"

The humans paled in the camera light. "He has a gun?" asked Vanilla.

Cortez clucked, unconcerned. "Probably just one of these." He patted his own nuisance gun in the holster around his waist.

"So...just a wildlife gun. A stunner," said Steve-whatever the cameraman.

"*Exactamente.*" Coffee Jerk said with a smile. "But okay, *mijo*, you can go first."

"THANK you," said Mercurio.

He pointed his flashlight off the marked path and stepped into Icarii's invisible scent trail. Only now, he enjoyed the crashings (it felt like) of Coffee Jerk and the news crew and their cameras and lights with every footstep he took. They would slow him down.

And it doesn't feel great knowing Coffee Jerk is armed behind me, either!

But some twenty minutes later, they were still all together, and Mercurio hadn't been shot.

"*Mijo*, how long since your Gorgon left the group?"

"Dunno, I don't have a watch. Why?"

"He moves awful fast for a human in the jungle in the dark," said Coffee Jerk, shrugging a wing back at the news crew, noisily crushing every leaf in the forest.

"I think he can see in the dark," said Mercurio.

"Humans can't see in the dark."

"Does that smell human to you?!"

"Got me there, *mi*—" Coffee Jerk stopped short as a new chorus of screeches rose out of the distant jungle. He held his hand up at the humans. They fell silent like squabs under a hawk's shadow, and all of them listened.

Not beacon calls. Some ground predator's on the move.

But there was a flourish in the call Mercurio didn't understand. Ground predator, yeah, but the flourish made it a specific one, almost as if the predator they were calling about had a name...The jag?

"No way..." Mercurio said to himself, just as Coffee Jerk grabbed him by both shoulders, brown wings mantled. "Which side did you come up? The east side? Did you leave the trail before this?"

Though Coffee Jerk's grip was just firm, not punishing the way Icarii's grip had been, Mercurio's injured side still twinged.

"No! I just cut across some rocks I couldn't climb."

"*Alcornoque!*" Coffee Jerk shoved Mercurio away. "That ground is jaguar territory!"

"Jenny's? I didn't scen—"

"It's her lanai, right on the edge of where she lives. You cross it, you get chased out. If you're lucky. And she just had cubs!" he said, eyes wide, ruff puffed. He whipped around to the news crew. "Let's go—turn around, back to the path, *ándale!*"

The crew did an about-face obediently.

"We don't want to be anywhere near this idiot right now."

Hot anger shot through Mercurio, but it immediately turned to cold fear. "What, you're leaving me? What—what about your film?"

The dark was already encroaching; as Coffee Jerk led the team away, the news crew's cam lights receded, leaving Mercurio alone with the super flashlight. Which suddenly didn't seem all too bright...

He raced through the hustling humans, squawking at Coffee Jerk.

"C'mon, *amigo!*—the tall Gorgon's scent—the jag won't—"

"Get lost!"

"Shouldn't we—" started Vanilla, but Coffee Jerk shook his head. "She'll hunt him down—and us along with him if we don't get out of here."

"At least leave me the gun!"

"NO!" Cortez snapped at Mercurio with his beak before coming at him in a flurry of wings. The blows pummeled Mercurio's already tender rib and shoulder and sent him squealing into the jungle. He might have run blindly into the underbrush if it wasn't for the faceful of clean, un-Gorgonated air hitting him in the face.

Right. Right.

He stood there a few minutes, panting.

Then he about-faced and began searching for Icarii's scent again.

I don't know where I am, the stupid jag's after me, and I don't have a gun. But the plan hasn't changed. I gotta catch up with Icarii.

The freaky scent hit Mercurio smack dab in the face. If the tall Gorgon's super-predator-from-another-world scent didn't scare off the cat, the gun he had sure would.

Mercurio beat tracks as fast as the bouncing flashlight would let him. Trees lashed drunkenly where his cams bashed into them, following the square.

All he had to do was keep moving.

Fast.

34
KEONAONA

THE RAIN HAD PAUSED, and finally Keonaona could lower his aching wings. A few plips and plops were rolling off the canopy above and splashing off his head, like firm taps from unseen fingers. They added to his pains, rudely awakening him to the other sensations of his body: so hungry (but *NOT* hungry; he had zero desire for food!), his empty stomach felt like it was peeled inside out; so cold, his drained legs felt like sodden puttees crumpled up and left in a cold corner to never quite dry.

And his head...felt like a tidal pool. Strange pushings and pullings in it.

Please come home! was the feeling one moment. And then that awful hollow pain would pummel him. Because the thought had come in Hana's voice. And Hana's voice was gone forever.

And then...this—some—a DEMAND yanked in opposition to his despair—insistent he was wrong, if he came back to the house he would find out—but he pushed it below. The demand was clear, but impossible! Impossible!

Keonaona held his head. He wanted to moan, but all he held now was silence within him.

His feet had stopped carrying him forward.

No. I have to keep going.

The promise of the river pushed him forward, and he let it.

Leaves brushed his shoulders as he proceeded. The scent of them was noticeably lusher. Plumper leaves. More water. He was on the right track. Had to be.

He ignored the distracting tugs in his head (*yes, it's all in my head, anyway, isn't it?*). Kept going. Kept going. He paused. Sniffed. Ancient habit.

That's when he heard the footsteps in the bracken nearby. Coming up on his side.

He turned his head. Nostrils wide open. Big Jenny?

No! Not Jenny!

Jenny he knew. Jenny was familiar. A part of home. A good way to die.

But the foul nightmare he'd just inhaled—

Otherworldly.

Terrifying.

The edges of it were sharp but the things it contained implied—his mental picture of it, he couldn't make ears nor tails of it.

A misshapen horror made of the blood of...he didn't know what. Darkness? And hungry.

It was hungry. But it wasn't Jenny. Alien.

In the dark, he saw leaves shifting, darker shapes moving against a less-dark background. His head pounded. His legs trembled.

To be killed by the jaguar would be natural. He knew, or could guess, where he would end up.

"Ho'okano, stop!"

It knew his name! This thing of dark, this abomination of blood—*it knew his name!*

His head pounded again. His name sounded between his ears, an echo of the horror behind the leaves.

He turned and ran.

35

GORGON

"*THAT WAS PAPA, THAT was Papa*! Mama—" Ho'okano's son scree'd the tracking call.

Jerimin, pushing aside wet leaves, caught only a glimpse of the fleeing father before the square ran off screeching. But he'd seen haunted eyes, edged in the twinkling veil lights.

Ho'okano's wife, left behind by her fleeing mate, turned, looked up into Jerimin's face. "Help me!" she said, and then ran after her husband.

Jerimin took off after her.

Oof. Jerimin tried to put on speed (and how grateful he was for the veil sight, else he would have tripped over these treacherous roots and biffed it long ago), but the terrain was too much and his previous nap not enough; he seemed to be chasing after the leafy wake of the red, never quite getting close enough to see him fully, let alone catch him.

The trees, though, were thinning now, wide gaps between them.

Ahead of him, a screech of alarm—in his head—and then a brief scream in the air, one that was cut off with a THUD.

"Careful, careful! STOP!!" screamed Ho'okano's son. He had been racing alongside Jerimin, but in this moment, the squab became a blur of ghostly speed; he threw out a teal arm in front of Jerimin, as though he were still solid, but Jerimin slid to a stop halfway through the squab's body. Luckily, that was still good enough to keep him from flying off the sudden steep drop-off.

All the living lights of the veil sight had been disorienting blurs as he ran through the landscape; the squab's knowledge of the area had saved him from taking a fall.

Panting, Jerimin peered over the edge.

Below him, the bank of the river, a flat muddy plane. Ho'okano lay facedown in it, mud outlining his body like a snow angel.

His wife crouched next to her husband.

"*Ipo? Ipo?*" she said.

But Ho'okano did not move.

That's not good.

Jerimin scanned the cliffside. *Where's the way down?*

Duh, you have a guide!

Ho'okano's son was watching his parents, frozen. Jerimin snapped his fingers. "Hey, hey—how do I get down? Show me!"

Luckily, the squab pulled himself together.

"Follow me," he said. The squab began running parallel to the drop-off's edge, and Jerimin followed. The drop-off was a sudden, steep bump in the regular curve of the bank, but a little further down, it sloped manageably down to the muddy plain where Ho'okano had fallen.

Just a few yards out from where Ho'okano lay, the river rushed by. The veil sight highlighted sticks and fish and things, all zooming by at a significant rate.

Jerimin rushed to Ho'okano, facedown in the mud; and his wife, who danced helplessly next to him, still calling to him.

The son left his side to kneel next to his father.

He's not dead, is he? I'd see him different, wouldn't I? With the sight?

The veil lights defining Ho'okano's form seemed sludgy, but they were there. *Maybe he's still alive now, but won't be if I don't get help.*

Jerimin bent down to check for a pulse when, to his shock, the square thrust himself up on his arms. His feet biked beneath him, spraying Jerimin with mud (*his legs are bare! No puttees. Good way to get hookworms out here, no wonder she says he's not in his daylight mind!*), and then he lurched to his feet.

He wobbled a second, then turned around.

His stunned gaze flew around Jerimin. And then, he *SCREAMED!*

The sound of it made Jerimin's heart shift into overdrive. Macoya's nuisance screaming back at the house had NOTHING on this throat-grating howl, powered by pure terror.

At first, Jerimin thought it the incoherent screaming of fear, but then his brain woke up and heard the Native words, stretched out and distorted though they were, for *DEATH! JACKAL!*

My scent! He thinks I'm Death itself!

Ho'okano turned away and stumbled for the rushing river.

"Lane Ho'okano, calm down, please!" Jerimin reached for him, only to have the square glance back, scream bloody murder again and stumble for the river.

Jerimin jerked forward in pursuit before he caught himself. He halted.

I can't chase him! He'll just keep running away!

Ho'okano's wife ran alongside her mate, grabbing at him—but her arms passed through his body, fruitlessly. Even so, she kept screaming at him to stop.

Tuning her out, but keeping his focus very deliberately on the stumbling Ho'okano in front of him, Jerimin reached back into the colors in his mind the way he might have once reached behind to tap the desk of a classmate behind him in the row.

/Ho'okano won't come to me. It's my scent. Is there any help nearby?/

He tasted, faintly, the residue of coconut milk on his tongue. The coil weight that was already settled in among the colors expanded out. He closed his eyes, but the veil lights still described the river and Ho'okano entering the water.

The perception expanded in an invisible globe around him, now encompassing the overhang, now encompassing the forest edge, now encompassing farther into the forest, where a couple of somethings were heading this way.

The closest looked to be Macoya, his three cameras (*are you serious?!*) (/Yes. His floating eyes./) hovering around him as he bulled his way through the jungle. His veil-lit figure suddenly paused to raise his beak and sniff like a hound.

/Okay, he'll do. But who's that other one?/

The sight moved to the second living thing headed their way.

Alarm fizzed in their heads, bright and sharp.

"Oh, yikes!"

A jaguar was parallel to Macoya, moving in a big cat's jog that made those huge, paddle-like paws flap inward as they kept pace with the auteur.

With a sensation like...a reverse blink? the entire jungle was lit up a moment, and then a nearby section was sharpened. He couldn't tell what she was showing him at all, until she sharpened the edges around the jaguar cubs even further.

Uh-oh. Angry mother incoming.

/Yes, one who can climb and swim./

He looked at Ho'okano. The square had stopped screaming, but every time he glanced back at Jerimin on the shore, he shrilled and splashed deeper into the river. The veil sight showed the river's depth: soon his feet wouldn't reach bottom. He would have to swim—but more likely, he'd be swept away by the river.

/The huntress is cutting the Mercurio off./

Perception expanded; the jaguar had pulled ahead of Macoya, putting on speed. Jerimin calculated its trajectory. If the beast was intent on cutting Macoya off, instead of escorting him off its territory, it looked like it would meet him...about where Jerimin had exited the jungle.

He sent a wordless request and perception reduced (but not the taste of coconut) until it was only the regular, forward-seeing cone of vision he could comprehend. He hightailed it up back up the drop-off, made another request, unholstered his pistol, but left the light off.

He checked the river. Below, Ho'okano splashed while his wife and child begged him to swim to shore.

/I will see if I can give him calmth./

The taste of coconut left his mouth. His head felt lighter, but the veil sight still let him see a good ten feet or so deep into the forest. Either Macoya would come out first, and Jerimin could direct him to help Ho'okano (who, he assumed!, wouldn't flee from a normal-smelling squargling), or he'd see the jaguar coming and shoot it down first.

Assuming the ammo is still good.

Paranoia seized him. He'd checked it back at the house, but...

He groaned, tilted the gun upwards and turned it to see the workings better, just like the Setsorea Corp trainer had taught. He pressed the magazine release button and the gel container slid neatly out of the grip into his awaiting palm.

Which is how the group of squarglings coming out of the jungle behind him found him. Their alarm screeches made him jump—and also slam the gels (*which had been just fine, idiot!*) back home into the pistol.

Suddenly, he was surrounded by a pack of squarglings, all squawking and trumpeting and smacking at him with their wings.

He staggered back, but kept the gun pointed upwards, away from them.

"No, no—jaguar!"

But his protests were drowned out by their shrieking. He searched their faces for Homeowner, but couldn't distinguish anyone familiar; no light meant no color discernment, and the veil sight made it hard to tell them apart.

He tried to turn around, to monitor the jaguar-Macoya situation. He might not be able to get away from the crowd, but he *could* see over all their heads.

The jaguar wasn't in view yet—but a flash of round light—visible, not veiled—wibbed out from the jungle a few yards away.

A second or two later, Macoya stepped out of the jungle. He shone Jerimin's own flashlight over the noisy scene before him.

Jerimin inhaled so deeply that he felt it in the bottoms of his feet. Just maybe, he *might* be heard over the mob.

He screamed at the very top of his lungs: "MACOYA!"

Miraculously, the blue head perked up. Macoya looked straight at him and winked.

Winked? Oh, for crying out loud—

Jerimin jabbed his finger at the switchback leading to the bank. "QUIT FILMING AND GO GET HO'OKANO! HE'S IN THE RIVER!"

And then—miracle number two—the auteur pointed his flashlight in the direction Jerimin indicated and got moving, his cameras bobbing gently after him as he ran past the crowd and towards the river.

Hope he has more luck than I did, Jerimin thought, before a bright set of lights threw his own shadow before him and set the mob squalling in pain and blinking. Using his free hand to shade his eyes, he turned around.

That brown square Cortez stood next to the Netron World News Association crew.

Harold ran up to Jerimin, shoved the microphone in his face.

"We were told you had a gun. So who are you planning on shooting, Icarii-sir?"

36

MERCURIO

Incredible! Whatever freak powers the tall Gorgon had, they'd led him right to Red!

Much as it pained him to abandon a scene as dramatic as a mob of wings harassing the tall Gorgon, Mercurio ran past them all, resetting Angel so it would follow him instead of Icarii. With that gun in hand, he could shoot Angel of the sky, anyway, so this was safer.

Where had he been pointing? There wasn't anything in the river over there.

Mercurio swung the flashlight around, sniffing. Water, water, jungle, mud, and...Oh! That distinct, fruityfloralriffic smell of Hoʻokano. He aimed the flashlight at the scent—and lo and behold! There was Red, up to his armpits in the river and wading farther in. Dude! It wasn't like the ʻEhuana was some little stream. No way he'd be able to cross it.

After shucking his memory sticks and stashing them behind a nearby boulder (and marking his scent on said rock with a quick rub of his cheek), Mercurio ran straight for the gold-combed figure—and stepped off into air. He squawked as he fell forward off the drop-off, then whistled in agony as his chest hit the mud, jarring his poor, aching ribs.

What the heck!!?

After a moment to recover, he scooched forward for the flashlight, intending to turn and see where the missing step ought to have been. Then he heard a sound like a giant gurgling drainpipe, and an explosion of predator warning screams from above.

Great, the stupid cat's here! Bet it's safer in the water. Cats hate water.

He snatched up the flashlight and charged into the river.

Whoa! was his first thought. *That's some current!* Even though his feet touched bottom, the constant current swept him parallel to shore like it was a push broom and he was old popcorn, stronger than any lazy river he'd encountered in the water parks he'd reviewed. Instead of struggling against the current by walking on the bottom, he tucked his knees close just to be floating and leaned forward, reached his arm out for the first stroke.

"AAGH!" He yanked his arm back. His injuries couldn't be ignored anymore.

He clutched the still-glowing flashlight to his chest with his arms and used his tail and legs to propel him through the water. Any sound of Ho'okano splashing was drowned out by the combined ruckus of the panic onshore and the rushing river itself. And, submerged beneath him, the flashlight didn't shine far in the underwater murk. This was a job for the snoot. Arching his neck, he got his beak a little higher out of the water and sniffed for Ho'okano's scent.

The whiff stuck out like a neon sign against the duller scents of the muddy river. Mercurio struck out for it, kicking his legs.

It was rough work. Red was downstream, but since the current was carrying them both at the same rate, Mercurio had to swim hard in order to catch up with him. His ribs ached with every move—whose idea was it to connect them to his leg movements, anyhow? At least the cool water helped soothe the laser burn on his back and the new bruise(s?) forming on his leg from the fall.

"Hey! Ho'okano! Wait!" He followed his Standard words up with some nest talk—*"Safe, friend, come back!"* But paddling his legs was stealing his breath and he couldn't really get his usual volume behind the calls. It was all he could do to keep his bearings on Ho'okano's scent, also being carried away by the river.

MaxCam hovered just above the water, focused on Mercurio's face, sensors keeping it safe from the wet for now.

Mercurio checked the status of his cameras in his contact lens. Wideshot was high up and hanging back. Angel, however, hovered faithfully over his shoulder.

If I could just get a look at Ho'okano, I could put Angel on him—that'd help, I bet!

He sniffed furiously, holding the flashlight beneath him like a giant, hard-shelled egg. It was tempting to ditch it—the swim was hard enough without the awkward thing adding drag—but one, he'd hate to think what the Gorgons would do to him if they found out he lost it; and two, the glow'd make a handy beacon for Ho'okano to find him, if the bean-brain would just turn around and look!

And I guess it'll help 'em find my body if anyone comes looking for me!

Find his body? No, he would survive this. If there was any question of it, Mercurio'd ditch the mission. Red wasn't worth dying over.

Kick, kick, kick...And then, a snootful of heaven, a glimpse of red and gold, courtesy the submerged flashlight. Mercurio blinked quickly, putting Angel on Red's trail.

The metal ball swooped past Mercurio. It didn't have filming lights on it, not like the pro cams of the human news teams, but in this dark, two half-moon little red and blue nav lights on its edges shone distinctly. Track Angel, and you were tracking Red. Easy!

Except the swim still wasn't—but at least now he didn't have to spend his breath snuffling out Red's scent trail. Maybe he could give calling him another shot.

He inhaled as deeply as he dared, but slowly. His chest twinged anyway.

Don't even try it, buddy, the injuries seemed to be saying. His lungs were as full as they were gonna get. Mercurio blasted the call out as far and loudly as he could.

"*Safe, friend, come back!*" Feeling his limits, he inhaled, called out again. "Come back to shore with me, it's safe! Let's talk!"

No answer. But a strangled sound of desperate panting broke out from the general water noise, and now he could really go for it, especially since he knew Angel's follow parameters: it would always stick to the left shoulder of the subject, at a distance of about one foot, give or take. Mercurio leaned forward and lashed his tail in the river, following Ho'okano's wheezing. He splashed noisily when he kicked now, his mouth mostly in the nasty water.

Just when Mercurio thought he'd caught up with his subject, he heard Red take a deep breath. A very deep breath. And then he saw Angel's lights dip.

Down into the water.

Mercurio screeched—it was too late to disengage Angel, the cam was already dunked, following its programming straight into a watery grave.

He almost dove himself, just to give Red a piece of his mind, but caught himself in time—MaxCam would do the same as Angel if he dove now.

Mercurio treaded water. Or tried to, anyway. Like the lazy rivers at those water parks he'd reviewed, the current kept him moving even though he was upright. The lights on the riverbank were getting smaller and smaller at an alarming speed.

So is Red coming up? How far away can he swim? Why won't he just listen to me? Jerk!

Mercurio scented the air again, gearing up to pounce on the cam-killer the instant he surfaced. He wouldn't put it past Red to swim as far away as he could and surface silently.

It's what I'd do if I was trying to get away!

Instead, just a few feet past him, the square broke the surface of the water with a deep gasp. Mercurio pirouetted in the water and stealthily kicked his way over. The super flashlight showed Red's back, and his dripping shoulders hitching as he coughed.

Wedging the flashlight into the crook of his bad arm, Mercurio grabbed for the runaway. Red shrieked as Mercurio's claws closed on his shoulder.

His eyes ran over Mercurio in a series of starts and stops, like he couldn't believe what he was seeing. *Who was he expecting?*

Red turned in the water to face Mercurio. Mercurio put his hand back on the other square's shoulder.

"You're not *it*," he said. Mercurio couldn't tell if Red was relieved, or confused.

"No, it's me!"

"Why are you following me? I don't want to see anyone!"

"Gorgons want you."

"Gorgon!" Red's eyes bulged in horror—then his brow fell in anger. "What does the Gorgon care about me?"

"It—well—it's—can't you come back to shore and we'll talk there?!"

"No." Red turned away, but Mercurio still had a grip on him. Hoʻokano gaped his beak, ready to bite.

"Look—they came after you 'cuz your wife and kid asked them to!"

"WHAT?!"

Now Mercurio really couldn't tell what that face was. He was glad MaxCam was getting this.

"You're lying—trying to get me on film again—"

"No, brah, I saw them!"

"SAW THEM?! LIAR!"

Hoʻokano suddenly grabbed Mercurio with both hands. He screamed in his face before raking his wings through the water. The resulting wave came at Mercurio like a punch, flooding his beak and mouth with the bracky, silty taste of river.

Hoʻokano pressed upon him, beating his wings, sending up wall upon wall of spray, until all Mercurio could see, hear, smell, and taste was the wild water.

They squawked and screamed and struggled, but not for long.

Mercurio's legs were getting heavy, and his chest and shoulder were really aching now. But Hoʻokano didn't look so hot, either. Panting after his watery assault, the flashlight glow showed dark rings around his eyes. And ever since he let go of Mercurio, he wasn't as high up in the water like before.

"Red, c'mon—let's go back to shore. You got neighbors there waitin', if you're scared of—"

"No, I don't wanna see 'em!" The red flipped around onto his belly and tried swimming farther out into the river. But with every stroke, he sank lower, and lower...until he stopped for a second, kinda upright...and then he just *dropped* in the water, like a marble dumped in a glass.

Mercurio treaded water, stunned for a second. Then, something left his mouth—*Mother help us!*, maybe?—and, crushing the flashlight to his chest, he dove under.

The water was cloudy and swift. It fought Mercurio as he kicked himself downward. *This is crazy. This is crazy.* How long would Superflashlight hold up? Hopefully long enough for him to spot Red's bright hide here in this silty brown fog.

He squeezed Superflashlight as tight as his bad arm would let him and began reaching out with his good arm, probing the cloudy mess in front of his face.

C'mon, Red, c'mon, Red. He lashed his tail, surged forward. He'd need to surface for air soon, but if he did, wouldn't the current just carry Ho'okano farther off? He forced himself to hold out, sending his good arm in a wide arc in front of him. His eyes stung with grit.

No good. I gotta go up.

He fought himself. He could do this, he could hold out—just...just ten seconds longer, come on!

Superflashlight's beam dimmed. Mercurio's lungs burned. His groping hand felt nothing.

But then...he felt something cold on his shoulder.

Cold and *solid*.

A hand?

He turned his head to see who it could be, but the cold hand pushed him, turning him as the flashlight flickered—

He saw it; just a glimpse of berry red, and then the flashlight died.

Mercurio clenched his beak, let go of the flashlight, and beat tail, feet, wings, arms forward, towards the last glimpse of Ho'okano.

He reached a hand forward—

And caught him. Ho'okano flailed weakly, like he didn't want the help, the ingrate! But Mercurio closed his fist tight and kicked, managed to blindly wrestle the other square into his arms. His lungs were screaming at him to take a breath, and his head hurt, so he pointed himself hopefully upward and swam with everything he had left, Red hugged tight to him.

Water rushed past, but not fast enough.

Mini lens flares began dotting Mercurio's vision...

He felt cold hands swooping him upwards, one fast push!

And then, they breached the surface, splashing and choking.

Mercurio breathed a second too early, sucked in disgusting river water that sent him into a coughing fit, but he never lost his hold on Red.

Father Moon still wasn't showing his face. It was still too dark to see. When he recovered, Mercurio turned his head, mouth gaped, trying to scent who'd pushed him to the surface.

Thank Mother, those hicks got out here! Now someone else can take him off my hands!

But there were no scents of other squarglings. No splashing. No calls, either. They were still alone out here.

Then who pushed us?

Red moved in Mercurio's arms. Mercurio couldn't tell if the square was doing it on his own, or if it was just the current catching his limbs and pulling them along.

Then he felt Red's belly pushing in and out against his arms. So he guessed he was breathing.

Still. He was awful *quiet.*

Mercurio needed his breath back, needed to start calling for help...those dodos on the shore, they'd have to hear him and come running. Sure!

He caught as much breath as he could—tricky, 'cause he still wasn't fully recovered from the coughing fit, or the struggle to find Red underwater, but he'd just get tireder if he put it off. Then he released the jangly sound of a casino jackpot—but it whoofed out short, way too short, and deffo not loud enough.

Red dragged them both down in the water. Mercurio churned his feet. But now that he had him...he couldn't let him go. Right?

For right now he could keep them both afloat.

Please don't make me let you go. Please, Mother, let 'em hear me!

He switched over to nest talk, simple words, loud cries no one could ignore.

"Help! Water! Tired. Help! Water! Tired!"

He kept crying the words over and over.

Overhead, Wideshot watched, unwavering, unblinking.

37

KEONAONA

KEONAONA DRIFTED IN THE dark. At last. Nothing to worry about.

Then:

"*Help! Water! Tired!*"

Kai? Was Kai in trouble?

Keonaona stirred, unable to ignore the deep instincts the plaintive calls needled. He allowed himself a single, weary breath. His bones felt like rubber. The fur ruff on his cheeks was cold and clammy plastered to his face.

Cold and clammy?

He paid attention on his second breath, noticing the river smell, and the sharp caffeine-and-ambition scent enfolding him.

Then it all came back: though he had called desperately for Him, the Great Jackal had not rescued Keonaona from the abomination on the riverbank. Now he was out on the river, and the feedster was ruining things again.

"Let me go," he said to the feedster, but the cockleburr ignored him, kept the nest talk going. Him, not Kai. Kai was gone.

Even though...

But no, that had to have been river weeds he'd felt beneath him. River weed or maybe junk (old smuggling crates?) somehow bearing him up, keeping him from going down like he wanted.

Not his son beneath him, grabbing his ankles and lifting like he used to in an old swimming game, one where the little squab tried to flip his father in the water.

"Let me go," he said to the feedster, when the bluebeak (but all was dark out here) had to take a breath.

"No," said the feedster. "*Help! Water! Tired!*"

He wasn't quite as loud now.

Keonaona supposed if the feedster wanted to drown with him, that was his business. He went limp again.

The inevitable would come.

38

GORGON

JERIMIN HAD PINCHED HIS eyes shut against the glaring filming lights, but the veil sight still let him see the scene: the microphone shoved in his face by Harold, her cronies, and that Cortez square behind her, backs to the jungle, whose starry-edged leaves overlapped in a visual mess he couldn't currently make heads or tails of. But the jaguar would be coming out of it any second now.

A blip of orange alarm. The veil sight expanded so that, even facing forward, he could see behind himself. The squarglings were all jumbled, too, but his Queen brushed them aside and instead outlined the drop-off beyond them in painful, sharp, unignorable lines.

/I don't plan on running that way!/ he sent, just as the jungle-noise-mess parted, and the jaguar jogged through, coming straight for them. He was seeing a few meters into the jungle. It was would be out in the open in seconds.

/You may not keep the choice,/ sent his Queen, with the image of the news crew stampeding forward, engulfing him.

"JAGUAR!" he screamed, pointing.

He didn't know what he expected, but it wasn't for the squarglings behind him to go instantly silent and the news crew in front of him to turn dumbly around.

Idiots!

The cat must have heard him; its jog turned into a charge, and it burst out behind the camera crew with a gravelly roar that Jerimin felt in his sternum.

The other woman in the news crew screamed—the round-shouldered cat was nearest her—

Jerimin raised the pistol—

—the sights were shaking, but come on, this thing was smaller than a dragonelle!

But you could reason with a dragonelle! Stop and chat with it. Trick it. Who knows what this thing's thinking!

The jaguar looked every which way. The dumb newsgirl was still rooted to the spot, screaming—

And now the squarglings behind him were screaming, probably hysteria would take them in a second—

Jerimin tried to find the cat's center mass, but it was at an odd angle to him, mostly frontal, mostly legs, and the dumb newsgirl was too close, he could hit her instead—

"Nobody run!" someone said sharply.

And then Cortez—of all people, Cortez!—leapt out in front of the big cat, wings spread wide, waving his arms up and down and roaring back at the animal! And he was armed, too! Even if he was waving the gun around at the moment and not aiming with it...

Jerimin slid his finger off the trigger. Better to let a native deal with it.

The jaguar snarled at Cortez, then dodged around him...slalomed past Jerimin...and leapt off the higher elevation onto the riverbank below.

Jerimin, Cortez, and the news crew ran to the top of the switchback and stopped. There, they watched the animal from just a few feet above its head.

"Why isn't she attacking us?" he asked no one in particular.

/None of you are her prey./

He watched the beast snaking its head behind a rock, sniffing. Harold's cameras came on scene, aimed their spotlights so he could see, in vivid color, the orange and black cat biting, then then tearing apart something hidden behind the rock, something long and noodley. The long strands hung from its jaws like entrails. But when the jaguar's teeth cracked apart something on the noodle, the resulting piece that dropped from its mouth wasn't bloody or squishy, but hard-edged, and grey like—oh! They were Macoya's bands of memory sticks! Yikes.

/I eat the feeling./ Along with the sensation of being buzzed by an annoying fly, so vivid, Jerimin actually swiped the air with his hand.

The motion caught the cat's attention; it looked up path at Jerimin, eyes gleaming gold where the camera lights caught them.

That was one burly cat. The last big cat he'd been up and close with had been a cougar; it seemed rather lithe in his memory compared to this toothy chunk of muscle. It also had been possessed at the time, full of malevolent intent. But the eyes of this beast were simply wild, not vindictive.

Did he shoot? Should he run?

Instincts that were not his paralyzed his legs, kept him rooted.

/Stand your ground. You are a fellow predator. She knows this, but if you run, you will confuse her./

Next to him, Cortez raised his wings and roared again. "Jenny, go home!" He kept talking without taking his eyes off the jaguar. "Hey, *flaco*, help me out here, your stink can't do all the work!"

So tempting to push him off the switchback. "If you shot it—"

"You don't shoot Jenny unless it's life or death!"

"This isn't?"

"No, she just hates that blue-headed feedster, like the rest of us. Where is he, anyway? He wouldn't shut up about being your right-hand wing!"

"He's supposed to be in the river." Jerimin raised his gaze to look out over the water, but then the veil sight suddenly expanded in a bubble around him again, showing a vehicle approaching from the jungle behind them a good few seconds before he heard the throaty (combustion!!) engine.

Jerimin kept still, trying to keep his bearings as his Queen kept expanding the sphere of her perception all around him. Cortez, hearing the engine noise, jumped on the spot to face it, cheek fluff bristling. One of the cameras turned its spotlight on the vehicle as it exited the jungle, but the cameraman opted to keep the other one's beam on the jaguar.

"Zorin!" said Cortez.

Jerimin peeled enough of his attention off his Queen's work to see he addressed Homeowner, driving a four-seater side-by-side with huge all-terrain wheels. The mayor rode shotgun next to Homeowner, and Lase Likeke sat in the back. Some of the squarglings he'd seen on Homeowner's lanai were piled into and on the side-by-side, and more followed behind him on foot.

"Don't get out, it's Jenny down there."

Homeowner/Zorin's eyes widened. "She didn't get Keonaona, did she?"

"I don't know! Right now it's tearin' apart some feedster's mem sticks!"

Homeowner sniffed at the news crew, but his beak pulled his head like a magnet to face Jerimin. The concern on his black-and-grey splotched face went behind a sort of wall. "He said you wanted us out here to help you look. Where should we start?"

"He's in—" *the river,* he meant to say, before the coil weight in his head—previously sitting behind his temples, projecting the veil sight through his eyeballs and looking through them like he was a pair of binoculars—lashed forward.

His stomach floated and though his feet never left the ground, Jerimin's whole body felt feather-light upon it—

—and then he no longer saw the squarglings around him, but saw a scene of shimmering lights: it was Macoya, and Hoʻokano. They were in the middle of the river, farther out from shore than Jerimin thought was wise...and deep under the water.

The lifelights that made up Macoya were strobing, fighting to stay lit has he swam, blindly thrashing past Hoʻokano, whose lights were sludgy, growing dark around his body as he sank.

Circling them helplessly were the wife and son, swimming in the water with motions like the living. Nearby, a spherical shape sank—a camera of Macoya's...

Jerimin wasn't quite sure where he was in space, but felt something flowing from him, being taken from him, and then he felt—

no, was—

He *was* his Queen, and he was himself, unafraid of the water, and his Queen, knowing how to aid them all but terrified of the depths, was suspended, shuddering between her desire to help and her fear of the water.

Gently, he reached over-into her selfspiritimage and over-rode her fear with his own braveryeasefriendship with the water.

His reaching turned into her reaching.

Below the water, she touched the spirits

(distantly, he felt himself grow even lighter)

who became solid for a second or two—the wife long enough to turn Macoya in the direction of her sinking husband, and the son long enough to help lift his father and the feedster from their doom.

Then, the weight in his head and the weight in his body rebounded back into place. The veil sight constricted to just a body or two deep, but there was an itch, a weight in his head, where the two squares in the water had last been located.

The camera lights shone on him like a spotlight. All eyes were on him.

Homeowner and Cortez and the Likekes and Harold—well, everyone present, probably—were staring at Jerimin in utter horror.

"No not the water *Gott im Himmel* don't let me drown not the water not the water..." The prayer dribbled out of his mouth like sand spilling out of a broken hourglass.

He shut up, shook his Queen's fear off, took a step forward, almost fell face-first onto Cortez—the crowd *whoa*'d as one—but he caught himself without touching the bristling square.

Drunkenly, Jerimin pointed. "Ho'okano's in the river. Out there. With Macoya. They're not going to last long."

"Get in," said Homeowner. All the hangers-on jumped off the side-by-side. Mayor Likeke clambered into the backseat next to his wife, making room in the front. Jerimin staggered forward, caught the roll bar to steady himself. "They're out far," he called over the idling engine. "Do you have a winch?" He might have noticed, except his gravity, and all the goings-on in his head, and the reduced veil sight were making it hard to take in the finer details of what was in front of him.

"Yeah."

Jerimin reholstered, then scrunched himself beneath the roll bar and into the side-by-side's passenger seat. "How long's the chain?"

"Fifty feet."

Jerimin looked out over the river. While out-of-body, he hadn't gotten the clearest look at the shore, so his estimate was bound to be off. "That could work. But I'm not sure. We can figure something out when we get there."

Homeowner whistled a quick trill, almost like an ambulance shuttle, and the squarglings around him made room. He maneuvered the vehicle in a tight three-point turn that eventually got them onto the flat riverbank, facing the direction Jerimin had pointed.

Behind them, the jaguar roared.

The mayor twisted in his seat. "She's just warning us off."

Homeowner gunned the engine anyway. In that moment, Jerimin decided that he liked Homeowner.

"Zorin, you got any life jackets on this thing?" asked Lase Likeke.

"Yeah, should be float vests in the cans in back."

"Thank Mother you're always prepared."

Headlights showed the ground rushing past them, the river lapping to their side just a few feet away. Homeowner kept one hand on the steering wheel, the other on the gear shift as they hummed over the ground. All the while, the news camera above shone its light down into the open-air cabin. "When we get there," said Homeowner, "we can tie the vests to the winch chain and toss it out to them, then reel them in." A quick glance at Jerimin. "You'll tell us when we're there, right?"

"Yeah...But they may not be close enough to throw something out to them. They seemed far out there when I saw them."

"Just now?" asked Homeowner.

Jerimin nodded. The taste of coconut milk was fainter, the reduced veil sight dimmer than before. He kept his head turned towards that mental itch. It was moving downstream swiftly, and he feared losing it.

"Um," said Mayor Likeke, "Jenny's still chasing us."

Jerimin kept facing the beacon, so he only heard Lase Likeke turning around in her seat.

She squawked, dismayed. "That mama is not in her right mind!"

"Should someone shoot her? Maybe?" Jerimin asked.

"I'd rather not!" said Lase Likeke. "She just had her cubs, they need her!"

"But these are stunners, right?"

Squargling cries were coming out of the jungle side of the bank. Jerimin couldn't hear well enough to make out their meaning, but the major shrieked some sort of reply before his wife answered:

"Yes, but what'll they do to her milk, I'd like to know! If we go far enough, we'll be off her territory. She should go home..."

Jerimin didn't like the doubt he heard in the hen's voice.

"What about a warning shot?" said the mayor.

Jerimin was instantly back in the Firearms Safety 101 classroom again.

"You don't fire warning shots!" he said at the same time as Lase Likeke and Homeowner.

The mayor chirped twice. "Eesh, eesh, sorry!"

"But if she doesn't stop chasing us soon, we won't be able to stop either," said Jerimin. The beacon was just a minute or two away. "You may *have* to stun her—otherwise, how will we get to your equipment?"

They rode in silence.

Jerimin pointed. "We're coming up on them. Ideas?"

They sat without speaking.

The engine growled, and Jerimin thought he heard the cat snarl back.

They were at the right spot, and the cat hadn't gone away. "We're here."

Homeowner adjusted their speed to keep Jerimin's pointing arm parallel to them as the squares washed downstream. The veil sight showed them as distant shapes bobbing low in the water.

He couldn't swim out there...between helping the ghosts go solid and running around all night in the jungle, he didn't have it in him.

In the backseat, the mayor quawwed softly. "Jenny's still here."

Fishing them out with the winch still makes the most sense, but the cat'll be all over us if we stop.

/I've dug an idea,/ sent his Queen. /But if it works, it will eat the last of my power; you will be night-blind after./

"What is it?" he said aloud. The squarglings all looked at him.

The response was less words than sensation and image: if she could take control of the jaguar's body, *it* could swim out there for them.

/You sure that's a good idea?/ She'd once touched their pet rabbit's mind, and the animal hadn't reacted well.

/*Nein.* But there is...morehighersimilar brain to work with./

"Hold on. The Gorgon is trying something with your cat," said Jerimin, just before the jaguar unleashed a horrid scream.

"Whoa!" said the mayor. "Easy, girl!"

Lase Likeke shrieked in Jerimin's ear.

"Stop hurting her!" she said.

"We're not!" he snapped back.

/Nope, that didn't—/

/Idoknow./

"She's back on us!" said the mayor.

Jerimin risked a look back over his shoulder. The big cat was pelting after them full-on, teeth bared, eyes intent.

The veil sight flickered like an overhead office light on its last leg.

Jerimin turned back quickly to face the squares in the river—and startled when he saw Ho'okano's son standing next to the side-by-side. He was standing still...yet remained next to the moving vehicle. So much for physics!

"I saw!" said the son. "Tell her to try again, please! Papa isn't going to make it! He won't be happy dead!"

"It won't work!" Jerimin found himself yelling over the engine. He knew he must look mad, shouting out the side of the vehicle at no one. "Your cat won't let her in!"

"Please!" said the squab.

Behind Jerimin's eyes, his Queen shifted her view. Something Jerimin didn't understand well enough to describe surrounded the ghost. She turned his head further, to see the jaguar. Something similar surrounded it.

Realization hummed in his bones: *resonance.*

Jerimin found his mouth opening, his words clipped and overpronounced as his Queen spoke through him. "*You! Enter the cat!*"

"What?!" The squab actually lost pace (or whatever) with the side-by-side for a second, drifting behind the vehicle.

Jerimin bared his teeth and hissed, but he didn't fight it.

"*NOW! Enter the cat! You will swim out!*"

The squab reappeared next to the side-by-side's cab. His eyes and voice were hungry with hope. "I can save him?"

"*YES! GO!*"

The squab turned away; Jerimin twisted to see the squab and jaguar alongside one another.

Then...something else *happened*, but what it was, exactly, Jerimin didn't have the verbs or nouns for it. But when it was complete, the squab was gone, and the jaguar was no longer chasing them, but standing still, picking up its huge front paws, one after the other, staring at them in wonder.

The world went dark, save for the camera's spotlight overhead. The veil sight was gone. Jerimin's brain listed to one side as his Queen's power leaned out the side of it, straining to keep the squab packed into his borrowed body.

This time, Jerimin spoke. "Quit counting your spots and bring them in! We'll be up ahead, we'll try to throw you a rope."

The jaguar/squab looked up at Jerimin, met his eyes, then bounded into the water. In a few short moments, the jaguar's body was heading for the middle of the river, paws paddling powerfully, head up and sniffing. It zoomed along with the current towards the two squares, their location now only a faint prickle in Jerimin's head. He hoped it wouldn't fade.

Thunder broke overhead. Then came a rain, like mist.

Probably not good for her power.

Jerimin smacked the dashboard with the flat of his hand. The side-by-side had long since stopped. The squarglings, all gawping after the cat, came to.

"Drive up ahead of the current. They're not out of the woods yet."

39

MERCURIO

MERCURIO STRUGGLED ANOTHER RAGGED breath in. He could feel the water constricting in on all sides, each breath a little shallower. If he let Red go, well, that'd be one less thing horning in on his lung space. But now that he had Red, Mercurio couldn't stand the thought of letting him go.

He swung his tail in the water; their heads bobbed up a little higher. Ho'okano nestled against him like a newly-hatched squab.

It wasn't about what the Gorgon would do to him anymore; it'd just be *wrong*, somehow, to have him in hand, and then to just...let him go? Like...a quitter? Even with no one looking, it'd be the worst thing he could do.

Maybe Icarii was right, maybe there were some things more important than chasing dreams.

If you don't let him go, you'll die for sure, dummy!

Mercurio blocked out the scene in his mind: of himself and Red being carried along the 'Ehuana River, like two misplaced banana leaves. The news cams ashore, the lights, the jag, the Gorgon—those were long gone behind them.

MaxCam had drowned when Mercurio dove for Red.

It was just them and Wideshot, alone on the river.

It could go one of two ways.

    EXT. SOMEWHERE ON THE 'EHUANA RIVER - NIGHT

    Rain bombards the swift river, which is CHURNING
    fatalistically.

    A struggling MERCURIO releases RED from his
    arms.

The fruit seller floats down the river, out of sight, never to be seen again.

Mercurio DROWNS anyway, completely alone on the 'Ehuana, winding up in the same watery grave as Red.

> MERCURIO (V.O.)
> Your humble correspondent died doing nothing useful at all.

He rewound the scene to the beginning.

Alternate ending:

EXT. SOMEWHERE ON THE 'EHUANA RIVER - NIGHT

A struggling MERCURIO lets RED go.

Red sinks below the river, never to surface again. But the cavalry arrives just in time to pull the humble correspondent from the water...

EXT. SOMEWHERE ON THE BANKS OF THE 'EHUANA - NIGHT

Mercurio, wrapped SHIVERING in a blanket, is approached by the TALL GORGON.

> TALL GORGON
> What happened to Red?

Mercurio lifts his head. But he can't look the tall Gorgon in the eye.

> MERCURIO
> I let him drown so I could survive.

And the tall Gorgon would understand, and wouldn't punish him, but it wasn't about what the Gorgon—either of them—would do to him anymore, nuh-uh.

Red was real, in his arms. Cold, but with a heart beating against Mercurio's hand, and an envy-inducing scent that was washing away, weaker with every minute they floated along...He was *real*, more real than the viewers he narrated to, real like Tutu had been, someone he was responsible for...he hated it! But if he let go, he'd hate himself more.

He reset the scene a third time:

EXT. SOMEWHERE ON THE BANKS OF THE 'EHUANA - NIGHT

MERCURIO, now DEAD, is pulled free from the river by the residents of Crooked Neck—but he still holds RED's corpse tightly in his arms.

Well, it's a better ending than some lame movies I've seen!

So they floated down the river. When Red's beak sank below the waterline, Mercurio would kick, and they'd rise up again...but his right side was killing him. And he was getting tired...

He looked up. No Father Moon, but Wideshot hung in the air, lights gently strobing. With a few blinks of his eye, Mercurio maneuvered it close. He crooked his free arm over it. The propellers roared beneath the squarglings' weight.

It wouldn't last long, but it'd keep them afloat a little longer.

Rain fell from overhead. The air grew misty.

Just what we need! More water to choke on!

The rain was too much. Wideshot's propeller's stuttered, then finally gave out. Mercurio kept it close in his arms. Little comfort, but still some.

He swashed his tail again, used it to chirp out a weak "*Help*," in nest talk.

Nothing.

Or so he thought at first. He gasped in another breath, caught a familiar scent in the muddy air. The jaguar's stink made him jerk his head around in fear—

He saw two golden glints above the water, perfectly round, staring right at them.

Coming for you, you mean!

Huge paws paddled. The glowing eyes were getting bigger. The jaguar was closing in fast.

He tried to scream it away, but hardly a whistle came out. It was almost on them now. Close up, his eyes could finally make out its blocky head in the gloom.

They were dead meat.

Ho'okano turned his head. "Jenny?"

The paddling beast redoubled its efforts, lifting its fanged head higher out of the water.

Then...

No me digas! Couldn't be! I'm going nuts!

But Mercurio heard the jaguar garble back, and in that garble, if you listened well (and why wouldn't you? There was nothing else to hear out on the water outside of the rain-mist and your failing breathing)...if you listened well, and weren't going crazy before you died...well, he could have sworn somewhere in that garble he heard a distorted version of the nest talk chirp for *Papa.*

"Kai...?" said Ho'okano.

Mercurio sank lower in the water—from shock, from fear, from exhaustion, who knew?

But the jaguar swam closer, close enough to touch...

It turned around so its back faced them.

Still paddling, it looked over its shoulder at them and garble-chirped, "*Papa, come!*"

Ho'okano *reached out* to the dang thing...

And it let Ho'okano get his hands around its burly neck. The jaguar kept its height in the water.

Mercurio could feel the wake of all four jaguar legs churning in the water. Since Ho'okano'd left him to go to the jag, Mercurio was up a little higher, but not by much.

Wideshot's round casing pressed under his bruised arm. It hurt.

No way he could swim to shore alone. A twist ending?

Red lives, but not me? Now that'd be a movie he demanded a refund for!

The jaguar's jaws gaped again. "*Friend, come.*" Is that what it'd said? Or had it just choked?

Ho'okano released one arm from around the jaguar's neck, reached out to Mercurio. His whole arm shook.

"*Come*," he managed to chirp.

Mercurio released Wideshot from his grip and swam to Ho'okano. The red square replaced his arm around the big cat's neck, and Mercurio wrapped his arms around Ho'okano's shoulders.

The jaguar began swimming through the mist. The scent of its wet fur filled Mercurio's beak.

I can't believe this. I can't believe we're really moving.

The mist surrounding them showed nothing. Getting close to shore? Farther away? Mercurio had no way of knowing.

I have to be dead, this is ridiculous! A jaguar that speaks garbage nest talk is not towing us to shore!

He couldn't believe. So he just kept breathing.

Time stopped existing.

The mist didn't clear. The jaguar kept paddling.

All three of them, Mercurio noticed, were gradually sinking lower in the water.

It's strong, but not...a supercat. Whatever.

"How far's shore?" He might be able to swim a little ways on his own, but not far.

"Don't know," said Ho'okano.

"Should I let go?"

Ho'okano didn't answer.

Above them, thunder rolled.

They sank a little lower. The cat scooped its jaw up, swallowed water. It didn't look like its nose was much above the surface.

Rain came down harder. It stung now, at least, the parts of him that were still above water.

There was nothing out here. No cams, no ropes, not even a log to grab. The...freaky jag was their only hope. If it went under, that'd be THE END, roll credits. But if it and Ho'okano made it to shore, maybe they could send help back? Or the jag could drop Red off, come back for him? Maybe he could just float, just float, until...until...

Until what?

The current hadn't stopped, and the rain was thicker than ever. Even Red's wings and golden comb were hazy like blurry stained glass on his vision. Cool effect. But with rain that thick, Mercurio didn't think anyone'd be able to pick up a scent to track him. Yeah, the tall Gorgon had powers, but who knew where he was now? If Mercurio let go, how would anyone ever find him?

The nest-talking jaguar suddenly bucked in the water. Like it was desperate to stay up above the surface.

Ho'okano murmured something, but Mercurio couldn't hear the words over the hissing, stinging rain.

His aching side was throbbing. Soon, he wouldn't have a choice.

So who am I gonna be? The deadweight that torpedoes the mission?

No. No, not him.

One of us should get out of here alive.

And he wanted it to be him—so badly! There was so much he hadn't done yet, so many films to make, places to see!...but...it just...wasn't going to be.

He relaxed his arms, began sliding them out from around Red's shoulders.

Red turned his head to look, but Mercurio bowed his head to the water, avoiding his gaze. Already, the jag was swimming a little higher.

This was it.

His sides were quaking with fear.

Alarmed, Red began scolding him, the same turbulent *rrr!*, *rrr!*, *rrr!*, over and over, a warning straight out of the nest, a *don't you DARE do it!*

Mercurio closed his eyes and let go.

He drifted, unattached in the water for a full second.

And then he heard a new voice, trumpeting from shore.

"Head's up!"

Mercurio opened his eyes to see a bright, yellow, blurry shape flying towards the jaguar in the mist.

It landed near it with a watery PLAP.

Whatever it was, it *floated*!

The jaguar lunged towards it, all claws out, and Mercurio lunged for Red with his own claws, and all three of them clung tightly to each other as they were hauled to shore.

Mercurio's heart pounded in his ears, relief flooding him.

But over that...he could have sworn the rain sounded like applause.

40

KEONAONA

KEONAONA KEPT HIS BEAK buried in the jaguar's neck as they were pulled to shore.

My brave egg. My brave egg.

The words filled Keonaona's head the same way the wet Jenny fur filled his beak, excluding even the rain world around him and the gentle river current tickling his belly, legs, and tail from below. Even the feedster clinging to his shoulders may as well have been a dream.

Because even though the tang of Jenny's scent hadn't changed—not for one second—Keonaona was convinced his son was now, by some miracle, here with him, in the jaguar's body. Because who had ever heard of a full-grown, wild predator cheeping words like it belonged in the nest? Let alone offering herself to be, well, ridden upon, like she was tame, when she had always deigned to avoid her squargling neighbors, living unseen like a ghost, her scent and claw marks the only sign of her?

No. Mother had sent Kaimana for him. And since his body was laid up at Ria's place, she'd let him use Jenny instead. By what means this had happened, he didn't know. But clinging to the rosette-stamped neck, Keonaona was certain he was no longer alone.

The pelting rain let up a little. Keonaona's feet found shore just after Kai's did. The cat released its clawed grip from the makeshift buoy and the three of them separated to wade through the shin-high water onto the muddy riverbank.

There were wings there—plenty of them—but Keonaona couldn't keep his eyes off the jaguar, now panting, head hung heavy, bowed towards its muddy paws.

An ear twitched as though somehow the animal felt itself being looked at, and then it suddenly looked up at Keonaona, eyes bright.

Keonaona bent, put his hand on the cat's head. "I'm proud of you, Kai-in-the-sky. You did it. You saved me. So don't feel bad about your mama, okay?"

The cat bowed its head. Heaviest sigh.

Keonaona whistled, sharp. "Hey!"

The cat started, stared up at him again with such surprise in its eyes Keonaona felt the memory of laughter brush past his beak.

But this was important. Kai was always too hard on himself. He couldn't let his egg be haunted by this.

"Listen me. Kaimana, It wasn't your fault."

The cat looked around.

Keonaona waited.

Finally, the cat turned looked into his face again. Out of its thick, spotted throat, it managed, "*Yes,*" in nest talk.

"Good boy." Keonaona stroked the cat's neck. He opened his beak to say more, but a terrible, bloodcurdling, otherworldly scent filled his head, and a shadow blocked the shore lights. The abomination!

Keonaona rose up, wings spread, *BACK OFF!* scream ready in his throat until he saw that it was just a human—a very, VERY tall human—but no, it couldn't be, no human ever smelled like this!

"*Hello,*" chirped Kai, in the jaguar. He looked at Keonaona. "*Papa, friend.*"

Pieces of the puzzle fell into place.

Keonaona swallowed the scream away. "You're...the Gorgon?"

The tall man nodded once. No, it was more like his head sagged. And now that Keonaona was seeing him up close with his eyes and not his beak, he saw how tiring even that gesture was for the strange...man. Dark circles under the eyes, soaked head-hair, frayed, sweat-and-jungle-smelling clothes...

He's run himself ragged...looking for me?

He handed Keonaona a large sheet of foil. "Wrap this around yourself." Then the tall man, the Gorgon, turned to Kai. "You need to get back in that jungle right now."

A steel bolt punched through Keonaona's heart. "Can't I say goodbye?" What kind of cruel beast was this Gorgon to bring his son back to save him, then not give them any time together?

"You'll say your goodbyes at the house."

The shaking in Keonaona's knees doubled. He'd get to say goodbye? Like the war mourners?

The tall man spoke to Kai again. "She knows how to get back to her cubs. Make sure she doesn't hurt anyone on the way. Then you get out of her. Understand?"

Kai nodded that heavy, beautiful head over and over.

"Keep *no* plans to stay in her." The tall man's voice had suddenly changed; it was accented...and strained. "Or return in her. I didplant you in there, I can uproot you. And if I must to uproot you, I will refuse to make you like-alive."

Jenny's body seemed to lower itself into a bow. "*Yes!*" Kai chirped.

"We'll meet back at the house." This in the man's normal voice.

The Gorgon stepped back, tossed his long arm towards the forest. "Go."

The jaguar sprang for the treeline. A few alarm cries followed it before it was swallowed up by the blackness of the forest.

Keonaona stood with the Gorgon, trying to peer through the mist where his son had gone.

"He'll be safe."

Keonaona looked up into the tall man's face again. He spoke so calmly, with real reassurance, yet his scent seemed to promise violence and all things awful.

Kai had called him "friend." What would Hana have made of him?

He supposed...He supposed he could ask her.

Back at the house.

Keonaona pulled the foil tighter around him. Little beads of rain banged against it, rapidly, so the sound quivered like a drumroll. He swallowed.

"I want you to stay with me. Both of you. As my guests."

Rolling his eyes, the tall man leaned back, facing the dripping heavens, arms thrown out like Keonaona's words had literally struck him. When he was upright again, he seemed to struggle to say something—his mouth didn't open but his lips worked.

At last, he said, not without a little exasperation, "Good!"

Then his mismatched eyes jumped over Keonaona's head. He stepped away quickly, into the dark and out of the path of the blazing shore light floating this way.

Keonaona stared at it dumbly. He was too tired to do anything more about it. It seemed to have peeled apart from the other, higher shore lights—two were low—maybe one of Zorin's side-by-sides? Now that Kai was gone, his beak was paying attention, filling out the scene as best it could with the rain, and he thought he could smell Zorin's scent pooled nearby like the motor oils he sometimes worked with on the weekend.

And he could scent others, too: neighbors and strangers alike, all here onshore. Why so many? For him? That thought made him squeamish.

But now the light was on him, the glare erasing all vision apart from it. It seemed familiar, somehow, but in a way that raised his ruff—

And then the smell of vanilla human perfume emerged from the screen of rain. The newswoman. The microphone she held was suddenly under his jaw.

"Ho-oh-kah-no-sir, what can you tell me about the events of last night?"

Keonaona froze, staring at her.

What could he say? How could he explain everything that had happened? Could he even make her understand?

Footsteps arrived next to him. And a familiar scent that made his wings tense with dread.

41

MERCURIO

MERCURIO STEPPED BETWEEN RED and Vanilla Woman, pushing the mic away and lifting his decent wing as much as he could to shield Red from view.

"Hey." He croaked once. "Turn off the cams."

Any squargling would have recognized that croak as meaning serious business. But instead, Vanilla Woman put the mic under Mercurio's beak.

"And you are?" said Vanilla Woman. She looked at him expectantly, like a co-star waiting for him to pick up his cue. Like she knew what Mercurio would say next.

Well, after an exhausting swim, hours in the jungle, being shot, scraped up, and bludgeoned by his own equipment, your humble correspondent doesn't feel like saying his lines. Even with millions of views handed to him on a platter.

"I'm tired," he said. "So's he. He doesn't want to talk."

The microphone was still there. The cams were still recording.

"Shut it all down." He paused. "Or do you think the Gorgon will let you off easy for keeping him up all night?"

The mic pulled back, a little. "It's three in the morning," said Vanilla Woman.

"Exactly. You wanna be the reason he didn't get to bed till five? 'Cause he ain't patient when he hasn't slept. I got the laser burn to prove it."

Vanilla Woman's face dropped in shock. But then the mic rushed towards Mercurio's face.

"Tell us more!"

Mercurio opened his hand for the mic.

She didn't hand it over at first, not till he made the intergalactic sign for "hand it over": the grabby claw. She handed it over.

Mercurio turned and threw the mic in the river.

He lowered his slumping wing. Red was positively gawping at him.

What, I can't do something nice for the sap whose life I just saved?

Whatever.

"Come on, Red. Let's get you home."

The cam lights followed them to Garage Hound's open-air ATV.

Mercurio gingerly climbed into the back bucket seat next to where the tall Gorgon was folded up awkwardly, watching everything.

Red took the front, next to the driver's seat.

Voices and clucks buzzed all around them, but Mercurio didn't hear any of it. He stared at his folded hands for a while, completely still. Not really thinking. Just...sitting.

After a time, Garage Hound swung into the front seat. The gas engine *zummed* to life, blowing fuel smell into the air.

Something occurred to Mercurio. Before Garage Hound could drive off, Mercurio leaned forward.

"Hey-uh, cousin," he said. "I left some equipment, uh, back up the shore, behind a rock. Think we could swing by and get it?"

Garage Hound glanced back—at the tall Gorgon. Mercurio's last hope dimmed at the look they exchanged.

"Were they mem sticks?" said Garage Hound.

"Yeah."

"Jenny got 'em, brah. *Kala mai i'au.*"

"It...got 'em?"

"Yeah. Ripped 'em apart, I heard."

"What about my screen?"

"Probably got her claws in it before we drove away."

Mercurio sat back, stunned.

It wasn't enough he'd used the last of his money and lost all his equipment. No, he had to go and make mortal enemies with a wild cat.

"This was before his son entered the cat," added the tall Gorgon.

Mercurio looked into the tall Gorgon's face. He felt a twitch in his eye. *Was that supposed to make me feel better?*

Garage Hound spoke again. "The way she tore 'em apart, cuz...well, I wouldn't go out in this jungle alone no more, okay?"

Mercurio nodded.

Garage Hound shifted into drive. With wet cracks like snapping plastic, the ATV's wheels turned on the riverfront. In seconds, it was trundling over the jungle track it had crawled out of, moving steadily, but slowly, away from the river.

42

KEONAONA

THE PISTON ENGINE NOISE cut off.

Keonaona jerked out of his doze. The sound of rain and murmuring filled the gap the now-quieted engine left. The pungent tang of liquid fuel joined the familiar mix of soothing flowers, staunch cubbat-quality turf, and time-worn wood; scents that made up Keonaona's front yard. The smells of...him, his history, his lineage...his family past—of sitting out here with his own father and mother, drinking lemonades and playing cards during muggy summer nights—and family present, of watching Kai climb his play cube like a monkey while sitting with Hana on the lanai...

He blinked hard—he must have been dozing open-eyed in Zorin's side-by-side—looked up at his house through the black roll bar that cut his home's underside and the bright grey sky into three different sharply-angled pieces. Was it dawn already?

He sat up as Zorin came around, his oil-and-metal scent brushing past Keonaona's face in the air. The wide-shouldered mechanic opened his door...and then bent over to gather Keonaona out.

Keonaona waved him away. "I've got it, Zor," he said...and then promptly felt his rubber legs give out on his first step out of the vehicle. Zorin caught him, then helped Keonaona not make a fool of himself stumbling up onto the lanai, where he scented Lani, Analū, and...he looked up, to confirm his beak's guess with his eyes...well, that must be the other Gorgon, looking over the scene in his favorite blue wicker chair, scent just as strong and otherworldly as her mate's.

They had been waiting for him.

329

Lani rushed him, scolding him with sharp *gaks* like he was a nestling. Behind her, Analū stood. Lani and Zorin quickly set Keonaona down in his vacated chair.

Now that he was sitting out on his lanai, Keonaona could see all the wings coming up the drive...more than the whole town had come out. Strangers had searched for him. Like the strangers in Pillars Beach had recovered his poor little family.

The wings, familiar and foreign alike, came up the drive, and behind them the forest was noising awake in the drizzly dawn with screeing birds and hooting monkeys.

The forest where the jaguar was nested with her family. The jaguar touched by that otherworldly...person...sitting in his chair nearby, and by the tall man, now stumping up the lanai porch with head forcibly raised, but undeniably wobbly. From fatigue. But did Keonaona look any better?

The tall man stood beside the seated Gorgon, and their scents fit together like razor-edged puzzle pieces.

His neighbors were coming up onto the lanai. Some of the visitors took this as an invitation to join them but were roundly scolded to stand back on Keonaona's marshy front lawn. Far behind them, some squabs had discovered Kaimana's play cube and were scrambling about it, but the adults were washing up to his lanai like waves to the shore.

And here came Griffon Cortez, marching up the drive, Lono and Rosie and that Netron news crew in tow.

The blue-headed feedster stood at the bottom steps of the lanai, one hand on the carved banister. One wing hung, injured. Boy, he looked young, now!

His neighbors had Zorin and Lani and Analū surrounded. Questions came, fast and furious. What had Keonaona been doing in the river so late at night? Was it true his family hadn't come home with him from his trip? Was he moving away? What was the Gorgon doing on his lanai? And what about Jenny? Wings were saying Jenny had acted strange...

Everyone had come out for Keonaona.

He owed them an explanation.

It wouldn't put things back the same. But if they had the answer, maybe they could be satisfied, and he could be alone for his goodbyes. Maybe he wouldn't have to put on a gracious face as they sat in his parlor with the Gorgon, saying their own, worthier goodbyes.

Lono's distinct whistle-tune parted the crowd, and he and Rosie came up the lanai unchallenged, though the questions previously leveled at Zorin, Lani, and Analū were now aimed at the couple.

The Likekes ignored them to come up to Keonaona. Lono opened his beak, but Keonaona didn't want him to say anything.

Quickly, he stood. And fell back into the chair again (the cushion puffed a cloud smelling of wood lacquer and persistence and soursop; they'd put him in Hana's favorite chair), but he grabbed the sturdy metal armrests and pushed himself up again to his feet.

Unsteady steps took him to the post at the top of the lanai stairs. Clinging to it, he looked out over everyone again. So many eyes on him.

He was guilty. It had been an accident. He didn't deserve to be aboveground, breathing the fresh wet air of the rainy season, tasting sweet pineapple *atole*, scenting new people and places and things. He wasn't supposed to be alone. He wasn't supposed to be doing those things alone. Not without his family. How could he tell them that? How could he tell them how wrong it all was? How could he explain it all the right way?

The grey air brightened a second, casting shadows, then went wan and dull again.

Maybe he couldn't.

But he supposed he could tell them what had happened.

"My name is Keonaona Ho'okano. I own this house. Me and my family were supposed to take in the Gorgon a few...days? ago, for their visit.

"The plan was for you all to say your goodbyes here. But—" He couldn't say anything for a while. The only sounds came from the distant jungle and some of the squabs playing on Kai's cube.

He swallowed hard.

"But my family is dead."

He could feel all of Crooked Neck on his lanai, holding their breath, utterly silent.

331

"We were on—I was on a business trip just before. They came to visit. Stayed two weeks with me. At the end of it, instead of coming back here, like we planned, I went elsewhere to work a little longer. I thought I could earn some extra jen and we could go back for another vacation, no work, just have fun.

"They stayed in Pillars Beach. I wanted them to come home. But they stayed there while I went to another city to work some more. They went out swimming alone in the ocean, someplace quiet. They..." He had to swallow again, twice. "They told me the ocean took her against some rocks, and my egg swam out to save her, but he...he couldn't..." He couldn't do this, he couldn't tell this story.

"I wish we had all come home and followed the plan. I wish I hadn't taken the extra job. I wish I'd made them come back. I wish I wasn't mad at her for not coming home like I wanted. I'm mad at her now, but I love her. I...I wish I could die now. But that is not the path Mother has chosen for me.

"I'm sorry you all were up all night looking for me. I'm not worth it. I just didn't want to be seen. *Mahalo nui loa* for looking for me, for caring. I'm supposed to be the best host in town, but right now I can't be even a good stranger. I'm sorry for that. Thank you for coming."

More silence. Even the squabs' clamor faded away, softer than the awakening jungle.

Then, from somewhere out on the lawn, a mourning keen rose up, a single voice which somehow seemed to contain all Keonaona's devastation and bewilderment and sorrow and anger.

Lani gave the answering cry, a wail long and haunting, that spoke to Keonaona's heart: *we understand, we see your pain, we will not pass you by, we will stay with you while you are suffering.*

Keonaona raised his head as the mourning songs mounted like ocean waves. He looked over them, the guests of Crooked Neck, all come to mourn a loss. He'd thought his loss separate, different from theirs, but perhaps all loss was flavored from the same spring. His loss hadn't come from the war, but that didn't mean they weren't singing the same pain.

Perhaps he wasn't the only one here that didn't wish to be seen...but who needed to be.

The songs of sorrow exhausted themselves. The yard was not silent again, but it was quiet.

Keonaona looked over all the wings again.

Life was not normal. It would never return to its former shape. Never again.

He didn't know. He didn't know how he would get through this. He didn't know what shape his life would take on from here on out.

So much to not know.

He closed his heavy eyes.

But there were a few things he did know. He knew he would get to say the things that needed to be said to Hana and Kaimana. He knew how to be a good host. And he knew right now he was too tired to be one.

"Lani?" he said.

"Yes, honeysuckle."

"Will you help me?"

"Duh."

A tired smile dragged itself onto Keonaona's face. He scratched his claws twice against the post, then opened his eyes.

The feedster was the first one that he saw.

"Where are you staying?" asked Keonaona.

"Who? Me?" said the feedster, softly.

Keonaona nodded heavily.

"Motel."

"Room?"

"On the lanai."

Keonaona turned to Lani. "He can come in. And so can you two, of course," he said, keeping a hand on the post to steady himself as he turned around to address the Gorgon. "I'm sorry about earlier."

They said nothing. But the woman-shaped one rose from Keonaona's favorite chair. Her eyes were startlingly blue as she watched him.

"Lani?" said Keonaona. "Send everyone else home. We'll do this the way we meant to, Lono," he said before the square could protest, "but I need some time before I can do it right."

"How long?" he asked.

"Lono!" Rosie hissed.

"As much time as he needs," said Lani, warning note in her voice. "And if anyone complains, they can come talk to me."

"—Or me," added Analū.

"Got it?"

"Got it," said the Likekes. Rosie's was the resolute voice. Lono's, deflated.

Hearing them reply together made Keonaona ache for his Hana, but didn't make him want anyone else. Nobody would replace her.

"Go to bed, honeysuckle," said Lani. "I'll take care of things out here for you."

Keonaona trudged to his front door. He opened it, went inside. The scents of home embraced him painfully.

The feedster followed him in. The Gorgon entered next. Then shut the door on the world behind them.

43

GORGON

JERIMIN STOOD IN THE tastefully dim Hoʻokano parlor, glowering at Harold and her crew as they checked the setup they'd left behind four days ago. Since he and his Queen had spent the last three days in bed (both sleeping and...not), they hadn't gotten around to wrecking their equipment, so everything was in order for the interview. Which is why his face was all...heavy and stiff and just plain weird-feeling under all this "camera-ready" makeup.

He wriggled his itchy nose, reluctant to get the stuff on his fingers by scratching it normally.

The itching sensation disappeared as his Queen, out on the front lanai, scratched her own nose, transmitted the sated skin sensation back to him.

/AHHH! THANK YOU!/ he sent a flood of pink love and gratitude and memories of good-tasting food along with the words. He felt her grin and affection as she gathered it all to her like a bouquet of sweet flowers.

He smoothed down the front of his black linen button-down, grateful (first) that Hoʻokano owned an iron, and (second) that Lani the Lunch Hen had been able to find said iron in one of the many closets tucked away in the enormous mansion. Even if his hair was shaggy, he should look semi-presentable for a Netron audience: his shirt was smooth as a frozen lake and the creases in his pants knife sharp.

More importantly, he didn't think he'd bring down the annoying wrath of the royal stylist upon himself. Image *was* everything with this current court.

/They keep no vow name of ours. We can still refuse./

/No. I like the plan. Just hate the makeup. And her./

335

He looked across the room, at a closed door they hadn't been behind before. The news crew had Plattman in there.

Now that they'd spent time...not-sleeping,

/Prude!/

conserving power was no longer a concern. With just a glance out the side wall, his Queen had spotted the girl the moment she rolled up with Cortez in his golf cart. That had been just a minute or two after Lani the Lunch Hen had let the crew inside.

Thought they were being clever.

Well, they were in for a rude awakening.

Stevenson, the cameraman, caught Jerimin's smirk. He stepped away from his camera and faced him, shoulders square. "Something funny?"

You won't think so.

He smoothed his face into a nice, bland expression. "Not at all."

The cameraman scowled and returned to his camera.

Jerimin leaned against the wall, fingers drumming on his crossed arms. The colors in his head thrummed, deep hues of happiness. The heat out on the lanai in the early mornings pleased her, despite the lack of sun. He let himself drowse with her a while while the crew adjusted and readjusted studio lights.

The colors roused, like stirred silt clouding a beaker of water.

/The doorbell will ring, but it is not them. It is a package./

The doorbell rang. Lani left the kitchen where she was cleaning up breakfast (tea, fried potatoes with veg), drying her three-fingered hands on her apron as she strode towards the front door.

/A package? Is it my mobi?/ He'd asked if Nika could take a look at it the first morning at breakfast with Macoya, Analū the general store owner, and Lani. Poor Ho'okano had still been sleeping then. The store owner had taken it, but Jerimin hadn't heard anything since.

At least Lani let him borrow her screen to send a message to Lyle, but three days later, his scentmod still hadn't come in. He was completely out, which meant Jerimin would be sitting in sessions later today with every squargling treating him like a rabid dog.

/I cannot see in./ A rectangular parcel wrapped in yellow paper appeared before his eyes—and a sort of diagram, blue chevrons bouncing off the paper like it was a light shield. /A one willed it a surprise while wrapping it./

/Hunh. So...if I focus really hard when I'm wrapping gifts, I might stand a prayer of surprising you someday?/

/Youdowish./

He chuckled. The cameraman stopped to glare over his shoulder at him.

Clown!

He resisted the urge to bare his teeth at him (*wrong instincts!*) and just pointedly rolled his eyes instead.

The cameraman harrumphed and turned back to his task.

Hgggh. Wish they'd start soon.

He leaned back against the wall just as nail-clicks on the wood flooring heralded a squargling entering the area. He turned to look, expecting to see Lani's creamy orange hide; instead, it was Macoya, carrying a tan duffel bag over one blue-dappled green shoulder. He saw Jerimin looking and twittered softly.

"They said I could watch," he said. "You know—tricks of the trade."

This surprised Jerimin a little. He'd seen little of Macoya the past few days,

/Because sleeping. And NOT slee—/

/YES, thank you./

He shook her laughter to the back of his head.

Where was he? Oh, right. He'd seen little of Macoya, but when he had seen him, he was at Lani's side, following her orders to chop this, strain that, for dinner, or even washing dishes. And he was (probably for him) unnaturally quiet. Whatever had happened in the river had clearly affected him.

"You're going back to the feed game, then?"

"Dunno," said Macoya. He winced when he shrugged; one wing didn't go up as high as the other. Was Jerimin...feeling bad for him? Maybe not quite. "It's just...a rare opportunity."

Jerimin nodded.

The cameraman motioned the square over. After a quick, questioning look at Jerimin, Mercurio set his duffel bag on the floor against the wall and began following the cameraman around the set while he pointed out different, probably technical things. Macoya looked interested, even asked questions from time to time, but Jerimin couldn't see any of the fire that had once been in the square's eyes. Would he ever regain it? Jerimin would most likely never know. It was like that, traveling town-to-town like this, always meeting people, getting fragments of their stories, never any follow-up. It wasn't like you could send the Gorgon a postcard on the road—not that anybody cared to.

Well, this was their bed.

He mentally ran through as many possible interview questions he could come up with. Hopefully they wouldn't catch him wrong-footed.

Hopefully.

Eventually, the sound guy approached, tiny clip-on microphone in hand.

Jerimin, having had this done to him before, for *Deniba!*, pushed off the wall quickly.

"Why don't I sit down?" Having some hostile stranger stand on tiptoe body-to-body with him, fumbling for his collar wasn't Jerimin's idea of fun. And being Netron, he'd be fumbling a while, wanting to get it *just* right. Ugh.

"Tandon-sir, put him over there, please," said the producer, pointing out the chair opposite Harold, who was seated and reviewing her own notes.

Jerimin sat. As expected, the dolt took forever getting the thing clipped where he wanted. Then there was some last-minute bustling while filming concerns (he reckoned) were taken care of. A last dusting of powder on Harold's beaky nose, a quick examination of her no-nonsense chignon, and the camera's recording light switched on. Lani left the kitchen—he could hear her nails clicking; would the microphones pick that up?—but Macoya stood silently behind the cameraman, watching.

The producer sat behind Jerimin, in a chair that must have been off-camera. He twisted in his seat, saw her gaze meet the reporter's. He was surrounded.

/Wish they'd show up already./

A mental thrum of reassurance. /I will send them to you as soon as I can. You must to keep the interview alive until then./

Harold's eyes met his. All business, all professionalism. She wasn't one of the top TV anchors on his world for nothing. But he was a traitor—and worse, he was a traitor who had escaped punishment, and he had no illusions that everyone hated him for it. There was no forgiving that where he came from.

He straightened, tried to keep the easy, unconcerned interest in his own gaze. Not as easy as it used to be.

The recording lights switched on.

Harold started in.

The first questions weren't quite what he'd planned for. They were innocuous, factual questions—where did he grow up, where had he lived, did he have any siblings. To...soften him up? Maybe to put him at ease, though he was certain such a tactic would only be used to get him to show some soft underbelly before they struck.

He was right; the questions quickly turned to the events of the past two years. He stopped her before she could finish the first sentence.

"I've already spoken about that to the Osidern authorities. I'm not repeating myself. Bring it up again, and this interview's over."

He saw her jaw tense as she bit down. But then she began summarizing what she called "the Plattman incident."

He forced himself to relax in the chair. It's what a Gorgon would do. Not look at all concerned with the idea of some mealy-mouthed media puppets

/marionettes/

dragging her name through the mud.

Mealy-mouthed media marionettes. That wasn't half bad.

Harold's eyes narrowed at the little smile that he slipped out. "Do you find the thought of tying up young women amusing?"

"No," he said. "I'm happily married."

Her expression didn't change, but a blush raced up Harold's face, up to the roots of her hair.

"I wasn't implying anything like that," he said smoothly. "But it's interesting to see where *your* head is at, miss."

[Ausgezeichnet. Spoken like a true Gorgon.]

Well, the last Gorgon had used innuendo to throw people off balance, and Jerimin knew firsthand that it worked. Why mess with the classics? "I repeat, I did not tie up, harass, bother, or in any way molest Plattman-miss. It's unfortunate her psychological immaturity won't allow her to let go of a minor inconvenience she encountered on her vacation. Perhaps she needs to see someone."

"Like whom?"

"Like a professional therapist. Someone who can get to the root of her insecurity. Or insecurities, if that's the case. She won't ever find genuine happiness until she does. She'll just keep lashing out."

"Here's something from her written statement. Quote, 'He put his giant hand around my neck and squeezed until I started choking. My friend's little sister was next to me, screaming. The girls I was with were too afraid of him to make him stop.' End quote. Does that sound like lashing out to you?"

"Accusing someone of actions one has no proof for can count, yes."

"So you never attempted violence on her."

Violence! I used to be beaten so badly I had to wear long sleeves in to work in summer like a battered wife and she wants to talk to ME about violence?!

"No. Never."

"Never laid a hand on her."

"No. Never."

"Never threatened her?"

"No. Never."

"Then why would she accuse you?"

"Yes, why *would* she? She has no evidence, and yet her unfounded accusations single-handedly brought no fewer than four news networks to a small town in Osider. What is your opinion, Harold-miss?"

"I am here as a neutral party. Our viewers are interested in your side of the story."

"Then I'm afraid your viewers will find themselves bored, because my story is a dull one. Our host for that night could not take us in, so we accepted the hospitality of Plattman-miss's faerie friends staying nearby. To Plattman's disapproval."

"In her statement, Plattman-miss said those fae were terrified of you."

"She may say that, but to my knowledge, none of those fae have come forward to confirm her story."

"It's possible those fae are too frightened of you to come forward."

"That's one possibility. The other is that their friend is acting irrationally and they want nothing to do with her anymore."

He thought he saw Harold's gaze slip over to the side. A signal with the producer? He went on swiftly. "This young lady says she was strangled, but has no handprints. She says she was tied up, but has no ligature marks. She says her friends were afraid, but none of them have stood by her side. This seems to be a classic case of 'he said, she said.'"

The door handle to the back room was turning. But the door didn't move any further.

Harold spoke next. "In her statement, Plattman-miss said you took all their mobis. How could she document evidence without one?"

"Her statement should say this all allegedly took place in a twenty-four hour period, ye—right?"

"It does."

"They had a bus to catch in the morning and left then. *With* their mobis."

"Mobis she said you held for ransom."

"Allow me to address this first, please."

Harold nodded, barely. "Very well."

"Without their mobis, they couldn't have gotten on their bus. But ticket records should show that they were all aboard."

"They do."

"So she's safely away on a bus with her own mobi, allegedly with injuries on visible places on her body—but she didn't think to photograph them? That doesn't make any sense."

"Well, she was very upset."

Jerimin knew this schtick from past viewings of Harold. He kept himself level.

"She had five friends with her, all with mobis. None of them thought to record her alleged injuries?"

"She says they were all very upset."

"They were surrounded by neutral, if not friendly parties on the bus. The Osidern people are very caring. If something was wrong with her, someone would have noticed, and if someone noticed, they would have said something and tried to help her.

"Instead, these young women boarded their bus and went home. The fae went their merry way, and Plattman cooked all this up for the attention."

"That's what you think happened," said Harold. The back door was opening.

"Logic leads me to those conclusions." He stood up as Plattman entered the room, carrying her ugly grey backpack, followed by Cortez.

Before he could be scolded, he sent, /I know a Gorgon doesn't bow to anyone and probably shouldn't stand when a woman enters the room, but it doesn't hurt to look polite on camera. Part of 'the show.'/

Agreement, in a deep turquoise color, spread through his head as from a puff of smoke.

Stools were pulled up, and Plattman and Cortez—as her lawyer?—took their seats. Jerimin sat back down.

Plattman's dark, frizzy hair had been pulled back, but all the TV makeup in the world couldn't add much besides extra color to that round, plain-Jane face with its cockeyed hairline. She'd dressed—or they'd dressed her—in a white top and grey pleated skirt that evoked a Secondary school uniform without actually looking like one. Aged her down. Made him look like a bully. Whose idea had that been, he wondered.

"Then why did you make us pay a ransom to get our mobis back?" said Plattman.

"It's interesting, the sorts of dramatics a deranged mind can come up with," he said, addressing the reporter.

"You made Seppy pay two hundred ninety-five to get her mobi back. One forty-five for Jewel's. Forty-two fifty-three for Sizzle's. Even Treasure had to pay seven—she only had twelve jen, and you made her pay!"

"Making up random prices doesn't seem to prove anything."

"They didn't go home with that money!"

"Oh? Is that reflected in their bank statements?"

"It was in cash, and you know it! You held it in your hands!"

"If it was cash, then how they spent it won't be recorded. As I recall, the youngest mentioned she spent her money on candy."

"It wouldn't be recorded—except in receipts!" said Plattman with relish.

"Except in receipts," he replied calmly, ignoring the cold patches of sweat growing under his arms. He already knew where she'd go with this, and the argument wasn't weak.

Plattman went on. "You'd see a bank statement before the trip showing what we pulled for travel. Minus all the receipts we collected by spending and eating. Then count the money they had at the end. There'll be a huge amount unaccounted for, of money you stole from us!"

Harold turned to the girl. "Do you still have your receipts, Plattman-miss?"

"I do! I do!" said Plattman, bouncing in her chair. "I printed them out!" Paperwork from a folder under Cortez's wing was passed to Harold.

The reporter tried handing it to Jerimin, but he left his hands in his lap, shook his head. "Receipts can be doctored, and cash can be hidden. No matter what the receipts say, her 'what I was left with' number could easily be faked. Hidden inside her backpack until all this is blown over, then retrieved and, if she wished, redeposited."

"That's just the sort of scheme a deviant person would come up with," said the girl.

"I agree," said Jerimin, keeping his face bland. "So why did you come up with it, Plattman-miss?"

She seemed to inflate with silent rage. Then she ripped her backpack up off the floor. "I brought my pack. I haven't touched it since we left the house. Here." She thrust it at him. "Search it."

"No, thank you."

The girl suddenly hugged her pack like she was strangling it. The makeup couldn't hide her reddening face. "We didn't want you in that house! None of us did!"

"You still haven't explained why you would hold their mobis for ransom, Icarii-sir," said Harold, but just then, Jerimin heard the front door open out in the foyer. The sound was followed by a pleased red color filling one side of his head, and the chiming and buzzing of faerie wings down the hall. Towards them.

Jerimin turned to the sound tech. "You'll need some more microphones," he said as Plattman's faerie friends floated into the interview. All four of them, the tall siren, the shorter pixie sisters, and the pixie chef, were dressed like they were going into a Netron courtroom, in pastel polo shirts buttoned all the way up to their necks and charcoal pleated skirts with hemlines just below the knees. Confetti Wings wore a neon green scrunchie on her wrist where a watch might have been, but otherwise, they all appeared completely respectable—completely *credible*—to a Netron audience.

Microphones were rushed to the fae. After some sound checks, they sat down on barstools pulled from the kitchen in a row beside Jerimin.

Only Confetti Wings dared glance at Jerimin, but was swiftly and surreptitiously nudged by big sister.

At the reporter's request, each of the fae introduced themselves. Chef ended with, "We were at the house with Lisa during Her Ladyship's visit."

"Excuse me. When you say 'Her Ladyship', you are referring to this man?" Harold pointed to him with her stylus.

The fae all nodded. "Yes, ma'am," said Chef. "That's the Gorgon."

Harold nailed him with a raised eyebrow. "And you accept being referred to as a lady, Icarii-sir?"

"Of course. My title's always been styled this way. Far be it from me to question royal protocol."

Harold turned to the fae again. "Your friend Plattman-miss has made a statement that just last week, the Gorgon—this man—came to the home you were staying at for your vacation, allegedly strangled and tied her up, then made all four of you pay a ransom for your mobis. We'd like to hear your version of what happened during that visit."

The faerie girls all faced the Chef, and the Chef spoke to the reporter. "Well, none of that stuff happened. I mean—*we* mean—the Gorgon came to our vacation rental, and we let them stay the night, but nobody laid a hand on Lisa. Neither Gorgon." The other girls were nodding along in agreement. They certainly looked sincere!

And Plattman was *fuming.*

"No—no. Excuse me, but Treasure," she addressed the youngest, Confetti Wings, "you were screaming next to me! Right while he did it, he had his hand around my throat, you remember!"

And—bless that little pixie—Confetti Wings looked right back at her with a puzzled, *why are you saying these things?* expression—completely convincing!—and slowly said, "No...Lisa...you made that up."

"He said he'd feed me to *her*, to the other Gorgon! You were right there! —You all were!"

The fae looked at her solemnly, and the siren, Deception, said, "Yeah. We were all there, Leese—and nothing happened."

Plattman's dark brows dropped in a scowl. She raked it across all four girls' faces. "I can't believe this."

The fae squirmed.

Her head snapped to the reporter. "They're all afraid of him and you know it! We all know it!"

Incensed, now she turned to Jerimin. "You did this somehow!"

"It's not my fault if the cameras make them nervous, Plattman-miss. And without any physical evidence to prove harm was done to you, it's our word"—he circled his hand to include the fae—"against yours. Face it. You've come up short."

Her mouth gaped and closed but no sound came out: Check and mate.

"Would you like to end this interview now?" he asked.

"No." Then her eyes narrowed; absolute hatred was in them. "You're a scab, a detestable, lying blackleg. I hope you get the needle someday. It's just what you deserve. —You and that disgusting, subhuman *thing* you married!"

The whole room froze.

Jerimin checked Plattman's face. Her sneer remained. Not a shred of contrition to be found.

In her mind, the words she had just said about his Queen—his very best friend in all the universe, the heart of his heart, his partner in crime—were justifiable.

In her mind, she was right to insult his wife to his face.

In her mind, she thought she could insult the Gorgon's wife *to his face* and get away with it.

Wow. You really are THAT *stupid.*

Now, he'd been expecting something like this, and so was able to quickly tamp down the flare of rage that jetted through his body, but something must have shown on his face, because Harold suddenly lunged sideways in her seat, as if to put herself between Jerimin and the girl. The fae were silent, wide-eyed, looking at Plattman like they expected her to be struck down right then and there.

They were waiting for him to fire something back.

Instead, Jerimin turned to Cortez, watching unperturbed from his stool next to Plattman.

"I wasn't going to say anything. But...I noticed something."

The fae turned white as bone.

"Lane Cortez, it was your house we all stayed at, right? Plattman, her faerie friends here, and myself and the Gorgon."

"Yes, Lane," he said, suddenly and immediately sounding like he was in a courtroom.

Jerimin turned to Harold. "And your team, they've been staying at the Cortez house, too, correct?"

"Yes..." She answered with a quick glance behind him, at her producer.

Jerimin went on. "I was wondering...while you've been staying, did you or your crew happen to come across a large wooden bowl?"

A shadow crossed Cortez's face.

"Beautiful thing, about nine inches in diameter, maybe...four inches deep?" He molded its shape in the air with his hands as he spoke.

Harold's eyes flew across her crew's faces, but Jerimin could see them shaking their heads out of the corner of his eye.

"No? That's interesting."

Now Cortez was frowning.

Plattman sneered. "Why's that interesting?"

"I find it interesting—and you might, too, Lane Cortez—because I ate cereal out of it when these fae hosted us—but after you all left, I didn't see it anywhere."

"You were there," said Plattman. "I washed it."

"So you *were* the last one who had it." He turned to Cortez. "Have you seen it since you returned?"

The tiger-striped squargling's back was steel-girder straight. "No. And with all the guests, the wash has been going twenty-four seven. I should've seen it by now."

Jerimin nodded silently, letting that sink into the room. When he felt the thoughts had steeped long enough, he went for the kill.

He looked at Cortez. "Do you think it could be there in her backpack?"

The camera nodded to look at it, in Plattman's arms.

Plattman's eyes bulged in fury.

The square reached for it at the same time Plattman pulled back, but Harold got up off her chair and took the bag off the girl's lap. It didn't matter. If anything, it was better that she, a neutral-to-hostile party, be the one to do this.

"If you'll allow me," said the reporter.

Plattman's puffy fingers turned to claws, gripping her chair seat. "You don't have my permission!"

"You have probable cause!" Cortez shot back.

Plattman turned to him, injured. "You really think—"

"Excuse me, Plattman-miss," said Harold. "In the interest of time...Please, allow me."

"Fine."

Harold unzipped the main compartment and slid her hand inside. She began digging around.

Now, she could, theoretically, find it, but refuse to acknowledge it. But if she does that, I'll just make sure Cortez gets to take a look.

But it didn't come to that. He actually saw the moment the reporter discovered it; her teeth suddenly grit together, like maybe she'd cracked a finger on the one solid thing hiding among the yielding clothes.

Harold lifted it out. It was unmistakably the same bowl Jerimin had just described, the same one his Queen had stuffed in there that morning as a little farewell surprise. Plattman stared daggers at him. But Treasure gasped aloud, and dismay was clear on the other faerie faces.

No acting there.

"I'll take that, thanks," said Cortez. The reporter handed over the bowl. He promptly sniffed it. "Yes, it's mine."

Deception looked at the girl. "Why'd you take it, Leese?"

"I didn't do it! I told you, I haven't unpacked yet! YOU!" She jabbed a finger at Jerimin. "You did it, somehow!"

"I didn't. And you can't prove that I did."

Plattman whipped around to Cortez. "Doesn't it smell like him?"

"The whole place reeks like them! But *you're* the one who had my bowl in your backpack!"

Jerimin turned to the fae. "I'm very sorry about your friend. She doesn't seem to be the person you thought."

Plattman sputtered. "You—you two were alone with it—with my pack! You put it in there—"

"Why?"

"To make me look bad!"

"Again, *why?*" said Jerimin. "We never expected to see you again, Plattman-miss. You're a nobody. As far as we were concerned, the second you left the Cortez house, you were out of our lives. *You* were the one who called this circus together."

Harold had her reporter's mask of neutrality back on. The faerie girls all looked upon their human friend with horror—oh, it was *beautiful!*—and Cortez had a look of disdain on his face, sharp as the tip of his beak.

Plattman looked from face to face, completely lost.

Ha!

"Cut."

The lights on the cameras shut off; the hovering ones floated back to the cameraman's awaiting hand.

"I think that's a wrap," said the producer.

"What? No!" said Plattman. "No, you can't possibly believe him! Please! Harold-miss!"

Harold stood up. "The makeup comes off with facial oil and water," she said. Around them, the news crew was coiling wires, checking screens. Even Macoya, watching over the camera-man's shoulder this whole time, looked at his feet, refusing to meet her face.

"Cortez-sir, you have to beli—"

"My drivee's full up with the crew," he said. "You'll have to find your own ride back into town."

Plattman gasped in shock.

Jerimin sent his grin out onto his Queen's face. *Bet you weren't planning on that!*

Plattman turned to the fae. "You'll fly me back...right, girls?"

They shook their heads, didn't say a word.

She cupped her hands together, addressed the tall siren. "But I'm your roommate! Seppy?"

Nothing.

Jerimin stood, stretching.

Finally, Plattman rounded on him.

"You!" Her mouth worked. Whatever insults she wanted to hurl didn't seem to be making it down the passage from her brain to her mouth. "YOU!!"

"Excuse me," he said. "I'd like to take this makeup off. Are we finished here?" he asked Harold.

Her lips pursed grudgingly, but then the reporter nodded.

"You have some of that facial oil?"

The producer came to him, wordlessly slapped a package of wipes in his hand.

"Thank you," he said to her back. The media marionettes no longer seemed interested in him. Good.

Jerimin began walking across the interview room into the kitchen. The fae curtseyed one by one as he passed.

He had a wipe out and the kitchen sink running when Plattman followed him in.

She stood like a monolith, eyes boring into him.

A set of fruit-cutting knives lay within arm's reach of her. No one was looking.

He sent a request razor-edged with urgency.

"Don't do it," he sang softly.

Plattman grabbed the biggest knife and came at him.

Or tried to, anyway. She dropped to the floor on the first step, screaming in pain, grabbing her head.

Everyone in the other room ceased what they were doing and ran towards the commotion.

/Sheesh. Was I that loud?/

Busy, came his Queen's thought with a shadow of the pain she was spewing into the girl's head.

The fae, Jerimin noticed, kept their distance, opting to silently watch Plattman thrashing and begging on the floor. And the first time the screaming Plattman took a wild swing in the air, knife still gripped in her hand, the news crew backed off, too.

Two minutes later—when Jerimin called it off—Plattman came to, panting on the wood floor, smelling of urine.

/Tell her she's dead the next time she screws with the Gorgon./

He didn't feel his Queen sending those words; just saw Plattman cringe into a tighter fetal ball as the message was delivered, undoubtedly with some additional pain to make sure the message stuck.

She came out of it again a moment later, trembling and teary-eyed.

He glanced up from her. There, hovering level with his face, was one of the news crew's cameras.

The recording light was on.

It didn't matter what he did or didn't do. As far as his home-world was concerned, he was the devil, and that was never going to change.

Might as well do a good job of it.

He looked into the lens, and spoke as blandly as his beating heart would let him.

"There's clearly something's wrong with her," he said.

Then he turned back to the sink.

He finished washing his face clean while, at his feet, the defeated girl wept.

44

MERCURIO

MERCURIO SHIVERED AS THE tall Gorgon brushed by him, exiting the parlor. His creepy scent was extra thick, extra *threatening* in such close quarters.

Somehow, what Mercurio had just seen happen to the Plattman girl had made getting shot and walloped by the Gorgon look like a tender cuddle in a warm nest.

I dunno what happened, and I don't wanna know!

He watched the fae leave, taking their tense sweat smells and fruity perfumes with them.

At least now, well, he didn't have to worry about seeing the Gorgons anymore. The river'd gone down, and the buses were back up and running. While the producer took the Plattman girl away to get cleaned up, Vanilla Woman drew the curtains open, and a brighter, if still overcast light filled the darkened parlor.

Mercurio felt a little better. Not that he had anything to celebrate, besides getting out of town.

"What's next for you, *mijo?*" Coffee Jerk—*Cortez, I guess*—stood there running his hands over his smooth, patched bowl. "Going to go back with one of the news crews? Bet they could use an intern."

Nearby, the cameraman lifted his head to listen. But Mercurio just shrugged.

"Dunno. Auntie Lani loaned me money for a bus ticket back home. I'll figure things out there."

Cortez grunted, sounding unimpressed.

"Yeah, well...running full speed towards something doesn't make sense if you're not sure it's the thing you want," said Mercurio. *Wait, did that even make any sense?*

Before Cortez could call him on it, Mercurio went to his bag where he'd left it and nestled it against his good shoulder. The bad one was better but still didn't like being jolted around. He turned towards the hall.

Cortez clucked at him, surprised. "You leaving *now*?" he asked.

"Yeah. Lani's got her wings coming up to help during good-byes. Don't wanna get in the way." Show's over. Nothing left for him here now. Coulda thrown Tutu's money into the garbage and saved himself the trouble.

"If you can wait, I'll come back, give you a ride to the station after I get them home." He lowered his wing from Vanilla Woman and her crew. "For you, only five jen."

"I can't pay you. Sack lunch from Auntie Lani, only got money for the bus. I'll walk there."

Cortez whistled, low. "You'll be Jenny sack lunch!"

"I'll stick to the road."

Mercurio drifted out of the parlor. Here was where he'd been shot. This floor...it could've been cool B-roll. And here was the grand entryway, with chandelier and the carpeted stairs. Red had gone up them after they'd all come inside from the river, but Mercurio didn't think he'd been back down since.

Beneath the comforting scent of Hoʻokano's walls, a faint smell of grease and plantains clung to the banister. Lani'd been taking food up—and also down the back hall to the new room where the Gorgons had bedded down. Eegh.

Mercurio took a sec to make sure his paper ticket and cash were still in the duffel pocket he'd zipped it in—they were—then opened the front door onto the lanai.

He blinked hard in the dazzling light, then got a second shock before his eyes adjusted; above the scents of wood and damp grass and plants came the immediate scent of Red—Hoʻokano—into his snoot. And other scents were mixed up in the air, too—the Gorgons *and* the fae?

He turned towards them all. Finally, his eyes adjusted. Red wore a solid black lavalava, and a maile lei around his neck, probably the first of many he'd be wreathed in today. He held a wrapped box in his hands.

"Have a minute?" he asked.

Mercurio's gaze flitted around the lanai: the Gorgons and the fae were a silent, yet expectant wall behind Red—Keonaona. He couldn't read the the Gorgons' faces—neither of 'em—but the sugar-scented, rainbow-winged faerie looked kind of excited. Something was up.

Mercurio guttered. "Guess so," he said.

"Here. I...want you to have this." Red offered him the box. Mercurio took it, trying not to think about everyone watching. He slit the paper with his claw, peeled the wrapping off.

A camera. A good one, easily twice the cost of MaxCam, and that'd had the most bells and whistles. Pro grade, like something the cameraman inside would use.

He stared at it.

Suddenly nervous, he looked up—first at Red, then—weirdly—at the tall Gorgon. "Is this a joke?"

A sad, sort-of smile appeared on Red's face. "We weren't friends. But you didn't let me go on the 'Ehuana. I owe you something for that."

Mercurio thought about that for a while. Yeah, he guessed he coulda died—but he didn't. And he wasn't so sure if Red owed him or not. But he guessed it was nice, that he'd do something for Mercurio, especially after he'd sent the news crews after him.

Mercurio brought the box to his beak, sniffed it, caught just a hint of the metal inside.

"I...if you want, you can have it enchanted right now. I've asked"—Red shrugged both wings back, indicating the fae (and the Gorgons?) behind him—"and they said they would."

"I can silence the fans and weatherproof it for you," said the tallest faerie, in a pale orange shirt. "Including the lens."

"And we can make it so the battery and fans never overheat," said Rainbow Wings, in a sherbet pink shirt.

Was this really happening? That was hundreds of jen worth of enchantments!

"Uh...uh...okay. Yeah, sure." Mercurio fumbled the camera out of the box. The tallest faerie held out her palm, and Mercurio put it in.

She rolled it between her hands, sending up sparks that smelled like oranges, then stroked the lens—*she'll smear her finger oils all over it!*—before handing it over to little Rainbow Wings.

She rolled it around, too, but there were no special effects. Then she asked Mercurio sheepishly, "Um, is the battery still in the box?"

He checked. "No, but..." he helped her find the pop-out slot where the batteries were, one for fans and the one for the cam. She took them out, gave the other to Purple Shirt, who smelled like her sister. They held them close to their lips and inhaled, and then Purple Shirt did the same to the fans, once he pointed them out.

Grinning, they handed the batteries back, and Mercurio put the camera back together.

This. Here in his hand.

"*Ma—mahalo*, Red. But...what do you want me to do with it? Your town mascot got my screen."

"I don't kn—" Red stopped talking and turned to look out over the front drive.

It was Garage Hound, driving up in his noisy ATV.

Red waved once. "That's Zorin," he said.

The wide-shouldered square—Zorin—pulled up beside the stairs and parked, engine rumbles going quiet. He got out, an open brown box in his hands, and jogged up the lanai stairs to join them. In the shadow of the lanai, his olive-and-black mottled hide was dark as motor oil.

The square leaned into Red, wrapped his wings around him gently. "Keonaona, how you doin' with yourself?"

Red sighed. "I don't know. But I'm doing it one minute at a time."

"Well, I know I said before I'd be staying home for all this, but I'll stay with you today to help, if it's cool with you."

Red just nodded. He looked choked up. Mercurio rolled the camera in his hands.

Garage Hound stood up, refolding his wings. He turned to Mercurio. "Hey! You recovering, brah?"

Mercurio nodded. "Yeah. I'm fine."

Garage Hound snuck a glance at Red. "Well, I got something for you," he said to Mercurio. "I think you'll like it!"

Garage Hound reached into the box...and pulled out a beefy-looking black screen, easily a thumb thick.

"Keonaona asked me to track down your gear. When I drove back, your sticks were toast, but Jenny only clawed the front of your screen glass." He held the beefy screen up. "*I* woulda just replaced the glass and called it good, but Keonaona here's a prince." (At this, Red shook his head.) "He had our guy Nika recover the drive and put it on here. Happy Pāheahea!" He handed the new screen over to Mercurio.

Mercurio goggled at it. A new, ruggedized screen was one thing, but a new screen that had all his old shortcuts and programs and files on it?? Really??!!

He switched it on. And let out a kettle whistle of joy seeing his wallpaper and shortcuts whizz into place.

He could've cried, except that just...no. No.

The fae were hopping into the air and clapping. Yeah, it felt like that. Then Rainbow Wings did a somersault in midair, whoo!ing. No, it felt like THAT!

Mercurio laughed, despite himself.

"Does this mean you can film something now?" asked the tall Gorgon.

The fae dropped to the lanai with clunks.

"Y—yeah, sure," said Mercurio, curling his bad wing in protectively.

"Because after the hit piece they're going to put out on me," he said with a dark look back towards the parlor inside, "we could use a balanced portrayal going ahead of us."

Next to him, the big Gorgon was looking at Mercurio and nodding. Icarii went on. "I think you'll know what to record, Lane Macoya. After all, you've seen us in a...variety of moods. What do you say?"

"He has to get permission first from the mourners—if he's going to film any of them," said Red.

"Agreed," said both Gorgons at once. "But that doesn't preclude him from filming a Q and A with me," said Icarii.

Wow. Wow. It'd be different than what he had planned be-fore...but it could be better.

"Okay. Yeah, sure. I'll do it! And I won't...I'll be...you know."

Icarii raised an eyebrow at him. "Respectful?"

"Yeah, yeah, sure, sure!"

The tall Gorgon slid a...worried? nah, *concerned* look at the big Gorgon. But her head was turned away.

Almost looks like she's looking at someone next to her.

Then she turned to Mercurio. "Your tutu says she is proud of you, *'cuervito'*."

Mercurio froze. Freaked out, yes! Happy? Well, maybe when he thought back on this later, he'd get the warm and fuzzies. Maybe.

"Got a few more things in here," said Garage Hound, after shaking off the spooky feeling in the air. He lifted out a mobi, offering it to the big Gorgon. "For you," he said, only to have Icarii—up on his tiptoes, crazy relief on his face, snatch it out of his hand.

"Thank you!"

Garage Hound quickly reeled in his bristling wings. "...and this," he said, holding up a scentmod vial the size of a Jukee can with a paper note taped to it.

Icarii pounced a second time. "Lyle! Oh thank the gods!" he said, holding it up like it was a bar of gold. "Be right back!" he said, and dashed into the house.

The fae all went rigid, fear turning their scents sharp like burnt human bread.

Mercurio looked where they were looking: at the BIG Gorgon.

Well, yeah! He's dangerous sometimes, but SHE'S the one who eats people!!

One of the shorter fae, who smelled of roasted vegetables and nonstick pans, caaarefully turned to the big Gorgon. "Well," she said, "If milady has no more need of our services...we would be off?"

"A word first." The fae's backs stiffened. The big Gorgon went on. "Idohope you four will remember the many mercies of the Gorgon. We let you out of the house unharmed..." She paused for a moment, eyes darting away as if mulling something over...then she blinked and came back. "Scot-free. Your machines were returned. And you enjoyed traveling lunch on us. It was only that Plattman's hunger for spotlights and revenge that brought us together, here, now. Without her, we would have had no desire to call you back. A vital lesson in choosing friends, yes?"

The fae were nodding on fast-forward. "Yes, milady," they chorused.

"A lesson Idohope we will not have to teach you twice."

"Yes, milady!"

She turned away, spoke the next words towards the house. "Good. Be away and be loyal."

The fae instantly dropped into curtseys. "Thankyoumilady!!" They turned and bailed from the lanai, wings blurring. Streaks of neon light followed the paths of the fire fae as they shot into the sky.

So cool!

...

And he hadn't gotten any of it on film!

He screeched. "*Ay yi yi*! Outta my way, I gotta charge this thing!"

Mercurio clutched the camera to his heart and dove back into the house.

45

KEONAONA

Keonaona closed his eyes and breathed in the last sweet wisps of the fae as they flew into the bright clouds. The next breath he drew, though, was heavy, full of the scents of the memories the lanai held, and Zorin, and, of course, the Gorgon.

When he'd come back from the river, he'd retreated to his and Hana's room and just slept. Then days were marked only by Lani bringing him food. It had been a cloudy, muddled clump of time. During it, he tormented himself in the dark with the same questions as before. But then Analū had come by last night, apologizing for not seeing Keonaona's need (Keonaona had accepted the apology; after all, it wasn't fair of him to be annoyed that his friend hadn't seen the pain he'd been intent on hiding), and asking if he needed anything before his goodbyes with Kai and Hana.

He'd told him no.

But after Analū left, Keonaona had found a sheet of paper and wrote down the painful questions and the tender things he'd never meant to leave unsaid.

Keonaona opened his eyes and pulled the paper out of his lavalava pocket.

Or at least some of them.

He still wasn't sure it was enough. Maybe it would never be. It seemed just as soon as he thought he'd written all he wanted, some new thought would come to him, one he just had to tell Hana, or else, how would she ever know?

And now the time was upon him.

Zorin's claws tapped the wooden deck as he came over to Keonaona's side. "You all right, brah?"

Keonaona nodded unconvincingly. And then, thankfully, Zorin just stood there.

Keonaona looked out over the banister towards the jungle where Jenny and her family lay. He thought of Kai.

Behind him, the front door opened with a soft click. A new scent, intricate and grounded and warm, breezed by as Lane—no, Gorgon—Icarii came onto the lanai again. Beneath the scentmod, Keonaona could still pick out notes of his true scent, the unnatural one that had frightened him so...but scenting it now, with the mod added to it, it seemed it seemed only like a nightmare fading in daylight, just another bad dream in a lifetime of nights.

He turned around to look at the Gorgon. Another mated pair.

Taking on The Visit now meant they'd be in the house together. For weeks, possibly longer.

Gorgon Icarii saw him looking, tilted his head in a doggish way, asking with his odd eyes if there was anything Keonaona would like for him to do. The other Gorgon—he would have to ask what she wanted to be called—watched him, gaze level and silent.

Silent. Keonaona thought he would like that tendency in them, in the difficult days ahead.

Tires crunched over the gravel of his drive. Keonaona turned outwards.

Here came the Likekes in their drivee, and Analū following in his yellow one. He waved, not yet ready to whistle greetings or smile.

A big, out-of-towner family was squeezed together in the carts, including a little raspberry-colored squab that looked like a photo of Keonaona's great-grandfather in the living room. She or he reached out in the air, clutching for Kai's play cube.

They parked beaks-in to the front, next to Griffon's drivee and Zorin's side-by-side. The family scrambled out of the vehicles, only to stop and crowd together, warbling anxiously at the sight of the Gorgon up on the lanai.

Guess I'll have to say something, he thought, but then, to his surprise, the woman Gorgon stood from her chair and went to the railing. Her red robes swung gently as she stopped next to him.

"Fear not," she said to the crowd below. They stared at her. "Idokeep a better condition for you today."

More staring.

"In other words, you will not see my other shape."

Some of the tension left the family's wings.

Then she pointed to Keonaona. "But first comes this one, our host."

She looked at Keonaona. The sky above rumbled. Hot rain began falling, but in her blue eyes, Keonaona thought he saw clear skies again.

"Shall we?" she said.

The family was settled in the parlor behind him, speaking softly to one another. They took up every sofa, every stool, every bench. Lani and Zorin and Analū and the others would take care of them.

Keonaona stood before the door that led into the living room. The Gorgon was in there now. He took a breath, struggling to steady himself. His paper crackled in his hand.

Funny. He'd wanted this so badly, yet right now, he felt like running away again.

No use putting it off any longer.

Keonaona opened the door and entered.

The heavenly scent of Lani's famous melon salad hanging in the air of the parlor behind him disappeared with the close of the door.

Now he was drowning in the scents of Hana and Kai. Their scents had long pooled into the walls, the chairs, the sofa, the portraits. The very air tasted of them. Pain ripped through Keonaona again. He gripped his paper hard, heard his claw tear a hole in it.

No light came through the windows; the storm beating the house outside had turned the sky the color of lava rock.

He took a halting step in.

"A little dark in here, isn't it?" came Gorgon Icarii's voice. A click, and a single lamp was on, beaming warm light onto the faces of the pair.

The coffee table had been moved to the side. Three chairs had been arranged, two facing one.

Keonaona took his seat across from the lady Gorgon, and Gorgon Icarii keeled back into his seat from where had leaned over to get the lamp.

The rain clattered all around them.

For a moment, they all looked at one another. Their faces were softer than Keonaona had expected.

Icarii looked at the dark-haired woman in the red robes a long time. It struck Keonaona again that they were a married couple.

"Ready, Lane?" said Gorgon Icarii. Without that awful scent getting in the way, it was easy to see the kindness in his eyes.

Keonaona looked away, suddenly embarrassed. His gaze landed on a picture of Hana and Kai on the photo ledge.

He looked away quickly.

"I don't know," he said, just to be saying something. He glanced up again. They both seemed to be patiently waiting.

Keonaona didn't realize how long he had kept them waiting until Gorgon Icarii finally said, "You don't have to do this. You're allowed to change your mind."

"No, it's not that. It's—I don't know." Keonaona took a breath. "I'm still mad at my wife. And I feel like...even though I made the mistake that killed us—killed them...I'm still mad at her! What'll she—what will *they* say to me? They...saved me at the river—or I guess I mean, you saved me at the river, because of them...But if you hadn't, I'd be dead, and with them, and—" He forced himself to stop before his voice broke. It broke anyway. "Did they not want me with them?" He had to clench his beak shut a while before he could go on. "I don't know how to feel about all this." He held up his paper. "I wrote down the things I wanted to say to them, but—" When he spoke again, his voice was very small. "But I'm afraid it won't be enough, it won't be the right things."

Thunder murmured through the silence as if trying to keep quiet in the next room.

Gorgon Icarii turned to his wife. "Do you want to field this, or shall I?"

"First, you," said the red-robed Gorgon.

The tall man turned back to Keonaona.

"All right. First off...none of the times I've seen your family did they seem angry with you. I wouldn't worry about that. As to why they wouldn't let you die...well, before she"—he cocked his head at the robed Gorgon—"put your son into the jaguar's body, he said you wouldn't be happy dead."

"But I'd be with them! I'm not happy here! 'Wouldn't be happy'!" Keonaona squawked. "What does that even mean?"

The woman reached out, gripped Keonaona's arm tight. His wings flapped, startled.

"What do you feel?"

Confused!

Her eyes darted up above Keonaona's head, then back to his face. "Physically."

"...Your...hand."

"And beneath you?"

"My...chair? And my feet on the ground..." She was still holding on. His tail tip squirmed, nervous.

"Yes, and youdosmell rain, and us, and this place. And youdidtaste breakfast, hm?"

The Gorgon's words seemed like demands.

"Yes. I do..." Lani's melon salad was still syrupy in the back of his throat.

The woman Gorgon released him. Then, before he could stop her, she swept out of her chair and swiped the family photo Keonaona had looked at from off the mantel.

She held it up. "Youdosee them."

"Yes."

"But you cannot touch them, scent them, any longer."

Keonaona swallowed back a sudden sob. "No. It's just a picture."

"So it will be when you die, Keonaona. You will see and hear them and this entire physical world, but all will be..." her face screwed up, "flat. Your son had to be set into the cat by me because he could not affect the physical, though he direly wished to.

"So it would be for you. There is no happiness watching a world pass by. There is no happiness being unseen, not in that way."

Rain ticked the wood overhead.

"So," said Icarii, "it sounds like he'd be with them, but unable to interact with them? Almost like...living with a recording of them?"

She dipped, then tilted her head shoulder to shoulder, a strange gesture.

"Sort of, then," said Icarii.

"No and yes. What he must to know is that there is a reason the dead do not linger here. I have to call them from elsewhere, when we sit these sessions."

"Wait—you're saying...when we die, we'll just be...these shades? Somewhere else?" said Keonaona. It sounded awful to him, a horrific doom.

"For a while. Until all this"—she made a strange undulation with her whole body that Keonaona thought indicated the entire room—"is remedied."

She paused. "I am unable to say more. But while you keep breath in you, Keonaona, you can affect things, do good, or make up for mistakes." Her husband was nodding now. "This is why they did not want you dead with them. Far better to be alive and feeling and able to do a thing, than to be a spirit with only a whisper of influence."

"But I miss them!"

"*Of course you do!*" she thundered. Keonaona jumped.

"You loved them! Things fall in gravity, and death hurts when you love a thing! Do you wish to be exempt? Then stop loving!" She finished this tirade with a snap of her teeth.

Keonaona sat, stunned for a few minutes! But eventually he was able to think back on what she had said.

"They...saved me because they wanted me to be happy," he tried.

"Yes," said both Gorgons at once.

"And they're not mad at me?"

"No," she said.

"'Death is the lens that adjusts all perspective.' Apollo Marinakos." said Icarii.

Her eyebrows raised. "A Netron spoke wisdom on death, and your committees thought it important enough to teach to memory in their schools?"

Icarii just shrugged. "They can't censor every thought."

"I reel from shock," she muttered, setting Keonaona's photo on the coffee table alongside them.

Icarii stopped smiling at her and turned to Keonaona, sober again. "You're never going to get all the answers you want," he said, nodding at the paper in Keonaona's lap. "Or say everything you want to say. But you're getting a rare opportunity to hash a lot of things out."

"I'll get to say goodbye," said Keonaona. "Even though they didn't die in the war."

The robed Gorgon growled. "Count that rarest. You are our host, suffering extraordinary circumstances. Other requests, we will refuse." Icarii was nodding ferociously, brow suddenly iron. "I do not use my power lightly."

"I understand," said Keonaona quickly.

Icarii's brow smoothed; his wife leaned back in her chair. They all three sat quietly while the rain flung itself against the house.

I'll get to say goodbye. The goodbye I really mean.

Keonaona looked down again at his paper without reading it. He covered the words on his lap with his hands. They would be there if he needed them—but he'd never needed a cheat sheet to talk to Kai and Hana before. Why start now?

He looked over at their photo on the coffee table. It'd be a good one to use at their funeral. But that would come later.

He looked at the Gorgons, still waiting.

"Thanks. For talking with me."

"Our pleasure," said Icarii. "Thank you for hosting us."

"At last," added his wife.

Icarii bumped his body against hers. "Be nice."

"You first," she said. Their eyes met before they shared a wicked laugh.

These are not the people I expected to host.
They quickly settled back into silence.
But that's not necessarily a bad thing. Kai called them friends.
And Hana sent them to save me.
Keonaona studied his family's photo again.
"I'm...I guess I'm ready now," he said.
The lady Gorgon pulled her hood over her face.
She offered Keonaona her hand.
And Keonaona took it.

PRONUNCIATION GUIDE

This novel uses a number of real Hawai'ian words and names. Here's some tips on how to pronounce the non-English letters you'll see:

The *kahakō* (vowel with a line over it): If every syllable is one beat, the ā (or ū) indicates you hold the vowel sound for two beats instead of one.

The *'okina* (') is a Hawai'ian letter indicating a glottal stop. Most US speakers of English do one when they say the word "mountain." The "t" gets swallowed up so the word is pronounced more like Moun'n.

Sadly, ebooks are unable to render a proper *'okina*. A single left-facing curly quote has been used as a substitution.

I'm no Hawai'ian expert, but I hope these tips help! For more detailed instructions please consult your local linguistics teacher, Wikipedia, and How to Speak Hawai'ian books.

Any language errors in-book are mine and mine alone.

On with the words!

A'ina Muliwai: ah-EE-nah MOO-lee-why
'Alohilani: ah-loh-hee-lah-nee
alcornoque: ahl-kohr-NOH-keh
amigo: ah-mee-go
Analū: ah-nah-loo
ándale: AHN-dah-leh
atole: ah-TOE-lay
cáscaramida: KAHS-kah-rah MEE-dah
cuervito: kwehr-VEE-toh
danke: DAWN-keh
'Ehuana: eh-hoo-ah-nah

'Ewalani: eh-wah-lah-nee
exactamente: ehk-SAHK-tah-mehn-teh
Gott im Himmel: gawt eem HIM'll
Hana: hah-nah
heissa hopsasa: hye-suh hope-zah-zah
hedor: eh-dohr
Himmel sei Dank: HIM'll zye dahnk
Hriana: hree-AW-nuh
ipo: ee-poh
ja: yah
Keonaona Ho'okano: keh-oh-nah-OH-nah HO-oh-kah-no
Kahananui: kah-hah-nah-nu-ee
Kahele: kah-heh-leh
Kaimana: kye-mah-nuh
Kapekolo: kah-peh-ko-lo
koa: koh-uh
Kōko'olua: kooh-KO-oh-loo-uh
Lane: rhymes with *pain.*
lanai: luh-nye
Lani: lah-nee
Lase: rhymes with *pause.*
Lono: loh-no
Likeke: lee-kay-kay
nein: same as *nine.*
Nika: nee-kuh
mahalo: mah-hah-lo
mijo: mee-ho
Mo'o: moh-oh
'ohana: oh-hah-nah
Osider: AH-said-her
Pali: pah-lee
Pāheahea: paah-hey-uh-HEY-uh
pono hana wikio: poh-no hah-nah vik-ee-oh
sanft: zahnft
serape: sair-AH-pay
tagein, tagaus: tahk-eyen, tahk-owss
wahini: wah-hee-nee
weliweli: weh-lee-weh-lee

CROOKED NECK DIGITAL SOUVENIRS

After you finish a book, you're usually only left with a the memory of the story. But with this novel, you can get more!

These digital souvenirs will let you keep a little piece of *Crooked Neck* on your desktop, device, planner, or even on your wall!

Here's just a few you might enjoy:

- The **Crooked Plumeria Digital Wallpaper Set**—set of 16 themed colorways includes "Smoky Purple", "Bananas Bananas", "Garage Hound", and "Ocean's Truth"

- *The Art of The Guests of Crooked Neck* browser presentation

- Illustrated **jaguar** and **coati** digital wallpapers AND printable posters

- Tropical organizer sheets

- "Movie poster"-style printable files featuring Keonaona, Mercurio, and Jerimin

- ...plus many more!

Visit **shop.pixelvaniapublishing.com**
and select *Digital Souvenirs – The Guests of Crooked Neck* to
view the entire collection.

SPECIAL THANKS...

...to Miracle Forest on YouTube, for creating the amazing ambient videos I listened to while writing this.

...Paula A., for helping me name Crooked Neck's resident state.

...Paul B., for answering my news crew questions.

...Big Cat Rescue, for answering my jaguar paw question.

...Linsey D., for being a FRIENDLY READER and also for being my MORAL SUPPORT while painting the cover and developing the Kickstarter.

...Malia H., for helping with surname pronunciation.

...and to all those who contributed to the early release of this novel on Kickstarter, including these "Kingly Coati" and "Completionist Coati"-level backers: Ben Kauer, Brooke D., Connor Brewster, Eron Wyngarde, Eva Holmquist, Francesco Tehrani, GRIFFIN FAMILY, Kristina H., Linsey Duncan, and TD. I thank you all immensely!

A LETTER FROM DANIELLE

Hi! I'm Danielle Williams, and I wrote this novel. Thank you so much for reading. I sincerely hope you enjoyed your time in Crooked Neck!

I write refreshingly different sci-fi, fantasy, and horror fiction. If that sounds like something you'd like to read more of, please sign up for my free newsletter at

https://www.subscribepage.com/daniellewilliams

It only comes out a few times a year to announce new releases, free goodies, or Kickstarter launches.

Reviews help other readers find books. I appreciate all reviews, whether positive or negative. And if you know someone who might enjoy this book, please share it with them!

You just read the second full-length novel in the *Worlds of Everlush* book series. As of this writing, there are two other titles in the series:

- *Growing Shadows in the Desert*, a prequel short story

available at https://books2read.com/growingshadows

- *Steel City, Veiled Kingdom*, the epic-length novel that started it all. You can grab the Complete Edition ebook at https://books2read.com/steelcitycomplete

Wanna read an excerpt from *Steel City, Veiled Kingdom?* You're in luck! Just turn the page to get started.

Thank you as always for sharing and supporting. Until next release, I wish you good health and happy reading!

Danielle Williams

Please enjoy the following excerpt from Jerimin's origin story...

STEEL CITY, VEILED KINGDOM

Available now at your favorite digital retailer.

OCEANS AT THE EDGE

I ONCE TRIED TO run into the sea to drown myself, but the water never rose higher than my skinny fourteen-year-old calves.

It didn't take long before I found the end of the sea, a glass wall at the very edge of the tower. Jets pumped recirculated water through slots aimed at my ankles. I stared through the glass at the steel city before me. If climbed over, I could jump, and if I jumped, I'd fall. I'd close my eyes and pretend I was flying—at least, until the first autokinet smashed into me. It'd be a quick death—the machines never stopped in time—and a better one than the injection in store for me when I failed my final set of tests.

At least this way I get to choose.

My palm had just kissed the glass when my father grabbed me from behind.

I twisted, but he was too strong. He hauled me, his only son, through the water, back to where my mother screamed and people avoided looking at us. My escape had failed.

I'd been paying for that day's cowardice ever since. You see, I didn't score low enough on my final Kakuri-Majinuri tests to warrant death—but my numbers weren't high enough to declare me a safe member of society. I fought the judgment for a couple years, but I eventually got the message and stopped.

Fifteen years later, there was no water. And no wall, either. I'd found another edge, on an unfinished street. No one would see.

The autokinets thundered at the base of the skyscraper city.

I took a breath, closed my eyes...

And swore. Why did I have to do this? I never did anything wrong! I never hurt anyone—never wanted to! I'd just been judged unfairly—the tests were wrong!

But my anger changed nothing. The KM numbers made me unemployable, so I was penniless. The numbers made me dangerous, so I was friendless, even among the other city castoffs. And, worst of all, the numbers made me honorless, so I had no family.

The numbers had stolen my future, and I couldn't get it back. It wasn't fair, but I saw no other solution.

The world grew dim as dusk arrived. I took a step towards the edge—

—and was grabbed from behind again.

But instead of being dragged away, I was swung to the ground. Dazed, I stared up into the face of a pale-skinned woman with wild black hair. Her hand pressed on my heart, pinning me down.

"Do not," she said. "I need you."

ABOUT THE AUTHOR

Danielle Williams is the author of six novels and more than a dozen other refreshingly different tales of wonder, horror, and humor, the latest being the slow-burning morsel of surreal, psychological *Bona Ossuaria: A Home Renovation Horror Story.* Her work has also appeared on the NoSleep Podcast.

Visit PixelvaniaPublishing.com to explore her full collection of stories.